Thanks for Nothing, Nick Maxwell

Thanks for Nothing, Nick Maxwell

Debbie Carbin

St. Martin's Griffin
New York

THANKS FOR NOTHING, NICK MAXWELL. Copyright © 2008 by Debbie Carbin. All rights reserved. Printed in the United States of America. For information, address St. Martin's Press, 175 Fifth Avenue, New York, N.Y. 10010.

www.stmartins.com

"Tubthumping" Words and Music by Alice Nutter, Louise Watts, Judith Abbott, Nigel Hunter, Darren Hamer, Allan Whalley, Paul Greco and Duncan Bruce © 1997, EMI Music Publishing Germany GMBH & Co KG, Germany. Reproduced by permission of EMI Music Publishing Ltd. London WC2H 0QY

Library of Congress Cataloging-in-Publication Data

Carbin, Debbie.
    Thanks for nothing, Nick Maxwell / Debbie Carbin.—1st St. Martin's Griffin ed.
        p. cm.
    "First published in Great Britain by Black Swan, an imprint of Transworld Publishers"—T.p. verso.
    ISBN-13: 978-0-312-38368-8
    ISBN-10: 0-312-38368-1
    1. Single women—Fiction. 2. Pregnant women—Fiction. 3. Travel agents—Fiction. 4. Chick lit. I. Title.

PR6103.A715 T47 2008
823'.92—dc22

                                                                2008013019

First published in Great Britain by Black Swan,
an imprint of Transworld Publishers

First St. Martin's Griffin Edition: August 2008

10 9 8 7 6 5 4 3 2 1

For Mum – I wish you
could have seen this.

Acknowledgements

I need to thank most of all my two extraordinary children for being conceived and inspiring me. And of course my husband, for his input.

Thanks must also go to everyone who read this story and gave me such fantastic feedback and encouragement; the book is now far better than it would have been without you: Richard, Ruth McKenna, Manda Fear, Tracey Owen, Suzanne Allen, Sandie Hines, Annika Dann, Lucy Coates, Irene Carbin, Carol Ward, Jackie Hawker (and your mum), Lois Whipp, Chris Dann and Colin Dann (thanks also for all the advice!).

Thanks to everyone at Transworld, who have been wonderful and sooooo patient, particularly Lydia Newhouse and Linda Evans.

And finally a huge thank you to my good friend Greg Snow, who liked it first; and my lovely agent Laura Morris, who ran with it.

Chapter One

Last year I was happy, hurtling through my life in a dizzying tornado of hot dates, sexy outfits and dirty dancing: in flashy cars and happening hot-spots with slick lipstick and must-have hair, lights bright on my highlights. I was surrounded by gorgeous men who wanted me to let them do anything for me. I was fabulous, flirty, sensuous, sexy and seductive. I was at the top of my game. I was at the top of everybody's game.

Then it all stopped.

My life ended at precisely the same moment as a new life began.

It was a really hot Friday night in July, one of those nights when you just can't get cool, even with nothing on and all the windows open. Look, there I am, in the living room of my little flat. No, look on the floor. See me? On the rug in front of the sofa. Those are my feet on the edge of the coffee table. My hands are on the floor above my head, so you can see my elbows sticking out. The rest of me is underneath Nick Maxwell, from Personnel.

Can you make me out now? I know, not much of me is showing but you'll see more of me later. For now, I just want you to look at my face; look at the expression. Hold it, right there, freeze. Now, just look at that. Look at my eyes, just little slits. In fact, they're actually closed, I think, aren't they? And my mouth, smiling but not too broadly, lips slightly parted, pale pink and beautifully glossed. I have good lips. Anyway, what do you make of it? What does that expression bring into your mind? Looking at that face, I think, Bliss. It's a blissful face, isn't it? And like most bliss, it was, back then, deeply rooted in ignorance.

Oh, here we go. Looks like Nick's activity is drawing to a close. You can tell because I've put my hands on his back. If we could see Nick's handsome face, I'm sure it would show an expression of deep and serious concentration. The rest of him is pretty good to look at too, don't you think? Even though he's quite shiny now, with all that exertion, it's quite manly, and downright sexy. Oh yes, Nick Maxwell was *the* office catch, and I damn well knew it, lying there.

OK, it's all over now. Let's leave them a moment, in the name of dignity. There are few things less graceful than rising from the floor after a passionate sexual encounter. I'll take this opportunity, as the lovers disengage, to tell you a bit about myself.

My name is Rachel Covington. I am twenty-five and single, although what you're seeing are the events of a year ago, when I have just turned twenty-four. I think I look pretty hot, most of the time. I've got short blond hair, with these gorgeous gold and copper highlights, and I'm quite slim, with long legs. Good lips, as I've said. My nose is not so good but I've been told it's quite cute and buttony. I suppose my dream is one day to be married and settled down, but not right then, not at that moment, on that hot July night when tall, sweaty Nick Maxwell was picking his way through our abandoned clothes towards the shower room, wearing nothing but his socks.

I work at Horizon Holidays, in the Telesales department. Selling holidays, in case you didn't work that out. 'Good afternoon, Horizon Holidays. My name is Rachel, how may I help you?' It's not rocket science but then I'm not a rocket scientist.

Oh God, look at Nick coming out of the shower room now. Doesn't he look like an aftershave advert? Running his fingers through his damp hair, staring off pensively into the middle distance, not a hair on his caramel chest. Those baby-blue eyes – you could die in them. Oh, look, look, he's dropped to the floor to do some press-ups right there in front of me. And one-handed, no less. Biceps like Brad Pitt's buttocks. Dazzling.

Anyway, I quite like selling cruises and all-inclusives and short breaks to people. I get to leaf through the brochure every working day, which is lovely. Horizon don't stint on the paper like some places do, and I think it makes a real difference.

'A million copies of that brochure are printed,' Jean the supervisor says, 'and two-thirds of them are taken to someone's home. Hundreds of thousands of people look at that brochure, but only 1.79 per cent of those people are actually interested enough to pick up the phone. Only 32 per cent of that 1.79 per cent who phone in actually book a holiday. So you cannot afford to let even one of those get away! *Read* your brochure, *learn* the alternatives, offer something else and make a sale.' The first time she said that to me was during my training course when I was seventeen. To me then, she seemed like a kind of President or Prime Minister, eloquent and powerful on a podium, with bright red hair in spite of pushing fifty, a permanent smoker's cough and a selection of really tight T-shirts and miniskirts that she always wore with black tights, winter and summer. There were certificates around the walls proclaiming Jean's achievements – 'Most Sales in a Week', 'Most Sales in a Month', 'Cruise Sales Record', 'Long-haul Flight Record', 'All-time Yearly Sales Record'. Apparently, no one has beaten that one, even now. People have tried. There was a performance chart, listing everyone's names and showing how many sales they were making each month; Jean's name was always at the top, holding the record, even though she doesn't sell any more, she stopped eight years ago when they made her supervisor. But the record she set eight years ago hadn't been beaten then, when I started here, and has still not been beaten now. Eight years ago, can you believe it? She must have been an amazing sight, flicking those brochure pages like her fingers were on fire, thumping out names and addresses on that keyboard, firing out every possible add-on you could ever think of, like an outside cabin so it had a window, a sea-view hotel room, all-inclusive when the client had rung up for half-board. When she was training us (I started at the same time as two other girls, Chrissie and Val) she took a couple of calls in the sales room, just to demonstrate what she meant by add-ons. I didn't think it was possible to persuade someone to pay for something they may not have really wanted when they called in, but she did it.

'You're not forcing them to do anything they don't want to do,' she said, after convincing a woman who had rung up to book a three-night city break in Prague for her and her husband's fortieth wedding anniversary to book a fortnight in the Dominican Republic instead. 'Oh yes,' she'd said into her mouthpiece, nodding to us as she closed down the Prague page on her computer, 'Prague is lovely, really sweet and suburban. The ideal anniversary destination – for the fifteen-yearers. But you're in another class, aren't you? These crystal anniversarians think they know what it takes to keep a marriage going, but they haven't got a flaming clue, have they? They don't know what it's like to be *old* together. That takes fortitude, determination. And patience. My God, the patience that you need to last forty years. There's a reason why you get rubies and they get a set of wine glasses! Ruby. A real, valuable gem, not some cheap crystal copy. Now, does that say Prague to you? Because I don't think it does. I think for two steadfast, long-standing lovers, for better and worse, you deserve a real chance to relax and be romantic again. I think we're talking Caribbean.' She had turned to us and winked as she'd opened up the Dominican Republic page. 'If they didn't really want it, they wouldn't book it.' That was her maxim. I had never seen anything like it. I still haven't.

I'll show you my office later. Make sure you have a look at the performance tables. They're over by Jean's desk, pinned up on the wall. You'll see that my name is always in the top three, week in, week out. Everything Jean showed me, everything she said, everything she taught, I have used, and honed and perfected. I am the one who has come the closest to beating Jean's eight-year-old sales record. I missed it by thirty-two sales. Just thirty-two. Oh come on, that's not many, you know, not for a whole year, not when we're talking about more than three thousand sales. Oh yes, I'm the only other person, in the history of

Horizon Holidays, to go over three thousand in a year. That's how I know I'm going to beat that record of hers one day. She must have been over forty when she set it, and I'm only twenty-four, so I've got years and years ahead of me to get better and better and better. Sometimes, when she's writing up the stats at the end of the day and she totals up my sales for the year so far, I see her looking worried. She doesn't realize I see it and it's only there for a flicker, but I've seen it and I know I'm going to be the one.

Well, all seems to be dignified perfection again, if you want to look now. Don't you think Nick's shirt is fantastic on me? I look like a Bond girl in that, I really do. When he was taking it off earlier, I made a mental note of where it landed, so I could grab it and look all sexy and Bond-girly in it. Just as well you weren't watching at that moment as there was nothing attractive about my frantic nude scramble over the back of the sofa. Anyway, it was worth it, and he'll notice in a minute. Hang on, he's going to say something.

'You are so sexy, Rachel,' he says, gazing at me. I know I look fabulous in a messy, just-had-sex-on-the-floor way, and I smile and lick my lips seductively. 'Glad you came out with me now?'

I don't answer straight away. Of course I am glad I went out with him, who wouldn't be? Look at him, he looks like a cross between Enrique Iglesias and Hugh Jackman, with no shirt on. Crikey, it's hot in here. But you can't be too eager, can you? You've got to play the game. After all, Nick Maxwell was the major catch in the office, lusted after by all, including Jean the supervisor and her assistant, Graham. But if there was anyone not lusting

14

after Nick Maxwell, you can bet your life they were lusting after Rachel Covington. We were perfect for each other.

I have worked at Horizon for about six and a half years. Nick has been there for two months. In my six and a half years here, I have easily been the best looking person in telesales, if not in the building. I'm not being big-headed, it's just the way it is. But then Nick arrived, and I knew I had met my match. As soon as I first laid eyes on him I knew that we would be together. Chrissie knew that we would be together. Val and Jean knew that we would be together. Martin and Mike, best friends and inseparable to the extent that you never saw one without the other, so no one was ever really sure which one was Martin and which one was Mike, knew that we would be together.

'Oh my God, Rachel, you have got to see this new guy who's just started in personnel,' Chrissie had said. 'He's the sexiest thing I have ever seen in a suit. Including Richard Gere in *Pretty Woman*. I bet he'd fancy you.'

I had shrugged. I was pretty wary of Chrissie's taste in talent. Her standards were decidedly lower than mine, but she was always trying to set me up with someone. Mum says she lives vicariously through me, which means that because she's quite – well, let's say she's a 'large' girl – it's pretty unlikely that she's ever going to get a bloke of her own, so she tries to get them all to go out with me instead. It's like almost really dating. Quite sad really.

Anyway, I had been down this road before and I wasn't going down it again. She was always, 'Oh you must come and meet my really sexy cousin/neighbour/milkman. Just wait till you see him – he's so totally gorgeous, you'll be perfect together.' Enter some lanky blond freak, grinning enthusiastically in Tesco's jeans. Yeah, right.

She hustled over to me then, her tangerine tunic growing larger and brighter as she got nearer. I had to slit my eyes a little. 'Just see him, all right?' she persisted, actually taking my arm. 'Just take one look at him. You'll see.' And then she put her other hand on her chest and rolled her eyes dreamily skywards with a sigh.

'All right!' I raised my arms in a gesture of defeat, but really just to get her to take her doughy hand off my skin. 'I get the message. I'll take a look, but I'm not going out with him, OK?'

Well, she'd been right, of course. But you can't blame me for being a bit wary.

It's eerily quiet in there, isn't it? Just the sound of Nick blowing out gusts of air and sucking more in over his teeth as he completes his second set of fifty sit-ups. These are the kind of sit-ups you do with the bottom half of your body raised above your head, so you're actually sitting up uphill. Not quite the same when you've balanced your legs against a cream faux-leather beanbag.

This bit's quite dull, really, just fifty more sit-ups, followed by fifty more push-ups. We can skip over this to the end. There's a moment just as Nick is coming to the end of his fiftieth push-up. He's two-handed this time, but he's taking both hands off the floor at the apex of each push and clapping them together once, then twice, then three times. I'm on the sofa, smiling, eyes glued to his torso. But then suddenly there's a change, an almost imperceptible flicker as the expression on my face alters for a tiny moment. Did you see it? Let's go back. There. Just for an instant I've glanced away, looked down, frowned, apparently remembering something, thinking about the significance of what it might be, and it's a big something, it's huge, but then Nick manages to clap four times and I've forgotten immediately what I was trying to remember, I'm clapping along with him, laughing, the memory, the danger, all forgotten in the joy and exuberance of the moment.

In another place that I can't see, changes are already beginning to take place. It's a battle, a contest with only one winner and only one prize. In a race that demonstrates survival of the fittest at its most relevant, one contender is already beginning to set himself apart from the others. He pushes on, focused on the goal, knowing only the goal. All around, his comrades fall in their legions but he does not stop and he does not mourn their passing, for this is a fight to the death and the weak are eliminated. Finally he senses his prize is near. He knows that this is the most difficult test of all as he is battling against the best of the best. On he goes, faster, reaching her side at last as his final rival falls away. She embraces him, whispering, 'You're the one, you're the only one.' They join together in a fantastic collision of beings when their two selves become one for ever.

This story is about how everything got started with me and Nick Maxwell – and one other. There was a chocolate cake, some wine, a little romance, a lot of lust and some sperm. Well, just one actually.

Chapter Two

Yeah, you've got it. OK, not clever. But I did say I wasn't a rocket scientist. Excellent family planners, those rocket scientists. Well, they've got to be, haven't they? You can't find out you're accidentally up the duff the night before the long-awaited five-year expedition to Mars. You can see all those bespectacled geeks at NASA throwing their clipboards on the floor and going outside for a furious fag.

The worst thing about my situation was that I had actually almost known what I might have just done. Remember that moment, that little worry line that flitted across my face as I was doing my Bond-girl in Nick's shirt on the sofa? That was actually me thinking, Hang on, what's the date today? Then Nick did his four claps and I was lost again. I was already lost by then anyway.

Well, you can imagine how little sleep I'm getting. Look at me, three in the morning and I'm still lying there grinning, eyes wide. Nick, you will notice immediately, is absent, which is just as it should be. I don't like to sleep with someone straight away.

I don't think there's any point watching me lying there for hour after hour, so we can skip to the next day if you like.

Oh, no, there is one more thing that I'd like to show you from that night, just so you can understand what happened after. It's quite quick, and then we can move on.

Let's go back to the moment after the four claps. I'm smiling on the sofa, watching him walk over and sit down next to me. He touches the collar of his shirt (it's on me, remember) then runs his fingers down towards the top button. It's not done up, of course – no point wearing a man's shirt if you look like you're going to the office in it – and he pushes the fabric apart with his fingertips. Naturally the second, third and fourth buttons aren't done up either, so the material slips back on my shoulders. I'm leaning back now and that blissful expression is back, look. I've closed my eyes in anticipation and then he says, 'Give over, Rachel, I'm trying to get my shirt back.'

My eyes fly open. Not a good look, even from here. I think we'll just gloss over this bit – it's embarrassing. Suffice to say that I gave him his shirt back and put a tight T-shirt on instead, which is almost as good as the shirt.

A very few minutes later, Nick's standing fully clothed in the hall and I'm leaning sexily against the open door. I can do a lot of things sexily. Mum always says that some people have just got it, and I am one of those people. It's not like I don't have to try, because I do. It's just that when I try, it's really easy for me to do it well. I'm not being big-headed or anything, it's just how it is. Sometimes I do it without really meaning to, like when I'm out with just girls. They get a bit annoyed with me, but it's worse when their husbands/fiancés/boyfriends are there. I can't help it, it's like a kind of habit.

Anyway, from here you can see that Nick is also really

good at doing things sexily. He's got the top four buttons of his shirt open so there's a good deal of chest showing, and his jacket slung casually over his shoulder, like a model in a Freeman's catalogue. This is the last chance you'll get to see his flesh for a while so drink it in while you can. His hair, still slightly damp from his post-coital shower, is floppy now and charmingly unstyled, and he has a hint of a five o'clock shadow, even though it's only one a.m. He's so close I can smell Lynx, mixed with shower gel, sweat and sex.

He's moving nearer now, bringing me inside the circle of his own heat. The warm scent of him is damp and intoxicating. He leans in further and puts his mouth to my ear. His sandpaper face gently scratches mine, making me shudder slightly. The feel of a stubbly face grazing lightly against my own overwhelms my senses; then his hot breath on my cheek and earlobe brings me out in goosebumps all over. You'd be able to see that if I turned round.

He holds this pose – his mouth against my ear, gently breathing – for three, four, five seconds, then very lightly, *excruciatingly* lightly, just touches his lips on to my ear. Well, not my ear exactly. It's the little lumpy bit that juts out of your cheek into your ear and holds your earphones in. It definitely classes as more cheek than ear, whatever Chrissie may have thought. What would she know anyway? She's never likely to get a kiss like that from anyone. She's probably still a virgin.

Sorry about that. It was a bit catty. I didn't mean it, particularly the bit about her being a virgin: she definitely isn't one. She just really really annoyed me when I told her about that kiss.

'On the *ear*, you say?'

'Technically, I think it counts as chee—'

'Well, fuck me, I've never heard of being kissed good-night on the ear before. What the hell do you think made him do that? Didn't like the look of your face after all? Maybe you had repugnant black eye-bogeys that made him want to gag every time he looked at you?'

Classy, isn't she? Eye-bogeys, for goodness' sake. In Chrissie's world, eye-bogeys are the gelatinous blobs of mascara that coagulate in the corners of your eyes when you are out late. Chrissie gets them a lot and I think she assumes that because she gets them, everyone does. Well, I don't. It all comes down to the brand of mascara you use. Personally I prefer to spend a bit more than £3.99 on my products. Anyway, I have my eyelashes dyed and starched every three months so mascara is a thing of the past.

I was a bit puzzled by Chrissie's smug outburst. After all, she was the one who had suggested Nick to me in the first place and practically forced me to meet him. Why would she be so delighted in thinking she had found a flaw in our breathtaking encounter? Mum says that Chrissie is jealous of me, which is why she says this kind of thing. It wasn't a flaw anyway. If you have ever been kissed like that, you'd know what I mean.

Back to the hall. You'll notice that the whole time he's pressed up against me, breathing in my ear and kissing my *cheek*, he has the car keys in one hand by his side, and the other hand holding the loop of his jacket, up by his shoulder. He doesn't touch me with anything other than the very tips of his lips, if there is such a thing. I mean he doesn't press down with his mouth or squash his lips on to me; and he doesn't wrap his arms round me and try to squeeze the life out of me or stuff his tongue down my throat. It's a sweetly intense moment that crackles with the promise of things to come.

Look, there he goes. Gone. And look at me now, closing the door really softly, then bounding off around the apartment like a hyperactive boy with a pogo stick on Christmas morning, when he's forgotten his medication and had loads of really highly coloured sweets and coke before breakfast.

You can meet my brother later. He's ten.

So here we are, back to me lying in bed, staring wide-eyed at the ceiling. Actually, that's no good at all, not if I'm expecting to see Nick again tomorrow. My eyes will be all red-rimmed and bloodshot. I won't need eye-bogeys to make him gag.

I close my eyes. Yes, that is definitely a good idea. So I'm still not sleeping but at least my eyeballs will keep moistened.

Well, seeing as how I'm not going to be getting any sleep anyway, I'll explain to you how we came to be writhing like eels on my carpet after I'd told Chrissie I wouldn't go out with him.

You'll remember that I had agreed to take a look at him? OK. Well, I expected this to be on my terms because it usually is, but Nick Maxwell beat me to it and took me completely by surprise.

Earlier that day, I had been let down by Martin and Mike, the two friends of inconclusive sexuality I mentioned earlier. They bring me a coffee from the machine by the lifts around two o'clock every afternoon – it's a ritual that's gone on for the past two or three years. They go right past the vending machines every day on their way back from Data Processing, so it's not exactly a hardship for them to stop and pick me up a light mochaccino as they pass. And it saves me walking all the way over there myself when I could be on the phones, making sales. After all, as Jean's always saying, Sales are the pillars that hold up the cathedral of Horizon Holidays. Without Sales, there would be no After Sales, no Data to process, no Personnel to manage, no product to Market. So if those boys in Marketing start to think they're big and clever, or those pale-faced nerds in DP throw a tantrum about some figures that don't add up first time, they need to remember just where their jobs start: where ours ends. Sales is like oxygen for Horizon.

Martin and Mike collect the morning's stats until twelve, then stop for their lunch. They never vary that, always a twelve o'clock break. They're back from lunch by twelve forty-five, and start collating the stats they collected in the morning. When they've finished, they take them down to the light-deprived bods in DP in the basement. The whole trip takes about forty minutes, including the extra couple of minutes it takes for them to get my coffee, so they arrive back at my desk, steaming cup in hand, at two o'clock.

Only this day, 28 July, the day I first laid eyes on Nick Maxwell, the day I accidentally set in motion the cataclysmic chain of events that would change my life utterly and irrevocably, they didn't. By 2.05 I was getting worried. Well, perhaps worried is a bit strong – I know it's a long way down to the basement from the third floor but they were grown men and they were together. But I was mystified. They had never been so much as a minute late before – not for work, for lunch, for meetings, training, coffee. Whatever. They had synchronized their wristwatches with the wall clocks to ensure this. I glanced at the clock repeatedly, checked my own watch, checked the time on my computer screen. They all said different times, but each one was definitely showing after two.

In the end, I switched my turret to 'B' for busy, unplugged my headset and stood up. Val who works next to me saw me get up and automatically checked the time, then looked at the door, expecting the punctual pair to appear, but still they didn't. I could see her looking expectantly at me and I had the strong feeling that she had worked out, by M and M's non-appearance, where I was off to, and was going to ask me to get her something from the machine while I was there. Her eyebrows were raised meaningfully as she snagged her handbag with her foot and dragged it across the floor towards her, but she couldn't speak to me directly because she was on a call. I heard her say suddenly, 'Oh, could you hold the line a moment, my screen's just gone down', but by the time she'd looked round, I was out the door. As I entered the corridor from the sales room, I could just hear her voice saying sadly, 'Oh, no, it's all right, it's come back up again.'

I know, I could easily have got her a drink; I'm not lazy or thoughtless. The truth is that she always has hot chocolate, which takes about forty seconds longer to come out of the machine than tea, coffee or soup and those forty seconds are precious to me. It's all about the sales.

So I'm off up the corridor like Kelly Holmes in a kitten heel, expecting to see M and M heading towards me at any moment, but they're not in the corridor. They're not even in the lift that arrives with a ping as I girl-run past it. I stop and wait by the doors for a second, thinking it might still be them arriving, but it's just a tall man in a dark suit.

24

'Good afternoon, then,' he said to me, smiling broadly and inclining his head slightly towards me. I glanced at him just long enough to know that he didn't interest me, then hustled on.

'Lovely to meet you,' this same guy is saying genially. I ignore him and continue on up the corridor – I've had to learn to do that. It doesn't come naturally to be rude, but quite frankly I haven't got the time or the brain cells to indulge everyone who wants to talk to me. It's just self-preservation.

'See you again!' he was calling to me as I walked away. Well, he might see me, but I wouldn't notice.

When I got to the drinks machine, there was a man standing there. He had his back to me, white shirt, sleeves rolled up. Even from a small distance away, and from the rear, I could see he was the sort of man that I did notice. I slowed down my approach – you can't be sexy while walking fast – and wet my lips as a kind of impromptu lip-gloss. I didn't have a chance to do much more as he turned suddenly so that I almost walked straight into his chest.

'Oh, sorry,' I said, feeling a bit flustered, which is totally unlike me, but I had just caught my first glimpse of those breathtaking baby-blue eyes, and I was floundering. These are the clearest, lightest blue eyes I had ever – have ever – seen, framed with really long, really thick, black eye-lashes, and now staring at me intently. I felt penetrated by them. He smiled at me and the edges of his eyes crinkled up slightly.

'Hello there,' he says, smiling down on me like the sun.

'Hi,' is all I can squeeze out. My mind is a wasteland. Not that I'm renowned for my pithy intellect and witty repartee, but I can usually manage a sexy innuendo on a first encounter.

'I'm Nick,' he says, putting out a hand, and all I can think about is what that hand will feel like on my skin.

'Of course you are,' I say as my small hand is encircled and engulfed by his. It's cool but not damp. Strong but not insistent. He doesn't let go straight away, just presses my fingers gently with his own.

'What do you mean by that?' he says, almost laughing. I've got completely lost in this conversation and have no recollection at all of what I've just said, so can't even think about explaining it. Come on, brain, get with it. A lone dog barks in there somewhere.

I shrug instead. He buys it. 'And you're Rachel Covington,' he says smoothly.

'Yes.' It doesn't even occur to me to ask him how, or why, he knows that.

'You work in Sales, don't you?' he asks, still pressing my hand in his.

'Yes, Sales. That's right.' Tumbleweed skitters past in the barren desert of my intellect.

'And you always get a cup of coffee at two o'clock.'

'Yes.' I'm standing there like a child looking at Father Christmas. I'm not even concentrating on my posture. At the back of my mind, like someone else's mobile phone ringing in the distance, is the thought that he seems to know a lot about me, where I work, what time I have coffee. But of course if he was waiting by the vending machine at two o'clock today to meet me, he just got lucky because I wouldn't usually go down there. Any other day, he would have been standing here holding hands with Mike or Martin.

'Well, Rachel Covington from Sales, I have been told that I should meet you, and now I have. I'm very glad that I have. Everyone was right about you, what they said.'

'Mmm-hmm.'

'Except I couldn't have imagined you would look like this.' He looks me up and down blatantly and shakes his head, apparently in wonderment. 'You're totally gorgeous.'

I nod and his eyebrows rise. Well, I think false modesty is really unattractive. If I went around saying, 'Hello, I'm very ugly, nobody look at me,' people would just assume I was fishing for compliments, or that I was as mad as a bag of curlers.

'So. They say that Rachel Covington and Nick Maxwell ought to get together.'

'Do they?' It came out as a bit of a croak as my voice had totally shut down in order to send vital fluids to other areas.

'They do. They say that Nick and Rachel could be the Brad and Angelina of Horizon Holidays.'.

'Ah.'

'Personally, I think they've got a very good point and it shouldn't be ignored.'

'Plus they're expecting something now.' Finally! I've found my voice. Nick inclines his head with a smile in a gesture of admiration.

'You're so right. We can't let them down, can we?'

I shake my head. 'It wouldn't be fair. They've got their hopes built up. We owe it to them.'

'I agree. Out of consideration for them, I will invite you out after work.'

'And because I am such a caring, thoughtful person, I will accept.'

I went back to my desk without the coffee. That's how much he had affected me.

So here I am, the morning after. For the first time ever, I feel like *I* got lucky last night. Usually, if I decide I like the look of a bloke, it's all over bar the pouting. No challenge, no sport. For me, anyway. But this Saturday morning, I am floating around my flat with my feet two inches off the floor. Forget cloud nine: I am on cloud nine million.

Oh, look, that's my cat, Cosmo. Isn't that a great name? I named him after a magazine. Mum thinks it's really clever, because it does actually sound like it's a real name. I've had him since he was a little kitten. Cute, isn't he? I love cats. They don't need much looking after and they're so much sexier than guinea pigs. Nothing that has the word 'pig' in its name could ever be considered sexy.

This particular morning, I am not feeling all that good physically, not having had much sleep. My mental high is more than making up for that though. Look at my face, grinning away like a loon even while I'm prising those pungent, shiny jellified lumps out of the cat food tin into Cos's bowl. They stink out the whole flat so I'm opening the French doors.

See that bit of garden through there? It's mine. That is, it belongs to this flat, so I get exclusive use of it. Cosmo comes and goes through those doors, as you can see. He's quite familiar with the garden and all its hidden delights. Actually, most of the delights out there have been hidden by him, so I tend to stick to the paved area by the doors.

My dilemma on this gorgeous sunny day is this: shall I shower and get dressed straight away, or shall I wait in case Nick phones? It's warm in here, even with the double doors open and all the glorious sounds and smells of the garden flooding in – glorious except that one, Cos, thanks – so if I get showered and dressed and then he phones, I'll have to shower and do my hair again, which is a pain. Especially if my hair goes really right first time, and then I have to wash it and start all over.

What I could do is loll around in my PJs for an hour or two, just until he phones, then I'll get dressed. But what if the postman knocks with a parcel? Am I expecting any parcels? No.

So I make some breakfast and bring it into the living room with a magazine – *Elle* this morning. This room, the living room, is my favourite room of this whole flat. Well, there's not much more to it, to be honest: just the bedroom, which you've seen; a little shower room, which you don't need to see; and the kitchen up the back there, which you can see on the other side of the counter. Mum says it's perfect for a single girl, and I agree. She wasn't too happy when I told her I was moving out, but she helped in the end. All the walls are quite plain, aren't they, and I do prefer a bit of colour, but it's in my tenancy that I can't paint without the go-ahead from the landlord and I'm not bothered enough by cream everywhere to find out from him if he would approve of my choice in colour. He's quite attentive, but a bit creepy sometimes, you know? I do wonder whether that's because of, you know, me being so attractive.

Mum's pretty good at picking out bright stuff to cheer up a room. I found that old standard lamp in a second-hand shop – I know, you can't tell, can you? – and Mum bought the red shade to go on it. She says it's chic. It's certainly less plain in here with that on. It looked like the red-light district last night, especially with two naked bodies twisting on the floor. Can you see the expression on my face as I'm looking at the bit of carpet where it happened? Looks like my insides are melting over a low flame.

Usually on a Saturday, I do all my chores and go out for a run or a bike ride. I have a list of jobs that need doing every day, every week and every month. It's laminated – Mum did that at work for me – so I can cross them off with a water-soluble pen every time I do them, and then rub the whole thing off and start again. Chores in the morning, small lunch if I feel like it, then exercise in the afternoon. Some Saturdays I'll go out for a drink and then a club with Chrissie and Susan in the evening. Susan doesn't work at Horizon but we were all at secondary school together and we've managed to keep in touch. Yes, I knew Chrissie before we started at Horizon together. We've known each other since we were about six. At primary school we weren't really friends but then at secondary school we got together with Susan and Sarah and became The Fruity Four. Chrissie was a lot thinner in those days.

Sarah doesn't come out with us on Saturday nights. You'll meet Sarah very soon.

This particular Saturday my rock-solid routine has crumbled to dust. I can't concentrate on anything. I didn't even get the list out of the drawer. If Mum had come round and said, 'Rachel, why aren't you working through your list?' I would have said, 'Who are you?' You see how already Nick Maxwell is starting to screw up my beautiful, organized, productive life? The seeds had already been sown. As you know.

Let's move forward a couple of hours. Here I am still,

on the sofa, flicking through a magazine in my PJs. It's now eleven thirty and the phone is still maddeningly, sickeningly silent. I've even got it on the sofa next to me, just in case I wouldn't hear it from the coffee table in front of me. The thoughts going through my head are utterly mad, although I look quite sane and peaceful sitting there. I'm thinking things like, Can't go out for bike ride, might be blinded by the sun and veer into the path of an oncoming bus, and, Can't push the Hoover round, might dislodge the floorboards, fall in the ensuing hole and break my ankle. I'm in denial, basically. I really don't want to admit to myself that I am still sitting in my PJs at eleven thirty, not doing chores or carrying out my time-honoured Saturday routine because I am doing nothing other than wait for a call from Nick. I don't want to admit that I am waiting by the phone; that I'm making no sound in case the phone rings and I don't hear it; that I'm not even dressed so I don't have to do my hair twice. It would be unthinkable to admit to myself that I have become one of the sad skinnies that Chrissie introduces me to, who wait for weeks for me to return their calls. I cannot admit that for the first time in my life, someone else is in control.

Christ, did you see me jump then when the phone started ringing? I look like I've just woken up on Christmas morning and Santa has left me the thing I've been yearning for for years, and is now on the phone to tell me how great I am. So why don't I answer it, you're wondering? Well, I do intend to answer; I just have to get ready first. I'm sliding down in my seat to make me feel sexy; no one looks sexy sitting rigidly upright like a doctor's receptionist. I've half closed my eyes, fluffed up my hair and licked my lips, even though no one can see me. The point is that I can picture what I look like, and that helps me to feel sexy. And no doubt Nick on the other end of the phone is trying to imagine what I look like at this end, so it would be totally wrong for me to look like a bag lady.

Finally I'm ready. I reach for the phone, then snatch my hand back suddenly. Don't answer it straight away! Never, ever answer a phone until it's rung at least . . . oh fuck it. 'Hello?' I say throatily, trying to sound like I'm wearing a black négligée.

'Have you got a cold?'

This is not Nick. It is a woman's voice, but not Mum. I ponder for a few seconds, then I hear the sound of shrieking in the background and I realize suddenly, with plummeting heart and sinking spirits, that this is Sarah. The one who doesn't come out on Saturdays any more.

'Hi, Sarah. Why do you say that?'

'You sound funny. Got a sore throat?'

I hoist myself up in the seat again. 'No, no, I'm fine. How are you?'

'I'm fine. Jakey's had a bit of a cold the last couple of days, running a temperature of 38.5 for most of Thursday night, but he seems to have perked up a lot this morning. Can you hear him? He's been marauding round the house since about six o'clock this morning so I'm totally shattered. He always gets a bit hyper when he's feeling better after being poorly.'

I'm losing interest in this conversation at an inverse proportion to the length of time it goes on for. That's an expression I learnt from M and M. It means that something is decreasing at the same rate that something else is increasing. I glance around for something else to occupy me, then spot the magazine that I put down when the phone rang and begin leafing through it again.

Sarah McCarthy, née Lincoln, is the fourth member of the Fruity Four. Me, Sarah, Chrissie and Susan. We did everything together back then – the vomiting, the hangovers, the VD – Virginity Donations ('We didn't lose it, we gave it away!'). In those days, me, Chrissie and Susan pretty much relied on Sarah to come up with the ideas. She was the one who suggested that we run topless through the town centre one night, a terrifying but exhilarating experience that had nearly landed us all in the back of a police car. Sarah was the first of us to part with her virginity, choosing the romantic setting of up against my front door for this landmark moment in her life, while I stood unfortunately not quite out of earshot staring at the garden, terrified that my parents would wake up. Sarah could carry on drinking long after everyone else was throwing up on someone's lawn. Sarah introduced us to pot. But then, only a year after leaving school, Sarah met Glenn McCarthy, a civil servant with a Cavalier, and everything changed. Sarah couldn't come to the pub, she was meeting Glenn. She couldn't sleep over, Glenn was expecting her. She couldn't go away to Butlins for a girls' weekend, Glenn wanted to look at a house. She started saving hard for a deposit and tasteful tableware and then the unthinkable happened: they got married. I remember the day with bitter regret. A sad day for friendship, that had been. I wore black (well, very dark navy: black is so draining). Chrissie got hold of some pot and brought it to the reception and she, Susan and I got high in the marquee then threw up on the grass. It was the end of an era. We were all just eighteen.

A year later Sarah was so excited and happy to announce over a speedy non-alcoholic drink after work that they were expecting their first child. If I'd thought Sarah as a prospective bride was bad, Sarah pregnant was a hundred times worse. Now we got, 'I can't come out tonight, I'm too sick,' then, 'I'm too tired,' followed by, 'I'm too fat,' and inevitably, 'I'm too sick, tired and fat.' For old times' sake, we all continued including her in the arrangements, even though we knew she probably wouldn't come. And even if she did she was all 'You're not smoking that near me, it's toxic, blah blah blah'. When the baby finally arrived, we all felt the anticlimax of a long-expected event simply happening, as expected. Like after Tuesday, you know it's going to be Wednesday. We weren't excited or thrilled, in spite of what we claimed on the ward. Susan even said, 'Fucking hell,' later in the car park as she ground her butt out under one of her mules.

That was five or six years ago and she's never been out with us since. And once the Fruity Four were down to three, we found that our group couldn't easily support the change and our evening revelries tailed off from weekly to fortnightly to monthly. Now I can't even remember the last time I got together with the other two for a night out. Chrissie's changed a lot over the years, of course, and isn't as fruity as she used to be. At least not in a good way. She does tend to look literally like fruit now. And Susan's always starting some serious, long-term relationship or other, which seems to make her less keen on wearing the tight tops and trousers she's always looked so good in. At least in public.

Oh God, the phone's gone silent. You can tell because of the look of panic on my face. This means that Sarah is waiting for an answer or a comment or something and I can't give it because I haven't been listening. I improvise.

'Oh, sorry, Sarah, what was that? Cosmo just knocked the phone out of my hand.'

'Again? He's always doing that. Sounds to me like he craves your attention too much.' There's a pause, then Sarah's voice becomes muffled and distant. 'No, not now, Jakey, Mummy's on the phone. I said wait a minute. Just a *minute*, will you?'

'Everything all right, Sarah?'

'Yes, yes, just Jake. He can't bear it when I'm on the phone. Always picks that very moment to need the loo or sneeze all over himself or want a drink or something.'

'Oh.' I really hate it when mums speaking to their children refer to themselves as 'Mummy'.

'Anyway, are you coming or not? I need to know the numbers.'

'Coming?' Hmm, my left middle fingernail could do with touching up a bit.

There's a long, exasperated sigh. 'To Jake's birthday party. It's the nineteenth, that's three weeks today. You're not going to let me down, are you, Rachel? You are his godmother, you know.'

Yeah, when does she ever let me forget it? Can you believe it, me a godmother? I know, I didn't think it through. When she had asked me, Jake was three months old and an adorable soft little bundle who smiled and burped and slept in my arms and went straight back to his mum for everything else. Over the years I have observed with horror how he's morphed into a tall, blond, smart-mouthed, demanding, noisy, disobedient, self-centred boy who seems to do nothing for his mum and dad except stress them out. I have no idea what to say to him or how to interact with him. I am probably the worst godmother that has ever existed. I can't even remember his birthday, even though this one must be number four or five. I wish I could resign the position, particularly at moments like these when I'm watching a whole Saturday afternoon evaporating before my eyes.

'Of course I'll be there, Sarah. What sort of godmother do you think I am?'

'I know exactly what sort you are, Rachel, and I regret it daily.'

While she is undoubtedly right there, it's still quite hurtful to hear that she regrets asking me. 'Thanks.'

'Oh, look, Rachel, I didn't mean it. It's just that . . .'

I'm starting to worry about how this call is clogging up the phone. What if someone else is trying to get through? If he got an engaged tone, would he try again in a few minutes, or would he give up until this evening? Or worse, leave it until tomorrow? I'm glancing at my watch now, acutely aware that this call has already lasted more than five minutes and now looks like it's going to drag on for another five. If only I'd paid attention at the start of it, maybe she wouldn't be droning on at such great length now.

'. . . So they moved him on a level in the end, thank goodness,' she's saying. I insert an 'Uh-huh', every now and then but I'm up and walking towards the bedroom. I have a plan.

'I told her he was bored with what they'd given him. It was far too easy for him. I said to her, "He's bored. How can you expect him to sit still when he's bored?" She didn't seem to agree, so I told her . . .'

'Uh-huh.'

In my bedroom, I've found my handbag on my dressing table and got my mobile phone out of it. No new messages; no missed calls. OK, disappointing, but that's not why I've picked it up. Using one hand, I'm scrolling through the menu, looking for 'Ring tones'. Aha, found it. Select. Now there's a long list of all the ring tones my phone holds. God, which one have I got it set on at the moment? I can't remember.

'. . . work he's doing is so far above his age group. When you compare it to the other children, there's no comparison . . .'

'Uh-huh.' Doesn't matter which one the phone is set on. Sarah doesn't know, or won't remember, what my phone sounds like. I press something called 'Ibiza Party', and it starts playing immediately.

'. . . just needs to be properly challenged. What's that noise?'

'Oh, Sarah, my mobile is ringing. I'm going to have to go. It's bound to be Mum. If the phone's engaged when she rings, she always rings the mobile.' This is actually true.

'Oh. Have you changed your ring tone then?'

'Oh, no, no, that's the one it's set on for my mum. Listen, what time is Jake's party?'

'Three o'clock, for the third time.'

'Right. And what—?'

'The nineteenth,' she cuts in, 'three weeks today. Don't forget.'

'I won't, I promise. Must go. Bye.'

She's gone. I fling myself face first on to the bed in relief. Oh crap. I've agreed to go to Jake's bloody party in three weeks' time. Or was it two weeks? I jump up. Must write it on the calendar before I forget. Ninth of August.

There's a calendar on the kitchen wall just above the kettle, so I can look at it in the morning as I make my breakfast coffee, and make sure I don't forget any urgent appointments or meetings. For the most part, the days have just got men's names in them, with times next to them. I'm not promiscuous or anything. I just go out with a lot of different people. All I'm doing is looking for 'The One', and now I think I might have found him.

I take the calendar down from the wall and turn the page over to August. Well, it can't be the ninth because Sarah definitely said it was a precise number of weeks from today, which would make it a Saturday, and the ninth is a Wednesday. Was it the ninth of September, then? I flick over a page. No, that's a Sunday. What did she say, for heaven's sake? I turn the pages back and accidentally flick two over, to July. With a smile, I look at yesterday's date and write in 'Nick Maxwell, 7 p.m.', even though it is already in the past. Looking at yesterday's date, I notice that there's a big black cross on it, and the two days before and after it. Oh, hell, that means . . .

A wonderful thought occurs to me. What if I take Nick to Jake's party with me? I lay the calendar down, still open at July. Yes, that would be perfect. It wouldn't be a wasted Saturday afternoon after all. In fact, it would be better than if we spent the day alone together because I could show him off to everyone there, and then we could go out somewhere afterwards and imagine what it would be like to be parents, then thank God we aren't and then have lots of hot sex. What a brilliant plan, and still three weeks to convince him to come along.

Aha, three weeks, that's it. I pick up the calendar and quickly write 'Jake' on 19 August.

Let's move on a bit again. The day is going by so slowly. By half past eight, I'm really very stressed out. You can see that I've showered and got dressed at last. This is because the sudden and horrifying thought occurred to me that Nick might unexpectedly turn up at the door with a huge bouquet of flowers and tickets to something. He would not be impressed with me in my PJs. Well, he would be impressed, but maybe a little put off if it was three o'clock in the afternoon.

I've done a few chores but can't really settle to anything. I've watched a bit of an afternoon film, then some quiz programmes, but they're not holding my interest. I tried reading a magazine on the sun lounger on the terrace while sipping white wine, thinking it would be so sophisticated to be doing that when he phoned. I didn't have any white wine, just the dregs of a bottle of red, and the lounger cushion was soaking wet so I had to sit directly on the plastic slats. I lasted about three minutes before I was back indoors tipping the revolting contents of the glass down the sink and putting the kettle on.

Mum did ring but I managed to get her off pretty quickly. I usually have at least one meal round there each weekend but today I said I had plans both days. She was not surprised. She tells all her friends how popular I am with the boys. It's embarrassing.

Tea is two slices of toast. I know it's a small flat but I really can't bear to be away from the phone at all, so I take it with me into the kitchen while I make the toast. My mind is buzzing now, all sorts of stupid thoughts whizzing round inside, all of them desperately trying to block out the possibility that he's not going to phone today. I wonder whether Sarah will hire a clown like she did before? I suppose I should get Jake a present. But how old is he? Will Glenn's mysterious brother turn up this time?

You are surprised that I am occupying myself with thoughts of Jake and his upcoming birthday? Me too. But I am desperate. This waiting is a difficult job that I have never had to do before, so I'm really not very good at it.

So here I am, gone ten o'clock and still heard nothing. This cannot be normal. Or is it? Maybe this is what countless women are going through all the time, waiting and waiting for the gorgeous bloke they met the night before to call them up after an amazing and perfect evening. They know that he had a good time. They know that the two of them got on really well because they both laughed and chatted all night. They know that he was definitely attracted to them, from his behaviour. It was romantic, caring, thoughtful. They know that they are the ideal couple, that they will be perfect together, for ever. So why, why, why doesn't he phone?

When the call does come, I'm brushing my teeth. No, I'm not in the bathroom, I'm there, in the living room. I realized as soon as I'd put the toothbrush in my mouth that I had left the phone so I came back in here to be with it. I've waited all day, I am not missing the call because I'm in the other room.

So I'm wearing my orange terry-towelling dressing gown and I've got a mouthful of white froth. This is the moment the phone chooses to ring. Look at me, I'm frozen, staring, wide-eyed at the irony of it. The white froth is running down my arm and dripping off my elbow. Distractedly, I wipe my mouth with my arm, only managing to spread more white around my face than I remove. I am transfixed, unable to work out how to go about answering the phone with a mouthful of foam. I know, I know, I could easily spit it out into the kitchen sink, it's only a few steps away. Look, you can see me glancing that way, thinking about it then rejecting the idea. The phone has rung three times already – if I go to the kitchen, spit and come back again, it might stop before I get there. I consider spitting on to the floor but that's disgusting. Plus I might lose my deposit on the flat if there's a nasty white stain on the carpet when I move in with Nick.

It's rung four times now and is getting ready to stop, I can feel it. I glance around one last time but find no suitable receptacle to hand so out of sheer panic and desperation, I swallow the froth with a cough and dash to the phone. My throat is burning and I'm struggling not to splutter. As I seize the handset, I catch sight of my Father-Christmas face reflected in the mirror above the shelf in the living room, and smile.

Nick Maxwell knows when he is on to a good fling. Here he is, standing in front of the mirror in his room, checking his appearance one last time before going out. That hair is a work of art, isn't it? It should be, it's taken him long enough.

He's feeling smug; you can see it in his face. The girl he's just started seeing – me – is so gorgeous-looking, and she was at home on her own at ten-fifteen on a Saturday night, waiting for him to call. He smiles to himself in the mirror. It means that she is mad for him and will be available to him whenever he wants her to be. He gets an extra kick

41

out of the fact that she is quite a bit older than him. Her personnel records show that she's twenty-four, and he's only nineteen, on a gap year before going to Hull Uni next year. But he's never had any problems getting the girls he wants, and this one's no different. He had been told she was hot, but unlike most men that didn't intimidate him. He couldn't wait to get his hands on her, so he had engineered a meeting the previous afternoon, making sure the two dipsticks that usually brought her coffee at two o'clock were busy on another errand in Personnel at that precise time. It had gone better than he could ever have hoped and now he was going to get a repeat performance. He really enjoyed dating older women. They were much more likely to have their own flats.

'Nicky! Do you want some apple crumble?' a voice calls up the stairs. 'I can warm it up for you if you like?'

'No thanks, Mum,' he calls, jogging lightly down the stairs and into the kitchen. 'I'm off out.'

'You sure, love? There's ice cream to go with.'

He leans forward and kisses her cheek, then walks to the door. He throws his car keys into the air and catches them. 'Night, Mum.'

Chapter Three

'Rachel! Hang on a sec!'

That's Chrissie's voice calling me, but as you can clearly see I'm in a bit of a rush right now. I'm getting my coat on and shutting down my terminal at the same time, so I can't really stop to talk to her. I know exactly what she wants to ask me, though.

'Rachel, are you ignoring me?'

Trying to. 'No, Chrissie, of course not, I'm just rushing off.' It's Friday afternoon a week later and I've got another date with Nick. I've seen him every day since last Friday. I'm starting to think I'm heading towards being in love with him. I know that I have never felt this way about anyone before. And I've never had physical symptoms before. Just thinking about him makes me feel dizzy and light-headed, and that's pretty much all the time.

I turn towards Chrissie, who's standing there with one hand on her fake Gucci bag handle just below her shoulder – the bag itself is not visible – and a cigarette in her other hand waiting to be lit. Today she's a fruity vision in off-the-shoulder cerise, white flared trousers and pink stilettos. She refuses to de-emphasize by wearing muted colours like black or navy. Her lips are always gaudy pink or red, and her hair is a huge mass of dyed auburn curls falling on to her bare shoulders. So obvious.

'So, what's going on with you, then?' she asks me predictably. 'We've not seen you for lunch all week. Got another job?'

I laugh. She knows that I'll never leave Horizon. 'Course not.'

While we're here in the sales room for a moment, take a look at the sales league tables over by Jean's desk. Remember I told you I was always in the top three? Well, have a look now. Can you see my name anywhere? Look down a bit. It's at sixth place. The funny thing is, I don't even care. I've got much more interesting things to think about every waking moment than how I am going to beat Jean's old record.

Jean spoke to me about it on Wednesday. M and M had obviously reported to her that my figures were slipping, although no doubt she had noticed this herself anyway.

'You all right, Chick?' she had asked, exhaling a hot cloud of stale smoke breath over me. Horizon Holidays is a no-smoking building, but Jean just smells of smoke all the time. She has to go all the way down in the lift to the ground floor and out into the car park for a smoke, so she doesn't go very often and when she does go she smokes three, one after another. When it's very busy in telesales, she can go for hours without leaving, but her mood worsens the longer she goes without a puff.

'Fine thanks, Jean,' I replied, swallowing as my mouth filled with saliva. I had to fight with every nerve the violent impulse to gag. Jean's breath had never affected me like that before. It must be the lack of sleep.

Do you think I'm in denial? The signs are all there – the

symptoms, the dates, the calendar – but still I don't add it all up. It's so much easier not to acknowledge something unpleasant in the hope that it will go away on its own eventually and we never have to do anything about it.

'Sure, lovey?' Jean went on. She was not terribly maternal and this was about the limit of her caring. 'Your figures are down a bit. Anything we should know about?'

I glanced up at the tables. At that point, on Wednesday, I was fifth. I looked back at Jean. 'So I'm fifth out of forty-five instead of third? Do you see that as a problem? Am I skiving off, not pulling my weight, not putting the effort in? Why don't you speak to Val?' Val's head came up at hearing her name and she looked over at me nervously. 'Val's lucky if she makes it above *fifteenth*. I'm doing probably twice as many sales as her in a week, every week, even when I'm fifth. So if you want to have a go at someone for not cutting it, have a go at her.' I realized a bit late that Val might have found this slightly offensive, and looked over at her. She had gone very white and her mouth was slack as she stared at me in horror. She looked devastated.

Mum says people overreact to what I say sometimes because they don't like the fact that I'm better looking than they are. Maybe this was one of those times. Val cut off the person she was talking to, tore off her headset and rushed out of the room.

Jean and I watch her go in silence, then Jean turns back to me and stares at me for a few seconds. I'm wishing she would just go and get her foul breath away from me and eventually she says, 'Right, I'm off for a smoke. Graham.' Poor Graham flinches in his seat, then reluctantly stands up and begins patrolling slowly around the room, doing

Jean's job of making sure no one's on 'Busy' when they should be on 'Free' or 'Incoming'.

I turn back from the door to my desk and realize that the room has suddenly gone rather quiet. There is the muted sound of people on calls but they are all trying to talk really softly. Anyone not on a call has swivelled in their seat and is staring at me. I look straight back at them.

'What?'

Gradually, they all return to their work, some with a sad shake of the head, some with severe frowns in my direction. I'm standing there with my hands out, like, what's the problem? Eventually, Chrissie comes over.

'You can be a real bitch sometimes, Rach.' You know Val's got problems at the moment.'

'What?' I mean, I sit next to the woman at work, we're not married.

Chrissie sits me down at my desk and pulls Val's chair over to park her own wide load. 'Her mum's dying, for fuck's sake. Come on, surely you knew that? She's in a hospice, got days to go, apparently. Val is in a shocking state. She spends every spare minute hunched over the bed, waiting for her mum to breathe her last, and you sit there and have a go at her for only being fifteenth in the league.' She shakes her head at me. 'Jesus, I knew about it and I don't sit next to her. Don't you ever speak to her?'

'Oh yeah, like you're a walking saint.' I don't need to be lectured by anybody, least of all Chrissie, who makes sure she is abreast of all the gossip in the office and passes it on to anyone who'll listen. She's overlooking the fact that *not* knowing all the ins and outs of someone's very private and personal circumstances is actually to my credit. I don't bother to say this to her, though. Actually, she'd already walked away so I couldn't say anything else.

When Val came back to her desk about twenty minutes later, eyes red and puffy, I tried to smile at her but she didn't make eye contact.

Anyway, that was Wednesday. It's now Friday and I'm trying to get out of the office quickly. I have a dinner date with Nick at seven thirty and it's now five ten. If I allow fifteen minutes to get home and an hour and a half to get ready, that will leave me with about forty minutes to get a taxi to the pub, which is ample. In fact, it will give me more time to get ready, which I'll probably need because I haven't decided what to wear yet.

'So?'

Ah. Yes. I'd forgotten about Chrissie. She's still standing in front of me, unlit cigarette between her scarlet-tipped fingers.

'Chris, can we walk and talk? Only I'm going out later and I need to get ready.'

'OK.'

'Right.' I hesitate just once more before walking off towards the lifts. 'Night, Val.'

Val just moves her head to acknowledge that she's heard me. I shrug and walk, Chrissie tottering along behind me in her pink shoes.

'So? Where are you off to tonight?'

'Dinner with Nick. At La Bougie.'

She's silent for a moment. I knew she would be like this. Disappointed, I mean. For some reason, she desperately wants my relationship with Nick to go wrong. Like when she was laughing about that soft kiss on my ear. Mum says she wants to be me and have my life, so the next best thing is to hope my life turns to crap. We reach the lifts and I thump all three down buttons, then stare up at the lights as if hoping to bring the lift more quickly by sheer will.

'La Bougie. Wow, that's a bit posh, isn't it?'

'I know.'

'Got something nice to wear?'

I turn slowly and look at her for a few seconds. 'Yes.' Not that she'd know. She's got about as much style as a Punch and Judy tent.

When we reach the pavement, she pauses for a second. She's got the lighter out in her hand already so the time it takes for her to light the cigarette, take a deep drag and snap the lighter back into her bag is a mere two or three seconds. I'm making my getaway, though. She hurries to catch up.

'You going to Jake's party next week?'

I stop. 'Next week? I thought it was the nineteenth?' Christ, this means I'll have to go out tomorrow and get the present, which means I might miss Nick when he calls.

'Oh, yes, you're right, it's a couple of weeks yet, isn't it? You going?'

'I am his godmother, Chris. Look a bit off if I wasn't there, wouldn't it? Why? You going?'

She nods, her lips encircling the white filter of her cigarette. When she takes it away from her mouth, the end is covered in pink lipstick. 'It'll be better if you're there. We can have a bit of a chat. Out the way somewhere.' She takes another drag, and we arrive at my car.

I drive a lovely little burgundy Clio. It was only a year old when I bought it and I've really looked after it. Dad wrote me out some maintenance thingies I have to do once a month or so, like the oil and the water, tyre pressure, windscreen washer, and anti-freeze in the winter. Mum laminated that one too, and it lives in the same drawer as my chores list in the kitchen.

Chrissie looks at my car with obvious contempt then smiles. 'Have you seen my new car? Look, over there, the grey one.' I follow the direction she's pointing but I can't pick out which one she means. 'It's a BMW,' she says.

'When did you get that?' She's had a Volkswagen Polo for years, and loved it, as far as I was aware.

'Oh, few days ago. Finally managed to get the deposit together. What do you think?'

I nod distractedly. 'Yeah, it's lovely.' I'm so focused on the time and getting home and what I'm going to wear and what we'll do after the meal that I don't really give this any thought. It should have occurred to me to wonder how she could possibly afford a car like that on our wages, even including commission, but it didn't.

'OK, I'll see you later, Chris. Have a good weekend.' I get in, slam the door and head for home.

So this is La Bougie. Mum told me that's French for The Candle. What I love about this place is the fact that they light the whole thing with candles. They're on the walls, in the light fittings, on the tables. Thousands of them. There's no electric light anywhere. It must take them hours to light them all every day. Mum reckons that some of them are fake and they're actually gas fittings on the wall that light automatically when you turn them on. But even if that's true, it's still a real flame, isn't it, so it's the same.

There's my Nick, enthusiastically sawing through a thick piece of steak. I've got Caesar salad but I'm not really eating it. I'm just staring at the man sitting opposite me. Even with a mouthful of chips he's sexy. He grins at me, and winks. There's a little drop of ketchup on his bottom lip and I have a sudden really strong urge to kiss it away. Can't do that here, though. Bit too posh.

He's surprised me a bit tonight, actually. Although he's driving us both home afterwards, he's still had a couple of pints of lager. I suppose it doesn't matter, if he can take it. Some people just can't drink and drive, even if it's only one or two, but obviously Nick isn't one of them.

This is so lovely. We're not talking much but we're just so comfortable being in each other's company, we don't need conversation. You can see that just by looking at us, can't you? That's what really matters in a relationship – compatibility.

I don't have a dessert, but Nick's having one of those Knickerbocker things. I thought he would probably go for the cheesecake, but I was wrong about that, too.

When he's finished we split the bill and stand up to leave. Nick is such a gentleman, he comes round behind me with my jacket and helps me into it. He leans down over my shoulder and nuzzles into my neck, inhaling deeply. I close my eyes.

'You smell beautiful,' he says against my skin and I breathe in the scent of him, his warmth against my back, his hands light on my shoulders.

'You smarmy git!'

My eyes snap open at this loud, coarse voice intruding on our private moment. Nick's hands are gone from my shoulders and in an instant he has moved two or three feet away from me. I turn to see who has spoken, and find a young man of about eighteen standing there, grinning broadly, looking from me to Nick and back again.

'You old bugger, Nick! What the hell are you doing? All right, love?' he says to me as an afterthought.

I don't like the look of this character. Look at his hair – so short you can see his scalp. There's a faded tattoo on his forehead that looks a bit like 'SINKS'. He's got a pin through his eyebrow, too, and the type of green anorak that always makes me think of football hooligans. I take a small step backwards and look at Nick. What I see disturbs me a bit. He's looking very nervous, his eyes darting about, frowning at this person.

'Hi, Sean,' he says quietly. 'You all right?'

'Yeah, mate, tops. Who're you here with? Your m—?'

'No, not my mates,' Nick says quickly. 'I'm here with a lady friend. Now, if you'll excuse us . . .'

Sean's previously grinning face falls into a confused frown. 'What you on about, you poncey tosser?' A weaker, less convinced version of the grin appears briefly as Sean steps forward and punches Nick on the shoulder. Nick steps back hurriedly, turning away, taking hold of my hand. He looks really uncomfortable now and this makes me feel anxious. Maybe this Sean is part of a gang and maybe somehow he thinks Nick is involved? Nick's hardly looked at me since Sean appeared, but his hand is gripping mine tightly. Maybe Sinks is the name of the gang? I step closer to Nick's broad back.

'Look, Sean, we're just leaving so I'll see you round, OK?' He walks quickly towards the door, dragging me with him. I glance back towards Sean whose face is now screwed up with anger.

'Yeah? You can stick that right up your arse, you

ignorant wanker!' he calls after us, accompanying this comment with a hand gesture. I feel Nick flinch but he keeps walking, head down.

We walk like that all the way back to the car. Nick's got a long stride, so it's quite difficult for me to keep up. By the time we get there, I'm actually a bit fed up with him, and I've started frowning. He lets me in and as soon as he's in he turns to me and touches my face. I forgive him.

'I'm so sorry about that,' he says. 'Did it ruin the evening?'

I shake my head, sinking into the touch of his hand against my cheek. 'Who was that?'

He drops his hand and stares out of the windscreen. 'Sean lives near my parents. I sort of grew up with him.'

Immediately I shake my head. Something's not right. 'But he's only about . . .'

'No, I know, he's eighteen. Obviously there's a few years between us.'

'Oh.'

'But we lived near each other. I used to play with him anyway. Poor kid didn't have many friends so I kind of let him hang around with me, you know.' He laughs but it's a shallow, forced laugh. 'He was an irritating little so and so, always wanting to hang round the arcades, or play on the waste land on his bike, making ramps and things to jump over out of old bricks and bits of corrugated metal. This one time, we found an old tyre, so we hoisted—'

'You did that with him?'

Nick stops abruptly and looks at me. He nods.

'So how old were you then? If he's, what, six, seven years younger than you?'

He shrugs. 'Well, it wasn't . . . I mean, it was mostly me, you know. He's just a kid. I was probably about seventeen or eighteen, he was probably ten or eleven. Something like that.' He's not looking at me.

I nod. 'Oh.' But something is definitely wrong. His voice is different, he's nervous and agitated. Is this Sean some kind of threat to Nick now? Is there more to their friendship than the 'big brother' picture that Nick has painted? Did they get up to more than just building ramps for their bikes? Illegal activities, or something dangerous?

I know it's ridiculous and immature but thinking about that is a bit of a turn-on. Suddenly there's a side to Nick I don't know about, a dark side, and it excites me. I put my hand on his leg and he turns to look at me at last. 'Let's go,' I say, my pupils dilated and my breath laboured. He doesn't need telling twice.

Let's move on to next morning. You don't need to see what happened next. Suffice to say that he didn't stay over. He never does. I don't know why – it makes perfect sense to me seeing as he's got decorators in his own flat at the moment. That's why we always come here, and that's why he has to go home each night, to make sure they've locked up and turned everything off properly. And then he has to stay there the night so he can let them in the next day. He says he pays them extra to work all over the weekend, so it should be finished soon and I'll get to see it at last.

It's Saturday again so naturally I'm working through my chores. There's the laminated list on the counter top in the kitchen – see it? You can see I've crossed out the first third, which is not bad going seeing as it's only just gone one p.m. Look at me though, compared to last Saturday. What a difference! I'm together again, and collected, now that Nick and I are definitely an item. On top of that, I've got this new feeling of temporariness about this flat now, so I'm not putting as much effort into the cleaning as I used to. It seems like only a matter of time before I'll be moving in with him, so I'm a bit more relaxed about the list. In fact, I have crossed a few things out without actually doing them. I really don't see the need to wipe round the edge of the kitchen clock every week. It's only Mum that looks up there anyway. I'll do it five minutes before her next visit.

Ooh, there's the phone – that'll be him. Although we've been official for a week now, it still gives me a thrill when the phone rings and I get all bouncy and excited again, even with Marigolds on.

'Hello?' Please please please.

'Hi there.' Yes!

'Hi, Nick.'

'Hi, beautiful. Feeling OK this morning?'

This morning? I glance at the clock, but I know what the time is. 'I'm fine but it's not morning, Nick. It's quarter past one.'

There's a moment of silence, during which I check all the clocks in the flat, thinking I was the one who had got it wrong.

'One fifteen? Are you sure?'

'Yeah, absolutely. You must have slept—'

'Shit. I'm dead. *Shit.*' There's a muffled rustling at the other end as if Nick is trying to do something with his other hand. 'Look, Rachel, I'm sorry, I'm going to have to go. I didn't realize . . . I've got—'

'Is something wrong?'

'No, no, everything's fine.' He's breathing heavily and

moving around a lot at his end. Something clearly is wrong. 'I'll see you later, OK?'

'OK,' I'm saying, but he's already hung up. 'Bye then. Love you too, darling. Kiss kiss.'

I stare at the phone for a moment. That was a really odd call. He obviously rang me for a reason, but then never mentioned what it was. In fact, as soon as he realized what the time was, he was off. But how on earth could he not know what the time was? Not even to have a vague idea, like whether it's morning or afternoon? Either he'd have to have spent all morning somewhere with no access to a telephone, clock, radio or television, which is highly unlikely, or he'd literally just woken up, rolled over and dialled my number without even looking.

I like this alternative. It tells me two very important things. One: I'm the first thing he thinks about the minute he opens his eyes in the morning; and two: he knows my number by heart, because surely if he'd had to go and look it up, he would have spotted the time somewhere.

I'm smiling now. But then frowning again. Why would he possibly sleep in until one fifteen in the afternoon? We weren't out that late last night. He left here at about one a.m. again, so if it took him, say, half an hour to get home, he could be in bed by two. Surely no twenty-five-year-old healthy male needs eleven hours' sleep?

An interesting thought pops into my head. He didn't go straight home after leaving here. That's the only possible explanation. Bumping into that Sean freak really disturbed him, so I have no doubt at all that that is where he went after here. He had to go and smooth things over with the Sinks gang. And now he is late for a meeting that could cost him his life. He had definitely said, 'I'm dead,' when he realized he was late. I'm getting all goosebumpy just thinking about the danger that he might, even now, be facing.

I'm still holding the phone and on impulse I dial 1471. The number's there, and she tells me he definitely rang at one thirteen p.m., so I was right about the time. I write the number down quickly. Never know when I might need that.

At Nick's house, he's in a fluster. 'Mum, have you seen my bloody football kit?' he calls down the stairs as he frantically pulls on some clothes. His mum didn't wake him up at twelve like he asked her to, even though she knows very well he has footie on Saturdays. He looks well annoyed. He shakes his head, smoothing his hair with his fingers. That's going to have to do. Doesn't matter anyway, he'll be having a shower straight after the game.

Sean is going to kill him. He is supposed to have picked him up nearly half an hour ago and Sean's already going to be pissed off after Nick blanked him in the restaurant last night.

He runs downstairs to find his mum holding his shorts and shirt, clean and pressed. He grins at her in relief. 'Thanks, Mum.'

As he's stuffing his football boots into a bag, he's actually deciding that our relationship is over. Look at his face though – no hint of it. So cold. Obviously I wasn't aware of it at the time, but basically this is it. He's in trouble with his best mate – Sean – because of me, and now he's late for footie, also because of me. Had I known that he was feeling like this, maybe I wouldn't have asked him last night to go to Jake's party with me in two weeks.

Although I didn't know it, Nick's Saturday afternoons are always taken up with footie, followed by hanging around with his mates in the arcades for a couple of hours. Then most weeks, he and Sean will come back here and play on the PlayStation and eat Pringles.

Jake's party, as it turned out, was the final straw.

Chapter Four

Eight days later. Sunday the thirteenth of August. Sainsbury's.

Here I come across the car park now. I hate doing the shopping on Sundays. There's something really depressing about the supermarket on a Sunday. Here are all the loners buying their two chicken breasts, three apples and seven tins of cat food. All the families, all the happy people with loved ones, are at home on Sundays playing Monopoly while the chicken roasts.

I'm only here because I was too tired and depressed to come out yesterday. I'm still tired, tired like I haven't slept in a week, but I'm out of cat food so this trip couldn't be put off any longer. This fatigue is bone-deep and I drag my feet as I trudge across the empty disabled bays, muttering under my breath. I feel like I've had to walk two miles from my car to the entrance, yet here are five, six, seven empty spaces.

The trolley that I select doesn't come out of its stack when I pull it. I've already put my pound in the slot so I'm not giving up on it. I give it several more hard tugs, my fury increasing in direct proportion to the violence of my tugs. There is nothing visible holding this trolley there, which means either it has been welded to the next one as a kind of sick joke or some ghostly hand is refusing to let go. I put my other hand on the trolley behind, the one my trolley was inserted into the last time it was used, and push with that hand while pulling violently with the other hand. I'm grimacing now, my teeth gritted, leaning into the pull, digging in my heels, eyes narrowed, grunting.

'Here you go, have mine,' says a voice just behind me. Abruptly I stop pulling, drop my hunched shoulders and turn. A tall man in a dark T-shirt is standing there holding a trolley, which he pushes towards me with a smile. Then he walks over to one of the other rows of trolleys, inserts a coin, slides the trolley out easily and strolls off towards the store.

'B-but your pound?' I call out to his retreating back.

'Don't leave the country,' he calls back with a smile, and disappears into the store. I scowl at the unrelenting trolley, then let it go. I am beaten.

Things are no better inside the shop. Sundays are also popular for the very old, have you ever noticed that? It's a kind of social occasion for them. Sometimes they're not even buying anything, they just get a trolley, wheel it into the middle of an aisle and then stand and chat for three-quarters of an hour.

'. . . my daughter, Ruth, she lives in Australia, she's bringing the kids . . .'

'. . . doctor was one of those Pakistani types with really lovely eyes . . .'

'. . . *Countdown*'s just not the same, now that Richard Whiteley's gone . . .'

Can you see me? I'm still at the top of the first aisle, wondering if I stand any kind of chance at all. All the way down to the milk at the end are trolleys arranged in a loose zigzag across the aisle so that a straight pathway is not visible. I need some pasta too, but it's on the bottom shelf, tucked in behind yet another trolley. I'm exhausted, miserable, queasy and stressed. The perfect temperament.

"Scuse me,' I call out loudly, and walk in a straight line down the aisle, ramming willy-nilly into trolleys, legs, feet and handbags. Magically, a path appears through the four-wheeled forest. The people scatter, some swearing, others bleeding, all moving more swiftly than even they thought possible. One trolley remains stubbornly in my way, its owner holding a conversation on his mobile phone.

'Yes, yes, I won't forget. It's on the list . . . I will . . . Yes . . . Now, do you fancy pasta?'

'Just what I was thinking,' I say harshly, barging into his trolley, which rolls obligingly away.

Unfortunately, I haven't noticed that that's the man who's just given me his trolley outside. It's a bit embarrassing. As I walk away, I do hear him say, 'No, no, I'm still here. Sorry. Just got a bit distracted for a moment.' The expression on my face says it all, doesn't it? Men who can't do the shopping without their wives on the other end of the phone telling them what to buy are nothing more than performing dolphins. She's probably saying, 'Now reach up and touch the white bleach bottle with the end of your nose. There's a clever boy! Have a fish.'

I'm off round the corner by now, getting bread and eggs. The way my appetite's been going the last couple of days, I could probably manage for a week on nothing more than that, but I do need some cat food and should get some fruit and veg. I don't need much else so we can go forward to the point where I'm at the till, queuing up to pay.

This is the biggest test of all. In front of me in the queue is a tiny old lady in a beige felt hat who practically has to climb into the trolley to reach the items at the bottom, which is everything because she's got such a small number of things. I wonder idly why she didn't use one of those shallow trolleys designed for people just like her. Anyway, it takes her three weeks to retrieve each item from the trolley, and then she has to put both hands on everything as she puts them on the conveyor, arranging them beautifully and patting them affectionately once she's happy with their placement.

God, if looks could kill, I'd be stepping over her life-less body and loading my stuff on to the belt. You can see how fed up I am by the foot-tapping, hand on hip sighing I'm doing. Trouble is, I think Yoda in the hat there is a bit deaf, so all my impatient noises are lost on her. Either that or she's intentionally winding me up for some reason. Quickly I check her lower legs to see if any tell-tale traces of trolley injury could explain this torture. Unfortunately her legs are so close to the ground they are completely obscured by the trolley.

Finally her single layer of food and lavender-scented toiletries glides slowly away, exposing three inches of empty belt at my end. I grab handfuls of stuff, piling it all up two, three, even four items deep, cramming it all into that tiny space, cat food tins on top of tomatoes, bread squashed under bleach. This does me no good at all as I am no nearer getting out of there. Yoda is packing her stuff away into her trolley bag at the other end like a game of Tetris. This is taking an agonizingly long time and I am edging closer to aggravated assault. For relief from the torturous activity going on in front of me, I look up and away to the customers at the other tills.

The man with the mobile phone is two tills away, chatting easily with the little checkout girl, who is giggling like a teenager. She *is* a teenager. Her bright eyes are fixed on him earnestly. He's leaning slightly towards her, gesticulating with his hands, obviously recounting some story that is making the girl smile as he talks and laugh enthusiastically when he stops. As I'm watching, somehow my ears tune in to their conversation and I hear the words, 'How about pasta?' and then, 'Just what I was thinking,' and I realize in one sickening moment that he is talking about me. His hands are doing a trolley-ramming gesture as he says those last words and they both laugh together, united in the enjoyment of ridicule. My face has gone red, look. It's not clear whether that's from anger, humiliation or a combination of both.

Just at that moment he looks round for some reason, almost as if he could feel me staring at him. Suddenly he finds my horrified eyes and we gaze at each other for a few seconds, accuser and accused. He has the decency to look a little abashed before I look away and focus on getting me and the shopping out of there and back in my flat as soon as I can. Inexplicably, tears are threatening and my throat starts to ache. Not again, I tell myself. I am not going to cry again.

Ten minutes later I'm back in the car park, packing my shopping into the boot of my car. I have my back to the rest of the car park, so don't notice the mobile phone man walk past with an empty trolley, obviously returning it to the trolley park. He spots me and slows down, almost stopping by my car, apparently about to say something, but then thinks better of it at the last moment and walks off.

What I do notice, though, is that chap over by the cashpoint machines, the one in the red vest. It's the red that attracts my attention and I smile briefly at it. Well, it's not good on him, is it really? I start to turn back to the shopping, but something about this man has rung a bell with me. There's something intensely familiar about his gait, the style of his hair, the shape of his face, even though I can't make out the features from this distance. I stare harder, narrowing my eyes, racking my brains. I know him, but where from?

I continue to watch him as he jogs back across the car park towards a dark grey car. He reaches it, opens the driver's door, and then suddenly it hits me. The man in the red vest, now getting into the car, leaning over to the silhouette of his passenger, and giving her a deep, passionate kiss as I continue to gawp is Glenn McCarthy, husband to Sarah, father to Jake. But that's not his car he's smooching in and that woman is most definitely not Sarah.

This sight is almost unbelievable. My eyes feel like they're extending three feet from my body and making that 'BAROOOOOOOOOGA!' noise like in a cartoon, and I blink a few times to make sure they haven't made the whole thing up. But as I stand there, the car reverses out of the space and drives off down the lane adjacent to the one I'm standing in so I can see more clearly now that it definitely is Glenn in the driver's seat. His passenger, though, is obscured and try as I might I can't get a good view of her.

Glenn McCarthy having an affair? There'll be monkeys

in space next. I turn back to my car and close the boot distractedly. This is irrefutable proof that there are at least *two* women on the planet that find him attractive. That's if you can still count Sarah on that very short list, after something like six or seven years of marriage. Perhaps he's improved with age. I shake my head. Incredible.

At the trolley park, the trolley won't go far enough into the trolley in front for the chain on it to reach the coin slot on mine. I ram it several times viciously – look at that ugly snarl on my face: if I could see that expression, I might think again about using it – but still it won't slot in. It occurs to me then to check if there's a reason why it won't fit and I lean forward to look at the trolley in front. Sure enough, someone has left a small black mobile phone hanging from the metal loop at the front under the handle. I unhook it and look at it. It's a nice little model, obviously expensive, very slim. It's switched off at the moment and the blank screen reminds me of a sleeping face. Which makes me remember how dog tired I am and a wave of exhaustion breaks over me, almost knocking me over. The trolley slides in the rest of the way now, so I retrieve my pound and go back to the car.

Sitting in the car, I look more closely at the phone. I switch it on. What I probably should have done is hand it in at the Customer Services desk, but that's all the way back in the shop, which is a two-mile walk from here. At least, it feels like a two-mile walk. Anyway, it doesn't matter because I have no intention of keeping this phone. I know I'm a lot of things, but dishonest is not one of them. I go into the menu and search through the address book, looking for an entry that says something like, 'Home', or 'Me'. I find 'Me', but when I ring it I just get the voicemail for this phone. What kind of idiot would programme their own mobile phone number into their mobile phone, for God's sake?

I keep searching. There's nothing for 'Home', so I go through the entire list alphabetically, to see if there's anything promising. Mostly just a lot of different names. Dozens and dozens of them. This person has got more contacts in their mobile than me, and that's saying something. Admittedly most of mine are one-time acquaintances, but I like having lots of names in there. Anyway, you never know when you might fancy getting back in touch with someone. I'm at the Cs now. We've got Castle, Carlos, Chester, Cray. On to the Ds. Design (*Design?* Is that someone's name?), Danny, Debs, Darlington. The Es are much the same. In fact, it's like that through the whole thing, just a lot of names, some of which I suspect are surnames, some are place names and some aren't even names.

I did have an idea though. Under 'I', I noticed an entry called 'ICE'. I've read about this somewhere. After the London bombings it was recommended that everyone programme some In Case of Emergency details into their mobiles, so that if you're involved in an incident, you can be more easily reunited with your family and friends. I select the ICE name and bring up the number. It's another mobile number. That'll do so I press the 'call' button. The phone's switched off too, so the voicemail comes on. I hadn't even thought of what I was going to say and was totally unprepared when the beep came.

'Oh, er, hi. Sorry to trouble you. Erm, you don't know me but I've got a mobile phone that belongs to someone you know. I'm calling you from it. I found it today, in

Sainsbury's car park. Hooked on a trolley. So, um, if your friend wants the phone back, they'll have to call me to arrange a time, or something.' I pause. This message sounds completely dim. I'm wondering if there's a facility on this phone of pressing a button that will erase the whole thing so I can start again. Then I realize that of course it doesn't matter what I sound like because this person doesn't know me and will probably never see me again. If at all.

It occurs to me at this point that there's a chance this phone could belong to the man I had encountered on his phone, who had been making fun of me at the checkout. If that was the case, his opinion of me was already very low anyway. I leave my home number and disconnect, then switch it off and drop it into my handbag. That's that.

As I'm driving along the bypass on my way home, my phone back at the flat starts ringing. There it is, on the coffee table in the empty flat, which, you may notice, is not looking as tidy and well cared for as it has in the past. It's not what I would call dirty exactly, just a little unclean. A few coffee cups are standing on the table next to the ringing phone, and some of them have obviously been there a day or two. There are also a couple of dirty plates that look like they might have held toast. The magazines are no longer piled up neatly on the table, but are now spread on the floor and sofa in a clutter. There are a few things on the floor that weren't there before – my kitten heels that I usually wear to work, a light lilac cardigan, a pair of socks. Like I said, it's not total devastation, but it's not great.

The phone's rung three times now, and it sounds like

I'm outside, trying to get my key in the lock. Of course, I'm also carrying a bag of shopping in each hand, and rushing to get indoors and answer the phone. Bear in mind it is now eight days since I have last seen or heard from Nick, and the only person that has rung me up in that time is my mum.

Obviously I've heard the phone ringing, and have got my door keys in my mouth as I'm elbowing my way through the external door, arms full of shopping. 'Huck, huck, huck.' I drop the bags of shopping in the corridor outside and frantically try to get the internal door open before the phone stops. Oh, there I am, and how different I look from the exhausted woman in the car park. Look, there's a flush on my cheek, a sparkle of hope in my eyes, eyebrows raised in an expectant smile. Clearly I am convinced this is going to be Nick calling me at last with a fantastic but totally credible explanation for why I've heard nothing for over a week.

I'm in, I'm running, tripping, stumbling to the phone, reaching out my hand, and it stops ringing just at the moment my fingertips brush plastic. I snatch it up anyway and put it to my ear.

'Hello? *Hello?*' I shout insistently, angrily, demanding that the person damn well comes back here and talks to me. '*Nick?!*'

You've got to feel sorry for me really. This whole waiting for him to phone was bad enough when I was only waiting for a day, but now it's been a week, and it's all new to me. I am so used to being in control of this kind of thing. I can be cool, even cold, standoffish, when I know exactly what's happening. But I'm in the dark here, fumbling around helplessly waiting for him to come and turn the light on. And still I am fighting back the encroaching feeling that he's not going to.

Please look away. This is me at my lowest, collapsed on the floor, sobbing on to the carpet, pathetically saying his name over and over. I am not proud of this moment, and thankfully it doesn't go on long.

Three things occur to me as I'm lying there on the floor, each one contributing equally to my rising from that position. One: the front door is wide open; two: the frozen chicken is defrosting on the carpet; and three: although I didn't get to the phone in time, just the fact that he's called me is an enormous, tremendous relief and source of sudden joy. I practically leap up on to my knees and seize the phone again, keying in 1471, just to check that it was definitely him. I know his home and mobile numbers off by heart now, so when the number I'm starting to hear does not match either one of those, I frown and snatch the phone away from my ear, switching it off quickly and throwing it down on to the floor as if it could do me harm. I stare at it for a moment, fighting against the growing wretchedness threatening to knock me down again, then I switch it back on and dial 1471 again, sure I have made a mistake, or the phone has.

Neither of us had. Except me, of course, for thinking, hoping, it was Nick in the first place. Just in case he's rung me from someone else's house and will need to prove this later, I jot the number down in my notebook, underneath his home number, as the electronic woman is saying it. I kneel there for a few long seconds, hands flat on the floor, head hanging low, trying to get the energy, or enthusiasm, or whatever, together to go and retrieve the shopping and start putting it all away. Then wearily I get to my feet.

*   *   *

Another working week goes by, and now it is Friday. I don't see Nick at work all that time, although I deliberately go down to the vending machine and get my own coffee every day. He's never there. He knows I usually have coffee at two so obviously he's getting his at one thirty, or three o'clock or whatever, just any time other than two.

If I had one single gram of sense this week, I'd have realized that of course Nick will be getting his coffee or light snack from the selection available in the identical vending machine that is located on the sixth floor, where he works. But I haven't. This is where I met him two weeks ago, so this is where I think I am most likely to meet him again.

He doesn't call me either. If you watch the whole week, you would see me rushing to the phone to dial 1471 every time I come in, to see if his number is on there. The same number from the Sunday has rung me three more times, so the possibility still exists that Nick has gone away for a few days and is trying to get hold of me from a different phone, but I'm not really clinging to that with much hope. We haven't had any contact now for two weeks, and if he was going away, surely he would have told me beforehand? And I've had no texts or calls from his mobile.

No, I know exactly what is going on here, and I'm trying to accept it. I have been on the other end of this kind of behaviour enough times to recognize a silent dump when I see one, and I know from my own experience that the most important thing is to keep your dignity.

I have had people calling me three, four times a day, sobbing, trying to understand what they did wrong; I have received flowers, chocolates, perfume, death threats, all in the name of 'Why?' I have watched so many people dissolving into sub-human blobs of helpless incapacity, it turns my stomach. I am determined that won't happen to me. That is why I have not gone up to Personnel, I have not tried going for coffee at a different time, and I have not called or texted him. Not that I haven't wanted to, but of course the entire office knowing everything about what's going on does have its plus side. I have maintained an impressive dignity in front of everyone. They're not even sure who's the dumper and who's the dumpee.

Also, I've got this illness that I'm fighting. This past week, I've been making a concerted effort to get back up the league tables at work. My two-week fling with Nick (yes, I know technically it was only one week, but I'm counting the second week because it might not necessarily have been over by then, he might just have gone a bit quiet) has had a bad effect on my sales figures, and I'm now ninth in the league. Still not too bad out of forty-five sales staff, but there is the fact I didn't mention earlier that fifteen of those forty-five are part-time and only work evenings, so they don't really count.

I've managed to scrape back one place from tenth, but it's not been as easy as it used to be. This profound, bone-aching exhaustion I've been feeling has not improved. I haven't been sleeping well, what with all the sobbing, and I know that I am depressed, which Mum says makes you feel sleepy. Still, it's affecting my mind, too, so I'm finding it really hard to concentrate for long. I find myself flicking rapidly through the brochure towards something, and then I slow down, suddenly realizing that I've got no idea at all what I was going to suggest. I can't even remember what the client requested in the first place.

'I'm sorry, did you say Isle of Wight or Isle of Man?'

'I just want to speak to someone about travel insurance, you dozy cow.'

And that sort of thing is making me feel awfully close to tears, which is very unlike me.

By the Friday, I've decided I need to see the doctor, urgently. A couple of weeks ago, a day or so before I met Nick, Jean asked me to go and meet some clients in reception who'd just come back from their holiday in Nairobi and wanted to lodge a complaint. I get picked for this kind of thing all the time because of my appearance. I don't mean just my physical looks, I'm talking about my style, my dress-sense, my personal grooming. We don't usually have to see clients face to face, but I always dress smartly in a skirt and blouse and do my hair every day. Val always wears jeans and an old T-shirt, I've noticed, and ties her hair up with a rubber band, which is why she never gets picked for anything.

Anyway, I've been feeling peculiar pretty much since then, give or take a day or two, so it must be some revolting African bug I've picked up from that pair of whingers. And the thing about these tropical bugs is that they spread really quickly, particularly in confined air-conditioned offices, so for all I know, I am infecting the entire working population of Horizon Holidays. If I'm honest, I am also pretty scared. I've never had symptoms like these before.

So I did what I have done only twice before during my time at Horizon: I made an outgoing call. I'm not one of those people that think this kind of thing is OK. I know that Val's always doing it, but as we now know, she does have a legitimate reason. And on this occasion, I feel that I, too, have a good reason. I need to make an urgent appointment with the doctor. I'll even go during the day and leave work for the appointment if necessary.

'Next Thursday afternoon, love?' the receptionist says.

I pause. That's nearly a week away. 'But it's urgent. Did you hear me say it was urgent?'

'I heard.' I get the sudden and inexplicable feeling that she's looking into a compact mirror as she's talking.

'The thing is, I've had contact with people who have just come back from Africa, and now I'm feeling dizzy, nauseous . . .'

'When was this?' I'm gratified to hear her interest suddenly increase.

'Um, about three weeks ago.'

I hear as she exhales loudly and slumps back in her seat again. 'Well, if it was an African strain you'd probably be dead by now. Got any sores?'

'Sores? Well, no.'

'Mucus? Any pus at all?'

'Um, well, no, not as such.'

'Well then, I can do three fifteen or five thirty.'

I perk up. 'What, today?'

'No, love, next Thursday, I told you. Three fifteen or five thirty. Which?'

I book the five-thirty appointment and hang up.

Two hours later it's five p.m., the end of the day, and the end of the week. Tomorrow is Jake's birthday party and I have got him no gift. I can pop into a newsagent on my way over there tomorrow afternoon and get a card and then stick a tenner in it. That'll do. Christine is approaching me but I'm so tired and listless, I just want to go home. I hide behind Graham's desk as Chrissie passes and she stops to ask Val if I've left. Val shrugs – she clearly doesn't

72

give a flying rat's backside where I am – so after one look at my deserted desk, Chrissie totters off.

I walk so slowly back to my car that most of the other cars have already ·gone. There is no sign of Chrissie. Wearily, I drive home. I'm holding the steering wheel with only one hand because I'm too tired to lift the other one. I change gear as infrequently as possible. My eyes are so hot and heavy I let them unfocus on the so-familiar journey. I'm sure my Clio can find its own way home. My head lolls back on to the headrest and my hand drops to the lowest part of the wheel. A large red object rushes up suddenly in front of me and I stomp on the brakes, stopping inches away from the stationary Post Office van.

Now I do close my eyes, my heart thumping painfully, blood rushing noisily in my ears, tears coming. That was so stupid, I'm thinking to myself, so stupid and so *close*. The P.O. van moves off, but I stay where I am for a few moments, breathing deeply to calm down. Come on, concentrate.

I drive the rest of the journey exaggeratedly carefully, indicating early, braking often. 'Better late than *the* late,' Mum always says. 'Better to die quickly in a crash than to run out of oxygen,' Dad always replies.

The first thing I do when I get home is *not* check 1471 straight away. I manage to last five minutes before checking it, which is a thirty-second improvement on yesterday. The voice tells me I was called today at thirteen fifty-two but the caller withheld their number. I'm not sure how to react to this news. I do feel a sudden surge of hopeful joy, thinking that Nick had called at last, but at the same time the two weeks since I last spoke to him keep getting in the way.

I decide not to make a decision but to keep an open mind. Or perhaps I could ring him, just to check whether it was him or not?

I sit down on the sofa and put my bag on my lap, hunting for the little notebook I jotted his number down in, and my hand falls on to the slim black mobile phone I found at Sainsbury's. I take it out and balance it in the palm of my hand. Whoops. I had forgotten all about it, and now the owner has been without it for six days. Anyone watching me would assume that I was intending to keep it, but I swear I'm not. I really did just forget about it.

I switch it on. I bet the owner has been ringing it frantically, and has now assumed that I've decided to keep it, particularly since it's been switched off all week. They probably think I've taken their Sim card out and put mine in. When it's on properly, I am very surprised that no signal comes through from the network to say there are loads of messages. How odd.

As all my remaining energy ebbs from me, the phone slips from my fingers and my head falls back. I close my eyes, just for a few minutes.

I am woken up by an unfamiliar trilling sound. At first I think it's my alarm clock, but it can't be, surely today is Saturday? No, wait, it's not Saturday yet, it's still Friday afternoon and I'm on the sofa. I fell asleep when I got in. So what's that noise? It's not my mobile, or the land line ringing. I struggle to sit up and open my bleary eyes, looking around me, patting the sofa as if somehow that is going to help me locate a sound.

But it does. My hand touches the strange mobile and it's vibrating as it rings. I snatch my hand away in surprise, then quickly grab it and press the 'Answer' key.

'Hello?' Too late I realize that this call is almost definitely not for me.

'Aha!' says a man's voice. 'There you are, at last!'

I clear my throat, still trying to shake off the last threads of sleep. 'Oh, no, sorry, look, whoever you think you've got hold of, you haven't. I mean, this is not me. No, no, it is me. I mean, I'm not the person that should be me. I'm not the person who should be answering this phone.' I sigh. Why can't I seem to make any sense?

'I beg to differ. You are exactly the person who should be answering it because you are the one who is holding it.'

Well, that seems logical. 'Um, I suppose so. But you really—'

'Ah, no buts, please. Let's get to the business of the day, and that is, what are your demands?'

Look at my face now! It's a kind of comical puzzlement. I'm even standing up, to help me to understand what's going on. 'I'm sorry?'

'As well you should be. Thanks to you, I have lost a massive contract worth nearly ten million pounds. What have you got to say for yourself?'

It's totally clear that he thinks he's talking to the owner of the phone, but he won't let me explain. And now apparently the phone's owner has caused him to lose a lot of money.

'I'm afraid it's really not me you should be talking to about that. You see, I found—'

'Yes, I know, you found the phone. It's my phone. I want it back, as soon as we can manage it. So, I want to know what your demands are?' He sounds like he's smiling.

With a sickening jolt, I realize the significance of what

75

he's just said. I completely forgot about the phone and it has lain dormant in my handbag for almost a week, resulting in this man losing a contract worth . . . My hand goes to my mouth. Oh my God. I am responsible. I was too lazy to take the phone into the store and hand it in to Customer Services, and because of that . . .

'Oh my God. I'm so terribly sorry. It's completely my fault. You see, I've not been all that well lately, and when I found your phone, I was too tired, too ill, to take it inside, so I just rang the ICE number but then I forgot all about it and it's just been sitting in my bag since Sunday.'

'Hey, hey, it's all right, think nothing of it. It happens all the time. Honestly.'

'*Does* it?'

'Absolutely. I lost the car keys once and the whole middle-eastern arm of our company collapsed. I'm sorry to hear you've not been well.'

See that comical puzzlement again? Is this man having a laugh, or what? Do you think he's winding me up? Because I really am not sure at this point. His voice is nice, really friendly and warm. Plus he sounds like he's smiling the whole time, which makes me think he is just trying to get a rise out of me.

'Um, well, thanks.' What else can I say?

'Not at all. Now, please tell me, what do you want to do about this phone situation? Because I am prepared to go to any lengths to get it back. Truly. I will ford rivers, climb mountains, cross deserts, you name it.'

I'm smiling now. It's a wind-up, got to be. Ten million pounds my arse. I think for a moment. 'That's really commendable. But are you prepared to . . . drive to the Ashton Business Park?'

He pauses before saying, 'Are you suggesting . . . the Blooding?'

I'm grinning now. 'I am.'

He sucks a long breath in over his teeth. 'Very well, but you ask a lot. What time, and when?'

When you come off the motorway at our town, there's a business park there, with lots of shops, restaurants, leisure parks and businesses. Furniture shops, computer suppliers, shoe outlets, that type of thing. In the centre is a kind of square, with a huge fountain in the middle. This fountain has caused a lot of problems for our council because apparently it cost them nearly two million quid. It was the main topic of discussion everywhere you went for a couple of months last year, but not because of the atrocious waste of money it was. This fountain is now a famous landmark around the country because it is the most hideous and offensive thing you have ever seen. It was made by a local artist, and this person was obviously a fan of fox-hunting, because she chose for her subject a twenty-foot-high cast-iron tableau depicting a fox being torn in three pieces by a pack of slavering hounds. You have to look quite carefully to see the fox, or what's left of it, but the really horrible bit is the dogs. They're very stylized so they've got huge bulbous eyes and elongated noses and these enormous fangs that are just dripping with saliva, or blood, or both. It's a fountain, so there's water running constantly out of their mouths. It's called 'The Blooding'.

Anyway, this is the place I am thinking about, and the Mobile Man has obviously realized. So almost without intending to, I am arranging to meet him. But I have to give him his phone back somehow, and I'm certainly not inviting him to my home.

'Tomorrow, three o'clock, call this number. No funny business.' This is definitely fun, even though I don't know this bloke. I like him, though.

He laughs out some air through his nose. 'Very well. Tomorrow, at three, I will call this number. And all business, should there be any, will be extremely dull.'

'Excellent. Till tomorrow then.'

'Till tomorrow.'

Now this is Hector McCarthy, sitting on his sofa, in his study, chatting to me on his mobile phone. I was right, he is smiling, and has been throughout the whole conversation. He is clearly delighted with how that went – look at him, he can't stop grinning. This little bit of unexpected fun has brought a fledgling ray of sun into the dark misery that has been engulfing him lately, and it feels good.

He stands up and stretches, still enjoying the memory of the phone conversation. The way that the Mobile Girl responded to his joke about ransom was really refreshing. Miranda, his ex-girlfriend, would never have done that. She wouldn't even have understood the point of it.

'But she didn't kidnap the phone,' she would have said, 'she found it. This is just silly.' Well, yes, she would have been right, it was silly. But it was fun and that is what Miranda wasn't.

He realizes suddenly that thinking about Miranda has not cost him a single moment of pain. Surely that can't have just happened in the past half hour? He wonders how long he has been free of it without noticing. It hurt so much, for so long, he had just got used to the pain being there. But now, apparently, it was gone.

He is just enjoying the giddying feeling of freedom

when he hears a crash from the other room, followed by muted but terrified whimpers.

He starts, and runs quickly into the dining room. The sight that greets him sends his newly joyous heart plunging once more into despair.

There is a pool of water spreading out across the floor from the remains of a vase of flowers. The table the vase was standing on is tipped over, as are three of the four chairs. There is a jumble of broken china and glass scattered around the floor, and Hector recognizes the dismembered limbs of his mother's cherished ornament collection amongst the debris, now no more than a grisly china holocaust.

Hector's face is no longer smiling. He looks around the room quickly and locates the cause of all this devastation. She is sitting on the fourth dining chair, her feet tucked up on the seat, her arms wrapped tightly around her legs. Her face is slick and white, her damp hair clinging to her head in clumps. Her wild eyes are darting around the room until eventually they settle on Hector and she begins to gesticulate.

'Get them out of here, Charlie, please, they're on the floor, look. Please, please, Charlie, get them out.' Tears stream silently down her face in terror as Hector moves across the floor in two strides and wraps his arms around her.

'Shhhh, love, come on, it's all right now, shhh.'

Still she trembles. 'Please, Charlie, get rid of them. They're everywhere.'

'OK, I'll do it now. Don't worry.' Swiftly he fetches a dustpan and brush and sweeps up all the china pieces, every last fragment, and tips them away into the bin in the kitchen. Only then can he coax her up from the chair and persuade her to go upstairs with him.

He sits down on the bed next to her and holds her hand.

'Are they all gone now, Hector?' Her dark eyes are looking at him, and this time she sees him, not his father.

'Yes, love, they're all gone. For ever.'

Her face is visibly relaxing. 'You're a good boy, Hector,' she says as her eyelids droop. 'Such a good boy. I'll ask your father to take you out fishing at the weekend. You'll like that.'

He smiles sadly, feeling the dampness in his eyes. 'Yes, I will. Now you go to sleep, OK?'

Her eyes are closed now. 'OK. Night night, Hec.'

He walks back to the door, then turns, smiling. 'Night, Mum.'

Chapter Five

Saturday 19 August. The next day. The day of my god-awful godson's god-forsaken birthday party. Here I am, gingerly pulling back the covers and hauling myself slowly out of bed, looking, even though I have to say it myself, like a corpse rising. Look at my face – sallow, lifeless skin, sunken eyes, graveyard hair. I've even got my hands in front of me as I stumble across the bedroom like one of the undead.

It's my usual habit to have a look in the mirror as soon as I get up to see what the night has done to my face. Generally speaking, I get out of bed looking as if I'm about to go out for dinner, but these last two weeks I have not been sleeping as soundly as usual and the extra tossing and turning during the night is taking its toll. Reaching the bathroom I brave a look in the mirror and am shocked by what I see: toothpaste splatters all over the glass. They're not huge blobs that distort the image behind them so apart from being surprised that they're there at all, I'm not a great deal affected by them. I'm leaving them there for now.

Some people don't bother much with areas of the house that can't be seen by visitors, like the bedroom or bathroom, but I think that is the height of sloppiness. I'll admit that with all the stress I've been dealing with lately I am not at the height of cleanliness any more, but I'm still on the ladder. I'm just coming down a rung or two.

I lean forward and let the white dots on the mirror go blurry, and my face sharpens into focus behind them. Immediately I wish it hadn't and I let it swim away again. It's ironic, isn't it, that on this day of all days I look exactly like a godmother?

Being a godmother brings no benefit at all and sounds almost exactly like grandmother, so the image in everyone's head is a sweet, grey-haired old lady. Or maybe a tubby fairy doing 'Bibbety bobbity boos' all over the place. I am neither of those things, as you know; although today, I might as well be. Looking at the blurred, ghostly shape behind the toothpaste splatters, I almost despise myself. Why am I reacting so badly to a silent dump? Is it because this is my first one? Surely it can't be as bad as this for everyone else?

I am reminded suddenly of Craig Someone who I went out with about two years ago. We were together for less than three weeks and then I had to let him go. He didn't take the silent treatment well at all.

'I'll see you tomorrow then,' he had said at the end of our final date. He didn't know it was our final date, of course. I had nodded silently, endured for the last time the wet, sucking black hole that was his rendition of a goodnight kiss and gone home relieved that it was all over.

He phoned from the pavement five minutes later. 'Just wanted to tell you that I love you,' he had said, blowing –

or rather sucking – wet noises down the line at me. 'You're gorgeous, did you know that?' Well of course I did; I'm not blind. 'Call you tomorrow, babe.'

He called eight hours later. 'Good morning, sunshine,' he shouted down the phone. 'How are you this fine morning? Can't wait to see you later, gorgeous. I've got a great big surprise for you, babe. You're never gonna guess what it is!' I put the receiver down on the pillow, rolled over to the other side of the bed and went back to sleep.

He called three more times that day and left messages on the answerphone, begging me to call him back, pleading with me to forgive him for whatever he'd done to upset me, promising to change, to be the way I wanted him to be. The next day he called seven times, professing undying passion, pure, worshipful love, never-ending devotion. The day after that he lobbed dog shit at my windows and sprayed 'BITCH' on my front door with red paint.

But he was a nutcase, I think. The day after the shitting, the police came and peeled him off the lamppost outside my block, where he'd stationed himself for over three hours. Stark naked. He had been reading out alternately from a collection of love poems he had written for me, and a list of all the different ways he was going to cut me.

Soft gentle Rachel, you curl like a petal,
I rest in your arms, my soul is at peace,
You are my world, my everything, my sun, my
    moon,
The light in my life that darkened too soon.
I'm going to fucking carve my initials in your face,
    you little bitch.

83

Touching, isn't it? I read all about it in the local paper a few days later – I think I was out shopping when all this was going on.

Obviously Craig was already a bit unstable when I started going out with him. Not everyone reacts like that, and I am certainly not going to.

I am going to have a shower and get dressed now, so let's leave me in peace and go and see what Sarah is doing on this fine sunny morning. This is the joyous anniversary of the day that she bore new life, the day that the wondrous and perfect form of Jake, her first-born child, the fruit of her love for Glenn, the joy of their union, was delivered into the world in a moving, magical and astonishing moment.

'*Fuck it!*' Sarah shouts as the hot baking tray she is just taking out of the oven slips from her fingers and crashes to the ground in a sausage-roll explosion. 'Oh fuck, fuck, fucking *fuuuuuck.*' She descends to the floor at almost the same speed as the sausage rolls and begins to grab them hurriedly, as if she thinks she can do it before the germs on the floor have a chance to climb on.

I'm looking at Sarah, squatting and sweating on her kitchen floor as she scrabbles around in the infernal heat of a kitchen with the oven on for two hours in mid-August, knowing that what she's working towards is a two-hour-long descent into hell this afternoon that will bring utterly no pleasure to her, only more work, stress and exhaustion and I am struck once again by the unshakeable, unconditional and incomparable power of maternal love. Makes for a crappy Saturday.

I think the world is divided into two kinds of people: those that have got children and those that haven't.

Neither side can understand the other, and each believes that they have got the best deal. Except for the people who have got children, who are all secretly wishing they were on the other side. They all pretend to be deliriously happy with cute little Joshy-Woshy or darling little Emilykins because to admit otherwise would be like confessing to Nazi tendencies or admitting that they like conducting experiments on little fluffy bunnies at the weekends.

But who could possibly prefer being up to their elbows in diarrhoea and vomit on a Saturday night to getting dressed up in a totally gorgeous and sexy outfit, heading out into a smart nightclub, having a few drinks and enjoying some fascinating conversation with some interesting and exciting new friends?

No one. That's the truth. But I'll bet if you asked any parent which they would prefer, they'd all say, in a weary, lifeless monotone, 'Parenthood'. That's if you can even make them hear you over the screaming. No one ever admits it because if even one person did, other people would start saying, 'Actually, I wish I was on the other side too', and before you know it, millions of people would be defecting and eventually that would mean the end of the human race.

Did you see that? Sarah's just eaten two of the sausage rolls that went on the floor. Ugh. I wouldn't do that even in my own flat where I know for a fact the floor has been washed and bleached within the past six months. Thankfully she's now tipping the remains into the bin, which is a relief. I had been wondering whether she was going to serve them up at the party later. Remind me not to eat anything when I get there.

Only kidding. I never eat the food at parties.

So in the name of the continuance of the species, Sarah is now carrying a kicking and screaming Jake to the car so she can go and collect his birthday cake. Did you notice that she's on her own this morning? It's Saturday so Glenn can't be at work, surely? Let's go back to first thing this morning and see what happened.

Oh God, no, let's go forward an hour – I don't think I can stomach watching the fixed smiles of Sarah and Glenn in their bed, as their newly six-year-old son lands knees first on their stomachs, even though the sun has barely left the horizon.

OK, this is better. Glenn is standing in the kitchen with his coat on while Sarah is laying out seventy-five frozen sausage rolls on a baking tray. They're not looking at each other.

'Come on, Sar, you know the money will be useful,' Glenn says.

'I'm not disputing that, Glenn,' she says, calmly and sweetly. 'I'm just saying that the money isn't the most important thing here and you could miss the overtime today, just for one day, because it's your six-year-old son's *FUCKING BIRTHDAY*!' She turns to face him for the last two words and shrieks them into his face. He jumped too – did you notice? Good one, Sarah.

'I can't talk to you when you're like this,' Glenn says. 'I'll be back by the time the party starts.' And he walks out of the front door.

I wonder where he's off to. Oh, don't be so naive, of course he's not going to work.

Oh look, now Sarah's crying. I hope the tears don't land on the sausage rolls. No, actually it doesn't matter, does it, because we know they all end up in the bin later anyway. If only we could tell her not to bother cooking them.

Back to my flat where I'm showered and dressed and making my way to the kitchen for some breakfast. I've left my hair wet today, to give it a rest from the dryer. Mum says I should do that – let my hair relax once in a while – so that it doesn't get too brittle. I normally do it on days when I'm not expecting to see anyone, when I'm at home and no visitors are coming round, but today I just can't get the energy together for anything much.

Cosmo is getting on my nerves this morning, weaving in and out of my feet as I walk. Normally, when he does this, I try to avoid stepping on him by dancing around as I walk – I do love him – but today I just tramp blithely onwards. If he's got any sense, he'll stay out of my way. I'm vaguely aware of some soft things underfoot once or twice but he's all right because he scuttles off. Eventually he comes to rest in the kitchen and sits down in front of the cupboard where his food is kept, staring at it intently. It's like he's trying to tell me what he wants just with his eyes, like Lassie or Flipper. What's that, Cosmo? There's a group of kids trapped in the old silver mine and they've only got three hours of oxygen left?

Screw the kids, his eyes say, give me Kit-e-kat.

Yeah, well, I'm hungry too, so I get a bowl out of the cupboard and start filling it with Shreddies and milk. Cosmo is up again and from here you can predict what's going to happen, can't you? I move towards the fridge to put the milk away and Cos gets right in between my feet as I move my back leg forwards. He's squashed between my calves but more importantly my forward momentum carries me on but there's no foot to receive the weight so I stumble forwards, collide belly first with the counter top, rebound off it, stagger for a terrifying second and then crash with a shriek on to the floor in a milk explosion to rival Sarah's sausage rolls.

'Christ, you stupid *cat!*' I shout, kicking out instinctively towards Cosmo. Unexpectedly, my foot is right on target and I watch in surprise as Cosmo skates across the floor in slow motion, feet splayed and rotating gently, his eyes wide with shock. When he comes to a halt he slinks away, belly low to the ground and ears flat.

I want you to know that this is totally unlike me. I have never been violent to Cosmo in my life and normally I would be horrified that this had happened. Cruelty to animals is one of my favourite charities.

Today, though, I couldn't care less. Cosmo is fine, just a bit winded, but he's still got a home and is guaranteed two meals a day, so what's he complaining about? If he hadn't been so insistent on being fed first, this wouldn't have happened. And now I've got to clear up all the spilt milk.

Stuff it, I'm leaving it. I'm so tired I need to go and sit down. I'm taking my breakfast with me to eat on the sofa.

I get comfortable with the bowl on my lap and settle into a nice long uninterrupted think about Nick. The bastard. What can I possibly have done to make him want to dump me? I thought I was the perfect girlfriend: sexy, punctual, enthusiastic, if you know what I mean. What's wrong with any of that? It's been a fantastically successful formula until now, so what's so different about Nick Bloody Maxwell? What makes him so special?

If you take a quick peek at what Nick Maxwell is doing on this Saturday morning in August, you'll see him standing in front of his mirror in just his underpants, facing the mirror sideways, holding a hairbrush. Actually, it's his mum's hairbrush – Nick always uses a comb – and he's borrowed it this morning for a specific purpose. He's standing very still, gazing into his own beautiful blue eyes, holding the hairbrush by his side, in his fist. Suddenly the CD player on his dressing table begins to emit music – it's the opening bars of Elvis singing 'A Little Less Conversation' and Nick raises the brush to his mouth, dips his chin, frowns into the mirror and begins to sing along.

He curls his top lip and thrusts his pelvis, his chest muscles jumping in time to the music.

Fortunately for me, sitting on my sofa, I can't see this performance. I'm having a hard enough time getting over him as it is and seeing that would probably make me swoon into a lust coma.

But I'm still no nearer understanding why he seems to have dumped me. There is absolutely no sensible explanation for it. I'm trying to remember the last time we spoke, the last time we saw each other, although my own experience tells me that a dump rarely comes as the result of a specific conversation. Unless it's something like, 'I'm going to live in Australia tomorrow', or, 'I prefer your best friend.' But neither of those things was said the last time I spoke to Nick. I do remember asking him along to Jake's party, but he just smiled and said he'd have to check if he was free.

Oh God, Jake's party. Wouldn't it be so great if I could turn up with Nick? It would be a very sexy spoonful of sugar to make the ghastly medicine go down. The afternoon wouldn't be such a dead loss after all and it wouldn't end until late tonight. I've got goosebumps just thinking about it.

Now I come to think about it, Nick has never actually said that he isn't coming today. Could I phone him, just to make sure? No, that's ridiculous, if he was coming he would have contacted me. But then my reason for phoning him is not actually to find out if he's coming, it's to remind him about me, so he hears my voice, and thinks about other parts of me and maybe is reminded of a couple of reasons why he started going out with me in the first place. At least it would be, if I was going to phone him. Which I'm not.

But then, why shouldn't I? I'm not turning into Craig So'meone, just by ringing up to ask very casually if he's coming to this party with me today or not. I would never deliberately collect dog shit anyway.

I'm going to phone him. It's a party, for a little boy, my godson, and I need to know if I've got a lift there or do I have to get there on my own. Right. Now where did I write down his number?

I've left my cereal bowl on the coffee table while I wander round the flat hunting for my address book. It's in my handbag, right there on the sofa where I was just sitting, so don't worry, I will remember eventually.

I'm worried about my memory lately. I can't seem to retain information the way I used to. I'm sure it's all due to this virus or whatever it is, or the lack of sleep lately, or maybe a combination of both, but I've become so forgetful. I'm worried I'm turning into one of those elderly relatives you hear people talking about who are constantly being discovered wandering along the B2046 in their underwear. I always wear matching bra and knickers by Jasper Conran, so if it does happen, it won't be too embarrassing.

Ah, here we are, I'm back on the sofa, rummaging through my handbag. As I do so, my hand brushes against the mobile phone and I wonder distractedly if the owner will ring again today. Of course he will, if he ever wants to see his phone again. Aha, here's the address book.

The number is surrounded by doodles of hearts and the word 'Nick' written in very artistic and flowery writing. Don't look too closely at the page because you might be able to catch a glimpse of the words 'Rachel Maxwell' written there. Before I have a chance to talk some sense into myself, I pick up the phone and dial the number.

This is Nick's house again, about half an hour after that mind-blowing performance in his room. I'm sorry to have to tell you that he's got dressed and come downstairs in that time.

'Nicky! Phone's ringing!' It's Helen Maxwell, standing in the kitchen, pouring boiling water on to coffee granules. The ringing phone, with me on the other end, is in a different room, somewhere behind her.

'Mum, I'm busy.' That's Nick's voice, coming from the same direction as the ringing phone. Sounds like they're in the same room.

'Yeah, so'm I, you lazy thing. Just get the phone, please.'

'I can't, I'm at a crucial point.'

'So pause it.'

'I can't, I haven't got any Save Game crystals. Can't you just—'

'Oh, for crying out loud,' she says, slamming the kettle

down furiously, and balancing her smoking cigarette on the edge of the ashtray. She marches into the living room, mumbling under her breath, 'It won't be for me anyway, don't know why I'm bothering,' but Nick doesn't notice: he's engrossed in shooting a T-rex.

'I'm not your bloody secretary, you know,' she says, picking up the receiver. 'Hello? This is Nick Maxwell's personal assistant, how may I—?' Nick glances up at her briefly as she listens to the caller speaking.

'Oh, no, I'm not really, it was just a joke . . . I'm Mrs Maxwell, who're you? . . . Yes, he's here, shall I . . . ? Oh, OK.' Nick looks up again, more interested. Helen stares at him as she listens. 'Well, you can tell him yours— All right then . . . Look, there's no need to get . . . I shouldn't think so, no. Right, fine. Bye.' She turns round and puts the receiver back on the hook.

'Who was it?' Nick says, resuming his game.

'I don't know. Some girl for you.'

He looks up. 'Did she say who?'

'No, but she was bonkers. Very upset. Kept saying she was sorry and didn't mean it.'

'Did you know her?' he asks, already losing interest in the conversation.

'Nope.' She walks back to the kitchen door and turns. 'She asked me to pass on a message. She says, she hopes you catch a disgusting disease and die from it.' She thinks for a moment, then nods. 'Yes, that was it.'

Nick sniggers and his friend Sean who is sitting on the sofa joins in.

Helen turns to Sean. 'Oh, hello, Sean, didn't see you there.'

'All right, Helen.'

'Still not sorted out your tattoo, then?' Helen says, eyeing Sean's head.

'Nah, it's not worth it. No one really notices anyway.'

Helen smiles. 'Well, at least it's less offensive than SKINS, that's all I can say.'

Back to me sitting on my sofa, staring at the phone in my hand. Of all the reasons for Nick not contacting me all this time, I had never once considered the possibility that he was married. I shake my head in disbelief. But then why should I be so surprised? He's an incredibly gorgeous bloke who probably has women after him all the time. In fact, I should have been more suspicious that a bloke like that was still single.

Now that I start thinking about it, it's disgust that overwhelms me, not misery. I have had sex with a married man. Several times. In his *car*. What if he had sex with his wife in that car? What if he takes his kids out to the beach in that car? No wonder he never took me to his place. Decorators, my arse. It all makes sense now.

I've got up suddenly. My face has gone a rather peculiar colour and I'm heading rapidly towards the toilet, clutching my hand to my mouth. I retch violently into the bowl, my stomach clenching to expel its contents, but there are only a few Shreddies so once they're out, I'm left straining and rasping drily, body racked with spasms over and over, eyes streaming, mouth drooling. Eventually, after what seems a very long time, it stops and I slide, weakened, to the floor, wrapping my arms around myself, and curl up, foetus-like, saliva dripping off my chin and snot off my nose.

Chapter Six

Sorry about this – it's not very interesting to look at, is it? It's the outside of my bathroom door. I'm still in there, feeling very poorly, but it would only make me feel worse if you could see me. As you know I was born with a gorgeous face and body, perfect, straight teeth, naturally glossy hair and almost no freckles, but there is so much more to me than just those things. I would be a fool if I thought I could get by in life with just the good looks I was born with.

Firstly, I have to go to the hairdresser every six weeks to have my highlights touched up. While I'm under the heat lamp, Shanelle does my eyebrow wax, and every second visit she does my eyelash starch. I have to have some other areas waxed too, and let me tell you, that hurts. I do a facial once a week, I have a manicure once a fortnight and a pedicure once a month. I exercise regularly and only eat carbs every other Tuesday. On top of all this work, you have to consider the hours I put in choosing fabulous clothes, creating gorgeous, sexy ensembles, finding the right shoes – and it's not just the colour that matters, it's the style too – accessorizing with a scarf here, a bangle there, co-ordinating bag, earrings, belt, jacket. Then there's the make-up. I have spent what must amount to years in front of the mirror, dabbing, rubbing, smoothing, practising and perfecting the 'not wearing any make-up' look. It hasn't been easy.

So my clothes, hair and make-up are all perfect. But it's still worth nothing if I am seen looking hunched and undignified. I have poise, elegance and glamour, carved out of the raw material that God and my parents gave me, and I will not sacrifice it by letting you come in and see me in this state. So outside the door you stay.

This behaviour is quite unlike me. Normally, I love to be watched, whatever I'm doing. Normally, I am in control of whatever I'm doing. This is a bit different.

I can tell you, though, even though you can't see me at the moment, that I am quite surprised, and pleased, by this violent reaction. My abhorrence of the situation I have found myself in, of being 'the other woman', is so profound, due to my deeply held moral conviction, that it has brought on this episode. I feel quite proud.

Those sounds behind the door tell you that I am up, and in the shower. All right, you can come in now. I have already had a shower today, as you know, but I am not going to appear at Jake's party in the clothes I wore to throw up in.

As I'm rubbing my head vigorously under the hot water, I start thinking about Nick. Well, actually it would be more precise to say I resume thinking about Nick. Nick and his wife, in relation to me. Could Chrissie have known he was married when she was urging me to go out with him? I think back to that moment, when she laid her hand on my arm. Was she giving any clues away, or did she look like she was trying to hide something? I close my eyes as

I rinse the shampoo away and try to bring back into my head Chrissie's face as she was talking about Nick. Aha, got her – big red hair, strong perfume, orange top. Right, but what was the expression on her face? Was it secretive and knowing? Complicit? Deceitful? I'm zooming in on her, looking really close-up, trying to spot those little tiny clues . . . Big red hair, strong perfume, orange top.

OK so I'm not the most observant person in the world. Not of women, anyway. But I do know one thing: Chrissie does not consider anything to be forbidden or out of reach, and that includes married men. In fact, I know that she considers a married or otherwise attached man to be a particular challenge, and a valuable conquest.

'Single men are easy,' she always says. 'They're not getting any, are they, so do you think they're gonna turn you down, if you offer it? Has that ever happened? Of course not. They'll take whatever they can get, no question. There's no challenge there – they're practically falling over each other to get to you. It's all just a bit too simple.' She adjusts her top, pulling the V down at the front a bit to let her cleavage out. 'The real challenge lies with someone who's got a girlfriend or wife at home and who can therefore, in theory, get some whenever he wants. You've got to persuade him either that he's sick of having steak every night and would like to have a nice, big, juicy burger for a change, or that what he thinks is steak at home is actually just a soggy old burger and he can have nice, juicy steak every night if he dines out. Now that's rewarding.'

'What if he's vegetarian?' Susan asked once, looking sidelong at me and Sarah, before slugging on her Pinot Grigio.

'Gay, you mean?' Chrissie said with a confident smile. 'Oh, Susan, you know they're the biggest challenge of all.' And she flicks her hair nonchalantly over her bare shoulder, as if to remind us that she has the power to turn every gay man she's ever met over to the dark side.

She tried to convince us all when we were sixteen that she had done it. Had sex with a gay guy. I was very sceptical, even then, and she was much more attractive eight years ago.

'Brian McManus,' she announced proudly, a few days after the alleged event. Well, it was easy to see from his purple trousers that Brian was gay, but I wasn't convinced she had really turned his head. If you get my meaning. Back then, getting a gay guy to have sex with you was the ultimate accolade and confirmed in the eyes of the whole school that you were the sexiest, most powerful and feminine girl there.

Susan gave me a quick nudge and produced a confused frown. 'But surely, Chrissie, if a guy fancies you who normally only fancies other blokes,' she said, apparently puzzling it out, 'doesn't that make you the one who is *least*—?'

'You gonna have a go, then, Sue?' Chrissie had cut in quickly.

Susan declined, giving her standard excuse that she had just started seeing some bloke from Iceland ('The shop, not the country'), but I did find out myself a few weeks later that Brian McManus wasn't remotely gay, and never had been. He just looked gay. George Clooney would look gay in those trousers. Trouble was, I couldn't denounce Chrissie without giving myself away too. Brian was not attractive – he had huge yellow teeth and smelled of pastry

– but he found that quite a lot of high-calibre girls like me were very keen to sleep with him, as long as he kept quiet about it afterwards.

So we know Chrissie has never slept with any gay men, whatever she might like to think we think. But I do know for a fact she is not averse to having a go at married men, and has dipped more than a toe into that pool. 'Your dad's a bit of all right,' she once famously said to my horrified reflection in our bathroom at a birthday party. But Chrissie wasn't the only one who was encouraging me to go out with Nick. Do Jean and Val and M and M all think it's OK to shag someone who's married too?

No, surely not. Not Val, anyway. The story about Val is that she split from her husband because of the affair he had a few years ago. Apparently, she thought he was doing the accounts in the spare bedroom, when he was actually doing the accountant on the upstairs landing. I've never spoken to her about it first hand, though. It's just one of those really private and personal things that absolutely everyone in the office knows. So I think she would definitely not have encouraged me, if she had known Nick was a married man.

So, what does that tell me? No one knows Nick very well? Yes, and I don't know Val very well but I still know about her cheating husband. If Nick was openly married, the office would know. Which can mean only one thing – he is masquerading as a single, available man in order to ensnare innocent, gorgeous young girls into his web of sex. And lies. But mostly sex.

I pause while stepping out of the shower as this realization hits me. Can you look away a minute, please? Give me some dignity. I'll snap back into action in a moment.

OK, I'm safely wrapped in a towel now. You can look.

Are you surprised to see me just throwing on any old thing today? Yes, you're right, it is unusual. Normally, it would take me at least an hour to get ready, if not an hour and a half. Choosing my outfit alone has been known to take me almost the whole hour, but today I am throwing on a pair of shorts and a T-shirt that says in really small writing across my boobs, 'If you can read this, you're too close.' I've towel-dried my hair, but am leaving it to relax today, as you know, so that's done. And finally, I'm not even bothering to put on any make-up – not a crumb. What's the point? The only bloke there will be Glenn.

That is most unlike me. Normally I put on my make-up and do my hair even if I'm going for a swim.

Outside the air feels intensely cool and fresh on my skin. It's invigorating and makes my face tingle. I realize that this is because I haven't been outside without foundation on since I was fifteen.

When I arrive at Sarah's twenty minutes later – after getting Jake a birthday card from the garage on the way – Sarah squints at me in the doorway, as if she can see there's something different about me but she can't tell what it is. Eventually, she hits on it.

'You look ill.'

In spite of my apparently obvious fragility, Sarah has asked me to pull the bouncy castle down the garden to the shed, where there is a power supply. I agreed. Did you spot my mistake there? Well, I'm thinking bouncy castle, full of air, will be light and easy to move, like a giant beach ball. I can bounce it down the garden, no problem.

So here we are in the garden. See that enormous mound of thick, heavy-duty vinyl that looks like a sleeping orange-and-white dinosaur? That's the un-bouncy castle. It doesn't become bouncy, apparently, until you put air in it, and that doesn't happen until you plug it into the mains, which is in the shed.

This is the exact moment that a headache starts. I don't know if the headache is made worse because of the awful task I've been given, or if the awful task is worse because of the headache. It feels like someone's put a bouncy castle inside my skull and they won't stop inflating it. Apparently their power supply was easily accessible.

Let's move forward ten minutes. I have had a really shit day so far, and the sight of me straining and sweating on one end of a rope is not going to improve things. Here I am, ten minutes later, and the shed is in sight. You can see that my face has gone two or three shades paler than before I started this, and the truth is I really do feel quite poorly. Iron girders are clanging backwards and forwards inside my head, pounding into both sides alternately making me feel really sick and dizzy. I stand for a moment in the shade of some random tree, rubbing my temples.

'You all right, Rachel?'

I open my eyes to find Glenn standing there in a yellow shirt and beige shorts, grinning. He looks all right, really, doesn't he? I don't mean my type, obviously – an image of dark, seductive Nick Maxwell in a crisp white T-shirt and black jeans drops down on to the lawn beside the smiley, banana-shirted Glenn and makes Glenn look, frankly, a little ridiculous – but he's normal, what a husband and father ought to look like. Yeah, smile while you still can, you lying piece of worm shit. I hope your knob falls off.

'Shall I take over?' he says pleasantly, so I walk away as an answer. Technically, this should have been done by him this morning anyway, but he was apparently 'doing overtime'. Uh-huh, and I was drinking tequila slammers with the Queen in a hot air balloon over Sandringham.

The first child arrives at ten to three, like a scout ant doing a recce for the rest of the group, who arrive en masse ten minutes later. Luckily for me, I get a nasty spasm in my belly at that moment and have to rush to the loo.

It's quite good timing, actually, because after being violently and painfully sick, Sarah said I could lie on her and Glenn's bed for the entire duration of the party. Well, actually she said 'a while', but I'm taking that to mean, 'until the party is over'. As I'm lying here trying to relax, I am assaulted by two things: one, the sudden, violent realization that this is the bed that Glenn and Sarah have sex in; and two, a lot of shouting, terrible loud music and forced adult laughter from downstairs.

Eventually, the first of those two thoughts overrides the second and I haul myself up, glancing at the bedside clock – it's just gone four – then looking away quickly. Suddenly, I find I don't want my eyes to land on anything in this room, just in case they see something they shouldn't.

Downstairs, an eerie silence has descended. No, actually it's not silent, is it? There are some noises, strange, sucking, squelching sounds, but they're difficult to identify. I hesitate by the front door and stare longingly through the patterned glass at the distorted shape of my car out on the road. Could I slip out and drive away without Sarah noticing? I take one step towards freedom, then realize that my handbag is in the kitchen, which is at the moment swarming with offspring, so I am stuck.

Tentatively, I enter the living room, and through the double glass doors at the other end I can see the dining room and the reason for the unnatural quiet: it's feeding time. Twenty or maybe thirty kids are sitting around Sarah's big dining table – which has got the extra middle bit in – using both hands to move food from the serving dishes to their mouths. Little of it is actually chewed and consumed, it's just moved, handled. The movement is ceaseless, a blur of chubby reaching arms like tentacles waving across the table, as if all the arms belong to one being. Sarah is scuttling worriedly around the table, trying to prevent food and drink from landing on the carpet. I say, let it. It will probably be an improvement.

Over there on the patio, just outside the glass doors, I can see Chrissie and Susan having a cigarette together. They are facing back into the house and we wave and smile to each other in greeting, but further communication is unwise. We don't want to attract the attention of this feeding massive. Instead, we stand and stare at the spectacle before us until suddenly the children rise as one, as if they have communicated telepathically with each other, and go outside to play on the now-bouncy castle until their parents arrive. It is such a swift and immediate exodus, you can see a cup of lemonade still wobbling dangerously on the deserted table.

That was the weirdest thing I've ever seen.

Little by little the children disappear from the garden as their parents arrive, until eventually there is just one left, bouncing away relentlessly, almost as if he's set himself the target of bringing up his tea. It's at least quarter past five and the party ended officially at five, so this is extremely rude of the parents, imposing on Sarah for a bit of free babysitting. The more I look at that little brat down there in the garden, bouncing away, the angrier I'm getting. If I wasn't feeling so weak and headachy, I'd go and speak to someone about it.

'Hasn't Jake grown?' Susan says, coming over to the sofa where I'm slumped, and I realize immediately that the child outside on the bouncy castle is Jake, of course, and is still here because this is where he lives. They all look the same to me.

'Mmm.' I've closed my eyes and don't bother to open them. Apart from the headache, it adds to the illusion that I knew it was Jake out there all the time.

'Are you all right?' Susan asks me and I feel her sit down.

'Wha's the mapper?' Chrissie's voice enters the room. She's eating something as she speaks – it sounds like a sausage roll. I imagine a snowstorm of pastry leaving her lips as she talks.

'Rachel's got an awful headache,' Susan says, rubbing the back of my hand. Yeah, that's gonna help my headache. 'One too many screaming kids, I reckon,' she adds quietly, as if I've been recklessly over-indulging.

'I'll get her a tablet,' Chrissie says, heading out of the room again, back to the kitchen where the food is.

'See if Sarah's got any migraine tablets,' Susan says loudly. 'I don't expect Hedex is going to do any good now. You need a bit of peace and quiet, don't you, Rach? *Sarah,*' she shouts out over my head, 'can you please bring Rachel a glass of water?'

Oh, God, I'm going to puke again. Oh Christ, here it comes. Oh, no, wait a minute, no it doesn't.

'God, Rach, you've gone ever so white. Do you feel sick too? It's probably a migraine, then.'

'I had a migraine once,' Chrissie says, coming near

103

again. I keep my eyes tightly closed – I know she is wearing turquoise today. 'I passed out in Woolies and threw up for two days.'

'God,' Susan says, and I imagine the expression on her face saying so much more, 'you get everything really badly, don't you?'

'Well once,' says Sarah's voice, entering the room, 'I woke up in the night with stomach pain that felt like I was being ripped in half. Glenn drove me straight to the hospital.'

'Jesus,' Susan says and from her voice I can tell her eyes are really wide, 'what happened?'

'When we got there, they cut my tummy open and pulled out a real, live human being.' She rams a cold glass into my hand and marches away.

Have you ever longed for something really hard for ages, and then when it finally comes, you can't face it? No, me neither. If I long for something, it's usually mine a few minutes later, and then I get sick of it quite quickly. Except for today, strangely enough. I have been desperate to get home from this party for three weeks, since I agreed to come, and now that I'm going, I find I can't face it. At least, I can't face the actual driving. The thought of going home is like waking up after a really disturbing nightmare full of evil little flesh-eating trolls with sharp teeth, to find immediately that it was all a dream and the sun's out. And you've got the day off and have lost four pounds overnight. And you've won the Lotto jackpot. Which was a rollover.

Here comes Glenn. He's a piece of work, isn't he? I can't seem to get out of my head the image of him in the car park with that woman, sucked in together like two pieces of vacuum-packed ham, which is not good given how rough I'm feeling already.

'Chrissie's said she'll drive you home, Rachel,' he says to my eyelids, all fake caring friend's husband. I nod in silence, already wondering how I'm going to avoid that turquoise caftan all the way home.

Here we are in the car, five minutes later. See what I mean about that colour? It's eye-splitting, especially in close proximity like this. When I look at Chrissie she's almost ablaze, her head just a shadowy silhouette. But surprisingly, I am starting to feel better, leaning my head against the cool glass. Of course, the fact that those thirty odd kids are miles and another year away could be helping.

'Christ, I couldn't be a mum, could you?' Chrissie says suddenly, as if she's read my mind. 'I mean, sweet as they are, those bloody kids make me want to slit my wrists. Or theirs.'

'Yeah, they were noisy – I'm sure that's why I've got this headache. Sarah's brave, inviting that many.'

'Oh, do you think so? I don't think eleven is all that many.'

'Eleven? Don't be ridiculous, there must have been about thirty of them round that table.'

Chrissie glances at me. 'Nope. Only twelve, including Jake.'

I'm staggered. All that noise and mess, and only twelve of them. Mum would probably say it's because the whole is greater than the sum of the parts. It means that when people work together they can achieve more than if they all work on their own. Those twelve kids prove it.

'Did you know you had a call on your mobile?' Chrissie asks. 'While you were on the sofa feeling bad. I heard a phone ringing in the kitchen and tracked it down to a bag that Sarah said was yours.'

'Oh. Thanks.'

She glances at me sideways. 'Do you think it might have been Nick?'

And at that moment, I get one of those sudden revelation things that show you the way things are, and the way to go, all at once in a blinding flash of light. Except for me it was more a blinding flash of turquoise.

Chrissie is the one who told me about Val's husband and the accountant; Chrissie is the one who told me about M and M being seen playing badminton with two women once; she told me about Siân's depression, Marion's huge debt, Keith from Marketing's gay wife. She even told me about Jean's cancer scare a couple of years ago. Chrissie is the one who knows all the gossip. And, more importantly, Chrissie is the one who passes it on. Nick has been pretending all this time to be single, and he must be stopped. I raise my head and, squinting a little, turn to look at her. See that expression on my face? That's determination.

Or is it revenge? It's difficult to tell, they're both new.

'Not a chance,' I say in answer to her question about the phone call.

'Really? You sound very sure – have you checked?'

'I'm telling you, Chrissie, it's not him.' Time to plant the seeds. 'And anyway, even if it was, I'm having nothing more to do with him.'

She frowns a bit. 'Look, I know he's been a bit uncommunicative the last few days . . .'

'Thirteen.'

'All right, thirteen days. But he might have an explanation. Maybe he's been in hospital, or poorly or something. You can't be sure he hasn't been in an accident and was just ringing then to explain . . .'

'He's married, Chris.' Light blue touchpaper . . .

She freezes, mouth still open, and stares at me.

I jerk my head towards the windscreen. 'Watch the road, will you?'

Here we are, arriving home. Chrissie installs me on the sofa then heads for the door. She is halfway through when she turns and says, 'Do you want me to do anything before I go?'

She's got one turquoise foot outside on the communal carpet. I am so tempted to ask her to make me a drink before she goes, but in the end I'm glad to let her go straight away, and I shake my head. 'I'm going to have a long bawl in a hot bath, maybe sob over a bit of telly, then cry myself to sleep.'

'OK then,' she says distractedly. 'Well, take care of yourself. Night night.' And she's out of there, a woman with a mission.

We could watch her and see where she goes, but at this precise moment, the phone in my handbag rings again. It must have been the mobile man that rang in my handbag earlier on, so this is bound to be him again. I smile as I pull it out but then wish I had prepared something to say. It's good fun, joking around, but this is probably going to be the end of it. I know I have got to stop playing and arrange the handover.

I click the 'Answer' button and say smoothly, 'You're late.'

'So're you,' he says without missing a beat. 'I called at the allotted time, or just after, but you didn't . . .'

'Just after? Just after sounds like late to me. That is not acceptable.'

'Dammit. How could you possibly have known?'

'Fourteen thousand microscopic cameras. They record your every move, and then my fourteen thousand staff report back to me.'

'Blimey, you don't mess around, do you? Obviously you're a very skilled and well-equipped phone-napper.'

'It's a living.'

'In that case, can I please have one more chance? It's my first time.'

I pause to give the impression of serious thought. This is a trick I have learned for genuine conversations. 'Do you think you deserve another chance?'

'Yes.'

'Oh. Well, all right then, one more chance.'

'That's kind. Thanks.'

'You're welcome.'

'So? What are the demands, then?'

'Oh yes, you wanted some demands, didn't you?' I rack my brain, desperately trying to think of something funny. 'Tell me your name.' Yeah, I know, not very inventive but as you know I have had a terrible day so far.

There's a long pause from the other end. 'My name? Hmmm. I've never been asked for that before. People usually ask me for jewels or cash, you know, in ransom notes.'

'Well, I need to know what to put on the envelope that the ransom note asking for jewels and cash is in.'

He bursts out laughing. 'That's a very good point,

Miss Abductor. Seeing as you put it like that, my name is Hector.'

'Hector.' I'm smiling at this. I think it's a fake name. 'Right.'

'So can I expect the demands in writing, then? Now that you know who I am.'

'No need for that. I can tell you them now.'

'Shoot.'

'OK. But you should know that is not a good choice of word when you're negotiating for the release of a hostage.'

He laughs again. I like that sound. 'You know, you're absolutely right. That's probably where I've gone wrong in the past.'

'Oh no. Bad outcomes?'

'The worst kind.'

'I'm sorry to hear that.'

'Thanks.'

'You're welcome.'

There's a pause. I'm waiting for him to speak. Eventually he says, 'So? The demands?'

It's ridiculous. He must have asked me for these five or six times.

'Oh yes. Right. Hmmm. Well, firstly I demand . . . um . . . equality and freedom from, um . . .'

'Oppression?'

'Yes, that's it, oppression. Yes. Secondly, I demand, um, justice for all.'

'Oh, well said. I couldn't agree more. Anything else?'

'My third demand is . . . er . . . world peace.'

'World peace. OK.' He says it slowly, as if he's writing it down.

'And finally, I demand value for money.'

'Value for money.' I can hear that he's grinning now. 'So you want all races and peoples in the world to live in harmony together, free to express themselves without fear of retaliation, for all to be treated equally with fairness and justice, and . . .' he pauses here for effect, '. . . and get really good value. Is that it?'

'Exactly. And if you ever want to see your phone again, you'll remember that.'

He chuckles. 'Got it. So where, and when, are we meeting for the exchange? Is it still The Blooding?'

'Yes, The Blooding. Thursday, six o'clock.' My doctor's surgery is in the Ashton Business Park, so I can combine my trip down there with meeting the Mobile Man and giving him his phone back.

'Thursday, eh? Fair enough.'

'Right then. Until Thursday—'

'No, wait. I need to know your name. You can't leave me in torment like this.'

Ah. I walked straight into that one, didn't I? I'm a bit panicky now. This is a complete stranger after all, and not only have I just arranged to meet him, he wants my name. A picture pops into my head suddenly of an axe dripping with blood, traces of human hair still clinging to the grisly edge, light glinting and flashing on its silvery surface, the heavy wooden shaft held tightly in a large, blood-spattered hand, which is attached to the arm of a hooded man standing outside the external door of my block, looking at the names by the doorbells, wondering if I am Laura, Leslie or Rachel.

'It's Ruth,' I say quickly, after a very lengthy pause.

'Ruth. That's unusual.'

'Oh come on. You said you were called Hector, for heaven's sake.'

He pauses. 'But I *am* called Hector.'

We need to go back to Sarah's house for a bit now. Only to look – you won't see me back at Sarah's place for ages yet. Back to the lounge, where it is still a scene of mild devastation. Truthfully, it never really looks clean, not to my or Mum's standards, but this is much worse. Look at all the paper plates everywhere, most of them still with half-eaten sandwiches on them. Sadly, the food remains aren't just on the plates, but are squashed, flattened and ground into the carpet in various places around the room. This is not immediately obvious, though, because at the moment the carpet and the food on it are covered with dozens of balls and crumpled sheets of brightly coloured paper, cardboard boxes and clothes. Apparently, Jake has torn open all his presents and left them and their wrappings exactly where they are.

Over there, upside down and scattered, is the set of books Sarah's granddad carried home on the bus last weekend after spending two hours shopping for something that would look as if it had cost more than the ten pounds he could afford to spend. Here's the screwed up T-shirt Sarah's aunt and uncle bought because they thought Jake would like the picture of a zebra on the front. Pens, pencils, plasticine and various other craft materials have been discovered and discarded, dropped carelessly on the floor in favour of the next parcel. Jake himself is nowhere to be seen.

He's an ungrateful little shit, isn't he?

See that man, just getting up from the sofa, looking very

pleased with himself? That's Hector, the Mobile Man, and he's just finished talking to me. He looks quite nice, doesn't he, in an early thirties, stubbly, slightly dishevelled kind of way. There is definitely a chance that this is the guy who gave me his trolley at Sainsbury's, and whom I was then rude to, but I'm not going to examine that too deeply.

'Thanks, Sarah,' he calls out, picking his way through the debris on the floor. The way he does that reminds me of Nick, picking his way through our abandoned clothes.

'Did you manage to get through all right?' Sarah comes into the room, dragging a bulky black plastic bag behind her. She looks a lot better now, doesn't she? Oh, wait a minute, is that a large glass of wine in her free hand? Yes. No wonder she's chilling.

'Yes, fine thanks,' Hector says, taking the bag out of her hand and crouching down on the floor to begin scooping up the rubbish. 'Why don't you sit down and put your feet up, Sarah? Glenn and I can do this. Least I can do.'

He sounds as if he feels guilty about something. Let's go back five minutes and see if we can find out why.

Here he is, five minutes earlier, inserting the corkscrew into a bottle of wine. Sarah is standing by, holding an empty glass. 'Oh, Sarah,' he says casually, twisting the corkscrew in, 'would it be all right if I quickly borrow your phone in a minute?'

''Course,' she says, extending her glass towards the open neck of the bottle.

'Oh great, thanks. I really need to make this one urgent call and I didn't have time to do it before I left the office to come here.'

She shrugs. 'OK.'

'Obviously, getting here for my nephew's birthday was

more important, and I thought you wouldn't mind lending me your phone when I got here.'

Do you think he's laying it on a bit thick? I mean, she agreed straight away, didn't she? There's really no need to keep on and on.

Clearly, she hasn't noticed, anyway. Her eyes are closed and her mouth is clamped on to the rim of the glass, sucking down chardonnay.

Let's move forward again, back to where we were. So he pretended it was an important business call, but he was actually calling me, a complete stranger, so he could have a bit of a laugh. And, let's face it, do a bit of flirting. He must have tried to ring earlier from his office, but of course I didn't answer it then and he had to leave it until he got here this evening. No wonder he's rushing round clearing up now – apart from stopping every so often to stare off into space and grin a lot.

'What are you grinning about?' Here is Glenn, now that most of the work is done. 'You must really enjoy clearing up after kids.'

Hector looks up at his brother. 'No, not really. I've just managed to set up a meeting on Thursday that promises to be really rewarding.'

Glenn does not look pleased about that, does he? 'Christ, you never bloody stop, do you? Even on my son's birthday you're setting up meetings, making deals. What's the matter with you?'

Hector stops mid-scoop. 'I'm sorry, mate. I realize it's his birthday, but this one was fairly crucial. I couldn't do it from the office because I wanted to be here with—'

'Oh whatever.' Glenn looks at his wife, who is scraping a squashed Fondant Fancy off the sofa, then says casually,

113

'Oh, Hector, could you come into the kitchen for a minute, please?'

Hector is tipping a plateful of apparently untouched food into the bin bag. 'Yeah, in a minute, I'm just—'

'Please, Hector.' The tone in Glenn's voice makes Hector pause. 'I want to ask you something.' Glenn glances quickly at Sarah, whose face is blank as she takes a large glug of wine, then he whispers, 'In *private*.'

Glenn walks out of the room towards the kitchen. Hector gets up to follow. 'Fancy a cup of tea, Sarah?' he asks at the door.

'No thanks,' she says, holding out her empty glass. He takes it from her with a smile and heads to the kitchen.

Sarah and Glenn's kitchen is huge. But it's a terrible mess here too. On the countertops are yet more paper plates of food, most of it barely touched. There are crisps all over the place, on the floor, the table, the counter. Cups of squash are scattered around, more than one tipped over with its contents forming a purple pool on the floor. In the middle of the table is the birthday cake – a huge fort constructed of chocolate fingers and white marshmallows – looking now more like a pile of kindling. On the wall by the table are some brown smudges that look suspiciously like little fingerprints. Let's hope they're chocolate. Glenn is standing by the sink, staring into the garden.

'What is it, mate?' Hector asks as he picks up the wine bottle.

'I'm sorry, Hector, but I need to borrow some money.' He doesn't hang around, does he?

Hector stops what he's doing and turns to face Glenn. 'What?'

'Look, I'm desperate. I need some cash and you've

got loads. You know I wouldn't ask unless it was really important.'

Hector looks down at the bottle again. 'Well, of course, Glenn, but what's it for?'

Glenn clenches his fists. 'It doesn't matter what it's for, does it? I've got myself into a little bit of debt and I'd really appreciate some assistance, if it's not too much to ask.'

Hector continues to focus on refilling Sarah's glass. 'So what does Sarah . . . ?'

'Hec, I'd really appreciate it if we don't tell Sarah about it. It's quite important.'

'Why?'

Glenn looks down at the countertop. 'To tell the truth, I've been an idiot. Spent more than I should have, told Sarah we were doing OK. I don't want to worry her, you know? Plus . . .'

'Plus?'

He shrugs. 'Plus, I don't want her to know that even now that I'm thirty I can't manage to support my own family without getting help from my big brother.'

Hector puts the bottle down on the table. 'Why don't you take this through?' he says, holding out the now full wine glass. Glenn hesitates, then takes the glass out of Hector's hand and walks out of the kitchen. Hector puts his hands on the table and hangs his head. From the living room comes the sound of Sarah thanking her husband for the wine he has brought her. Almost imperceptibly, Hector shakes his head.

Glenn reappears in the doorway. 'Oh come on, Hec, it's not that bad. I'm a loser civil servant on a crappy wage, that's all. It's not like I've gambled it all away or something. You don't need to despair over me.'

'I'm not despairing, Glenn, not at all. And you're not a loser. It's just that other people on crappy wages seem to manage. Why is it so difficult for you?'

Glenn shrugs and reaches a glass down from a shelf. 'You ought to try being me for a while, then see if you can go round being so bloody nice all the time.'

Hector watches as Glenn pours the last of the bottle into his glass without offering any to his brother. 'But what's so awful about being you? You've got everything, lovely wife, a healthy, intelligent son, beautiful home . . .'

Glenn snorts. 'Oh, just listen to yourself. Beautiful home. Hah! This is a hovel compared to your place.'

Hector frowns but it is not anger, it is bewilderment. 'No it isn't, you idiot. So my house is bigger, so what? You're the one with the family. Don't you realize how lucky you are? To come home from work every day to this, your home, your wife, your child? I come home to . . . Well, you know what I come home to.'

'Here we go.'

Hector shakes his head. 'No, no, Glenn, here we do *not* go. I am not complaining, you know that. I have never, *will* never, complain about having Mum there. I wouldn't have it any other way. Of course she must live with me, you've got Jake and Sarah to think about. But sometimes, sometimes, I just wish I could come home to something warm, something giving. Don't you think that I wouldn't give all the money and possessions in the world, just to have . . . ?' He trails off.

'I don't need to hear that, OK,' Glenn spits. 'You don't have to try to make me feel better. You have this massive, successful business worth millions, and I have . . .' he glances at the door, 'I have Sarah and Jake. Yeah, well, much as I care about them, big deal.' He takes a deep drink of the wine. 'I am just asking you for help, Hector. Do you want me to get down on my knees and beg you? Because I will. I have got no pride left.'

'No,' Hector says quietly, 'I don't want you to do that. I've said I'll help you and I will. Of course I will. How much?'

Glenn relaxes visibly, his shoulders slumping, and a small smile of relief appears. He claps his brother on the arm. 'Oh thank you, Hector. I really appreciate this, mate, honestly.' He looks a bit sheepish for a moment. 'I'm sorry for being a bit snappy – it's just the worry.'

Hector nods. 'So how much . . . ?'

'I think five grand ought to cover it.'

'Right.' Hector takes out his chequebook and fills one in, tearing it out and giving it to Glenn.

'Thanks, bro,' Glenn says, taking the cheque and pocketing it. 'Just remember, not one word to Sarah, OK?'

Hector nods but as his brother returns to the living room, he can't help thinking that he and Sarah are being deceived.

Chapter Seven

For the next few days, I stay at home. You can see a path in the carpet, like one of those sheep paths on mountains, from the sofa to the bedroom and from there to the bathroom. If I'm honest, I wasn't really thinking it was flu, or a migraine by now, but I didn't want to admit to myself what I suspected. I was just waiting for the doctor to tell me for sure on Thursday.

I have spent my days watching loads of daytime telly. For the most part, they're about silly young women getting pregnant accidentally and sobbing about their predicament in front of a live studio audience. Nothing like sharing your awful dilemma with four million faceless and indifferent strangers to make you feel better.

Can you believe I have missed four days of work? I haven't had a day sick from Horizon the whole time I've been there. I give the odd thought to my position in the tables now, but it flits away quickly. I can't see myself ever going back there at the moment. Right now, I can't see beyond the end of each day. I feel like I am in suspended animation until Thursday's appointment.

On Wednesday afternoon, Sarah arrives with Jake, and a slab of cake. 'This is the one I made myself,' she announces proudly. 'I didn't want to give it to all those ungrateful kids at the party, so I hid it. Here, try it.'

She unwraps a paper serviette, peeling it away in the places where it has stuck to the contents, and spreads it out in her hands like precious treasure. Nestling there in the centre is a lump of brown cake coated in bright orange icing and some random green nodules with fat yellow heads.

'It looks lovely,' I say, eyes watering and mouth filling with saliva. I manage a weak smile at Jake.

'It's Bulbasaur,' he says, meaninglessly.

I nod and smile, assuming this is kiddie speak.

'I had the vinewhip,' he goes on.

'Oh,' I say, not sure whether I should be happy or sorry for him. Is it some repulsive infection he picked up at the party?

'And Bulbasaur evolves into Ivysaur, and then Ivysaur evolves into Vinesaur, but only if he wins loads of battles.'

'Right.'

'And in Safari Zone one, you can catch a Nidorhino, already evolved. Normally you have to catch Nidoran and wait for it to evolve, which takes ages. Although you can evolve it with moonstone.'

He's not actually looking at me when he makes this announcement, which only adds to my confusion. For all I know, he's been possessed by some ancient and malicious evil spirit from Sarah's housing estate and is speaking in tongues.

'Is he all right?' I whisper to Sarah.

She nods, unconcerned. 'It's Pokemon,' she says adeptly. Either he's not possessed or she is too. 'He's fine. Go on, try a bit.' She's looking at the cake. 'The icing's got fresh orange juice in it.'

After I vomited up the mouthful of cake that I did try, Sarah took Jake and left.

So here I am, hunched in my doctor's waiting room at quarter to six on Thursday afternoon. It hardly needs saying that surgery is running late. The waiting room is stuffed with old people in slippers, swollen legs wrapped in bandages, painful twisted fingers holding on to walking sticks and handbags. I'm glaring at them through slitted eyes. Surely some of these people just need a hot drink and a good talking-to. The last person that shuffled off towards the consulting-room door has not been seen for fifteen minutes. I'm beginning to wonder if she's died in there. How frustrating if she has, taking up the doctor's time for nothing. She might as well have not bothered coming in at all, and left the consulting room free.

At five to six, I go in. Dr Kanthasinapillai is really nice. He always makes me feel like he's really listened to my problem, thought carefully about it and taken time over sorting it out for me, while rushing me in and out of his surgery at maximum speed. He looks up from his desk, where he's typing up notes with one finger, and smiles.

'Won' keep you a minnid, Rachel,' he says. In fact, it takes him three minutes to write up the notes from his last patient. I want to bat his silly slow finger out of the way and do it myself, but I resist the impulse. Eventually, he turns to me. 'Well, Rachel, you're looking a bid pale. Whad is the madder?'

While I'm telling him all about the nausea, the fatigue, the odd dizzy spell, I try not to think about what it all seems to be adding up to. It's got to be stress or depression.

'And I broke up with my boyfriend,' I add at the end, just to make it a possibility.

'Oh, I see,' he says. 'You had a boyfriend.' Damn. He immediately latches on to the part of my statement that adds in very nicely with everything else. That's why he's a doctor, I suppose. 'And when was your lasd period?'

I knew this would be coming. I have completely avoided working it out before now. I close my eyes. I can remember the day: I was at the pool with Susan. 'I'm on,' I'd said, 'swim's off.' We went clubbing instead, which is probably better exercise. That was the last time I spent an evening with Susan before I met Nick, but the exact date still eludes me.

'Here, can you urinade into dis please?' Dr Kant is saying, handing me a tiny plastic pot with a very narrow opening. 'You can use the toiled.'

I finger the pot and wonder for a second whether or not he's got a funnel in his desk drawer.

Five minutes later and he's smiling as he shows me a small white plastic rectangle. 'Dis is de condrol window, which dells us dat de tesd has been carried oud correc'ly.' I peer over the desk at the thing he's holding. There's a little blue dot in the window. My eyes leap to the other window, even before he says it. They work like a microscope, zooming in on the window, magnifying what they're seeing there so that my entire field of vision is filled with an enormous window, white on white, and nestling right in the centre of this area, curled and sleeping, apparently harmless but full of potential, is a big, fat, blue dot.

'And dis is de resuld window. Congradulations, Rachel, you're going do have a liddle baby.'

Freeze. Hold it right there, right at that moment. If you

look all round me, you can see that not one hair, not one molecule stirs. Suddenly it feels as though, for an elongated fraction of a second, the thick layer of nonchalance that coats me and forms a safety buffer between me and the outside world is stripped away and all my senses are magnified, intensified. I take everything in. Even the grinning GP in the consulting room is silent, unmoving.

While the doctor and I sit frozen in our seats, let's take a look and see what the other interested party is doing at that same, seminal moment. The news has been launched that Nick is about to become a parent and take on the unfathomable, miraculous and incomparable role of being someone's father, and here we find Nick himself close to tears. No, not with the overwhelming emotion of that incredible moment; it's something much more basic.

Look, there he is, in the kitchen, his left hand held, palm inwards, in front of his face, his right hand tightly clutching his left wrist. In front of him on the counter is a chopping board with half an onion chopped up on it. The other half has been abandoned, as has the large and apparently rather sharp knife, on the counter next to it. If you look more closely, you can see a large red dewdrop forming on the end of Nick's left thumb.

'What is it, what happened?' his mum asks breathlessly, rushing into the room. 'I heard you scream.'

Nick sinks towards her, holding out his injured digit, his mouth turning down like a clown's. 'I cut my thumb.' He squeezes his eyes shut as tears leak from them. 'These bloody onions,' he mutters, dragging his forearm across his eyes.

'Oh, Nicky, let me see. Oh, darling, you poor thing.

Come here.' Helen Maxwell wraps her arms tightly around her wounded son, and gently rubs his back, talking into his hair. 'And you were trying to get the tea ready for me, you little love. Any better now?'

Nick draws back, nods and sniffs.

'OK, good. Well, you'd better go and put it under the tap, quickly. Then we'll put a plaster on it, shall we?'

He slouches towards the sink as his mum takes up the knife and finishes chopping the onion. 'Thanks, Mum.'

Of course, sitting in the consulting room, I can't see all this. Perhaps it's just as well. Creeping numbness has taken over.

Dr Kant seems delighted to be giving me the happy news, doesn't he? He's grinning as he gives me a calendar to help me remember the date of my last period, apparently oblivious to my bloodless face and shocked silence. I stare down at the numbers, coaxing my mind to work. I can't remember my period, but I do remember the last time I had sex and tell the doctor that instead. It was the night we had seen that Sean person at the restaurant. We did it in the car in a layby on the way home, and again when we got back to my flat.

'Layby,' the doctor says slowly, apparently typing this on to my notes. 'And when was dis?'

'Fourth August. A Friday.'

'OK. And you're sure you had no other sexual pardners for a month before or afder?'

I nod. It's official. Nick's a father.

Unsurprisingly, as soon as I get out of the surgery my head clears a bit and I can remember everything. My last period was the fourteenth of July. That's why I put black crosses on my calendar fourteen days later, the weekend of 28 July, and for five days either side. I always do that. That was also why I had one or two embryonic worry lines while Nick was doing press-ups on my living-room floor. I knew. I had known at the time but I had overlooked it in favour of Nick's performance. That was the moment I let everything slide: the moment I defined the rest of my life.

By the time I leave the surgery, it's almost six twenty. I walk slowly back towards the car park. The beauty of having your surgery in the middle of a business park is that no matter what depressing and hideous news you've just received from your GP, there's always loads of parking. 'I'm so sorry, Mr Smith, you've only got two weeks to live.' 'Oh no, that's bad. Thank God we managed to park nearby.'

It's a totally gorgeous summer evening – warm and golden, with a very light breeze that is full of the scent of cut grass from the roundabout on the bypass – but I'm stumbling along blindly, eyes turned inwards – not literally, of course, that would be hideous – oblivious to all of it. Ahead of me is the fountain. The water oozing from the slavering chops of the snarling hounds looks cool and refreshing so I head for that and sit on the rim. The sound of splashing water behind me is very relaxing and I close my eyes for a few moments.

'Are you OK?' says a voice nearby.

I open my red eyes and find myself looking directly into a warm, brown pair that seem almost familiar. Their owner, a tall man with a dark suit jacket slung over his shoulder, is leaning over me, his face very close to mine. I lean back a bit. My head is full of insistent, unsettling images based on everything I have ever heard about childbirth – lots of poking and prodding, people peering into every orifice, scrapes and swabs and stretch marks, forceps, tears and stitches. Mentally, I am lodged firmly in a terrifying waking nightmare, suffering anguish like I have never known, teetering on the edge of a full-blown panic attack; and physically I am intensely, eye-wateringly nauseous, so tired I can barely hold my head up on my neck, and wracked by an explosive headache that is limiting my capacity to think clearly and shrivelling my brain.

'I'm fine, thanks.'

'OK then,' he says, and walks two yards away, where he sits down on the rim and looks at his watch. I ignore him and close my eyes again. After a while, the splashing, trickling noises sound like a large crowd chattering and it fills my head so I can't think about anything else.

Next to me, the stranger is glancing at me repeatedly. I'm not looking my best at the moment, as you see, but I'm still better looking than probably seventy-five per cent of all the people this man knows, so he's having a good look. Luckily I've still got my eyes closed.

'Are you sure?' says the same voice, a few minutes later.

I open my eyes again. He's not standing over me but has twisted around from where he's sitting and called across.

'Yes,' I say, glancing at him quickly, then looking away.

'All right then,' he says. He looks at his watch again, then takes out a mobile phone and dials a number. I give up on closing my eyes and decide that I had better get going, when my handbag beside me starts to make an unfamiliar sound. I stare at my bag for a second. Of course, it's the

125

mobile phone. With a lurch I realize that I have missed our meeting. I reach in to pick it up and press answer.

'Hello?'

'Hello,' says the voice next to me.

I turn to look, still holding the phone up to my ear. 'Oh,' is all I can manage.

He smiles gently. 'Hello,' he says again. I hear his real voice, then half a second later I hear his electronic voice in the earpiece. 'You must be Ruth.'

'Er, oh, yes, Ruth, yes, that's me. In which case, you are Hector.'

He nods. 'You can hang up now,' he says, his words travelling to the stars and back to reach me.

I'm still holding the phone to my ear, so I bring it down and switch it off. 'Well, you'd better take it then,' I'm saying, handing it over. He doesn't take it straight away. In fact, he doesn't take it at all.

'Would you have a cup of coffee with me?' he says simply.

This kind of thing happens a lot. I have learnt over the years to try and keep on the move when I'm out because when I stop, even for just a few minutes, I turn into a kind of target. They don't often just come up to ask me out, but they appear from nowhere like woodlice and start trying to make conversation. It usually goes along the lines of, 'You all right?' Yes, I'm fine thanks. 'Excellent.' It tends to dry up at this point and the lunatic grinning takes over.

This is a bit different from how it usually goes, though. For a start, he doesn't seem to have lost the ability to speak coherently. He's not grinning like a loon, but looking at me with a small furrow between his eyebrows and a concerned little smile on his face. As I look at him, I realize that it's almost fatherly. I look at my watch. It's just gone half past six. Well, I've paid for parking until seven, so I might as well. It will put off the moment of going home to think for another half an hour, if nothing else.

I nod. 'OK.'

'Thank you,' he says, as if I've just agreed to give him one of my kidneys. He stands up and holds out his hand and I realize he's offering to help me up. I take it, and he raises me up gently from the fountain. We don't carry on holding hands, though. He lets go of mine as soon as I'm upright, then does a sweeping motion with his other arm in the direction of a little café called Cream Tease.

I've seen this place from the outside loads of times, but I've never been in. Tea shops are not really my thing, to be honest. But I don't say anything as he pushes the door open in front of me. The first thing I notice is the smell. It's a rich, warm, hot chocolatey smell, with a hint of vanilla and something else that I can't identify. He guides me over to a table in the corner. There's a single yellow rose in a really narrow glass vase on the white tablecloth. It's very simple and plain but not entirely unpleasant.

'I'll get us some drinks,' Hector says with a reassuring smile. I nod, not really bothered about a drink at all. I'm just passing time before starting to think about what I've just been told.

He returns with two steaming mugs, each with a mound of whipped cream on top.

'Try this,' he says, putting one down in front of me and sitting down in the seat opposite. 'It'll perk you up.'

I look up at him. 'How do you know I need perking?'

He leans forward, reaches out his hands and puts them

on the table between us. 'Ruth,' he says kindly, 'I know we've never met before, but I don't think I have ever seen anyone more in need of a perk. Are you all right?'

I smile weakly. 'Yes, I'm fine.'

He shakes his head. 'You say that, but I'm not buying it. Are you sure?'

I look at him. I've got this tiny, enormous thing inside me that I haven't confided to anyone yet and I really need to offload. Why shouldn't it be this guy? He's a stranger so I never have to see him or speak to him again. I can talk absolutely freely without worrying about what he'll think of me, which I couldn't do if I spoke to any of my friends. I don't think I could bear to talk to Mum at the moment either. She's bound to be revoltingly emotional about becoming a granny and I don't want to think that far ahead yet. In fact, talking to a stranger is the perfect solution. He might even help me make a decision about what I'm going to do, and then my friends and family might not need to know that I ever was pregnant.

I take a sip from the mound of cream. It's hot chocolate, which seems a strange choice on such a lovely summer's day, but it's oddly comforting. He raises his eyebrows expectantly.

'I might be able to help,' he says by way of encouragement.

I lick cream off my lips and put the mug down. 'Well, I don't know about that, unless you're an obstetrician. You're not, are you?'

'I'm afraid not.'

'Doesn't matter. I've just had a bit of bad news, you see. I'm going to have a baby.'

'I see. And this is bad news?'

'Yes. Very.'

'I'm sorry to hear that.'

Oh God, now he's judging me. I pick up my bag. 'Look, this was obviously a mistake. There's your phone, thanks for the drink—'

'Hold on a minute. What's the problem?'

'Well, I am in a bit of a state at the moment and what I really don't need is you judging me. You know, if you're one of those pro-life people or something and think that all babies have some kind of right to life and therefore any pregnancy should be seen as a wondrous, joyful occasion, then I'm afraid that I've got nothing—'

'Oh no, no.' He's shaking his head. 'That's not what I meant at all. I'm really sorry, I honestly didn't mean to upset you.'

I hesitate. 'What did you mean then? When you said you were sorry to hear that me being pregnant was bad news?'

'Well, I meant exactly that. I'm really sorry that for you, it's bad news. It suggests to me that . . .'

'What?'

'No, it doesn't matter. It's really none of my business.'

How frustrating is that? I stare at him. 'Please tell me.'

'But I'm not—'

'Look, Hector, I've just come straight from the doctor so I haven't told anyone yet. Not even my mum. You, me and the doc are the only people who know, so technically it is your business, in a way. You asked if you could help and I decided to confide in you, for the simple reason that you are a stranger and can therefore give me your objective opinion without the complication of knowing me. Plus, I don't have to put up with sympathy or criticism. I mean, can you imagine my mum? The first thing she's going to say is, Oh Rachel, how could you let this happen? You should have taken precautions. Yeah, thanks, Mum, great advice, but how the hell does that help me now?'

'So you're . . . ?'

'I'm pregnant, and it's a disaster. Exactly. Now what I could do with is to talk it through with someone who won't judge, who won't sympathize, someone who I don't know so that if I tell you something really private it won't matter because by the end of today we'll both have forgotten all about it.'

He fixes his eyes on mine. 'I'm afraid that already that's not very likely.' He jerks a bit. 'I mean, I've just met the girl who stole my phone, and it turns out she's only recently discovered she's pregnant and she wants my advice. I'm not likely to forget that very quickly, am I?'

'Well, maybe not. But you get my point? I mean, it really doesn't matter what you ask me, or what I tell you, because we're strangers so I can't possibly be offended at anything you ask, and you can't be offended at anything I tell. Right?'

'Right.'

'Right. So tell me what you were going to say.'

'Ah. Yes. Well . . .'

'You won't offend me. I promise.'

'All right.' He clears his throat. 'All I was going to say was that the fact that the pregnancy is a disaster suggests to me that the father is not a factor in the equation. I mean, you're not in a relationship?'

'Is that all? I thought it was going to be something really personal.'

130

'That is really personal!'

'Not these days. Don't you watch Jeremy Kyle?'

'No, not really.'

'Oh. Well, no I'm not in a relationship. But I was, or I thought I was, when this happened.'

'Right. So you're on your own?'

'Yep.'

'So you've got to decide then, haven't you?'

I look at him questioningly.

'What I mean is, you've got to decide, fairly quickly, whether you are going to have the baby and change your life for ever, or terminate now and keep your life exactly the way it was.'

I think about those words for a few moments. Just like that, in a matter of no more than ten minutes, he's summed up exactly the enormous dilemma I'm facing. And having been summed up so precisely and easily, it no longer seems so enormous. It's become suddenly very simple. I smile and nod, a gleam of light just becoming visible through the cloud of despair.

'By the way,' he says, as I take another sip of the hot chocolate, 'it's cinnamon. The extra ingredient. It makes it somehow more comforting, doesn't it?'

'Yes, it does. It's delicious.'

'Good. I thought it would do the trick.'

We sip in silence for a few moments. Then he says, 'You mentioned your mum.'

'Yeah.'

'Is she a bit forgetful sometimes? Crashes the car a lot? Suffered a recent head injury perhaps?'

I frown. 'No. Why do you say that?'

He grins. 'Well, when you were talking about her just

now, she called you Rachel. Do you think she confuses you with someone else, Ruth?'

Here's Hector, later that same evening, just arriving home. He's still grinning and the anxiety he usually experiences on entering the house is suspended for a few moments. All seems quiet and he creeps up the stairs. Sure enough, his mother is fast asleep, curled up like a child, her feet sticking out of the end of the covers. He tucks them round her gently, then softly kisses her forehead before heading back downstairs to the kitchen.

He gets a glass from the cupboard and takes it into the next room, his study, where he pours himself a whisky from the cabinet. He feels peaceful, content. For the first time in many months he can imagine a future for himself, a future with someone special in it. He doesn't know how, or even if, this friendship with the mobile girl – Ruth, no *Rachel* – he's grinning about that again – might develop, but she had interested him. A great deal. Even her current predicament doesn't alter his feelings. In fact, quite the opposite. He feels more caring and protective of her because of the baby. So much so that he told her to keep the phone. He had already replaced it anyway, and changed all the stationery to the new number, so it was as good as useless to him now. She protested, of course – she had her own phone already, why would she need another? But he had convinced her that it would be useful, just in case her other phone ran out of charge or credit. Plus he would be able to call her on it without her having to give him any of her own numbers. And she could call him on it whenever she wanted to talk. All his work numbers were programmed in, and it was easy enough to add his home number. It was also very easy for him to keep paying the monthly charges. Eventually she had agreed to keep hold of it 'for now'. He didn't know how long that gave him, but he hoped it was long enough.

Chapter Eight

So Hector let me keep the phone. I've still got it. I wasn't really sure about it to start with. I mean, it's a really flash, modern little model, and he said he would pay all the monthly charges, which made me feel uncomfortable.

'No, don't feel uncomfortable about that,' he said, walking me back to my car. 'I would have had to keep paying it until the end of the contract anyway, which isn't for another ten months. And you're not going to be racking up some huge bills, are you? Just use it to call me, if it makes you feel any better. And I can call you on it, can't I?'

It was a cute way of getting my number, wasn't it? I mean, technically it was his number really, so he already had it. I didn't mind. He was good to talk to and surprisingly it had really helped to talk about it with him. Although it took me quite a long time to decide what road to go down, as you're about to see, I did make one decision that night. I decided not to tell anyone else until I had made that choice. So it was just me and Hector. That's partly why I agreed to keep the phone. For now.

So now I'm trying to get my life back to as normal as possible. Of course I can't follow my normal weekend routines, or spend so much energy on keeping the flat nice – to be honest, I'm suddenly not so bothered about the dust as I used to be – but I have gone back to work.

Here I am, on the phone, making a sale. Look at the league tables by Jean's desk. Yes, that's right, I'm twelfth. It's not too good, is it? But then I did have a whole week off, so it's not surprising. I'm doing my best now to get myself back up there, but to be honest my heart's not really in it at the moment. Listen.

'Can I interest you in upgrading to an exterior cabin, Mrs Whitehead? . . . Well, it means that you get a window for the whole cruise, so you get the benefit of natural daylight . . . Yes, it is more expensive . . . No? OK then. So that's an interior cabin, on the *Caribbean Princess*, departing Southampton on the fifteenth of May next year . . .'

Can you believe I let that one get away? Exterior cabins are a gift usually, but right now it just seems like too much effort even to try. Plus, of course, I'm very distracted.

I'm ten weeks gone already. It's nearly the end of September and I feel like I'm running out of time to make this horrible decision. My mum's face floats in and out of my nightmares saying things like, 'Get up, Rachel, you're going to miss the bus,' and 'What do you think of yellow?'

The intense nausea that I have been experiencing has metamorphosized into its own polar opposite so that instead of not wanting to eat because of it, I now only get queasy when I am hungry, which is most of the time. And that is the most intense, violent hunger pain I've ever had. It feels like someone's scooped out the base of my throat and neck and now there's nothing there except a great yawning vacuum that won't be denied. I have noticed

135

Val looking at me when I eat. She's not used to seeing that because I never really used to eat at work. Not every day, anyway. She's probably surprised to learn that I chew and digest food just like her. But now look at me, scoffing Bourbons in between calls. During calls, even. Well, it's either that or retching.

M and M don't bring me coffee at two o'clock any more. That's a bit of a blow. Not that I would want coffee at the moment – the thought of it turns my stomach over – but me not wanting it isn't the point. They could bring me a hot chocolate or soup instead, or something from the snack machine. But they stopped doing it when I spent that week going down there myself, when I was hoping to run into Nick.

Hector's phone is with me in my bag wherever I go. Don't read anything into that – my own mobile goes with me everywhere too. It's just that this feels like a kind of umbilical connection to Hector, as if he himself is there with me, in a small way. I have rung him a couple of times since our chat over the hot chocolate, just to tell him how sick I was being. Well, I was feeling utterly miserable and couldn't talk to anyone else. I needed some sympathy.

'Is there actual vomit?'

'Uh-huh.'

'On target?'

'Not entirely.'

'Oh, you poor thing. All that mess to clear up. Is there anything I can do to help?'

'Well, you could come and—'

'Apart from clearing up for you, of course. That goes without saying. We may be strangers but I draw the line there.'

He's funny. He knew that I didn't really feel comfortable giving him my home address anyway, but made it sound like he was opting out.

And then, of course, there's Nick.

He's ten weeks pregnant too, of course, although acting as if nothing has changed. I haven't seen him here on the third floor again, not since our first meeting by the drinks machine back in July. It occurs to me now – finally – to wonder why he came all the way down from Personnel, which is on the sixth floor, to Telesales, on the third floor, just to get a drink. We know there's an identical drinks machine up there, don't we, but I don't like the feeling I get when I think about him ignoring it and getting in the lift to come down three floors instead. Did he do that to meet me? It seems likely and I'm not comfortable about it. I can tell that you're surprised about that, and you're right. Normally I would find that kind of detour, for that reason, immensely pleasing. But this time it's different.

The problem is, I didn't know what he was up to. I wasn't in on it. I mean, he orchestrated the whole thing, from finding out a bit about me, to disposing of M and M at two o'clock precisely, so I had to get my own drink. He predicted me. I feel manipulated and I'm not used to that.

If you feel the need to focus your eyes on that gorgeous bod again, he can be seen most lunchtimes hanging around the fifth-floor corridors, no doubt hoping to run into one of those tarty girls from the art department. Here he is now, in the lift with Veronica Stapleton from Product Design.

'How's everything with you today, Vee?' he says, hands in pockets, leaning back on the wall.

'I'm fine thanks, Nick,' she answers, pressing the 'G' button.

He nods slowly. 'You said it.' He smiles and blatantly looks her up and down through half lidded eyes. 'I'll bet those Marketing boys thank their lucky stars every day that you walk in.'

Look at her, the cow. She's actually blushing. Christ, she must be old enough to be his godmother.

But why should that bother me? Am I annoyed that my Nick is chatting up other women? Because it's been well over a month since we were together, so what did I expect? That after a week-long fling with Rachel Covington from Telesales, he would decide there was absolutely no point spending his time pursuing women any more and would swear off them for ever because after he'd had the best everyone else would just depress him with their mediocrity and never quite measure up?

Well . . .

No, of course not. That's just silly.

So he gets to carry on with his life as if nothing's happened. Which for him, it hasn't. Apart from a brief but intense relationship with the girl of his dreams who would have been worth leaving his wife for, if only he'd given it a chance.

But of course there was more to that fling than he knows. He left something behind one night – just a small thing. Well, a few hundred million small things. But one of them decided to stay, like an unwelcome tenant with squatter's rights. I feel like it's being really naughty in there, refusing to get its shoes on and leave with the others.

But the question still remains. And does Nick need to be involved in the decision-making process? Part of me, a big part, wants very much to tell him, at work, on the sixth floor, in his office in front of all his colleagues, in a loud voice, and smash the pretty little glass bauble he's been living in. Now that's definitely a desire for revenge you can see on my face – I am starting to recognize it.

But if I do go and tell him like that, so that everyone up there hears, then everyone up there will hear. Which is not particularly what I want, even though I would get a few seconds' savage pleasure from the look on his face. But the decision is still to be made, and if in the end I don't go through with it, why should I bother to involve him in the process at all? If I end it, no one will ever know. Ever.

Except Hector, of course.

My plan now is to go to see Sarah and talk to her about Jake and the birth and being a mum generally. I don't know why I didn't think of this sooner. She loves to talk about it and has done almost without taking a breath for six years, but I've never really listened before. I remember that Jake was born by caesarean because Glenn always makes that joke about him having to get out of the car through the sunroof, but the rest is a blur.

It's Saturday and I'm in the car driving round to Sarah's. I'm wearing a smidgen of Lovely Lilac lip gloss today, just to give myself a lift, but apart from that I've not bothered with make-up again. My hair, strangely enough, is still relaxing. It's so much easier than blow-drying and waxing it every day.

I've chosen to go on Saturday so that Jake will be there. Yes, I know, this is a complete turn-around for me, absolute avoidance being my usual tactic with him, but

I need as much information as I can get and Jake might actually have some.

Glenn's car is not on the drive – did you notice that? No doubt he's out choosing a beautiful and thoughtful gift for his devoted wife, as a token of his appreciation for their wonderful years together, to show her how much he loves and respects her and to let her know that his life would be a meaningless wasteland without her. Or he could be banging his bit on the side.

'Hi, Rachel,' Sarah says suddenly, bringing me back.

'Oh, Sarah. Hi.' In a fleeting moment, I take in the greasy hair, baggy grey T-shirt, elasticated-waist trousers and, perhaps most disturbing, the small red mark on her cheek. I can't see the elastic on the waistband, but I know it's there.

'Well ,who did you expect? Madonna?'

I want to say, 'In a three-bedroomed semi on a second-rate housing estate with a bike on every front lawn and more velour trousers than you would use making curtains for the entire Albert Hall?' I don't. Instead I say, 'Well, I've looked everywhere else. Is she here or not?'

A flicker of a smile is visible on her face for a flash, then it's gone again. 'Come in,' she says listlessly, and then slouches back up the hall to the living room.

Her place is a bit messy as always but, like I said, my standards in that area have been on the slide for the past couple of months too. Maybe this is one of the adjustments I will have to make, if I go through with it – a messy, disorganized home. I look at Sarah's retreating back as I follow her into the room. And of course I can look forward to thinking tracksuits and trainers are an OK way to dress outside of the gym.

'Where's Glenn?'

She sinks into the armchair nearest the telly, which is on with the sound down. 'Working overtime.'

'On a Saturday?' It's out before I have a chance to stop myself. I mean, the man works at the benefits agency – they're not even open at the weekend, are they? I watch Sarah's face but apparently she's bought it.

'Yeah. It's not open to the public and the phones aren't on because there's no receptionist in, but they're updating some files or something.' She shrugs. 'I don't really understand what they're doing, to be honest, but the money comes in handy.'

Oh. So there is actually extra money appearing then? I wonder vaguely where Glenn is getting that from as it's so plain to me, even if I hadn't seen him in the car park that time, that he's not doing overtime today. He's obviously as good as told her that she can't turn up unexpectedly at the office, or try and call him there, because if she does, the office would look and sound exactly as if it was closed for the weekend. Which, of course, it is.

Chrissie told me that Val only found out about her husband and the accountant when she phoned the Inland Revenue to complain about the huge tax bill that arrived. Mr Val had told her that the accountant was coming every week because they were calculating weekly tax payments to avoid getting a huge bill at the end of the year.

'This is a mistake,' Val had said to the tax person. 'This bill has already been paid in instalments. My husband and the accountant have been doing it every week.'

There was a cold silence from the other end at that point, which gave Val a chance to hear her words echoing back along the line, and she had one of those blinding-flash things, like the one I had in the car. After saying, 'Oh, could you hold the line a moment please?' she left him.

No doubt it was obvious to everyone who knew Val what was going on, so how come Val didn't notice? Particularly when, according to Chrissie, Mr Val and the accountant were at it in the house when Val was downstairs watching *Bargain Hunt*. He was banging her for over six months, apparently. Does being married to someone prevent you from seeing them properly? I mean, look at Sarah, slumped on her sofa on a sunny Saturday afternoon, apparently oblivious to her husband's philandering in Sainsbury's car park, in spite of all the clues he's been leaving.

Anyway, I don't feel it's my place to tell her about what he's up to. Who knows, he might end it with the other woman any day now and Sarah will never need to know.

'So where's Jakey, then?' I ask, sinking down on to the sofa, then jumping up again to remove a large plastic stegosaurus from under my bottom.

'In his room in disgrace. Little sod. God, he makes me so bloody angry sometimes, I could throttle him.'

This isn't a good start. 'Really?'

'Yeah. Called me a stupid cow because I couldn't make Old Trafford out of Lego. I was trying my hardest, but apparently it's had some extra seats built in at the corners recently, which I didn't know about. So the little git lobbed it at me and called me a stupid cow.' She touches the sore spot on her cheek. 'I was bloody well trying to do what he wanted, you know? And of course he's not the least bit grateful. Anyway, I had to drag him upstairs to his room, with him screaming the whole time about how much he

142

hated me and wanted me to die so that it was just him and Daddy because then he'd be happy. He's so rude and unpleasant – sometimes I feel like I really hate him.'

'Little shit. I can't believe he can be such a horrid little bastard, Sarah. For God's sake, what does he want? Blood?'

Oops. I've made a huge mistake here. Did you spot it? I forgot that really complicated set of rules you have to remember whenever you're talking to parents about their children. 1). Don't ever, *ever* say anything bad. 2). This means that you can't even join in, or *agree*, when the parents are telling you how appalling their kid is. Don't even nod. Little Susie could be hammering you over the head with a house brick, but you still have to laugh playfully as the ambulance crew wheel you out, and slur something like, 'She's a strong little thing, isn't she?' And when darling Johnny looks up from the drain he's just emptied your handbag into and grins at you, you have to rub his head and say, 'What an inventive child.' Then borrow a phone to call the bank. And a locksmith. And a taxi.

Sarah's gaping at me. 'Don't talk about him like that, Rachel. He's a six-year-old boy, that's all. He's not much more than a baby, really. For God's sake.'

'Sorry, Sarah. You know I don't mean it. I think Jake's a lovely child . . .' Oops. I forgot rule number three; when they're telling you how appalling their offspring is, you can't even *dis*agree, and tell them that he's actually wonderful and charming, because then it looks like you are belittling, or don't understand, or both, the enormous amount of stress the parents are under.

'Well, you would, you don't have to live with him.

Honestly, Rachel, you've really got no idea what it's like, being a parent. You haven't a flaming clue.'

'No, well, I didn't mean . . . What I was trying to say was . . .' I should just give up speaking at this point – it's by far the most sensible, and safest, course of action – but I've come here today for a reason. 'He's not always bad, is he?' This seems harmless enough, and I want to hear about the good side of being a mum.

'No, course not. Sometimes he's a little angel. When he's asleep! Ha ha ha!'

'You don't mean it.'

'No, you're right. I love him to bits. I'd do anything for him, you know? I'd die for him. I'd kill for him. But he makes me more angry than anyone else has ever had the ability to do. Including Glenn. I don't think I was ever a particularly hot-tempered person at school, do you? I used to get angry now and then, but not the screaming-myself-hoarse, pounding-my-fists-on-the-wall, smashing-stuff angry that Jake makes me feel. I don't know. I think kids just make you experience all your emotions more intensely somehow.'

'Really?'

'Yeah. I mean, it starts with this love. The second I clapped eyes on my little Jake, it was like a thunder bolt or lightning strike that hit me. I could almost feel this huge thud into me, like an electric shock. I was lying there, exhausted, hurting, bleeding, and then they put this little bundle on me and I saw his face for the first time. I didn't feel it, and then I did. Suddenly I knew that I couldn't live without him. In that instant. Then you get this protectiveness. You get all aggressive and unreasonable if anyone says or does something against your child. Even when you know he's in the wrong. Like at the playground, when he's thumped some scrawny little two-year-old, and the mum comes over and says, "Your son this and that, blah blah," and you feel this heat surging up inside and you start snarling and actually want to thump her.' She smiles a bit. 'You even find yourself feeling proud of him for lumping the two-year-old, and start thinking, Good one, Jakey. That's my boy.

'And then of course comes the anger. Anger like I've never known. I didn't even know I had this inside me. I love my son to distraction, Rachel, but sometimes I fantasize about thrashing the little bugger.'

'Jesus.'

'Oh, don't look so shocked. There's nothing wrong with fantasizing, is there? As long as I don't actually do it, which I don't. The fantasies help me cope, that's all.'

I'm not shocked that she thinks about pounding Jake. I think about that a lot myself. What I'm shocked about is the fact that she could be made to feel so violent, apparently by the person she loves most in the world.

'So you're glad you had him?'

Sarah stares at me. 'Well, of course I'm bloody glad I had him. What the hell do you think?'

I think she's secretly wishing she's on the other side, where there are no kids. But she'll never admit it.

'No, well, of course I thought . . . well, I know you adore him, Sarah. You and Glenn. I know you wouldn't be without him.'

She squints at me. 'Where's all this going?'

'Nowhere. No, nothing. It's just interesting. You know, your amazing love, yet how angry he makes you. The two extremes of emotion, caused by the same person.'

She stares at me a bit then apparently decides to leave it. 'So, you're looking better now. You all recovered from that bug, whatever it was last month?'

'Oh, yeah, pretty much. Still a bit queasy now and then but nothing much really.'

'What was it?'

'Oh, um, nothing major, just a kind of parasite.'

She wrinkles her nose. 'Ughh. Jakey had those once. The kids pass them round and round at school. Did you know that something like half of all children under seven have them without realizing it? Jake's bum was itching like crazy, I don't know how these other kids aren't aware of it. I got down there with a torch in the end and pulled his cheeks apart—'

'Yeah, thanks, Sarah.'

'They're really difficult to see, but then suddenly I could—' She stops talking suddenly and cocks her head.

'What?'

She raises her hand to silence me, then shouts, 'Why should I?'

There's a short silence, during which I glance around, desperate to understand what's going on. Then she tilts her head back again and shouts, 'How many times have I heard that before?' There's another pause, longer this time. Then, 'This is absolutely your last chance, OK?'

There's a thunderous response to that one that even I can hear, as the sound of Jake's feet can be heard thumping along the landing and down the stairs. A second later my godson hurtles into the room and runs straight into his mum's open arms. She wraps them round him tightly and lowers her head so her cheek rests on the top of his head. From somewhere inside this tight bundle I hear the quiet words, 'Sorry, Mummy.'

I've come away. Well, they were both crying and hugging and kissing and telling each other how much they loved each other, I felt like a bit of a gooseberry.

There's my car, parked outside my flat. If you look closer, you'll see me still sitting inside, thinking. Talking to Sarah about Jake hasn't really helped, to be honest. It was difficult to get all the information out of her that I wanted without actually telling her why I wanted it, and I had to drop the subject in the end. It's frustrating, no one else knowing about it. Maybe I should have told her? I try and imagine what that would have been like.

'Sarah, I'm pregnant.'

'What did you s— No, not now, Jakey, Rachel's trying to tell me something. You're just going to have to wait a few moments. Because I said so. Well, go to your room then. I don't care, Jake. Oh, all right, give it to me, I'll do it for you. But this is the last time, all right? You mustn't come and interrupt Mummy when she's busy. Sorry, Rach, what were you saying?'

Forget that. What if Jake weren't there when I told her?

'Sarah, I'm pregnant.'

'Christ, Rachel, you're not serious? What were you thinking of? You're not married! In fact, you're not even in a relationship at the moment, are you? Do you think it's going to be easy? Because let me tell you, it's hard enough doing it with a loving partner and husband to help and support you, let alone if you're doing it alone . . .'

No, maybe not. I need to speak to someone who won't churn out all the things that are already worrying me; someone who'll be sympathetic and kind, and maybe even help me put things into perspective; someone who's a good listener and has got a lovely voice. Who on earth can I call?

Only kidding. Of course it's Hector I want to speak to. It's such relief to be able to talk freely about it every so often. I haven't spoken about the fact that I am pregnant to anyone since I last spoke to Hector, and it's a heavy burden to think about and worry about every day without vocalizing it.

I reach into my bag and pull out his little black mobile. He added his home number to the address book before giving it back to me at the café, so it's easy this time to call. I select 'Home' from the menu and wait for it to connect. After it has rung twenty-five times, I accept that there's no one there and disconnect. Dammit. I throw the phone down on to the passenger seat. I'm frowning again now, look. Hang on – it's Saturday, but maybe he works weekends? I grab the phone again and select 'Work' from the address book this time. It rings three times before the answer phone starts. It's Hector's voice.

'Hi, this is McCarthy Systems. I'm afraid the office is now closed but please call back Monday to Friday, 8 a.m. to 6 p.m. Alternatively, you can contact me on my mobile number, which is . . . 07904 . . .'

I start. When I heard the answerphone I stopped listening properly, not intending to leave a message. But now I leap into action, seizing my handbag from the passenger seat, rummaging around one-handed for a pen, still clutching the phone with my other hand.

'. . . 764 . . .'

I'm rummaging so hard with my left hand and not holding the bag that eventually I chase it off my lap and it falls into the footwell, spilling the contents all over the floor.

'. . . 659. Alternatively, you can leave a message and . . .'

I lean forward as far as I dare to look at the floor, but it feels very funny to bend in the middle like that and I get a bit breathless. I can just see what looks like a blue Biro underneath the clutch pedal and I stretch my free hand forward, my fingertips just managing to touch the end and push it further away.

'Arses arses ARSES *ARSE!*' I shout in frustration as I repeatedly knock the pen further and further out of reach. I am really starting to pant now and eventually give up on the pen and sit back up. I've had to lean my head back against the headrest for a few moments, just to get my breath back.

Once my head clears, I wonder why I am trying to reach the damn thing with my fingers when I can drag it to within easy reach of my hands with my foot. What a complete arse. I lean over and pick it up, then redial the 'Work' number and jot the mobile number down on the flesh at the top of my thigh.

It rings once, then his voice says breathlessly, 'Rachel?'

'Yes. It is.' Of course the number of the phone I am calling from is displayed on the handset Hector is holding, so he knew it was me as soon as his phone started ringing.

'Good. I mean it's good to hear from you. You all right?'

I nod. 'Fine. How are you?'

'Never better. You're not vomiting again, are you?' He almost whispers this question, as if he's talking about something illicit.

149

'No,' I whisper back, bringing the phone closer to my mouth. 'It's all right, I think that's all stopped now.'

'I'm glad to hear it. But why are you whispering?'

'You started it.'

'Did I? Oh, yes, well, I'm not at home and I didn't think all the other people here would particularly like to hear about your . . .' he lowers his voice dramatically, '. . . internal lack of self-control.'

I laugh. 'That's a very nice way of putting it. It sounds almost dignified.'

'It does, doesn't it? But no one here except me has been on the phone with you while you've been exploding, so I know exactly how undignified it was.'

'Oh, no, please don't remind me.'

'Sorry. It was rather ungracious of me.'

'It's all right, we're strangers, nothing you say can hurt me.'

He chuckles and I hear the clatter of cutlery in the background.

'Oh, Hector, I'm so sorry, I've rung you up in the middle of something. You're having lunch—' Oh my God. It occurs to me suddenly that he might be out with his wife, or girlfriend. I cover my mouth with my hand, wishing a big black silence would open up in the atmosphere and swallow up this conversation. Or maybe I could go back in time and not ring him. Actually, if I've got access to a time machine, I may as well go back to July and not shag Nick. But I would still like to find the mobile phone in Sainsbury's. Then I could still meet Hector and not be pregnant.

'Rachel, it's absolutely fine. You're not disturbing a thing, I promise. It's more of a business meeting than a lunch, anyway. I am very glad to be distracted from it for a few minutes, especially by you.'

There's a giant silent 'Whoops!' bouncing along the line between us, and I get the sense that he's biting his lip and screwing his eyes shut, as if he wishes he hadn't said those final three words. But it's out there now and I find I'm smiling because of it.

'Thanks.'

'Well, um. Did you want to talk about . . . ?'

'The . . . the . . . er . . .'

I can picture him nodding, that little crease between his eyebrows. 'The . . . decision?'

I expel a breath that I didn't even know I was holding. It's such a relief that he can put his finger straight on to the thing that's on my mind, without me having to explain.

'Yes. That's it. The Decision.'

'It still needs to be made, then?'

I nod. 'I just can't . . . I don't know if I could . . . how I would . . .'

'Mmm-hmm.'

'But then, if I don't, if I . . . how will I ever ⸱ . . could I ever . . . ?'

'I understand.'

'You do?'

'Absolutely. It's a real dilemma, both sides of which have got far, far-reaching consequences. But if you don't make up your mind soon, it will be decided for you, won't it?'

'Yep.'

'Are you on your own?'

'Yes. I've just been to see a friend. Sarah – she's got a little boy.'

151

'Excellent idea. Did it help?'

'Not remotely.'

'Ah.'

'You know, she talks about him in this jokey way, as if she can't wait to be rid of him, or she doesn't like having him around. Lots of parents do that about their kids, don't they? I hear it all the time at work, they pretend they've told the kids to go and play on the motorway, or they talk about longing for them to be eighteen so they can kick them out on their ears. But then she talks about this amazing love that she felt instantly the first time she ever laid eyes on him, like an electric shock or something, and that she knew right then in that second that she couldn't ever live without him. But then she's got this tosser of a husband, Glenn, and I think he's having an affair, so she's got—'

'Whoa, whoa, hold it right there. Did you say Sarah?'

'Yeah. She's my friend from school. I've known her since we were both about twelve.'

'And her husband is Glenn?'

'Yep.'

'And the little boy is Jake?'

'Yeah. I think he's about five. Hang on, how did you know . . . ?'

'He's six. In fact, it was his birthday last month.'

I've always thought it was really comical the way that people in films take the phone off their ear and stare at it when they can't make out what's going on, almost as if the handset itself is faulty. I'm doing it though. The fact that this stranger whom I barely know and only met because he left his mobile phone at Sainsbury's seems to know about Jake and Sarah and Glenn is incomprehensible. It's as if some higher force has taken hold of the two opposite ends of my life and tied them together.

'Rachel, are you still there? Rachel?'

'Yeh, I'm here. Sorry, came over a bit *X-Files* for a moment.'

'I'd like to have seen that.'

'Ha ha. So, are you going to explain how you know all about my friends and their little boy? Are you stalking me?'

'Hah! No, no, although I think that would be much more interesting than the truth, which is not very *X-Files* at all, I'm afraid.'

'Well?'

'Sarah is my sister-in-law. Jake is my nephew. Glenn McCarthy is my brother.'

'Your . . . ? So you're . . .? Ohhhhh.' I have heard of Glenn's brother. Some self-employed arsehole who lauds it over Glenn the whole time. Sarah always invites him to Jake's parties but I've never once seen him there. She pointed him out to me at the christening – 'The elusive brother' – but that was four or five years ago and I forgot about him almost instantly. He was of no interest to me. I hadn't even remembered his name.

'So you're *that* Rachel,' he's saying, a broad smile in his voice.

'What are you saying? What does that mean?'

'I have heard all about you from Sarah. And from Glenn, come to think of it. Most of what he's told me is true. I wonder how much of what Sarah told me is.'

'What did she tell you?'

'Oh, I couldn't possibly—'

'Come on! I need to know what your preconceived opinion of me is.'

He laughs lightly. 'I have no preconceived opinion, Rachel. She's said some mean things and some nice things, but I always make up my own mind about people.'

'Hmm. So what did Glenn say then?'

'Ah, now that would be breaking the gentlemen's code. No chance.'

'Ugh, you're far too discreet. It's infuriating.'

'You, on the other hand, are delightfully outspoken. You mentioned Glenn having an affair?'

'Shit.'

'I couldn't agree more. Now tell me everything so that I can go and make Sarah a nice new pair of testicle earrings.'

Chapter Nine

At the opposite end of our town and the landmark spectrum to The Blooding we have a lovely park called Fieldwood Park, which has a small lake in it, a cricket pavilion and a rather posh restaurant. The dining area looks out on to the lake, where three or four swans slide about on the glassy water and willow trees bend over to take a look. The restaurant is called Madeleine's and usually they get a bit sniffy about clients using mobile phones while eating.

Hector is having lunch here with someone. They're at one of the tables with the lake view, at the back of the restaurant. These are the best tables in the place. Hector's just clicking off his mobile phone, smiling and frowning at the same time. Although he's angry about his brother, he's greatly enjoyed talking to me again – you can see that in his face. He doesn't know yet that this is going to be one of the worst days of his life.

The waiting staff know Hector well as he comes here a lot. They also know that he always leaves a generous tip, so after fighting over who would serve his table, they have refrained from giving him the 'look' when his phone rang, and actually stayed away from the table during the call in order to give him some privacy.

155

His lunch companion is very elegantly dressed in cream and has impeccable manners, discreetly turning towards the window view of the lake and sipping tastefully on a white wine spritzer while Hector talks. Hector is evidently receiving some bad – or at least infuriating – news and his guest tries desperately not to overhear.

Hector himself is conscious of how rude he is being to his guest, but he can't help himself. He keeps his phone with him, switched on, at all times because of his mum, and when it rang nine minutes ago he picked it up, dreading to see his home number in the display. Instead, it showed his old mobile number, which informed him immediately who it was.

Let's pause a moment and go back nine minutes. I want to show you the moment when the phone rang and he saw that number in the window. Here he is, elbows on the table, nodding as his companion is talking. He glances up and smiles as a young waitress sashays past. Then – there – the phone in his jacket pocket rings and he reaches in and pulls it out. Focus on his face – anxiety, dread, maybe even fear. But now it's in his hand and he can see the display and – look at that! His brow smoothes, he smiles, excuses himself hurriedly and turns away from the table, flicking open the phone eagerly. The fact is, he had intended to leave all calls, except any from his mum, until after his lunch. His pleasure at seeing that number in the display drove the plan completely from his mind.

So now he's finished the call. He stares down at the now silent phone in his hand for a few seconds, as if it is something very precious, then puts it away in his jacket pocket. His companion turns back from the window at last.

'Everything all right?,' says Rupert de Witter, putting his glass down on the table.

Hector nods, then shakes his head. 'Brilliant and fucking awful at the same time.'

'That sounds interesting. Care to elaborate?'

'I just found out from someone that my brother is an arsehole.'

Rupert smiles. 'Which is clearly the bad news. So I'm guessing it's the person who told you that's the brilliant part?'

Hector nods. 'Oh yes, my friend. I'll tell you all about it one day. In the mean time, can we get on with the business, please? I feel a pressing need to pay a family visit this afternoon.'

'Fine with me. I can get a round of golf in if we're quick.'

From this moment on, you can see that Hector has become quite distracted. He's frowning a lot, so must be thinking about what I have just told him about his brother. When he's not frowning, he's smiling to himself, though, and looking thoughtful, perhaps remembering the conversation he's just had with me? Perhaps really pleased that I've called him again? Perhaps delighted with the way his business transaction with Rupert de Witter is working out?

Twenty minutes later and they're shaking hands in the car park before parting company – Rupert to the driving range for a quick eighteen holes, Hector to the bypass to tear his brother a new hole.

He looks furious and is driving far too fast, particularly as he is not concentrating properly on the road. Every so often, he gets an image of Sarah on her knees cleaning, and Glenn mysteriously absent, supposedly working over-time, which makes the blood in his head start pounding and his eyesight go all blurry, and he squints and snarls through the windscreen, banging his hands against the wheel.

He's talking now. His muttering starts off quietly, then gets louder as he becomes more animated.

'You're a selfish, mean, dirty little low-life, Glenn McCarthy. You're scum. You're the lowest, vilest, filthiest, spineless little belly-crawler who doesn't deserve to have a wife and son and be loved like that. Ugh, you little shit. You shit, you *shit*.' A moped suddenly appears in the road ahead, having pulled out of a side road directly in front of Hector's speeding car. His eyes widen and he stamps on the brake, then yanks the wheel violently to the right, skidding on to the oncoming carriageway. He struggles to regain control of the car as it swerves to the left and right, the tyres squealing on the tarmac, and he braces himself as the large shape of a parked lorry looms up very fast towards him. He closes his eyes and wraps his arms around his head, tensed for impact.

The smash doesn't come. After a second or two, he lowers his arms and looks around. His car has come to a standstill close to the middle of the road, at a ninety-degree angle to his original direction. To his left, the parked lorry is intact, a man standing on the pavement next to it looking white and horrified. Hector raises his hand to the man to indicate that he's all right, releasing a pent-up breath as he does so.

A sudden tapping on the driver's window startles Hector and he looks up. There's a youth standing there in a crash helmet, visor still down, indicating for Hector to put the window down. This is evidently the careless moped rider who had so nearly been knocked over. Hector presses the window button, feeling a tremor in his hand. As the window reaches the bottom, the moped owner raises the visor and Hector can see that it's not a youth at all, but an elderly lady.

'Oh my goodness, are you all right, my love?' she asks. Her lips are trembling and her mouth sags with worry, and she puts her hand further inside the window as if to touch Hector's arm. 'I did look, you know, I always look. I don't understand how I can have missed you. Harry keeps telling me I shouldn't be on the road any more, not if I can't wear my glasses, you know, with the helmet on, but it's so easy to jump on and go, you see. Are you sure you're all right? When I think what might have happened . . .' She shakes her head.

Hector smiles. 'I'm fine,' he says firmly. 'Absolutely fine. No harm done at all. I needed to turn round anyway.'

'Oh, heavens, aren't you nice? What a gentleman. You don't meet many like you these days, I can tell you. They're just as likely to stick two fingers up at you as offer you a good morning. Now look, are you sure I can't do something for you? Would you at least let me—?'

'No, no, really, there's no need.' He wasn't sure what she was going to offer to do, but he didn't want her to do it. 'I'm fine, you're fine, that chap over there is fine. We're all fine so there's no need for you to do anything, and you really don't need to worry. I was probably driving too fast anyway.'

'Well, you should be ashamed of yourself,' she says, suddenly frowning. 'This is a residential district, you know. You could have caused an accident.'

Hector blinks. 'Oh, er, well, yes, I suppose you're right. I'll be more careful.'

'I should think so.' She snaps her visor down and says, her voice muffled, 'Young people zooming around the streets without a single regard for an OAP like me out for a ride,' and wanders away, back to her bike.

'Cheerio then,' Hector calls out. She does not acknowledge him and he has the discomfiting feeling that her hearing is failing as well as her eyesight.

The engine is still ticking over, so he shifts into first gear and carefully pulls away, back the way he has just come.

He's realized suddenly that now is not the time to confront Glenn with the news of the affair anyway. It's Saturday afternoon – Sarah and Jake will be there, and Hector has no intention of allowing either of them to hear about it. Besides which, he's so angry with his brother, whatever he wants to say would probably not come out right. He shakes his head. No. He will call Glenn at work on Monday and ask him to come round in the evening. They can thrash it out there, with no danger of being overheard by Sarah. With any luck, Hector will be able to convince Glenn to break it off and that will be the end of the matter.

The usual cold dread begins to seep into him as he nears home. What is he coming home to this time? Unconsciously, his foot eases off the accelerator and his speed decreases as he drives reluctantly along the road towards his driveway.

When he pushes open the front door, everything is quiet. He creeps into the hallway, concerned about disturbing her if she's nodded off in the armchair. As he progresses along the hallway, he begins to notice a faint smell of gas, which grows stronger as he approaches the kitchen. 'Not again,' he says and runs quickly into the kitchen.

On the threshold, he stops dead and stares into the room, frozen with terror.

The gas ring is on and hissing gently. Smashed glass litters the table and the floor, along with some newspaper and, most disturbingly, a few dots of blood. One of the kitchen chairs is tipped over and underneath it Hector can see one of his mum's purple suede slippers. Quickly he turns off the hissing gas and approaches the table. With sickening horror he realizes that the slipper is still attached to her foot, and she is lying prone on the floor by the table, her face pressed against the cold tiles. 'Mum!' he calls out, dropping to his knees, reaching for her, rolling her over on to her back frantically. He presses his ear to her chest but hears nothing. 'Oh God, come on, Mum, come on,' he whispers, placing his face close, his lips millimetres away from hers. He strokes her hair back from her face and holds his own breath; eventually he feels a faint, barely discernible stir of air on his lips. 'Yes, thank you, God, thank you.' He grabs a cushion from one of the dining chairs and pushes it under her head, then pulls out his mobile phone and calls an ambulance.

She's taken straight into Accident and Emergency, jumping to the front of the queue of Saturday-afternoon sports injuries. Hector jogs along beside the trolley until finally he is prevented from going further and the last set of doors swing closed in his face. He stands there helplessly for a few moments until the man behind the desk calls him over to give his mum's personal information.

Look around the waiting room a moment. Can you

161

see, sitting at the back of the room, one well-toned leg extended and resting on a chair in front, someone who looks familiar? Black, floppy hair, baby-blue eyes. We know who that is, don't we? Look a bit more closely – are there tear stains on those smooth cheeks? And all for a sprained ankle. I wonder how he would cope in Hector's shoes.

Hector is pacing now. His hair is standing on end from constantly running his hands through it, the crease between his eyes has deepened and he is biting at the skin of his lips. He starts, realizing suddenly that he ought to tell Glenn what has happened.

There is a phone on the wall inside a clear plastic hood. Hector walks to it and dials his brother's number.

'What's she done this time?' Glenn asks. 'More burns?'

'Glenn, you *shit*, you get here this second.' A few people have looked up from their misery towards Hector, and he lowers his voice. 'Just get here now.'

'Right, OK, I'll come. Just give me an hour or so. I'll ask Sarah's mum if she can look after Jake for a bit, but it's going to take a little while to get him over there and then drive all the way back—'

'Jesus, Glenn, stop making excuses and get moving. Your mum is lying unconscious in Casualty. Nothing is more important than that at this point in time.'

Twenty minutes pass. Hector paces the waiting area, rubbing his head, checking his watch, jumping every time the doors open and a doctor or nurse enters or leaves. He tries to see through the doors, tries to locate his mum in the room beyond, but it's impossible. There are hospital staff everywhere and mingling with them are the friends and families of the sick and injured.

162

The outside doors open and Glenn and Sarah arrive, glancing around in dismay at the crowded room, the over-riding feeling evident on their faces one of irritation.

Hector spots them and strides over. 'Where've you been? Hi, Sarah, how are you?' He glares at his brother, then leans forward and kisses Sarah lightly on the cheek.

'We had to drop Jake off at a friend's in the end,' Glenn says defensively. 'Sarah's mum was . . .' He stops and dismisses this thought with a quick wave of his hand. 'Where is she then?'

Hector indicates the doors where he last saw his mum. 'They took her through there. No one's told me anything yet, but I suppose no news is good news.'

Glenn shrugs. 'Maybe. Depends on what your definition of good news is.'

Hector glares at him, but at that moment they are approached by a young woman with a hesitant smile on her face. Hector walks over to her quickly.

'Are you the doctor? What's happening? Is she all right?'

'Are you the son?'

'Yes, I brought her in,' Hector says anxiously.

'One of them,' Glenn announces, walking up. 'I'm the other one. What's going on?'

'Perhaps you'd all like to follow me. I'll explain every-thing, but let's find somewhere quiet, shall we?'

She walks away towards a door, beyond which is a room with three sofas and a coffee table in it. Glenn and Sarah follow her in but Hector doesn't move for a few seconds. The blood has drained from his face and he puts a hand against the wall to steady himself.

In the room, there are flowers in a vase on the table and

163

pictures of flowers and clouds on sunny days on the walls. The walls have been painted lilac. It is in here that the doctor explains in a calm, matter-of-fact tone that Hector and Glenn's mum had a massive stroke at home, and another one after she had arrived in the hospital. The second one proved fatal. Hector stares at a framed print of sunflowers as he hears her telling them that they did all they could, but she had never regained consciousness. She had not suffered at all. At least her death had spared her that.

Sarah cries out, 'Oh no!' and covers her mouth with her hand, sinking down on to one of the beige sofas. Glenn glances at Hector, then sits down next to his wife and cradles her in his arms. Hector is counting how many sunflowers there are in the picture on the wall. There are eight in the picture above the sofa, and each one has fourteen petals. He looks briefly at his brother and sister-in-law comforting each other, then he wraps his arms around himself and goes out into the empty corridor.

Twenty minutes later, Hector and Glenn are sitting on either side of their mum, holding her cooling hands. She *is* there, on that bed, but you can't really make her out because she's so very tiny. She hardly raises a bump in the sheet. All the tubes and wires that connected her to life have been taken away. If you can see her face, she looks peaceful, but she doesn't look like she's asleep – she's far too still to be sleeping. She is inanimate now and it's already hard to imagine that she ever did move. It's like looking at a representation of her; like a waxwork figure of herself, asleep.

Hector can't stand the unmovingness of her. He gazes at

her face but no eyelash flickers, no pulse beats, no muscle spasms, no nerve twitches; no breath goes in or out. She is as motionless as an ornament. He has read accounts of people looking at their lifeless loved ones, expecting any moment that the person will open their eyes and ask for a drink, but he has no such feeling. He can see that she is no more likely to move spontaneously than the equipment around her.

You'll notice that Sarah is no longer present. She went home in a taxi a few minutes ago. Hector is looking at Glenn as if he wishes he would go as well, but Glenn can't see that because he's got his head down on the mattress.

'I can't believe she's gone,' Glenn says quietly, his voice muffled.

'No,' Hector says simply.

Glenn raises his head. 'I mean, the way she's been lately, I've kind of been thinking that maybe, if she . . . But now that it's happened, I can't . . .'

'I know,' Hector says, putting his hand on his brother's arm. 'You shouldn't feel guilty for thinking like that, Glenn. She had hardly any quality of life left. She was just stuck in a time when things were happy for her. And now she's out of her misery.'

After half an hour or so, they reach an unspoken decision to leave. Each glances at the other and understands implicitly that it is time to go. Glenn kisses his mum's hand then lays it down beside her on the mattress, takes one final look then bows his head and leaves the room.

Hector stands. There are tears running silently down his cheeks. He leans over his mum and wraps his arms around her for the last time, clutching her body to his chest. She does not return the hug. 'Thank you, Mum,' he says into her hair, mouth distorted with grief. 'Thank you for everything you've done. I love you so much. I'm going to miss you every day.' He kisses her cheek, then kisses it again, lingering there a few moments before laying her down on the pillow again. He strokes her hair away from her face and says, 'Say hi to Dad for me.' Then he walks quickly away.

Glenn drops him off but doesn't stay long. He has to get back to Sarah and Jake. Hector understands and prefers to be on his own anyway. Glenn is moving back down the path towards his car really quickly. He's almost running, as if desperate to get away. He probably is desperate; Hector is in a depressive mood.

In the kitchen, Hector is standing staring at the place on the floor that has become his mum's last memory. He tortures himself, imagining what she experienced. Was there pain? Did she understand what was happening? Did she feel frightened? Did she call out for him? He closes his eyes as he realizes that if she did cry out, it was more likely to be for Charlie, her husband, dead for eighteen years, than for Hector.

Why did he go to lunch with Rupert? He didn't have to do it that day. It could have waited until the following weekend, or they could even have met in the office during the week. But he and Rupert were old friends and he was looking forward to conducting their business over a pleasant lunch.

Ten hours earlier, that morning, Celia had said, 'Where're you going?', touching his arm.

'To work, Mum. I won't be long.'

'Work? Who works on a Saturday?'

Hector had stared at her. It was extraordinary that she knew what day of the week it was. Perhaps it was just coincidence.

'Don't go, Hector,' she had said then. 'I don't want to be here all on my own today.'

He had smiled and kissed her. 'You're being daft. I'll only be a couple of hours, then I'll come home and make you some pancakes. All right?'

She had nodded uncertainly, but followed Hector around the house, as he had got ready to go out. He had felt irritated with her, but forced it down.

So her last conscious moments were alone in the kitchen, doing . . . what? The broken glass everywhere looks as if it used to be a thick mixing bowl. There is a carton of smashed eggs on the floor behind the table, and the gas ring was on underneath a large frying pan. Hector looks around at the pitiful last efforts of his sad and deluded mother. It looks as if Celia McCarthy had been trying to make pancakes.

He can't stand to look at it any more and heads upstairs to bed. He doesn't sleep but spends hour after hour remembering long-ago holidays, Christmases, school plays and poorly days. His mum had done her best every day to make the boys happy, holding their hands both literally and figuratively for as long as she could. He remembered her hand clamped on to his so tightly it hurt at his father's funeral eighteen years ago, when he was just fifteen. The shocked whiteness of her face that day would stay with him for ever, and he had been totally unable to make her feel better.

He thinks about her illness, the cruelty of early-onset Alzheimer's that started eight years after she was separated

167

from her beloved Charlie, when she was only sixty. He remembers the agony of watching as day by day she forgot her life, her family and her loved ones, finally retreating into the comfort of long-gone days when her husband was still alive, conjuring him up from her memory.

Finally Hector is asleep. It's just after three a.m. It's not a restful sleep and he tosses and turns all night, waking at eight o'clock the next morning to the realization that his mum is dead.

And now here he is arriving for work on Monday morning, forty minutes late. His face is drawn and grey and his eyes are red rimmed. Darren, his assistant, watches him as he moves slowly towards the door to his office, his shoulders slumped over, head low.

'Can I get you anything, boss?' he asks, but Hector shakes his head without looking up. He moves into the office and closes the door gently behind him. Darren goes back in the main office and tells the other two people working there, Moira and Carl, that something is very wrong. 'He seems very down and depressed, not his usual cheery self, and should probably be left alone as much as possible today, OK? He looks like he hasn't had much sleep all weekend, and I daresay—'

He is cut off suddenly by a loud explosion of laughter from the office behind that makes Moira start in her seat. All three turn to look at the door to try and understand this inexplicable change in attitude, then Carl and Moira turn to Darren, eyebrows raised. He is utterly baffled and can offer nothing more than a shrug.

Chapter Ten

Of course, I am oblivious to Hector's tragic day. At exactly the same time as he and Glenn are looking at the still, soundless shape of their mother in the hospital, I am prowling the flat, about to embark on a rather sad evening of my own. I've got a hunger pang, but there's nothing in the flat to eat. No, that's not strictly true. There's lots of food, but everything there turns my stomach over. Even bread seems just too . . . bready right now. I've tried to settle in front of the telly with a glass of water – tea and coffee are banned from the flat – but I'm so fidgety. I'm up again, heading to the fridge, even though I know exactly what's in there – a lump of cheddar, some cold ham, a jar of pickled onions, six eggs, a tub of margarine. I stare at them, imagining eating them, testing to see if I fancy any of them. I most decidedly do not.

I slam the fridge door in angry frustration. I know there are Bourbon biscuits in the cupboard, but in my head they feel like sawdust in my mouth. I need something less . . . biscuity.

I head back to the sofa and try to watch television. A woman has just won £32,000. Terrific, except she was on £125,000 and then said that *Pride and Prejudice* was written by Jane Eyre. I tut and shake my head at her stupidity, but I have no idea who really wrote it, or who Jane Eyre is.

At last the adverts come on. They're better than the actual programmes sometimes. I wish I could dance as well as that car.

Suddenly my attention is seized by the supermarket advert. I am alert, poised, ears pricked, nose quivering, tense and ready. The advert is full of delicious, fresh, juicy produce being sliced, diced, peeled and squeezed in short, mouth-watering chunks. I'm staring now, frozen like the hounds from The Blooding, water drooling from my mouth. I know now, more certainly than I have ever known anything, that satisfaction will only be had by the immediate, gluttonous, wet and crunchy consumption of cucumber. Cucumber in cubes, cucumber in slices, cucumber in massive, cold chunks forcing their way over the back of my tongue and down my throat.

Within two minutes I'm driving fast along the bypass towards Sainsbury's. It closes at ten o'clock on Saturday night, so I'm in a bit of a hurry. It's half past eight now, so in fact I've got loads of time, but I'm hurrying anyway. The thought of cool, delicious cucumber slipping between my teeth is eclipsing any other rational thought.

As I speed along through the darkness, I get an inkling of what it must be like to be addicted to something – the intense, obsessive longing for something, and the acute pleasure in the anticipation of knowing that that desire would soon be fulfilled. I had a boyfriend last year – Tom Brown or Black or Jones – who was a really heavy smoker. Thirty or forty a day. If we were on our way to bed in the evening and he only had three or four left, he would have to rush out to the offie to get a couple more packs, just so that he had plenty for the morning, or during the night. He made absolutely sure that he never, *ever* ran out. It used to irritate the hell out of me, this dashing out at all hours, because it made me feel second best to something. Here in my car on a Saturday night doing eighty miles an hour, I finally understand him.

He was dead sexy but stank the flat out. Plus, he put me second, like I said. He had to go.

I have never been in Sainsbury's at this time of night before. It's populated by people in shorts and cardigans picking up milk and wine. I feel like a gatecrasher at some stranger's party.

I head directly for the fruit and veg aisle and grab two cucumbers, hesitate and then pick up two more. They are hard and heavy in my hands, their skin faintly glossy. After paying I hurry back to the car, the weight of the fruit in my carrier bag deeply satisfying. The drive home is a blur, dominated by thoughts of dark green skin and pale green flesh. My eyes keep flicking over to the four heavy bars lying on the passenger seat and I imagine the cool paleness within. Their two-tonedness is intoxicating.

Here I come, struggling into the living room with my teeth round one of the cucumbers. I drop the carrier bag, purse and keys on the floor and sink down on to the sofa, cold watery flesh and pips coating my lips, filling my mouth. Nothing has ever tasted this delicious and in fact if you look closely at the expression on my face there, doesn't it look suspiciously similar to my face while Nick was on top of me, all those weeks ago?

I finish the first one and make a start on the second, less feverishly now but with no less enjoyment. The pleasure is in biting off more than I can decently chew, overstuffing my mouth, then swallowing it before it's really thoroughly mashed so I can feel its cold hardness going down my throat.

Two-thirds of my way through the second one, I've had enough. Just like that. The intense longing and passion has stopped, as if someone has switched it off. In fact, now I can't bear to look at the cucumber left in my hand. The smell of it is in my nostrils, on my fingers, down my clothes, and bizarrely, in my hair. I drop the piece I am holding and cover my mouth with my hand, feeling immediately nauseous and bloated. Standing up shakily, I stagger from the sofa along the hall to the bedroom, burping and hiccuping, and haul my swollen body on to the bed, where I fall asleep almost instantly and dream of my mum with glossy green skin.

Let's draw a veil over the rest of my weekend. Suffice to say that the following day, the Sunday, I am not at my best. By the end of the day, my skin had become green and glossy too. Actually, unless you've ever eaten almost two whole cucumbers in the space of about four minutes, you can have no idea of the pain they can cause. As I was writhing around in acidic agony that day, I couldn't help thinking about all those cheesy greetings cards that list the superiority of cucumbers over men – they don't monopolize the remote control, won't moan when you buy more shoes, don't need to have their egos soothed, etc, etc. Of course, if I had chosen a cucumber over Nick two months ago, I wouldn't be in the predicament I'm in. But if I had chosen a man over a cucumber last night, I could easily have made my heart cold the next morning. As it was, it burned all day and no amount of Gaviscon could help.

172

Let's move forward three or four days and catch up with me at work on the Wednesday after the cucumber incident. Hold on – that's my empty desk. I must be in the toilet. Oh, yes, here I come now. And walking relatively slowly, in fact. That's quite a change from the ridiculous and, let's face it, utterly inefficient slow stiletto sprinting I used to do to and from the toilet and the vending machine before all this started. I was so worried about not missing a sale, I actually used to pump my arms as I moved. I'm pretty sure now that I wasn't really running, I just felt as if I was running. Of course, any saleswoman worth her headset would be able to make enough sales in the time she was in the sales room, even allowing for toilet, cigarette, food, drink and EBay breaks. So I'm not charging around the place like a rhino in nubuck any more.

Oh, God no, not a rhino. A gazelle. With those fabulous long black eyelashes. And gorgeous legs.

Beep. My turret has just signalled the arrival of an incoming call, so I press the 'I' button and announce, 'Good Morning, Horizon Holidays. This is Rachel speaking, how may I help you?'

'May I speak to Marion, please?'

'Hold on a moment, please, I'll see if she's free.' At precisely this moment, the mobile phone – Hector's mobile phone – goes off in my bag.

It's interesting to note that there's no hesitation over which is the most important. I simply cut the caller off immediately, switch over to 'B' for Busy and snatch my handbag off my desk.

'Hello?' Why do I still answer it with a question, as if I don't know who it is on the other end? It's going to be Hector, every time.

'Rachel.' There's a long, deep breath in and out. He sounds relieved. I'm smiling before he's even said anything. 'It's Hector.' It sounds like he's got a stinking cold. It makes me want to clear my own throat.

'Well I know that, Dippy. Who else would ring his own phone?'

'Of course. Sorry. Not thinking straight.'

'You're forgiven.'

'Thank God. How are you, Rachel?'

'Oh, you know, fine. I've got millions of cells inside me dividing and aligning and forming an utterly dependant second person that is throwing my hormones all over the place while diverting some of my food, water, blood and oxygen away from me towards itself, making my heart beat faster and shrinking my brain. And a slight headache.'

'Oh, it's so good to hear your voice. I can't tell you how much.'

'Try.' I'm grinning a bit too much, which has alerted Jean. No one grins while they're selling holidays. She's staring at me from her desk, so I duck my head.

'No, I really can't. I'll explain to you . . . another time.'

I've finally noticed what you no doubt noticed immediately – his voice is a bit strained. He sounds quite emotional, even. Is my well-being really that important to him?

'Hey, I'm all right really,' I say, trying to ease his concern. 'I'm not feeling sick any more, except when I'm hungry, I'm not revoltingly fat yet, and I've still got loads of time left to . . . er . . . make the big decision. I'm trying not to think about it too much, actually. Just getting on with things, you know, kind of hoping the answer will pop into my head one day over *EastEnders*.'

'Well, if you use that as a guide, you'll decide to terminate, then won't be able to go through with it at the last minute, tell the wrong bloke he's going to be a father and when the real father finds out, they'll have a fight, one will club the other over the head with an ashtray and your innocent brother will go to prison for it to protect you.'

He's joking and I laugh, but there is definitely something not right with him. What do you think? He sounds, I don't know, sad, I suppose. And although he's speaking very quietly, his voice is all echoey, as if he's in the bathroom, or at the swimming pool. Or underground.

'You're right, perhaps that's not the best idea . . .'

'Um, can you hang on a minute, Rach, please? I just need to speak to someone.'

That's very odd. I'm a bit miffed, if I'm honest. I mean, he rang *me*, for God's sake. But I do like the way he's just called me Rach.

'OK. But make it quick.'

I glance up as I wait and find Jean frowning at me. She even looks as if she's going to come over, so I get up. While Hector is talking to someone else, I take the phone away from my ear and conceal it in my hand, then head quickly out of the room towards the corridor. I go into the ladies' loos and lock myself in a cubicle, just in case Jean is in hot pursuit.

When I put the phone back to my ear, Hector is apparently still chatting away to this other mysterious person. Irrationally, I hope it's not a woman. I hear a voice saying something about '. . . so very sorry . . .' but that's all I can make out. Weird goings-on at the local underground cavern.

.Eventually, he comes back. 'Are you still there?' he says quietly. 'Rachel?'

'Yes, I'm still here, of course, dangling on the end of the phone, just waiting for you to come back and speak to me again.'

I hear him release a long breath. 'Thank you. Thank you so much. I'm sorry to keep you hanging around. It's just . . .'

'No, it's fine. I'm locked in a toilet now, so I can take as long as I want. We women are known for it.'

'Yes, I'd noticed that.'

I can't see him, obviously, but from the tone of his voice it sounds as if he's rubbing the back of his head with his eyes closed.

'What's going on, Hector? Is everything all right?'

He splutters a bit, and sniffs, then falls silent. I'm wondering if that was actually spluttering and sniffing, or the sound of interference or static on the line. Perhaps we've been cut off.

'Hector?'

He clears his throat. 'Rachel, can I ask you to do something for me? It would mean . . . It would really help me.'

'You're not going to ask me to do something weird with a pantomime horse, are you?' I don't know why I'm still joking around, but I can't seem to help it. It must be the tension.

He snorts faintly. 'No, you're all right. Not today. Although I may want to explore that another time. What I want you to do today – now – is, well, just to stay on the phone. Will you do it?'

I've drifted into the *Twilight Zone*. This request makes no sense at all. He's rung me up to ask me to *stay on the phone*? I have to stay on the phone all the while he's on the other end, don't I? Unless he's about to say something really horrible to me, that would normally cause me to slam the phone down – or rather, furiously press the 'end' key – and he's making me promise that I won't.

'I will, but if you say something horrid, I can't guarantee . . .'

'No, no, I won't be speaking. That's the thing.'

'Eh?'

'Rachel, I'm calling you from St Stephen's church. In about three minutes, I am going to bury my mum, and I really don't think I can get through it on my own. It would help me so much if you could just . . . stay there, just so I know someone is there for me. Even though we're strangers, and I really don't know you well at all, I feel that somehow you're connected to me, to this, because of the message you left on my answer phone the other day, just when I was feeling at my lowest point.'

I've put my hand over my mouth. And there I was, joking around and being silly. 'Oh, Hector, of course I will stay on the phone. Of course. But isn't Glenn . . . ?'

'He's with Sarah, and Jake. They're a unit. It's fine, I don't mind. I just don't want to go through it alone.'

'I understand.' Something occurs to me. 'What message?'

'Oh, God, this is it. Hold on, Rachel, please. Just stay right there.'

So I do.

If we take a look at Hector, and the service he is enduring, we can see, at any point during the next hour, that he has his mobile phone earpiece tucked firmly in his ear. Apart from the few minutes that he spent standing at the lectern, reading some thoughts about their mum he and Glenn had put down on paper earlier that morning, he has one hand covering it. The phone itself is secreted inside his jacket.

Sitting in the toilet cubicle, tears are sliding down my face as I hear Hector's beautiful voice talking about the costumes his mum sewed for school plays and fancy-dress parties; the magical Christmases she created; the time their dad prodded her playfully with a fork and she sulked for two hours and refused to come down to dinner. He spoke about his dad's death too, and how strong his mum was, for the sake of her two boys.

'Mum,' he is finishing, and I can tell from his voice that he's letting himself cry in front of everyone, 'you did well. We never told you, but you were a great mum, and we had a fantastic time. Thank you so much.'

In the cubicle, I hear quiet steps as he returns to his seat, and then I can hear him breathing again, sucking in rapid breaths through his mouth, letting them out slowly. His hand is back on the earpiece again, almost cradling it, as if he needs to be in contact with it. His head is slightly bent over towards that side, as if he wishes he could lay his head on a shoulder.

Eventually, the congregation moves outside, and I too have to head off. Here I am, pulling the door to the Ladies open a crack and peering out, phone clutched to my head. About three minutes ago the door banged open and Jean entered. I know it was her because she shouted out, 'Rachel, are you in here still?' I kept absolutely quiet and still, like a child in a dinosaur movie, waiting for her to give up and go to look elsewhere for her prey. It took two minutes of shallow breathing, but eventually she went.

So now I'm up and out of there, heading towards the lifts. I still have Hector in my ear, breathing quietly, talking to other people who are expressing their sadness to him and then waiting for him to say something cheering and make them feel better. Why aren't they trying to cheer him up?

Every so often he says, 'Still there?' really quietly, and I reply, 'Still here.' And he breathes on.

Five minutes later, downstairs in reception. Can you see me? No? Good. I'm hiding in the stationery cupboard that's at the end of the corridor where the lifts are. No one ever goes in here because each floor has its own stationery supplies, so these are purely for reception. No one ever uses stationery in reception.

Upstairs in Telesales, Jean is going berserk. Look at her, her hair is practically on end. She's tapping a foot and her eyes are fixed to the clock.

'Graham, take over. I'm going for a cigarette,' she says, heading fast to the door.

Thank God I thought to hide in the cupboard down here, because here she comes out of the lifts now. Bloody hell, I am so in trouble.

'Rachel,' says the phone, and I start a little. I had gone into a bit of a trance in the dark here next to boxes of three-year-old brochures. Who wouldn't?

'Yes, I'm here.'

'It's over. They're all leaving.'

'Oh. Where are you now?'

'I'm standing here, next to the grave. She's in there, right at the bottom. Cold and on her own. How can I leave?'

'Would it help if I talk to you while you walk away?'

He doesn't reply, so I start anyway.

'I am in so much trouble now. Jean, my supervisor, has been pounding round the building looking for me. She even came into the loos with a torch while I was in there. Now she's got SWAT teams at every exit, and there are dogs and men with sticks and lanterns. They're doing a fingertip search of the carpet in reception at the moment. There's even a guy in a white paper suit, picking up Biros with tweezers and dropping them into plastic bags.'

I hear what I think, hope, is a faint snort of laughter, so I carry on.

'I'm not kidding. Jean really, I mean *really*, doesn't like us to miss the sales. When my friend Chrissie went to put mascara on once, there was an APB out on her and within five minutes her unmascara-ed face was on *Crimewatch*. She was annoyed about that, I remember.'

'What's APB stand for?'

'Um, I think it's something like, All Personnel Beware, or something.'

Again, the laughter. 'I'm sorry to have got you into trouble.'

'No, you haven't. They haven't found me, so I can sneak back upstairs and pretend I've been sitting at my desk the whole time.'

'Aha. That's a good plan.'

'I thought so. So tell me something. You said that I had left a message on your answerphone.'

'Hah, yes. It cheered me up so much, I can tell you. I don't know when you left it, but I got it the day before yesterday, when I went into the office.'

'But I didn't . . .'

'I was back to work after one of the worst weekends of my life, so you have got to imagine my state of mind. I was

180

very depressed when I sat down at my desk, but in spite of that I start going through my messages. There's one about some contract or other that needs to be adjusted, and one about a meeting I need to attend, and then suddenly you, all out of breath and agitated, saying "Arses". I think your actual words were "Arses, arses, arses, *ARSE!*"' He laughs, a bit more enthusiastically. 'Those four words, at that moment, summed up succinctly and absolutely exactly how I was feeling, and hearing you say them on my answerphone made me feel so much better. I was suddenly less alone. I actually laughed out loud, which I really didn't expect to be doing when I woke up that morning. You are such a tonic for me, Rachel Covington.'

'Thanks. I'm glad I could help.'

'You really did. And thanks for supplying the music, too. It was really comforting.'

'Music? What music?' What's he talking about? I can't have supplied anything because I didn't know until an hour ago that this funeral was happening today.

'Your humming. It was lovely. So appropriate.'

'Humming?'

'Honestly, Rachel, are you having another *X-Files* moment? Don't tell me you don't remember?'

'I don't remember.'

'Well, all through the service, while we were all saying goodbye to my mum and I was struggling to keep it together, you were humming "Lean On Me".'

Chapter Eleven

That's a bit embarrassing, isn't it? During that long, silent phone call, I was feeling well chuffed that Hector was leaning on me, to help him through that awful time, and apparently my thoughts were plainly audible. I didn't even realize I was doing it. I'll have to watch that doesn't happen again.

I didn't want that phone call to end, though. It gave me a good feeling to be doing something for someone else, especially when he's six foot three with crinkly brown eyes and a delicious voice.

Oh, by the way, I didn't really get into all that much trouble afterwards. When I came off the phone from Hector, I sneaked back into Telesales without Jean seeing me – I think she was chain smoking in the car park – and then told Graham that I'd been feeling poorly with 'women's problems', and he left it at that. The classics are still the best.

Just over a week later, on the Sunday, I'm round at Mum and Dad's for tea. I've been avoiding seeing them for quite a few weeks, assuming that my predicament will be so obvious on my face – if not elsewhere – that Mum will suss it as soon as she looks at me. I still dread telling her and don't see any reason to go through that trauma if I decide that I'm not going to have a baby after all.

So here I am now, standing at my parents' front door. This is the very spot where Sarah did it with Martin Kennedy, on her sixteenth birthday. I am horribly reminded of that incident every single time I come home. It's like Sarah's gift to me.

Mum and Dad are in the kitchen, chatting while they sort out the dinner. Actually, Dad's doing most of the work while Mum leans against the counter, sipping wine. Dad's turn to cook today. He's apparently in the middle of telling her a funny story and suddenly she explodes into laughter.

'Hi, Mum. Hi, Dad.'

'Rachel love! Hello.' Mum comes over and hugs me and I pray silently over her shoulder that she won't notice my belly or boobs. I'm twelve weeks now and believe it or not there is a very slight rise below my belly button. All my clothes still fit, luckily, but I am very conscious of it. No one at work has said anything, though, so I'm pretty sure it doesn't show yet.

But this is my mum. If anyone's going to notice that I've gained weight, it'll be her. And not only is she bound to notice, she'll not hesitate to tell me, too.

She's still hugging me and you can see how I'm trying to prevent my torso from pressing into her too much. If she could see my guilty, anxious expression, she'd guess what was up straight away, boobs or no boobs. Fortunately, she can't. Dad can but as far as he's concerned, I'm doing the normal 'Getting-a-hug-from-Mum' face – faintly irritated smile, itching to get away. He winks at me and pulls a 'she-just-loves-you' face.

My mum was sixteen when she got pregnant with me. Mum and Dad weren't married but they were deeply in love, apparently. They managed to get the wedding in before I appeared, which made my mum's parents much happier. Well, happy is too strong a word for it. I won't say they hung up their baseball bats, but they did put them down on the floor for the toasts. My dad is ten years older than Mum, so there was a great big scandal in the family about this twenty-six-year-old man getting Mum in trouble. When I was born, all of Mum's family offered to take me in, they were so sure Dad was going to scarper. All my childhood, whenever I've seen my aunt and my granny, they've said something like, 'It's so lovely in Weston at this time of year. Why don't you come and see what you think?'

It's twenty-five years later now and my granny still gives Dad the old-lady-curse stare when she catches his eye. It's like she's saying, 'Don't think you got away with it because you're still on probation, my lad.'

Anyway, Mum's always been really young, compared to my friends' parents. She was only just forty earlier this year. Having a young mum was ghastly when I was a teenager. I kept bumping into her in all the night clubs.

She's let go of me and is looking at me strangely. Here it comes, I'm thinking, tensing.

'Have you been doing all your chores properly, Rachel?' she says, out of the blue. Of all the things I thought she might notice, I didn't think she'd spot that one. It's amazing. How does she know I've been slacking lately? Is there an absence of bleach aroma around me? The skin on my hands is too soft? My fingernails are looking a bit too polished?

184

'Course I have. I've still got my list, tucked away safely in the kitchen drawer. Have you got any cucumber, Mum?' I'm saying, heading for the fridge.

'Mm, I think there's some in there. Have a look.'

Here comes James, my little brother. 'Hi, Slacker. You all right?' And there he goes.

'Yes thank you, James,' I say, although he's already gone. 'I am very well, thank you for asking. It's so nice to see you. How are you?'

'Oh, don't mind him,' Dad says. 'He's preoccupied with a project he's working on in the garage. It involves cardboard and Sellotape.'

'Say no more.'

The dinner goes a lot better than I was expecting. Dad's telling me about some new power tool he's just bought, like a kid with a new toy – apparently it can saw wood at a forty-five-degree angle, although what use that is I don't know – and Mum tells me she and Dad have started going to salsa classes on Tuesday evenings. I look at Dad but his face is blank. James fills in any gaps in conversation with boring claptrap about some computer game or other, but you can get away with not really listening to him. I smile at him fondly and thank God I don't have to live with him any more.

So it seems my secret is still secret. I'm relieved the visit is out of the way as I drive home later. If I'd left it many more weeks, I wouldn't have been able to hide anything. Now I can leave it for another six weeks or so before I go again, and by then . . . it'll all be over, one way or another.

The next day is Monday again and I leap out of bed, delighted at the prospect of the start of another week at work. Look at me, I'm bounding around there like a non-pregnant, unworried person. But today I feel fantastic. After my shower, I do my hair and it goes right first time. And it looks better than it has for ages. My skin is glowing and healthy, I have got bags of energy and I feel . . . I don't know. Unstressed. I can't say carefree because I know that I am still pregnant and I am still thinking about it, but now it feels like it doesn't matter. It doesn't show, I don't look fat or ill, why should it trouble me?

No more Shreddies for me for breakfast. I am well into fruit now and just eat half a melon. It tastes like it has been crafted by God using all the tools in Heaven to make it perfect. I smack my lips, throw down my spoon and trip lightly off to the bathroom, where I vomit the whole lot up again.

In the car, I start singing along to a track on the radio – 'I get knocked down, but I get up again, you're never gonna keep me down' – and I am still singing it now as I'm entering the telesales room. I'm even dancing a bit. Oh yes, it feels good to be back to my old self.

I boogie over to my turret and find Val there, pale and quiet as usual.

'All right there, Val? How are you on this fantastic morning?' I call out.

'My mum died,' she says, effectively ruining my mood for the rest of the day.

'Oh, oh no, how awful, I'm so sorry,' I say, crouching down by her chair. For fuck's sake, what's going on? Two mums, in the same week? What are the odds? I'm forcing my exuberance down like an excited animal that won't sit still. Val's poor mum has been in a hospice for weeks, suffering hideous pain daily, so it's actually a bit of a relief that she's gone, so Val says, but she doesn't look relieved. I rub her back, then stand up and go out of the door to get her a cup of hot chocolate.

Poor Val. As I head up the corridor towards the vending machine, I'm remembering that time when she had tried to get me to bring her back a drink and I pretended not to notice. I'm truly ashamed of that now. I'm so preoccupied with these shameful thoughts that I don't notice until the last moment that there's a familiar back standing at the vending machine. My heart does a little lurch, but I'm actually surprisingly calm. I slow down, though, hoping that he will get his drink and leave before he sees me.

Or have I slowed down because it's so difficult to look sexy when walking fast? Are you getting a sense of déjà vu? Because I am.

Did you notice the irony of Nick not being at the vending machine every time I went there to try and see him, and there he is today when I no longer care? He must have asked around and found out that my new habit is an early morning hot chocolate which is very pleasing. Not that I'm remotely bothered any more of course. No you're right, I am bothered. You know me pretty well, don't you? My heart is beating faster and I lick my lips as a kind of impromptu lip-gloss. Of course, the word is getting around now that Nick's married. I wonder if he knows it was me that spread it? He turns suddenly and sees me approaching. His face contorts in fury.

'You evil little bitch,' he says in a low voice. I'm guessing that he knows it was me.

'Hi, Nick,' I say. 'It's lovely to see you too.'

'You've been spreading rumours about me.'

187

'Have I?' I walk nonchalantly over to the machine – 'Excuse me, please' – and feed the coins into the slot.

'Yes you bloody well have, you vicious little slag,' he says, stepping politely out of my way. 'Telling everyone that I'm married. What are you playing at?'

'I'm sorry, I don't know what you mean,' I say, really casually. 'Why on earth do you think I would spend even thirty seconds of my life on you?'

The hot chocolate is ready, so I take it, flash him a smile, and walk away. I am so cool but inside I'm burning up. It's those baby-blue eyes again, and those lashes. And that body. And the hair, let's face it. He just makes me melt. I so hope he is watching me as I leave. I have a pair of really narrow, low cut trousers on.

After I've gone, let's linger a moment and watch Nick's reaction to seeing me. He's not buying a drink, so that means he must have been waiting there just to speak to me. And although his face is frowning and distorted with anger, his eyes follow my low-cut trousers all the way back up the corridor. He doesn't move until I've disappeared behind the door.

Back in Telesales, Jean is making an announcement. We are getting a new person. Sabrina Walker, who used to sit at turret eight, has finally moved to Portugal with her boyfriend. She has been saying she's going to do that for the past year and everyone had stopped believing it was ever going to happen. But turret eight is empty, so either she's in Portugal or she's left to make it look like she's in Portugal. Either way, we're one down and that sounds like more sales for me.

Actually, this afternoon is my first ante-natal appoint-ment, so I need to work really hard this morning to make up the loss. My appointment is at three and Jean's let me take the afternoon off. I've told her it's a hospital appointment for a woman's problem. She put her hand up at that point and didn't want to know any more. I wasn't going to tell her any more anyway.

'Make sure you make up the sales,' she growls at me. Like I need telling.

About quarter past two, I flick to busy, wave to Jean and head off to the Ladies with my handbag. There's one thing I need to do before I leave, and for old times' sake I'm going to do it in the Ladies. I lock myself in a cubicle, put my handbag on my lap and rummage around inside for the little black phone. I get to the menu and click on 'Work', but just as it starts ringing, I hear the door open and two girls come in, chatting animatedly. Quickly I switch it off.

'Oh my God, Lise, did you see that? He's fucking gorgeous.'

'Yeah, I know. Did you see those eyes? What do you reckon? Do you think I could pull that?'

'You do know he's married?'

'So what? I don't wanna have babies with him!' I can tell from her voice that she's putting on mascara.

'No, that's true.'

There's a pause. I'm getting an uncomfortable feeling that they're talking about Nick. But all I know about the person is that he's gorgeous and married, so it could be anyone. Perhaps I'm obsessing about him. While I wait for them to leave, I've decided to have a wee. By the time I remember I'm supposed to collect some to take with me, it's far too late. Bugger.

'I feel sorry for the wife really.'

'Really? What, having to go to bed with that every night? Yeah, poor cow, it must be hard on her.'

'No, seriously. Being the wife is boring. He's used to her, know what I mean? That's why he was looking at us like that. Plus, she must know that he can get any woman he wants. Did you see him looking down my top? God, just thinking about that has got me all horny.'

'All right, calm down. You've got drool on your face.'

They snigger and the door opens and closes again. Quickly I find the 'Work' number and press 'Dial'. While it rings I'm snarling over Nick apparently flirting with yet more people in the office when he's got a wife and a kid on the way. Although technically he doesn't actually know about the kid. And it might not have been Nick they were talking about. But he did fit the description – 'fucking gorgeous' – perfectly.

'McCarthy Systems.'

Have you ever dialled a number and then while it was ringing had a really deep, long think about what the gorgeous but married bastard from your personnel department has been up to, and then when the person finally answers the phone you've completely forgotten who it is that you've rung? Nor me. Until now, that is. For a moment I'm sitting there on the loo hearing this woman's voice announce that I've just rung something called McCarthy Systems, and I have no idea why I've rung them. I'm in *X-Files* territory again. Obviously I've just been returned to earth by the aliens who abducted me, and I'm in the middle of a phone call I know nothing about.

'Er . . .'

'What can I do for you?' the woman says. I'm frowning, trying to remember what I was doing. Then I remember. McCarthy Systems. Of course.

'Yes. Can I speak to Hector please?'

'I'm afraid Mr McCarthy is currently unavailable. Can I take a message?'

Bugger. I hadn't bargained on this. When I ring people, in a social context, they are always available. I've got my first ever ante-natal appointment in half an hour and I really want to talk to someone about it. And that person, of course, has to be Hector. Oh God, this means I am going to have to go down to the surgery without a pep talk.

'Do you want to leave a message?' the woman reminds me.

Do I? I only rang up to speak to a friendly voice before my appointment, so what's the point of leaving a message? In the end, I just ask her to tell him that I called and leave it at that.

So here I am, emerging from the loos, and look at the expression on my face. How would you describe that? Anxiety? Disappointment? Revenge again? I don't know – I'm useless at this stuff. But I know how I was feeling – bloody fed up that I haven't been able to speak to Hector before the appointment. I am starting to love the intimacy of him being the only one who knows about the baby, but at the same time it's a bit frustrating because if he's not available to talk to, I've got no fallback, nobody on standby.

The appointment is upstairs in my doctor's surgery. I've been at this surgery for four years but I've never been up here before. The stairs are very steep and the corridors are very narrow with low ceilings, so naturally this is where they decided to set up the ante- and post-natal examination rooms. Right. Anaemic women with intimate and tightly sewn stitches, leaking from every orifice, with possibly a bawling infant clinging to their backs, have to climb Everest stairs, and when – if – they reach the top, the corridors are all clogged with really fat women and prams. I'm betting it was a man who put it up here.

'Rachel Covington?'

This is it. I'm trying to look like I fit in with all the other expectant mums there, but of course I don't. Most of these women are wearing flip-flops. I follow the nurse into the examination room and she closes the door behind us.

'Rachel, is it?'

'Yes.'

'OK, then Rachel, my love, have a seat.' She's blonde and plump with an ill-fitting dark blue nurse's dress on that's straining at the buttons. Here's the plain evidence that the NHS really is short of cash. That dress was probably new in 1980.

I sit on the chair and she perches on the edge of the desk. She's holding a pink cardboard folder and she opens it and reads what's inside. 'OK, so you're, what, thirteen, fourteen?'

'I'm twenty-four.'

She smiles at me. 'Oh, I'm sorry, I meant weeks, my love. This is going to be your first baby, isn't it?'

I'm staring at the folder. Someone's written 'Rachel Covington' on the front, in the place where it says 'Name of mother'. I have been labelled as a mother. It's very disconcerting. I don't feel like a mother but it seems these people have decided I could do it. That I should do it. This pink folder is a map to motherhood. If I set out from here,

I will eventually arrive at a point where there's a baby. My breath is stuck in my throat.

The nurse has obviously noticed the absence in the room of brimming maternal joy and is bending in the middle to try and make eye contact with me. '*Is* this going to be your first baby, Rachel?' she asks kindly. I look up at her helplessly but don't say anything.

She slides off the desk and walks to the back of the room. 'Have you seen my letters?' she asks me. She knows I haven't as I have never set foot up here before, but I shake my head anyway. 'Come and have a look, then.'

I stand up and go over to the wall where she's standing. Pinned, sellotaped and Blu-tacked to cork boards, picture rails and even the bare paintwork, there are letters. Pink letters, blue letters, yellow letters, plain white letters, some of them hand written, some of them typed. Some of them have been printed on a computer and have got all the traditional baby-related graphics down the sides, in pastel peach, soothing lilac and cornflower blue: dummies, bootees, cribs, sleeping infant faces. No one ever includes white, panicky adult faces, or red, blood-shot eyes, do they?

'These all came from my babies. Or rather, from the mums and dads of the babies I have delivered. Some of them are just from mums.'

I lean forward to read one of the letters. 'Dear Katy,' it says, 'We just wanted to write and tell you how much . . .' It goes on to say how their lives have changed with the arrival of their little angel, how they couldn't have done it without Katy's support, how much joy the little angel has brought them. They say that they can't find the words to express how they feel, but they have a pretty good go,

193

rambling on to the end of the page. Right at the bottom is a tiny photo, stapled on to the paper. I have to lean forward to see it properly. It's a teeny little face fast asleep, a curled fist the size of a marshmallow, full butterfly lips and feather black hair.

'Isn't she beautiful?' Katy is saying. 'Her name is Annabel.'

I move on to the other letters, the other photos. I stop at each one in turn, some on petal pink, some on sky blue, and read the joyful words, gazing at the pictures, at the tiny fingernails, the long eyelashes and the deep, dark wondering eyes. At intervals around the room there are letters that are clearly just from mums. They're slightly different because they talk of the anxiety, the worry, the stress, and then the exhaustion of coping alone, the dread of a change of lifestyle, reluctance to let that happen. But each one finishes off by expressing the joy of the new arrival, how it far outweighs any problems that he or she brought along, how their lives have changed, but not for the worse. 'It's certainly different now, but in a lot of ways it's better.' They end by thanking Katy for her help and encouragement, and saying how, in spite of the obvious problems and difficulties to come, they wouldn't be without their little Chloe or Sam or Liam.

Which is what Sarah said.

Those photos! They're incredible. The tiny little perfection of a mini person, with its own little features. I wonder if this one will have Nick's eyes, then start as I realize I am thinking forward, to the point where it is a real baby, with eyes, and a nose, and hair. And for the first time, I understand perfectly that there is a real person growing inside me, entirely dependent on me for everything, including life. It's just there. It has no expectations, no hopes. Not yet. But I could give it that. I could bring it to life. I'm wondering now if it has hands and feet yet, and if it has decided whether to be a boy or a girl.

'What do you think?' says Katy from the desk.

I look round at her and smile faintly. 'They're amazing. I never thought—'

She puts up a hand. 'I don't want you to feel you have to make up your mind now, Rachel. It's a big decision and shouldn't be made in the space of a few minutes, on the strength of someone else's happiness. Having a baby is the biggest, most serious thing you can *ever* do, and you have to be ready for it. Better the baby should not be born at all than born to a mother that doesn't really want it. It's little more than a plant at the moment, trying to get purchase in a bit of fertile soil. It has no consciousness, no aware-ness, so in lots of ways it isn't a baby yet. But it does have huge potential.'

'I know.'

'Rachel.' She walks over to me and takes my hands. 'Whatever you decide, I will help you, but I cannot help you decide. I don't want you to feel under any pressure, for any reason. No one is judging you, no one will think badly of you, whatever happens. OK?'

I nod dumbly.

'Good. Got your wee wee?'

Fortunately, there is a loo in the corner of the room, so I go and produce what she needs. She dips a strip of paper into it, examines it and then writes NAD on to my file.

'What's nad?' Is it the female equivalent of gonad, I'm wondering?

'Nad? Oh, you mean N.A.D. It means 'No abnormality

195

detected. I just tested your wee wee to see if there are raised levels of protein or sugar in it, because that can mean there is something going on inside that we need to know about. But you're OK.'

I don't like the sound of that, frankly. It doesn't actually mean that there isn't something wrong, it just means that no one has spotted it.

'Right then, well, seeing as you're here, we'd better check you out, Poppet, just to make sure there are no problems so far. All right?'

I lie on the couch and she presses into my low abdomen, just above the pubic bone. Suddenly she says, 'Ah yes,' but does not elaborate and I don't ask her. She gets a piece of equipment that looks a bit like what I imagine a round drawer handle would look like if it was connected by wires to a large box on wheels with a red digital display on the front, and presses it into my belly, moving it around. Eventually I see some numbers flash up on the display.

'What's that for?' I ask her.

'Oh, I'm just checking the heart beat, Rachel. Everything's fine.'

'You mean, the baby's . . . ?'

'Yes, the baby's.'

'It has a heart . . .'

She smiles at me and helps me up. 'Right, you would usually need to have an ultrasound scan during your first twelve weeks or so to work out your due date, but I don't think that's really necessary as you've been able to be so precise with your dates. The next scan is in about four or five weeks to check up on the size and to make sure it's growing right. All right, my lovely?'

'All right.'

'Good. Now I'll just check your weight and blood pressure to make sure you're in good physical shape, in case you choose to take this step.' Don't you just love the way she sums up the whole astonishing process, from implosive and highly improbable egg and sperm fusion, followed by forty weeks of astounding and never fully comprehended growth and development, to the twenty-four-hour-long series of agonizing muscle contractions that result in the harsh and bloody expulsion from one's depths of a live human being, as a 'step'? God, if only it were that easy.

Outside on the pavement, I've gone into a bit of a trance. I've got a baby inside me. That's the overriding thought going round my head. If I'm honest, that's the only thought going round my head at the moment. All right, yes, you're right, I've known for quite a while that it was a baby. But until this moment, standing motionless on the pavement in the autumn sunshine, it's seemed more like a problem and less like a potential human.

Katy may have said that my options are still open, and that no one will judge me, whatever I decide to do, but clearly she's lying. Little more than a plant, she says, with no consciousness or awareness. It reminds me of that old nightmare we were all told at school, that if you accidentally swallow apple seeds, they will start to grow inside you until eventually the tree bursts out of the top of your head, apples and all.

Well, there were no apple seeds, and it's not coming out of the top of my head. Apart from those details, it's pretty much fact.

The letters from the single mums were uplifting,

though. What's struck me most about them is that they all said their lives were different, but not worse. It's like jumping from one track to another. The transition is bumpy and difficult and once you've made the jump, you can't get back on to the first track again. But the new track has its own benefits so you probably won't want to. The hard part is deciding to make the jump.

I can't believe I'm even thinking about this.

The phone in my bag has started to ring suddenly, and I know who that will be. I delve in there quickly to retrieve it. I can't wait to tell Hector what's happened.

'Hello?'

'Hi, Rachel, it's Hector. Whoops, sorry, you knew that, didn't you? I got your message. Everything all right?'

'Oh God, Hector, I don't know. She says it's just a plant, but really it's nearly a human, so even though she says I've got time and my options are still open, and that no one will judge, I really doubt it.'

'Uh huh.'

'And she says she wasn't trying to pressure me, and that I don't have to decide now, and that she will help me whatever I decide, but she can't help me decide. And then she shows me all these amazing photos of tiny little babies, with shiny black eyes, and tiny fingers and toes, so perfect, and really thinks that they aren't going to sway someone in a certain direction. If that's not pressure, then I don't know what is. Mum says that kind of thing is emotional blackmail, when you try to get someone to do what you want them to do by making them feel bad if they don't.'

'She's right.'

'I know. It's totally not fair.'

'And probably unprofessional.'

'Yes, you're right. Unprofessional too.'

'Rach, can I just get something straight in my head?'

'What?'

'What on earth are you talking about?'

'Well, the midwife, Katy. Who did you think I was talking about?'

'Oh, the midwife. I see. Your mum came in there for a moment and confused me.'

'She does that a lot.'

He laughs. It's such a great sound. 'Oh she does, does she? I'll have to be on my guard then.'

'I think that's best.'

We fall silent for a moment while I struggle to think of how to bring up the subject of his mum and the funeral and everything.

'Your mum sounds lovely, actually,' he says suddenly. His voice has gone a bit quiet.

'She's a pain in the bum. You'd like her.'

'What are you trying to say?'

'No, nothing, only that, um, if you ever did meet her, you know, by chance one day, or something . . .' Crap. That sounded terrible.

There's a pause, then he says softly, 'I think I'd like that. I mean, to bump into her by accident. Not prearranged or anything.'

God, could he be any clearer? 'Well, we'll have to see if we can not arrange it some day.'

'Terrific. Just name the day, and I'll keep it busy.'

'OK.' I hate the direction this is taking. I really can't tell whether he's joking or not, which is totally unlike me. I can't even tell whether or not he fancies me and that's unheard of. Usually when I meet a new bloke I can pretty much guarantee that he's going to fancy me – unless he's gay, of course – but it's all different with Hector. He's the only bloke I have ever met pregnant, and that does literally distort things.

'Thanks for helping me out with . . . mum's funeral, Rachel. It made it less . . . unbearable.' His voice has gone all hoarse and throaty.

'Any time, Hector. You know that. I'm glad I could help.'

'You did. More than you know.'

He sounds raw again and for the first time in probably my life, I can't tell whether he's horny, or whether he just misses his mum. And for the first time in probably my life, it doesn't matter, whichever it turns out to be.

'What . . . ? What happened to your mum?'

He takes a long breath in and releases it slowly.

'I'm sorry, Hec, I shouldn't have asked. It's none of my business. Can we forget I said it?'

'No, no, Rachel, it's fine. I want to talk about it. I want to talk to you about it. Of everyone I know, all my friends and colleagues, you're the one I want to talk to about it. I'm sorry. It's just . . . it's still hard for me to say the words.'

I wait, clutching the phone as if I was clutching his hand.

'On the Saturday, when you rang and let slip about what my dear brother has been up to, I was having lunch with an associate and friend. I didn't have to have the meeting that day. I could have waited until the following weekend, or done it during the week. Sometimes I have to work weekends, but I try not to because of Mum. *Tried* not to. Anyway, after I spoke to you, I went haring off to visit some wrath on Glenn, but I got distracted on the way and decided that it wasn't a good idea to go and confront him while Sarah and Jake were around. The thing was, I was out longer, because of that. I had told Mum I'd be home to cook her pancakes, but by the time I got home—' He breaks off. I'm feeling a coldness beginning in the middle of me, like a fire of ice. 'When I got home, she was on the floor in the kitchen. She was trying to make the pancakes herself, and she had a stroke while she was doing it. I called an ambulance but it was no use. She had another stroke in the hospital, and died without regaining consciousness. She didn't suffer, apparently.'

'Fucking hell.'

'Yes, that's what I thought. Anyway, I have tortured myself every day since then, wondering if I hadn't gone to lunch, if I hadn't driven halfway to Glenn's after lunch, if I had just stayed at home that day, would she have died? Was it the stress of being alone that led to the first stroke? Or would calling the ambulance as soon as it happened have prevented the second one?' He stops suddenly and sucks in his breath. 'Oh, look, Rachel, I'm sorry. I don't want to burden you with all this. You've got enough to worry about without me going on . . .'

I have no idea what to say. Is it best in these situations to be interested in what happened, ask a few pertinent and tactful questions to show that you aren't going to avoid the subject all together? Or is it best to avoid the subject all together and try and take his mind off it?

When my granddad died six years ago, no one spoke to Granny at the funeral. Well, to be fair, she wasn't actually there, but I think that's because no one told her when it was. It's one of the family mysteries, where Granny was when Granddad went to his final resting place. In fact, she was enjoying a game of shuffle board on the deck of the *Mediterranean Jewel*, which sailed out of Southampton a week earlier, with the captain and his wife. I know this because I sold her the holiday. I have never told anyone, least of all my mum, where Granny went that fortnight.

'Do you want to meet up?' is what I say finally, and it's not entirely what I thought I was going to say.

Hector, you can see, is amazed, and pleased. It turns out that I have managed to sense, without words, exactly the thing he wanted to hear, and he had been struggling to find a way to ask me the same thing. 'Yes.'

'Really? Great. Where and when?'

'How about The Blooding. Can you make it in half an hour?'

I look over towards the dribbling statues. 'I can manage ten minutes. How about you?'

'I can do it in five.'

'Make it two and you've got a deal.'

'You're on. See you in two.'

Would you say I had time to pop into Cream Tease and use the Ladies to do my hair and put a bit of lippy on, in two minutes? No, I don't either. But that's where I am. Apart from anything else, I really don't want to be sitting there waiting for him when he arrives.

Here he comes now. I can see him perfectly from my vantage point of the café doorway. He's very tall – taller than I remember. And now I come to think of it, he's quite nice looking, too. I mean, we're not talking the devastating, dangerous, dark *beauty* of Nick Maxwell – Hector's older for a start – but there's something very appealing about his messy brown hair and stubbly chin. He looks

202

generally a bit rumpled, too, not immaculately groomed like Nick. His jacket's slung over his shoulder again, he's not wearing a tie and his shirt is coming untucked at the front. But the sight of him, hurrying towards the fountain, checking his watch, looking all around, makes me smile. Why is that?

For now, I'm staying here, in the doorway out of sight. I'm just going to make him wait for a minute or two. He's sat down on the rim of the fountain, the place where we first met. He must have driven like a mad thing to get here this quickly. Mind you, I don't know where he's had to come from – maybe it's really near by. I prefer to think of him driving madly to meet me.

Right, time to go. I emerge from the doorway and walk over to him, smiling broadly. He spots me and looks up, then stands up; and that expression of pure delight on his face almost stops my heart.

'My God, Rachel. You look fantastic.' He takes hold of my arms and pulls me in towards him as he leans forward and kisses my cheek. For two seconds I enter his personal space, and he's inside mine. Everything slows down, almost stops, for those two seconds. I catch a scent of cologne or aftershave, and shampoo, warm and spicy, and his face scratches mine. Then he's away again. He's done this even before either of us has had a chance to think about it, and afterwards we look at each other, a bit surprised it happened. I know that it's made me feel a bit hot and weak in my belly, but what does the expression on his face tell you? To me he looks a bit disconcerted, flustered. Maybe even a bit concerned? I've never had that reaction to physical contact before.

His car is very near by in a car park – of course – so he

suggests we go for a drive. He's got a lovely car, actually. A big silver Mercedes of some kind, with leather seats and air conditioning. I lean back against the headrest and close my eyes as the cool air glides over me.

'So where shall we go then?' he asks me, glancing repeatedly over to the passenger side. Then as he's pulling away from the car park, he stalls the car.

'Sorry,' he says, restarting the engine. Then, as he tries to pull away again, he stalls it for a second time. 'God, what's the matter with me?' he says, turning the ignition key again. 'I'm all fingers and thumbs.' He doesn't meet my eyes.

'Well, there's the problem. You should be using your feet.'

'Oh, ha ha,' he says, then almost goes the wrong way round the roundabout and puts the windscreen wipers on instead of the indicator.

'Let's just drive, and see where we end up,' I say, smiling.

'So you're quite happy to stay here?'

We head out into the countryside and as he drives Hector tells me more about his mum, who was living with him, and the cancer that killed his dad eighteen years ago. I feel so sorry for the fifteen-year-old boy standing next to his mum at the funeral, holding her hand so tightly like a much younger child. He doesn't look at me while he tells me this, but I'm watching him and his eyes fill up. He blinks it away quickly and I point out the sheep through the window, pretending I haven't noticed.

We wind up at a little pub called The Frog in the Night-gown where the picture on the sign above the door sends us both into gut-wrenching laughter and we stumble through the door.

Hector watches me as I wipe away tears of laughter. 'You know,' he says, 'you are a different person to that sickly, pale little thing I bumped into two months ago.'

'Thanks. I think.'

He orders our food – salad for me, heavy on the cucumber – and I eat everything, fast and unselfconsciously. It makes me think of the last meal I had with Nick, that time we met that vicious Sean character. I had hardly dared eat anything, trying to look dainty and interesting. Hector is watching me eat but it doesn't bother me. Why should it when I'm not doing my best to look sexy the whole time?

On the way home, we sit and sing along in the darkness to the CD player. He's got one of those compilation CDs with loads of old songs on it, and I manage to find the track I had been singing to that morning on my way to work – 'Tubthumping' by Chumbawamba. While I sing 'I get knocked down, but I get up again', Hector sings 'We'll be singing when we're winning'. We bounce from side to side in harmony with each other, enjoying the music, feeling buoyed up by it.

'Hang on, hang on,' I'm saying, putting my hand on his arm. I've had an idea. He smiles down at my hand.

'What?'

'Listen, how about this. "I get knocked *up*, but I get up again." What do you think?'

He laughs delightedly. 'It's brilliant!' So we sing that instead. I am remembering being in Nick's car with him, and how tense and nervous I was the whole time, never relaxed, always trying to look my best, be my best. I look over at Hector who is now cheerfully humming along to 'Smack My Bitch Up' by The Prodigy and I realize that

205

since I put the lipstick on in Cream Tease I haven't thought about my appearance once.

'What are you looking at, you witch?' he says suddenly, grinning.

'Nothing. Just thinking about Nick.'

'Nick?'

'He's the . . . er . . . father.' I say it really quietly.

'Oh.' He glances quickly at me and then back at the road. He does not resume singing.

He drives me back to my car in the business park, the cheery, fun atmosphere suddenly dissipated. He's gone all quiet and sullen.

He's turned the engine off, so I say to him, 'Thank you so much, Hector. I have had such a lovely time.' I've said that loads of times before, but this is the first time it really means something.

He gazes at me, his eyes sad now. 'So have I, Rachel,' he says softly, then reaches out his hand and moves a strand of hair away from my eyes. He leaves his hand there, touching my hair. 'A truly lovely . . . time,' he murmurs, a bit distractedly.

'I'd better go,' I say, picking up my bag from my lap. 'Work in the morning.'

'Yes, me too. Look, can we . . . ?'

'Yes?'

'Well, perhaps we could . . . If you weren't . . . I mean, if you felt . . .' He runs his fingers through his hair, messing it up even more. 'What I am struggling to say is, do you think we could do this again sometime? Go out, I mean, not talk in a car park.'

I nod and smile, and his face brightens. 'Yes please.'

'Oh, good,' he says with a sigh of relief, and with his

hand still on my hair he moves towards me and very gently kisses my cheek again.

It's *not* my ear, or the gristly bit that sticks out of my ear and holds my earphones in, it's my cheek. And it's light, and soft, and I can feel his breath on me long after he's moved away again.

As I walk away from the car, I look back to wave. He's watching me intently but he's not smiling. In fact, he looks decidedly worried. I almost stop where I am, the expression on his face slowing my feet, making me frown. But then he's turned away to reverse out of his space, and I watch his car as it leaves the car park.

In the car, Hector is frowning as he drives. What I don't know is that he thinks that because I'm pregnant, I've just come out of a long-term relationship. He thinks that I must still have feelings for the dad. He thinks the dad will very soon realize what he's missing out on, and call me up for a tearful reconciliation. He didn't plan on kissing me, but he couldn't stop himself. He's cursing himself for that now because there is no point feeling what he's feeling when ultimately the best thing all round is for the parents of the baby to be reunited.

Chapter Twelve

I can't fathom him out, which is another first for me. Is Hector the first complex and deep person I have ever dated, who maybe has more on his mind than getting me into bed? What hope have I got of understanding him, if that's the case? He seems pleased to see me and we have such a laugh when we're together. But then, suddenly, he gets all quiet on me, and looks really fed up and worried when I walk away. I think about it for twenty minutes before dropping off to sleep.

It's the best night's sleep I've had for three months. I'm up the next day, bouncing around the flat, singing that same song again. In spite of yesterday's disaster, I'm having the other half of the melon this morning. Crafted in paradise by happy angels. I hesitate by the toilet, but nothing comes. Hooray!

This puts me in an even better mood. I finish getting ready for work – hair is getting longer but I quite like it – and grab my bag and keys from the table. I'm just heading out of the front door when my stomach does a sudden convulsion and I have to run back to the toilet to lose my breakfast after all.

Let's skip forward twenty-five minutes and wait outside

the lift doors on the third floor at work. The lift is just arriving with me in it. See that young woman in black, with the short, sexy haircut, standing there, waiting? Who do you think that is? The lift doors open, and there I am coming out, catching sight of the woman, who is waiting for me, it turns out, not the lift. She walks right up to me, as if she knows me, but you can see from the way I turn away from her and try to get past without engaging in conversation that I don't recognize her. And then all of a sudden, I do.

Have you ever seen in films where one of the characters looks at someone, then looks away without noticing something, but then apparently realizes that they haven't looked properly and have probably missed something crucial, so they turn their heads back really quickly? Mum says it's called a double-take. I've always thought that it's totally fake because surely if you're looking at the woman who a moment ago was a scruffy dyke in baggy jeans and a grey hoodie, and is now a stunning supermodel in a sheath dress and silver shoes, you're not going to glance at her, dismiss her and look away, then suddenly realize that's she's changed almost beyond recognition and suddenly turn back to feast your eyes on her new image, are you?

Well, that's what I did.

'Holy crap!' I shout. It's Chrissie – can you believe it? I mean, look at her! Doesn't she look different! At last she has abandoned those fruit-themed tops in flowing cerise and lemon, in favour of floaty black wide-leg trousers, black leather boots and a very tight red top with a plunging neckline. There's even a hint of black lace from her bra visible at the V of her top. I'm speechless. And how much better does her hair look? That long, curly mane falling on to her shoulders is gone. Instead she's gone black and short, feathered all over and curling forward in wisps by her face. It looks gorgeous. In fact, I'm touching my own hair self-consciously. It looked all right in the mirror this morning but now I am acutely aware that it hasn't been cut for almost four months, and the highlights are growing out. Bugger it – Chrissie is making me feel inadequate!

The last time this happened was nineteen years and four months earlier, when Chrissie's painting of her favourite story – *Ghostbusters* – got put up on the wall.

She's got different make-up, too. Much more subtle, nude colours instead of that brash red lipstick. She looks chic, slim and stunning! Not that she is slim, but these clothes emphasize her large bosom and draw attention away from her large hips and belly.

'My God, Chrissie, you look amazing!' I've quite surprised myself there. Generally, I don't like other people looking better than, or as good as, me, and undoubtedly Chrissie does. But it doesn't bother me at all. In fact, I feel delighted for her and smile at her, genuinely meaning it. She's looking sceptical though.

'Thanks. Anyway, I've got to tell you something. The new station eight is here. Just got in. Calls herself Paris, of all things. Fancies herself, you can tell. Bit of a tart . . .'

'What's brought on this change in image all of a sudden then?'

She stares at me. 'Nothing. Why should anything have brought it on? Why can't I just decide to change my look when I feel like it without being bombarded with a load of questions and stares?' She starts to walk away, then comes back suddenly. 'Quick, there she is now. Look at her.'

I follow the direction of Chrissie's discreetly rolling eyes to where a young girl, probably only about eighteen or nineteen, is standing just inside the door to the sales room, talking to M and M. She looks all right to me, long mousy hair in a ponytail, short skirt, white shoes. M and M look cheerful enough, smiling and chatting away animatedly. I'm about to turn back to Chrissie when I notice something that makes me freeze and my mouth falls open. Mike or Martin is holding a steaming coffee cup and as I watch, he gives it to the new girl, pressing it into her hand. She's all smiles and pretty acceptance, fiddling with her hair, wafting her eyelashes. And then, horror of horrors, I see from M's gestures – pointing with his elbow back along the hallway to the lifts, nodding emphatically, indicating his watch and the clock on the wall – that he is explaining to her that he and M go past the vending machine every day around two o'clock and can bring her a coffee back each time, if she wants.

I glance at Chrissie and she's studying me intently, obviously waiting for my reaction. Back at the doorway, this usurper is smiling prettily again, nodding, obviously saying 'Ooh, thank you so much, that will be just lovely,' and then she leans forward and kisses each one on the cheek, before walking off. As she's going, M and M watch her walking in silence, then turn to each other and do – can you believe this? – a surreptitious low five on each other.

'She's obviously very common,' Chrissie says as I stand and gape. 'Come on, you've got to get in there.' Other people are walking past us into the sales room, calling out 'Morning' and 'Hiya'. She takes hold of my arm and moves me along the hallway and through the door. Over at station eight, the new girl is chatting sweetly with her new neighbours, Jim and Penny, while they show her how her chair works, how to turn on her computer, how to activate the turret.

At my desk, Val is standing there, watching all this going on. She sees me and smiles. 'Hi, Rachel. You all right?'

I nod mutely and sit down.

'Don't like the look of her,' Val says. She's much more talkative now. We've become almost friends.

'Me neither. Want a hot choc, Val?' I stand up again and head off towards the vending machine.

The thing that's bugging me is that I have always had a certain status in Telesales. Well, not just in Telesales, all over the third floor. And other parts of the building, if I'm honest. My name means something in most Horizon circles, whether they love me or hate me, they're not usually indifferent. I am the one that gets the attention, the one that gets invitations, the one that gets the coffee, dammit. And now this Paris girl, who actually has very ordinary hair when you look at it, is trying to shoulder me out of the way.

At the vending machine, I have to stand for almost eighty seconds waiting for the hot chocolate.

Am I over-reacting to M and M simply offering to buy someone a cup of coffee every day? But they used to get me a cup of coffee every day. Yes, but I blew that when I was full-on obsessed with seeing Nick. But now that everyone knows Nick's married and we're not together any more, why didn't they offer to start up again? Maybe they meant to, but never got round to it? Or maybe they just couldn't be bothered any more. I have spent a fair bit of time lately in a foul mood, looking pretty hideous, so they've obviously gone off me. But did they ever fancy me in the first place – they're gay, aren't they? I don't know, are they?

Beep. The first hot chocolate is ready and I feed another pound in for the second one.

I don't think anyone knows the answer to that one, even M and M themselves. It doesn't matter either way. The point is that they don't do it for me any more, but they're more than happy to do it for *Paris.* So what? Why do I care? Why am I even having this conversation when I might be going to have a baby? Am I having a baby? Oh bloody hell, I don't know.

Beep. That's number two, so I grab it and head off back to my desk.

Val and I endure in silence all morning the fawning and simpering going on at eight. Jean does the talk about add-ons and sales figures and league tables and Paris sits and pretends to take it all in. I'm watching her, though, and I can see that while she's pretending to be listening to Jean, she's actually flirting with Simon, who sits opposite. It's cruel, that kind of thing, because Si is clearly delighted and thinks he might be in there, while realistically anyone can see that someone like him doesn't stand a chance with her. He's a lovely bloke and means well, but he wears tank tops. Still, all the while she's not listening to Jean talking about sales technique and client care she's not learning, which means more sales for me. I'm back up to sixth – did you notice that?

At lunch, Chrissie flips out a compact to touch up her lip-gloss and flick out her new hair and disappears out of the door, without even checking with me what I want to do. I'm a bit narked about that, as you can see by my face as I watch her go. Val always goes down to the staff canteen for lunch so for the first time ever, I go with her. She's thinking about getting herself a new sofa and talks about it non-stop on the way down. I'm fantasizing about the salad and fruit that I'm going to eat when we get there. Occasionally the image of one of the Ms giving Paris that coffee creeps in, but I focus hard on the imaginary apple I'm eating and make it go away.

When I get back to my desk twenty-five minutes later, there's a message for me that someone has called, and a number I should call them back on. I don't recognize the number and assume instantly that it must be Hector. Look at the delight on my face as I quickly dial the number.

'Lacey Ladies,' says a voice I recognize and I slump in disappointment. It's Susan's shop.

'Hi, Susan, it's Rachel. How are you?'

'Hi, Rach! Bloody hell, where the fuck have you been? I haven't seen you since Jake's party. I've missed you. How are you?'

'I'm fine, Sue. How are you?'

'I'm all right, as ever. But you were really ill last time I saw you – did you get home all right?'

Remember that Jake's party is getting on for two months ago now, so if I didn't get home all right, it's far too late for Susan to be asking me about it. She can't do anything to help me now.

'Yes, thanks, no problem. It wasn't flu, you know.'

'No, no, I know all about it. Chrissie told me everything.'

'Oh, did she?' Well, it's no surprise that Chrissie has told her – I did tell her about Nick being married on purpose so that she would spread it around Horizon. The Chrissie

214

telegraph is so effective, it's even reached the underwear shop in the precinct.

'Yeah. What a complete tosser that bloke is. You shouldn't have wasted any of your time on him, especially letting it make you ill, you idiot. Men are all the same – lying, cheating wasters who are good for one thing only and should be safely discarded after fifteen minutes.'

'Fifteen, eh?'

'Ten, then. If you're lucky. And that includes having a ciggie after. Fucking bastards, the lot of them. I just wish I could manage without them.'

'But we can't, can we? Where would the fun be in that?'

She sighs dramatically. 'No fun at all. No heartache either, but no heartache is not worth no fun, is it?'

'Erm, no. I think. Anyway, I'm all right now. Completely over him.'

'Really? Sure? Brilliant. Do you fancy a swim this afternoon then? See what's hanging around at the pool in Speedos?'

'Yes, all right. Shall we meet there?'

Before Susan arrives, I take the opportunity to scrutinize myself in my cozzie. There's a full-length mirror on the wall by the toilets so after I've locked everything away, I stand and inspect the damage. Well, my boobs are definitely a bit bigger, but considering there's another person hiding inside me, my belly isn't too huge. Sure, it's not as flat as it used to be, but you wouldn't guess what it was, if you didn't know. You'd just assume I was an overeater.

Bugger.

Susan arrives and looks at me sidelong in the mirror as I'm staring at myself. 'You look beautiful as ever, Rach,' she says, 'but you can see where you've missed the swimming recently.'

I manage forty lengths and stagger back into the changing rooms, legs like jelly. In the same time it's taken me to do forty, Susan's managed to do fifty and get a date with the life-guard. She glides into the shower, serene and relaxed. 'Wasn't that fabulous?' she says, washing her hair. 'Just what I needed. Phew!' I'm not sure if she means the exercise or the date.

We head to the café for our usual black, sugarless coffee, but today I'm having hot chocolate and a cinnamon whirl.

'That looks delicious,' Sue says, sipping her black coffee.

'Want some?' I say, offering it out to her, mouth full of pastry.

'God no. The animal fat in those things comes from . . . Oops. Sorry, Rach. You carry on. Anyway, you deserve a treat now and then, don't you? Doesn't matter what I think. You're probably in need of a pick-me-up anyway.'

I look up at her sharply. 'What do you mean?'

'I only mean after this man you liked turned out to be married. You were pretty cut up about it.'

'Well, to begin with, I suppose so, but now—'

'I know exactly what it feels like. I was in love with a married man once.'

'Really? I never knew that.'

She nods, taking another sip. 'I didn't tell anyone. It was a terrible time for me. I was a mess. As soon as I found out, I ended it.'

'Mmm.'

'Trouble was, I got pregnant.'

I almost choked on my bun. 'You *what*?'

'You're right, it was stupid of me. I was only eighteen. It was a disaster.'

I hardly dare ask the next question. 'So what did you do?'

'Do you remember me having a baby the same time Sarah did?' I shake my head. 'No, well, what could I do? I was eighteen, I had no money and the father . . . well, let's just say he didn't relish the idea of telling his wife the happy news.'

'Oh my God . . .'

'I've never stopped thinking about it, though. How old it would be now, what it would look like, that sort of thing. I see toys in shops and I wonder if I would have bought them for Christmas or birthday presents. I even choose things.' She's staring into space, distracted.

'Is that why you joined that pro-life group?' I ask her gently.

She comes back and looks at me properly again. 'No, no. The terrible thing is, I was already very anti-abortion, even then, so the decision I made went completely against everything I felt strongly about. I had created this tiny, precious thing that was desperately clinging to me for survival, but I couldn't provide what it needed. So I shook it off, and it fell away.' She swallows and takes a deep breath. 'I can't forgive myself.'

'Oh God, Sue, why didn't you say anything? It must have been torture for you when Jake was born.'

She nods, her eyes filling with tears. 'I didn't want anyone to know what I'd done. I felt like a murderer. Still do, actually. So I kept it to myself. Even my mum doesn't know about it.' She grins unconvincingly. 'Been looking for love ever since. Or forgiveness maybe.'

'So why are you telling me now?'

She smiles, sniffs and wipes her eyes with a serviette. 'I thought you might find it interesting. So, did you check out that blond life-guard? God, I really think this is it this time, Rach. He's the one.'

Has she guessed, do you think? I can't tell. Here I am, in the car driving home, and I'm going over and over what she said, about how she thought I might be interested now. And earlier when she said something about 'it shows that I haven't been swimming for a while'. Has she spotted the bump in my belly and linked it with the 'illness' I had at Jake's party? She's always been very insightful, Susan, so I wouldn't be surprised. I didn't tell her though. I'm still not sure, even after that.

One of those throat-scraping hunger pangs hits and I stick my tongue out of my open mouth, as if somehow that will help.

They say that in pregnancy, you lose all your dignity. This must be what they mean.

Saliva drips off my tongue on to my lap and I do one half-hearted little retch. I need food. What is there in the house? A parade of images marches through my head: a huge plate of spaghetti bolognese with loads of cheese on top; a steaming mound of chilli and rice, with loads of grated cheese on top; a plate of beans on toast, with grated cheese melting on top, but much quicker – only five minutes to prepare instead of fifteen. Or better yet, what about just toast, covered in hot, drippy butter, all soaking into the . . .

Oh bugger it, I've missed my turning. I stomp on the brakes quickly without thinking and from behind there's a loud squeal of rubber on tarmac, followed instantly by a deafening bang and a fierce jolt, which forces my car and my body forward violently, leaving my head to jerk sickeningly backwards into the too-small head rest. Hot bolts of pain sear up through my neck and shoulders, into my jaw and I cry out. On one level I realize that I have been shunted from behind, but on another my mind is spinning and I clutch the wheel tightly, heart thudding with panic. I close my eyes to beat back the encroaching nausea, but everything starts turning as if I've had too much to drink. I look up again and try to focus hard on something stationary to bring the spinning under control. I look out of the windscreen and focus on a red letter-box on the other side of the road. The only sound I can hear is the very faint whine of what sounds like a car reversing at speed.

Look at that car go! The bastard, didn't even stop to make sure I was all right. No doubt driving with no insurance, or no licence or both.

So now what do I do? Maybe if I stay here for a few minutes, the pain will subside and I can drive home. After thirty seconds of sitting as still as I can, I can't endure it any longer and feel I have to get out. If I could reach my bag, which fell on to the floor with the impact, I could call Hector. Or an ambulance. My mind is so confused I can't decide which one I need more.

I jump as there's a sudden tapping on the window, and then the door is opened from outside. Thank God.

'Are you hurt?' says a voice, the face just out of view. All I can see without moving my head is a beige cardigan with big brown buttons that look like wood. I try to nod, but white-hot knives slice through my neck.

'Yes,' I say instead.

'Where, love? Neck?'

'Uh-huh.'

'Anywhere else?'

I've been nodding and shaking my head for about twenty-three years, so it's really hard to stop myself from doing it. I try to shake my head – *ouch* – and then say, 'No,' in a pained voice.

'OK, love. I'm calling an ambulance now. Don't move.' Oh, do you think? I had been thinking about doing a spot of line-dancing while I waited.

He walks away from the car but I can't turn my head to see where he's going. I can hear his voice requesting the ambulance, although it's too low for me to hear it distinctly. After a couple of minutes, he's back.

'All right, love, don't worry, ambulance is on its way. My name's Frank, by the way. I live over there, right by the letter-box. That's partly why we moved here, you see. You wouldn't believe how convenient it is living right next to a letter-box. We get everything done in double quick time. Main thing is, you're OK. Oh look, here comes the ambulance now.'

The paramedics – Tom and Beth – check me over and ask me lots of questions, then put a huge plastic collar around my neck and lift me gently into the ambulance. Flat on my back with the weight of my head supported the pain eases a bit and I close my eyes. Suddenly I feel really sleepy.

At the hospital, they wheel me into the Accident and Emergency department, where not very long ago Hector's mum breathed her last. This thought crosses my mind disconnectedly as I lie and stare at the ceiling, unable to look at the people talking to me unless they put their faces right in front of mine.

'What's your name, love?' someone says.

'Rachel.'

'Hi, Rachel. I'm Clare, Staff Nurse. Now then. You hurt your neck, right? Don't nod, Rachel.'

'OK.'

'Right. Do you have pain anywhere else?'

'Not really. But I am pregnant. Will the baby be all right?'

'Well, you're obviously not very far along, so I expect everything will be just fine. We'll get you up for an ultra-sound, just to be on the safe side.'

'Thank you, Clare.'

'No trouble.' I hear her giving instructions to other people out of my line of view. Everyone is out of my line of view unless they're floating horizontally above my trolley. She's talking about abdomen, spine, neck, seat-belt, pressure, and I realize that I'm going up for X-rays.

'Clare!' I shout out loudly.

'Right here,' she says, six inches from my head.

'Oh, sorry. Will the baby be all right, with the X-rays and everything?'

'Don't worry about it, Rachel. There are quite a few medical types here – between us we'll think of something to protect it. I'm sure it'll be fine.'

But I'm not sure. Suddenly my head is filled with slow-mo close-up replays of my body flying forwards with the impact, my abdomen straining against the seat-belt, and all the pressure of my body moving forwards concentrated into that tiny area. I lie there and wait for someone to do something, all the time terrified that the little life I've made is detaching itself and giving up. I lay my hands on my belly and cup them around the tiny mound protectively, imagining the tiny body inside. I wish I could picture it. Does it have any hands yet, or toes? Or is it just a blob with a heart? I can't see if there's anyone near me, so I call out.

'Excuse me? Clare? Is there someone there?'

'Yes, love, what's the problem?' The voice is very near and she moves right in front of my eyes so I can see her. This is such a small attention that I appreciate almost more than I can think.

'Oh, thank you. Do you know what a thirteen-week-old baby would look like?'

'Do you mean a foetus, inside the womb?'

'Yes.'

'Don't try to move your head, Rachel. Now let me think. From what I remember I seem to think that at thirteen weeks, it's fully formed, just very small.'

'Fully formed. Do you mean arms and legs?'

She nods. 'Yep. And fingers and toes. It's all there.'

'How small?'

'Oh heavens, you're really putting me on the spot now. Let me think. Maybe the size of – oh, a plum, perhaps?'

'A plum. A little plum.' I smile weakly. 'Thank you.'

She smiles back and touches my arm. 'Try not to worry. I'm sure it'll be fine. They're a lot tougher than you think.'

During the X-rays, someone lays a very heavy, cold, piece of something over my belly. I still can't move my head so I can't check to make sure it's properly covering my plum. 'Have you made sure it's covering the baby?' I call out into what could very possibly be an empty room. 'Is this definitely sufficient to protect it?'

222

'Yes, Rachel, don't worry. We know what we're doing.'

'But I don't think this thing is over me properly. Can someone please check?'

At the ultrasound, the lady working it says that it is difficult to see anything because my bladder isn't full, but she says there's no apparent bleeding in the uterus and no bleeding externally, so she concludes there's nothing to worry about. I disagree. I think there's loads to worry about.

'Can you do another scan in a couple of hours when my bladder is full? Just to make sure?'

She smiles at me and wipes the jelly off my tummy. 'There's really no need, Rachel. At this stage, your baby is still so tiny, it's not likely to be affected by external pressure, unless it was very severe. It's cushioned really well in a huge sac of fluid. You really don't have anything to worry about, I promise.'

I catch sight of the notes she's made as she picks up the papers and just glimpse the letters N.A.D. No abnormality detected. Which doesn't mean there isn't one.

So they've put a foam collar round me and they're letting me go. I feel too fragile to be let go. There's no way I can drive.

'Is there someone you can call?'

It's almost eleven o'clock at night. Who can I call? My first thought is Hector, in spite of the hour. Maybe even because of it. They won't let me use the mobile in the hospital so one of the nurses takes it away and dials the 'Home' number from the office landline.

'Is that your boyfriend?' she asks when she comes back. 'Baby's dad?'

If only. 'Oh, no, no, just a friend, that's all.'

'Really? Well, he was very worried about you when I told him what had happened. He asked me to tell you not to worry, he's coming straight over. He said he'll take care of everything.'

'Did he? 'S nice.'

Let's watch Hector in his home for a few moments, as he flings the phone back down on to its cradle and runs the length of the hallway towards the front door.

'Please, please, please,' he's saying, as he looks all around him, patting his pockets, rummaging through other jackets hanging up, running into the kitchen and snatching up a set of keys from the table.

It is possible he was saying, 'Keys, keys, keys.'

He seizes a jacket from the hall cupboard, slamming the door shut carelessly and yanks open the front door. Just as he's stepping over the threshold, he pauses, turns, looks up the stairs and calls out, 'I'm just going . . .' Then he catches himself and stops shouting. 'Out to the hospital to help a friend,' he finishes quietly, and closes the door behind him.

I think it's worth watching for a few more seconds as he starts the car and drives it recklessly and fast through the dark streets towards the hospital. I particularly like the way he zooms through amber lights and pulls out in front of lorries at T-junctions, hunched forward on the seat.

The pain is subsiding a bit now, largely thanks to the vast quantities of drugs I've been given. ('Are you *sure* these are safe for the baby?') Through half-open eyes I can see that standing three feet away from my bed is a man in an elephant costume, like the one from the car insurance advert, and he's talking to the Queen, apparently. Suddenly, bubbles start rising out of the end of his trunk and in that moment I realize that it's a real elephant.

The nurse leaves me to doze on the trolley. After a short time, I can hear the sound of a familiar, deliciously deep voice talking to the doctor somewhere out of my sight. I blink a few times and the elephants – there are three of them now – melt away, to be replaced by Hector's face, horizontally six inches above my face, and I'm looking right into his crinkly brown eyes.

'Hello, sleepyhead. How're you doing?'

''Lo, Hec.' I close my eyes again, allowing myself to relax and drift away now that I feel completely safe.

'What have you been doing?' he says, rubbing the back of my hand with his thumb.

'Don't know. It was th'elephants. Had a crash.'

'The . . . Well, you almost caused another one, you know. I must have been doing eighty all the way here. I can't tell you what . . .' He trails away and I open my eyes again. He's looking at the foam collar round my neck, frowning.

'You're lovely,' I say, even before I meant to. 'Plum says thanks.'

'Plum?'

I stroke my belly. 'Plum. My baby. I'm having it. I'm having a baby.'

He looks at my whole face this time, his eyes circling my features – hairline, forehead, cheeks, nose, lips, and his gaze eventually lands on my eyes as he smiles. 'You're going to be a wonderful mum.'

Chapter Thirteen

Hector drove me back to my flat – he had to keep nudging me for directions – put me in my bed and then slept on my sofa that night. It's a two-seater and he's a big man – did I mention that? – so it can't have been very comfortable.

The next morning, when I get up, I've forgotten that he's there and I go and sit on the toilet, leaving the door open as usual. My neck's still so sore and gradually as I sit there, I try to replay what happened yesterday, culminating in Hector practically carrying me indoors, and—.

Crap, he's on the sofa, just yards away from where I'm having an enormous pee. Quickly I push the door closed with my foot, praying he's still asleep.

If I'd been awake twenty minutes earlier, I'd have seen that having barely slept all night, he'd crept out early to go home for a shower and change of clothes before work. He's left me a note on the sofa, though. You can see that little square of paper lying there on top of the folded blanket. When I look at it later on this morning, I'll see that it says, 'Dearest Rachel and Plum, I hope you're both well this morning. I'm so sorry not to be there when you wake up but I have an early meeting today and I must change my stinky clothes and scrape the filth from my limbs. Please, please, ring me if you need anything. I will call you tonight. H.x PS Plum, be good for your mum.'

It's a lovely note. After reading it, I fold it up and put it in my jewellery box.

Anyway, I have to spend two weeks off work with this sore neck, which is bliss. Have a quick peek at the office for me, would you? Has it all come to a complete standstill? Everyone vanished, furniture all packed up and gone, just a few stray papers blowing around in the breeze from all the broken windows, loose telephone wires sticking out of the walls and a family of pigeons settled in the corner?

No, I didn't think so.

Everyone is busy answering calls, sending out brochures, selling holidays and add-ons, in spite of my absence. There's Jean, looking like she's about to go for a cigarette break – she's always only half an hour away from a cigarette break – and there's Chrissie, leaning over her desk, engrossed in . . . hold on a minute. Who's that talking to Jean? Is that Nick Maxwell? What on earth is he doing in Telesales? Has he come down to see me, perhaps? But he's nowhere near my desk – in fact, he's making his way over towards . . . Oh for goodness' sake, look at Marion and Graham, staring at him like a kid looking in a toyshop window. Yeah, Marion, I said Toy, as in Boy. God, she must be in her thirties if not even older.

Hector is true to his word and calls me that evening. He calls me the next evening too, but not the one after that. The day after that, he calls during the day, and the day after that he brings me shopping and cooks me tea. During the second week, he calls only three times, each one in the evening. I am stuck in the flat so I spend every day waiting for his call.

Does this remind you of the day after Nick and I had got together, when I was hanging around the flat all day waiting for him to call, and pretending that I wasn't? Me too. Except this time, I am quite happy to acknowledge that I am waiting for his call.

After two weeks I go back to work. I'm still keeping my resolve not to tell anyone, even Susan. But even though keeping it from her makes me feel a bit guilty, I can't tell her, or anyone else, yet. The baby is nothing to do with them, it's just between me and Hector. Oh, I mean, me and Nick. Silly me.

On one of my first days back at work, I come home and find a brown envelope in the mail box. I turn it over in my hands, examining the post mark and the handwriting, but I can't guess what it is. Once I'm inside, I head for the kitchen and put the letter down on the countertop. I reach into the fridge for the orange juice, and the phone rings.

'Hi, Rachel. It's Hector. How are you today?'

I'm smiling as I'm talking. 'Hiya, Hec. I'm really well. Been to work, which was OK.'

'That's good. How's your neck?'

'Swan-like and elegant, thanks. Surely you knew that?'

'But you describe it so well, I can almost see it.'

'Is that why you rang me then? So I can describe various parts of me down the phone to you to help you build up a clear mental image?'

'No need. Every part of you is burned into my memory.'

OMIGOD.

'Oh, well, not every part, obviously. I mean, I haven't actually seen every part, so I would have to imagine . . . No, no, I don't mean that I've been imagining you with nothing . . . Which is not to say that I wouldn't like to . . . Um, I mean, what I'm trying to say is that I know exactly what you . . .' He stops. Finally. 'Shall I come in again?'

'Why don't you?'

'Give me a minute.' And he hangs up.

I'm doing that staring at the phone thing again. Except this time it's not so much with puzzlement, but more with a soppy fond smile on my face. Hector is so cute, even when he makes no sense. Especially when he makes no sense.

Ooh, the phone's ringing again. I'll leave it to ring a few times before answering, and use the time to get comfy on the sofa.

After it's rung five times, I press the answer key. 'Hello?' I'm doing a breathy, puffed-out voice.

'Hi, Rachel, it's Hector.'

'Oh, hi, Hec, how lovely to hear from you. I've only just got in – heard the phone ringing from the hall.'

'Oh really?' He's grinning. 'So where were you?'

'I was at my Circus Skills course in the Community Centre. We did unicycle today.'

He chuckles. 'What was it like?'

'Well, once you've learned how to climb on to something that has no brake and can't stand on its own, then balance on one wheel by pedalling rapidly backwards and forwards, steer using a combination of your body weight and the left and right pedals while flailing your arms wildly around in the air, worked out how to stop and got

229

over the terrifying feeling that a crucial part of it is missing, there's nothing to it.'

'Yeah. I picked it up in about twenty minutes flat.'

'As long as that? We're doing trapeze next week. That's a whole hour.'

'Is that wise, in your condition?'

'Oh, yes, it's fine. The doctor said some moderate exercise would be beneficial.'

'So, something like a nice walk in the park, a little slow dancing perhaps, slicing through the air at fifty miles an hour clinging to a two-foot-wide bar suspended forty feet above the ground, or a gentle bike ride?'

'Yes, he said any of those would be good.'

He laughs again and I snuggle down further on the sofa, enjoying the sound. Then he clears his throat meaningfully, as if to change the mood of the call. It works.

'Actually, Rach, I'm ringing for a bit of a favour.'

'Oh. What can I do for you?'

'Well the thing is, it's my mum's birthday today. She would have been seventy.'

'Oh, oh no.'

'Yeah.'

'What are you going to do?'

'What do you mean?'

'I mean, I think you should have a celebration. Just a small one. To remember her life, and birthdays gone past.'

'I don't know . . .'

'Look, I know I didn't know her, but I do know my mum would want people to smile and laugh when they remember her, not sit around all glum and miserable. What was she like about birthdays?'

230

'Well, she liked them, I think. She had one every year, without fail.'

'Seriously, Hector. I mean, did she ever let a birthday, yours or hers or Glenn's or your dad's, or anyone's, go by without doing something?'

He thinks for a moment. 'You're right. She would probably want some kind of party, even if it's just a little one.'

'Exactly.'

'Even if it's just a party for two.'

'I can't think of anything more lovely than her two boys getting together and having a few—'

'I meant me and you, Rachel.'

'Ah.'

'What do you think? I rang you because somehow it feels as though you are involved in this. I mean, I know you never knew her and I didn't really know you when she died, but I spoke to you that day, and then you left that message on my machine and came to the funeral – sort of – I just know that . . . I'd like to spend the time with you. It will help to take my mind off things.'

Can you hear the change in his voice? The intensity, the gravellyness? And his breath is really booming down the line, as if he's got his lips right up close to the mouthpiece. What does that say to you?

I'm picturing him sitting in his office, or on his sofa at home, hair all messy, tie askew, shirt crumpled and un-tucked, clutching the phone to his ear, thinking about me. No, I mean, thinking about his mum.

'Are you sure you don't want to spend this time with Glenn?'

'Huh? Not likely. I'm still pretty angry with him about

this woman, and I haven't had a chance to speak to him about it yet, so it would affect how I was feeling. I'd be all aggressive and hostile, instead of warm and slushy. Plus, he's got Jake and Sarah with him – he'll just spend the evening with them. I hope, anyway.'

'All right then. Why don't you come round here for a drink later, and we can break open a birthday cake?'

He sighs deeply. 'That would be wonderful, Rachel. You'll be saving me from being on my own in this horribly empty house.'

He says he'll be round about seven, when he leaves work. That gives me about an hour and a half to get to Sainsbury's and back.

It's 25 October, so naturally the store is decked out with Christmas garlands, twinkling trees and inflatable reindeer, and there's a CD playing that is probably called *Best Classic Christmas Hits EVER!* I grab a couple of bottles, one of wine and one of wine flavoured water, and head off to the bakery for a birthday cake. Incredibly there's one there that says 'Happy Birthday Mum' on it, so I grab that one and head home.

I'm back now, and have you ever seen me move so fast? I'm unpacking the cake and wine and frantically tidying the place up as I go. It's not too bad, but I have just had two weeks of not being able to move much, so there's a few things here and there to pick up. Mostly clothes. And dirty cups and plates. And magazines. And some empty crisp packets. And videos. And the post.

As I'm tidying, I'm going over in my head the conversation that Hector and I have just had. It's very exciting that we're having our first proper arranged date, even if it's only in my flat. Every other time we've seen each other,

232

it's been to support me in a crisis, or to support him in a crisis. So far, our relationship has been disturbingly like two friends, supporting each other in crises. But this one is different. It's pre-arranged and there's alcohol and cake, which makes it a party. A party for two. He said so himself.

But hang on. Isn't this just another crisis? His mum's birthday. He's feeling down, doesn't want to spend the evening alone in his empty house so he rings me for a bit of distraction. I stop mid-dust and straighten up. 'Take my mind off things,' he'd said, as the reason why he wanted to spend the evening with me. Oh crap. We're just friends, aren't we?

This is another new experience for me. This year is peppered with them. I have never had a male 'just good friend' before. Every bloke I've known, apart from family, of course, has pretty much wanted to have sex with me. I'm not assuming, or guessing – they tell me, sometimes straight out. Once I could see it in the guy's face. 'Will you have sex with me?' was written in black felt pen across his forehead.

So there's Nick, who did want to, and followed the norm as far as that, but no further, and now there's Hector, who apparently doesn't even want to. Doesn't even fancy me. I expect the fact that I'm carrying another man's child is putting him off a bit. Oh God, not again. For the second time in three months, I am falling for a guy who's not interested.

When the flat looks presentable, I bring the wine, two wine glasses and a candle to the coffee table. Then I take the candle back to the kitchen and put it away in the cupboard. It's not appropriate if he just sees me as a friend.

We can sit under the electric light and swap stories about previous loves.

How fair is this that twice in the space of three months I have got the hots for someone who is not interested? After all those years of irritating blokes who had the hots for me long after I stopped being interested. Mum would probably say it was ironic. Actually, I think I would have said that first, and she would agree.

So I'm curled up on the sofa, everything's ready. I'm looking repeatedly towards the front door, which is ridiculous. He's not going to suddenly appear there – he's got to ring the buzzer and come through the external door first. But I am imagining his tall form filling the doorway, those brown eyes crinkling with a smile as he walks towards me and puts his arms round me . . .

I've fallen asleep on the sofa. We can move forward two hours, unless you want to spend two hours watching me sleep.

No, please don't. I went out with someone who did that once. It's surprising how a face held motionless ten inches above your own for four hours can seriously interrupt your sleep pattern.

So two hours later, half past nine and the phone's ringing. It's woken me up and my head snaps up from where it was lolling on the sofa. My chin is wet with drool and strands of hair are stuck to my cheeks. I'm glad Hector hasn't repeated his trick in my dream and materialized in the doorway.

I lean forward and pick up the phone, confusion filling me. "Lo?'

'Hello? Rachel? It's Hector.'

'Hi.'

'Rachel, I am *so* sorry. I've been in a meeting with Rupert de Witter since I spoke to you and it took much longer than I expected. He's single at the moment, so he's got nowhere else to be . . .'

Suddenly I'm completely awake. 'Who did you say?'

'What do you mean? The meeting? It was just some bank guys and Rupert de Witter. He's the director of —'

'I know who he is. He's my boss.'

There's a silence. 'You work at . . . ?'

'Horizon Holidays, yes. Why were you in a meeting with him?'

'Well, he's asked my company to fit a new computer system for him, that's all. We were mates at school, so he's given me the job. Plus, I'm the best, of course. We had to meet-up today to discuss the applications and what sort of thing he wanted from the set-up . . .'

'Oh, right. Well. What a coincidence.'

'It's a small world.'

'You know, people say that but really it isn't.'

'No, I suppose not. Rachel, I'm so sorry for being late. Can I make it up to you? I've got the birthday cake. I could still bring it over, and we can . . .'

'Oh, look, Hector, I'm sorry, I'm really tired.' You're surprised, aren't you? You know first hand how much I was looking forward to seeing him tonight, and yet here I am, putting him off. But I am trying to sound really casual, like a friend. Not like someone who's gagging to see him. 'Can we do it another night? Do you mind?'

Look out of the window, up the street and go along the first right turn you come to. Recognize that car? The big silver Mercedes, with the air conditioning. Yes, that's how close he is to my flat when he pulls the car over to the side.

Oh, look at that, there's a bunch of freesias lying on the passenger seat.

When the car has stopped, he leans forward and puts his head on the steering wheel. 'Of course. You must be exhausted. You get off to bed, and maybe I'll speak to you soon.'

Back to me at my flat. I'm sitting there like stone on the sofa. He hasn't even tried to talk me round. That's that then. He definitely just wants to be friends and nothing more. And when I think back to the time we've spent together, all the gestures of affection have been really platonic. Little tiny kisses on my cheek; a hand held in the hospital, smiles and winks that any friend might give to a friend who's secretly pregnant.

'Right. Night then. And happy birthday to your mum.'

'Thanks, Rachel. Night.'

In his car, Hector clicks off the phone, then tosses it carelessly on to the passenger seat, where it lands on the flowers with a rustle of Cellophane. He pushes his hands into his hair and leans forward again, as if trying to soothe a bad headache. If we go back an hour to the drawn-out meeting with Rupert de Witter and the finance people, you can see him there sitting forward on the very edge of his seat, repeatedly looking at the clock on the wall, straightening the papers in front of him, fidgeting with his tie and saying things like, 'So, if we could move on.' Rupert, you can see, is nodding and agreeing with Hector. 'OK, next point,' but then within moments he's laughing at some story he's telling about his decorator. He and Hector look like negative images of each other, don't they? Hector, clearly and concisely going through his presentation in bullet-point form, getting his entire input done in less than an hour and a half so he could get away quickly; then Rupert, entertaining everyone by getting off the point and telling long rambling anecdotes about his painter's mother getting stuck for fifteen minutes under a desk in Furniture Village before anyone noticed.

So here he is now, looking pleasingly fucked off in his car twenty seconds around the corner from the flat. He makes a 'Nnnnhhh' sound from frustration, bangs his palms once on the steering wheel, then pushes the car into first gear and swings it round across the road, back the way he's just come.

The next morning, I'm opening the fridge and I'm stunned to find a brown envelope addressed to me on the shelf next to the margarine. I take it out and stare at it. How the *hell* did that get in there? Cosmo is weaving in and out of my feet, prrrping.

'What do you reckon, Cos? Super-efficient postman, or what?'

'Prrrp.'

'Right, OK, I'm doing it, don't worry.' There's a plastic airtight container in the fridge that holds the rest of the cat food from the tin that I opened yesterday evening. I take it out of the fridge and pull back the lid, then get a spoon from the drawer.

Would you say that the smell of cat food is one of the most repulsive stinks in the world? It's a thick, meaty aroma that you can almost see rising in greasy tendrils from the repulsive glistening chunks squatting at the bottom of the bowl. Suddenly without warning, I start shovelling the cold, meaty mass into my mouth as fast as I can, not chewing, just swallowing and shovelling, over and over, like a robot. It slides over the back of my tongue and down my throat slick and easy.

Suddenly, I reach the end of that particular road, just as I had with the cucumbers. I drop the spoon and the bowl in horror, much to the relief of the starving Cosmo who instantly starts to tuck into the spilled food. As I watch him, the wet lip-smacking noises he is making with the meat start to grate loudly on my ears and in that moment I become sickeningly aware of the soft, mushy lumps stuck between my teeth. My mouth floods with saliva and my throat and stomach constrict violently, sending me running for the toilet, where I am the most sick I have ever been in my life. The sight of the recently consumed cat food lumps floating around the toilet bowl brings on convulsion after convulsion until my eyes are streaming and my stomach muscles are screaming.

It's another giant leap away from the perfectly honed and maintained poise I have spent twenty-four years working on.

After a long, long shower and a ten-minute session with the toothbrush I feel cleaner and refreshed and about ready to head off to work. Just as I'm glancing around the kitchen, I notice the brown envelope from the fridge, still lying there on the side. I pick it up and this time I open it straight away. It's an appointment at the hospital for the ultrasound scan the midwife mentioned. Tuesday, fourteenth November, at half past two. Almost three weeks away. According to the letter, I need to drink two litres of water in the two hours preceding the appointment. I burp and unfortunately it tastes of salmon and beef chunks in gravy. Quickly I grab a glass and pour some water down my throat. Yet more time to be craved off work. Never mind – I can't wait to see little Plum on that screen.

As I walk into the Telesales room twenty minutes later, I notice a sudden hush, accompanied by the hurried movement of people, who are giving the impression they were grouped together moments earlier, returning to their desks. I glance around the room and notice that just about everyone has got their head determinedly down, focusing intently on their work. Even Val barely looks up when I arrive at my desk. The clock is showing two minutes to nine. This is unheard of, everyone, bar none – well, except me – starting early.

'Hi, Val. What's going on?' I ask, hanging my jacket over my chair.

'Don't be silly, of course not.' She hesitates and then says, 'I mean, nothing. What do you mean?'

I blink at her. 'Well, everyone starting early, heads down, not looking up. It all went quiet when I came in. What's everyone talking about?'

'I don't know. Oh, look, a call . . .'

She busies herself answering the call. I look around the room. Even Chrissie is already working, scrolling through the South of France. There's one noticeable exception, though. Paris, the new station eight, is absent, her terminal off, the screen dark and grey.

There are clues here that, if you look at me standing there stationary by my desk looking confused, I haven't got a hope in hell of working out. I could show you where Paris has gone, and I could explain what everyone was talking about before I came in, but I think that if I have to be left to puzzle it out myself, so should you be.

So I give up and get on with setting up my desk for the

day. Headset plugged in; computer on; turret switched to 'O'. Aren't I naughty, to be making an outgoing call before I've even taken my first call? It's 9.01.

I've managed to commit this number to memory and it rings once before being answered. 'McCarthy Systems, may I help you?'

'Is Hector there please?'

'I'll see if he's in. Whom shall I say is calling?'

I smile at this. I'm imagining an old lady sitting in some draughty hallway, or in a corner of the room that Hector rents for his office. She's probably a relative, an aunt maybe, or a cousin straight out of school, helping out by answering the phones to make the company seem more impressive. Whom shall I say is calling! I tell her my name and wait a few seconds while she checks, probably by peering over a partition or shouting out his name with her hand over the receiver – 'Hec! Are you in? There's a call for you!' – and then she comes back and tells me he's in a meeting and can't be disturbed for several hours.

Another bloody meeting! I'm amazed that he ever manages to make any money at all, the amount of time he spends in meetings. When does he do any actual installing?

I leave the Telesales number and click off. Before I switch my turret over to 'F' for 'Free', I pause a moment. Did Hector say yesterday that he was in a meeting with Rupert de Witter? I was so drowsy when he rang. He said he was installing a new computer system for him, didn't he? But that doesn't make sense – you don't need a professional installation company to put a new computer in for you, you can just pick one up off a shelf in Dixons. Or get one of the sales staff to do it for you. Maybe it's something to do with a home security system, or something then. Hector certainly gives his clients good service.

It's very strange to think about Rupert de Witter being one of Hector's clients.

I flick over to 'F' and instantly my turret bleeps and flicks to 'I' to receive the incoming call.

'Good morning, Horizon Holidays, Rachel speaking. How may I help you?'

'If I book a holiday with you, will you come with me?'

Don't panic, it's all right, it's Hector, not a filthy caller. Although I've had my share of those. There's a procedure laid down in the staff handbook that you have to follow whenever you get one. Basically, it involves disconnecting the call immediately. We don't always follow the procedure though – it's a good laugh to keep the guy going for a while.

Anyway, this isn't one.

'Hector! I thought you were in a meeting and couldn't be disturbed for hours.'

'Well, that was the plan. But I've just come out so I could call you. How are you this morning?'

'Fine.' I decide, in the interests of feminine mystique, not to tell him about the cat food. 'Actually, I'm quite excited. And I've thought of a way you can make it up to me for last night.'

'Oh, Rachel, I'm so sorry about that. It was so inconsiderate of me. Inexcusable. What can I do to make amends?'

'Well, it's a bit of a favour, actually. I've got this appointment, for an ultrasound, when they kind of look inside you to see if the baby is the right size and things. I had one done at the hospital after the accident, just to make sure

241

it was all right, but I couldn't see it because of the neck brace. So this will be the first time I'll see little Plum and I wondered whether, seeing as you're the only other person in the world who knows about the baby and therefore the only person qualified to be there without saying, "What in God's name is going on here?", if you'd come with me.'

There's an elongated silence. Yet again, I'm worrying that he's getting uncomfortable with how this is going, although this is no more than one friend might ask another. I'm chewing my lip while I wait for an answer.

'Erm, well, if I've understood you correctly, and I'm not entirely sure that I have, then I'll have to say, because of the fact that it's going to be quite a personal and private appointment and, if I know anything about obstetrics and sonography, might be fairly intimate, and us being virtual strangers and all, that wild horses won't be able to keep me away.'

What a tease! I thought he was going to say no. 'Well, that's not saying much. Wild horses are notoriously bad at security.'

Here I am now, on Scan Day, spending ages on getting ready, much like the old days. I told Jean it's Granny's funeral today, and then made a mental note to go and see Granny soon and make it up to her. I've got very little idea of what to expect, so what to wear is proving a problem. Most of my clothes are too tight round the middle now, so I'm left with a knitted woollen dress Mum gave me once that's little more than an act of penance, and a black lycra skirt that's always been a bit loose on me.

The only way to decide between the two is to enact the

scan by lying down on my back on the bed. Immediately I can see that the dress is a no-no. I would have to raise the whole thing up from the hem so everyone in the room – i.e. Hector – would see my knickers. The skirt then. Now for a top. This is a bit easier because my top half is much the same as ever, except for an extra D on my cup size. In the end I settle on a red V-neck T-shirt that hugs in all the right places but is stretchy enough over my enlarged boobs. I have a look at the whole outfit in the bedroom mirror, with jacket on and off, and I'm as satisfied as I can be. Now all I have to do is pop down to the sports centre and drink the swimming pool without peeing. Right. I've got an hour and a half before I have to leave, so I fill up a measuring jug and sit down to flick through *Parenting* while I slurp through it.

Did you notice the new direction my choice of magazine is taking? *Cosmopolitan* and *Elle* seem largely irrelevant now, and these parenting magazines hold an intense fascination. I can't stop looking at the photographs of women giving birth, even though I always slam the magazine shut and have to breathe deeply for a few moments afterwards to calm myself down. My overriding feeling about those pictures is amazement that anyone would agree to be *photographed* doing that.

Two o'clock and I'm heading out the door, even though it's only a fifteen-minute drive to the hospital. My car, by the way, is good as new – all sorted out by the insurance company while I was off sick from work. They even collected the car from my flat and delivered it back there afterwards. I was very impressed with the service, although, as I've mentioned before, I do tend to get good service if it's a man.

Anyway, I'm really worried about finding a parking space near to the hospital. Have you ever filled your bladder to its utmost capacity so that it feels like stepping on a small pebble will cause it to explode? Well, it's a first for me too. I have walked beautifully in some very difficult shoes in my time, but they were nothing compared to this. I feel like I have to glide along the ground, keeping my legs permanently bent so that I don't bob up and down at all. Fortunately, I find a space only twenty-five yards away from the door, which is better than I was expecting.

I'm meeting Hector here, but there's no sign of him. I make my way to the ultrasound clinic and check in. I'm fifteen minutes early, and the clinic is running fifteen minutes late. I've got to wait for half an hour.

'But I need a wee!' I blurt out.

'Yes,' says the receptionist, not looking up.

The waiting room is full of women slamming *Parenting* magazines shut. They've all got men with them, solicitously bringing them more water or lemon squash from large jugs on the table, asking them how they're feeling, reassuring them that it won't be long now. They're like worker ants, bringing nectar to the queen bee.

I wish I'd known I could drink some of the water here, while I'm waiting. I'm starting to feel real pain. I find myself thinking that I'll know better next time.

Next time?

Five minutes later, ten minutes early, a familiar voice says, 'Hello, you there, am I late? I haven't missed it, have I?'

I'm so relieved to see him, particularly as he takes one look around the waiting room, sees my agonized face and leans over to kiss me on the cheek. It's quick, automatic, the kind of kiss I imagine gorgeous six-foot-two husbands give to their wives all the time.

'Are you all right, bubbalugs?' He's slipping into this role so easily, it's just a heartbeat's work for me to imagine what it would be like if it was real.

'Yes thanks, Pooh Bear. Just bursting for a wee, and still twenty-five minutes to wait. But I'll live.'

'Well, I passed a Ladies on the way in. It's right outside—'

'Oh get behind me, Satan.'

'What?'

'I've got to have a full bladder. It helps them get a clearer image of the baby.'

'Oh. I forgot about that.' He looks at me, then reaches for the jug of water and a cup, fills the cup and drinks it straight down. He immediately refills the cup and drains it just as quickly.

'What are you doing?' I whisper.

'I'm putting myself in your shoes,' he says. 'I'm going to do everything I can to understand what this is like for you.' He drinks down another cupful of water, then immediately refills it.

All the other women suddenly look disappointed.

On the wall near the ceiling is an electronic board that scrolls out messages like 'Please turn off your mobile phone,' and 'Donate your unwanted cutlery'. Every so often there's a beep and a name flashes up; then one of the other women gets up and leaves the room. One by one, everyone in the room, including me and Hector, has fallen mute, as we stare up at this board, transfixed.

Beep. Helen Roberts.

All eyes scan the room looking for the lucky Helen. She gets up and waddles painfully away.

Beep. John Lithgoe.

Everyone is stunned and we all start looking around us quickly. Nobody had noticed that there was a man on his own in our midst, sitting in the corner reading *Men and Motors*. He puts the magazine down and gets to his feet somewhat self-consciously. We stare at him as he walks the length of the room and goes out into the corridor towards the examination room.

'Gall stones,' someone says, and everyone does a collective, 'Oh,' of understanding.

Beep. Roslyn Pike.

'Oh, Jesus, thank crap for that!' Roslyn shouts out in a broad Australian accent as she heads for the door.

'Lovely, lovely lady,' Hector says quietly after she's gone, closing his eyes and nodding.

'Don't make me laugh,' I warn him. I have a groaning dam inside me and one good laugh will collapse it.

'Sorry.'

Beep. Lara Croft.

'No way!' someone actually says out loud. We all turn eagerly to find out who is getting up. It turns out to be a heavily pregnant young woman with a scruffy blond ponytail and glasses.

'Don't laugh. I was Lara Croft long before she was,' she says to the room as she gets up. 'It's a bloody curse.'

'She'll be gone long before you, though,' Hector says kindly as she walks past.

'You think? She's already died once, but came back. How many more times?'

She walks through the door to the examination room

and we hear the muffled sound of her giving her name to the sonographer. There's another muffled sound, and then poor Lara has to say her name again, as if the sonographer didn't hear her correctly, or at least thought he didn't. Or maybe he's having a giggle at her expense.

Beep. Rachel Covingt.

Apparently there isn't enough space on the electronic display for my whole name. I glance around the room quickly, to make sure that Rachel Covingt isn't getting up, but she isn't so we head off into the examination room.

'Are you baby's father?' the scan machine operator asks the room, not taking his eyes away from his equipment. It's very dark in here; evidently his eyes have adjusted so well to years of working in such poor light that he can even see behind him.

The silhouette of Hector looks at me and I nod almost imperceptibly. He clears his throat. 'Yes I am.'

Hector comes to the bed and sits down on the chair by my head. He takes my hand and leans down to me so his head isn't so far above mine. His right arm and shoulder are pressing against me.

The machine operator does some fancy things with his machine that we can't see, and then he says, 'OK, here's baby.' And he turns the monitor round so the screen is facing us.

And there's my future, in two shades of green. Look at that. The scan man is pointing out all these things and I can see them all. There's the spine; there's a hand, with five stumpy little fingers; there's a foot; and there's the face. It's turned on its side and is facing right towards us now, as if it can see us on the other side of a window. I can make out two dark green hollows in a pale green oval, a faint outline of a nose and another hollow underneath.

'He's like you,' Hector murmurs, eyeing the inhuman skull-like image.

'Yes, he is beautiful, isn't he?'

'Who's his dad, the incredible hulk?' He's joking around, but he can't take his eyes off that screen, can he?

'It was a profoundly beautiful and intense moment.'

'Well, I want a divorce. He's clearly not mine.'

'It's really very difficult to tell at this early stage what the child will look like,' the sonographer interjects. 'The green hue is nothing more than the LCD screen the image is displayed on.'

Hector and I stare straight-faced at each other, both of us governed by our full bladders.

'Would you like a picture of baby?' the scan man says at the end, as if it's the most ordinary thing in the world.

Hector and I use the facilities while the picture is printing out. There are few pleasures in life that equal the sensation of emptying your bladder when it's been full for two hours.

When I come out of the Ladies, I see that Hector has finished before me. Look, there he is, standing by the door to the scan room. That's the humourless scan man, giving Hector a small square of paper, then retreating back into his shadowy domain. Look closely at Hector's face as he turns from thanking the scan man to look down at the picture he's holding in his hand as if it were made of spun sugar. His eyes widen, his mouth smiles very faintly and as it lies there on the palm of his big hand he raises his other hand, very softly lays his fingers down upon the image and strokes it gently.

Chapter Fourteen

What did that mean? Does he love my baby? Does he want my baby? Is he going to smother me to death with a pillow one minute after giving birth then snatch the baby and run off to Cyprus and raise it as his own?

It's a lovely thought, but somehow I doubt it. Much as I might like to fantasize about it, Hector is not the father of this baby, and never will be. As far as I know, no procedure exists that can unravel a pregnancy and start it again with a different sperm. But he looks like a father, doesn't he, standing there waiting while I put my coat on. Have you ever seen anyone look more like a father?

Just over three weeks have gone by since then and tonight, Friday 8 December, is the night of the Horizon Holidays Christmas Party.

These are usually really good dos, with a bar and disco, lights, fog machine and loads of blokes – some of them even halfway decent. Just between you and me, though, I have already been there with most of the decent ones. I never like to go back over old ground, but at least it means I don't have to buy my own drinks.

Here I am, in my room, throwing size-ten clothes

into a pile on the floor with no hope in hell of getting into any of them. Finally I understand what it feels like to be uncomfortable in clothes. I have got a new top to wear though, so all is not hopeless. While I have a quick shower, let me fill you in on what's happened since the scan.

Immediately afterwards, Hector took me out for some lunch, which was lovely. Nowhere posh, not like that Madeleine's place in Fieldwood Park that we know he goes to. But I wouldn't really be comfortable there. He did suggest La Bougie but I don't think I want to set foot in that place ever again.

'Why not?'

'I went there with Nick once, back in August. It would just bring back memories.' I'm thinking about that brutish friend of Nick's with the scary tattoo and the anorak, and I close my eyes and shudder a bit. Hector's looking at me and as I shudder we can just see him pressing his lips together and frowning.

'Fine, not La Bougie then.'

My eyes open and focus on him, but he's looking away now, impatiently jangling his car keys.

'I don't know about you, but I could go for some salad,' I suggest. 'What about Pizza Hut?'

He turns to me, his features softened, and smiles. 'Oh, Rach, I don't want to take you there. It's not remotely—'

'Not remotely what?' I've got this strange feeling he was about to say 'romantic'.

'Classy. I mean, is it? It's lunchtime so they'll have the buffet out and you won't be able to move for gargantuan fat people troughing off the food table. It's like a study in gluttony.'

Of course he wasn't going to say romantic. Why would he say that? We're 'just good friends'. Nothing more.

'I am prepared to throw a tantrum over this,' I say, folding my arms. 'One day, when you're pregnant, you'll know exactly how it feels to fancy something and not be able to have it.'

'But . . .' I've got the strange feeling he's going to say, 'But I already know how that feels, every time I look at you.'

'But I won't ever be pregnant, will I?'

Dammit. What's the matter with me, for fuck's sake? He is not going to seize me by the shoulders and tell me in a pained voice about the torture he's in, how much he wants to be with me, how it kills him every time he looks at me, and even though I am carrying another man's child he doesn't care and will accept the baby as his own when it's born.

'. . . car. Rachel? Rachel, are you in there?'

He's bending over to bring his face level with mine and I realize that he's been talking about something and I've been away in Mills and Boon land.

'Sorry, sorry, just feeling a bit distracted. What did you say?'

'I said, "Not unless medical science comes up with an amazing external womb for men to carry around with them, attached by an umbilical cord to their bellies so the foetus can get nourishment that way. But even if medical science did come up with a contraption like that, a.) the father would be unlikely to get all the same cravings and desires as pregnant women do because it wouldn't be such a tremendous strain on the body, and b.) I think I would walk a million miles before I tried it. I'll go and get the car."'

I blink. 'Um. All right then. I'll wait here, shall I?'

So we went to Pizza Hut. Seated in the booth, I take the picture out of my bag and lay it on the table. We pore over it, arms on the table, heads almost touching.

'He kept saying "he",' Hector says. I nod.

'I noticed that. What do you think it means?'

Hector looks up at me with a lopsided smile. 'I can't imagine, can you?'

'Could he have been saying it to cover all eventualities?'

He shrugs. 'I suppose so.' We both lean down over the picture again. Hector says, 'I couldn't believe how clear . . .'

'Me neither.'

'And the little feet . . .'

'I know.'

'Did you see his face?'

'Yes! He looked right at me.'

'And the hiccups!'

'Yes! I didn't even know that they . . .'

'Nor me!'

We both laugh and look up at each other. Our faces are very close and we both sit up a bit more.

'I wonder if it is a boy,' I say.

'Well, you're just going to have to wait till Christmas to open your presents, aren't you, little girl?'

'You're right. There's no way I can open this one early.' And here comes the waitress with Hector's pizza. Look at the way she's ogling him, for heaven's sake. Like he'd ever look twice at a waitress.

'Thank you very much,' he says, smiling warmly at the girl and maintaining eye contact for a second longer than was actually required.

252

'Ooh,' I say suddenly, clutching my belly. That got his attention.

'What? God, what is it, Rachel? Is everything all right?'

I nod. 'I think I just felt it move.'

Very near by but too far ever to visit, microscopic nerves caused tiny muscles to contract a tenth of a millimetre and a miniature limb like a curled prawn twitched in its first demonstration that it was alive, and in some tiny, subliminal way it knew that it was.

'Oh my God. Really? What did it feel like?'

I'm shaking my head because it's impossible to describe. How can you explain what something feels like if you've never felt it before and the other person never will?

'Oh, it's like, I don't know, like holding a butterfly in my hand. No, no, wait a minute; maybe more like someone flicking dust off my jacket. Oh, Hector, it's so hard to . . . Oh, there it goes again!' I lean back in my seat, my breath taken away by this new extraordinary feeling, and lay my hands across my belly.

A week and a half later, here I am sitting at my desk listlessly talking through the St Petersburg hotels with a customer.

'No, Mrs Sullivan, that one doesn't have a pool. Or a gym, no. Well, I don't think any of them do. I don't know why – maybe that sort of thing isn't very popular over there.' There's an opening here for me to suggest a more expensive destination, like Dubai, where all the hotels will have pools and gyms and air conditioning and saunas and spas and hairdressers, but I miss it.

I am interrupted by Hector's phone going off in my

bag. 'Oh, Mrs Sullivan, I'm awfully sorry, can you hear that sound? It's the fire alarm. I'm going to have to go now. Why don't you call back in an hour or two? If the building is still standing, I'm sure someone will be able to help you. Yes, certainly, my name is Christine. Thank you, goodbye.'

I flick to 'B' for Busy, grab my handbag and head for the door and the sanctuary of the Ladies. As I go I am rummaging in my bag to get the phone before it stops.

You'll notice that as I enter, I don't hesitate, even for a second, by the mirror, but head quickly into a cubicle.

'Hi,' I say as I lock the door behind me.

'It's me,' he says, as if we were really close.

'Hello, you. How are things?'

'I'm fine. How are you two?'

'We're doing well. Plum is still hiding and I think he's right. He can't face all the probing into his parentage that he'll face as soon as he announces his presence.'

'I can understand that. Little fella's entitled to some privacy.'

'He certainly is.' A sudden thought occurs to me. It's the office Christmas party at the end of next week. What if I invite Hector to come with me? God, I'd love to see the look on Chrissie's face if I turned up with him. She's probably never seen anything like him before. Outside of the Littlewoods catalogue.

There's something familiar about this scenario, isn't there? Remember when I asked Nick to come to Jake's party with me? Well, I didn't know it then, but that was the final nail in the coffin for our relationship. Technically, it was the only nail, but it was a big 'un.

'Hey, Hec, are you free next Friday?'

'What, the eighth? I think so, why?'

'Well, it's our office Christmas party and I was wondering if you . . . Well, if you would . . .'

'Come and perform? Yes, I would love to, thanks so much. But how did you know I was in a band? God, this is great! I can't wait to tell the guys. We haven't had a gig for months. They'll be stacked.'

This is utterly hideous. There is no way anyone wants a live band at the Christmas party. Unless it's U2. But then only if they promised to do 'Elevation'. And then leave.

'Er, Hector, I actually didn't know you were in a band. What kind of music do you do?'

'Mostly heavy slash metal, and some disco.'

'Oh. What's the band called?'

'It's called . . . um . . . Dead Funky.'

'Wow. The problem is that I don't think that Rupert de Witter will want that sort of music at—'

'Oh, no, it won't be a problem. He's a friend of mine, remember?'

Crap. 'Oh, yes, of course. That's . . . good, isn't it? Well. I suppose, in that case, that you—'

'Oh, Rach, I'm sorry.' He's laughing. 'I'm only teasing you. I'm not really in a band. It's a joke!'

I have to wonder at this point why he called me. Was he at a loose end and fancied having a good laugh?

'Right. Great. Good one. You really got me there.'

'I'm sorry. I just couldn't help it. What were you going to ask me about next Friday?'

But I've suddenly gone off the idea of asking him. I have to keep reminding myself that he's a friend, a mate, someone to have a laugh with, muck about with, not more. It's

255

clear from his little joke that that's how he sees me, and if I now go and ask him to come to the party, it looks as if I want it to become something more, which is not what he wants. And that, as I know from first-hand experience, makes me look sad and desperate.

'Oh, no, it doesn't matter after all. It's all sorted.'

'What, you sorted it while you've been on the phone to me?'

'Yeah. Someone's just put a note on my desk, so it's all fine now.'

'Really? Oh, well. Good.'

'OK then.' I'm making end-of-the-call noises because it's become quite hard to listen to his voice knowing that he thinks of me as one of the lads.

'Rach, I didn't mean to upset you.'

'What? You didn't. When?'

'Just then. That little joke. I'm really sorry if I hurt your feelings.'

'No, don't be silly. I'm fine. Look, Hector, I'd better go. There are search helicopters circling the building.'

'Oh, yes, of course. I'll speak to you soon, then.'

'Hope so. Bye.'

So here I am now, arriving at the party. The shirt I'm wearing is the new top. What do you think? I've worn the diamanté camisole underneath a couple of times but I don't think anyone here has seen it before. Anyway, to hide my little bump I've had to put this baggy gold shirt on over the top. I don't think it's visible really, is it? Looking at me from the other side of the room, in the dark and the fog, pissed out of your skull, you wouldn't notice any difference.

I'm not drinking, of course. It promises to be a laugh a minute for me, doesn't it?

Plum's movements have become really noticeable over the past three weeks. To begin with, I only felt it maybe once or twice a day, for a fleeting moment. And when it stopped, I got really sad and wanted it to come back. Now it's flickering away inside me like a candle flame, or like bubbles rising. It's a very peculiar sensation that feels almost like it's nothing to do with me.

As I enter the party, I start scanning the crowd for a glimpse of Nick. Well, come on, why do you think I spent so long getting ready? He's bound to be here – every department is here – so I'm desperate to spot him.

I don't want him back; you don't need to worry about that. Not even if he got down on his knees in front of me, wearing nothing but his boxer shorts, his skin shiny and damp, his hair all flopping messily, those stunning baby-blue eyes gazing up at me imploringly, or maybe just lustily, those full lips reaching up for a kiss, that sensual mouth—

Crikey, it's hot in here.

No, no, no. I just want to have a look at him. I haven't seen him since we last met at the vending machine by the lift on the third floor and he called me a bitch – presumably he made a special trip down from the sixth floor to say that – so I just want to have a look at him. Actually, what I really want is for him to have a good look at me while I am being devastatingly sexy, and for me to be utterly oblivious of him. But first I've got to hunt him down.

He should be easy to spot as there aren't many people at Horizon who look like him – there aren't many people in the world who look like him – but I can't pick him out. There are a few youngish blokes here and they're all wearing short-sleeve shirts and jeans. From a distance, Nick could be any of them. I need to get closer so I can study them more carefully, while looking like I'm not even aware of them.

Chrissie and Val are here, so I go over and stand with them. Chrissie looks like a tramp, doesn't she – short red skirt, black top, thigh-length black shiny boots; it's fantastic – and Val is wearing a very feminine floral-print dress and some peach lipstick. She looks different. We make our way over to the bar, but none of the blokes comes over to buy me a drink, which is unusual.

'Where is everyone?' I shout to Chrissie.

'What do you mean? Everyone's here.'

It's not until we get to the bar that I realize why it seems there are fewer blokes here than usual: they're all grouped around someone sitting on a bar stool. And guess who it is?

Paris.

She's had her hair cut, look. It's short now, and brushed forward around her face. It looks ridiculous, frankly. And so does she, flirting, batting her eyelids, simpering, giggling, thanking people so much for getting her a drink. For God's sake. I fist my hands as I imagine pushing her off the stool in her little strapless basque and sateen skirt.

It's a possibility that Nick is somewhere in that crowd, but I don't want to get any nearer. That would be too obvious. I move away and notice that even Chrissie, in her trampy way, is getting some of the attention. She and Paris giggle and put their heads together, like two people who have been friends for twenty years. I turn away and watch the dancing for a while, my eyes darting around, looking for those shoulders, that hair, those eyes. I'm not drinking so the hilarious antics of the couples and singles just make me squirm. I can't bear to look at one of the Ms with his shirt off, shimmying in front of Val, whose eyes are darting desperately around the room – anywhere, in fact, but at his shiny bare chest. But at the same time, I can't take my eyes off this spectacle. It's utterly riveting.

By eleven o'clock, I've had enough. Somehow, Nick is the one who has been oblivious to me while I have peered into every corner looking for him, and I'm crushingly dis-appointed. My head is pounding, I'm tired and the music is too loud. I leave the office and head towards the lifts, intending to sneak away without anyone noticing. But as I move along the deserted corridor, I spot a flash of move-ment with the corner of my eye. It was far down the end of the corridor that leads away from the lifts.

All is bright and familiar at the lifts, and my car waits at the bottom to take me home to bed. But I hesitate. Was that another quick movement at the end of the corridor? It's very dark down there. It must have been my imagin-ation. But in an action that is more like something Hector would do, I'm heading down there anyway, tip-toeing, can you believe? As if that's going to make any difference with the noise of the party just a few doors away.

I think I hear a short burst of soft laughter, and a rumbling sound that could be furniture being dragged across a floor. The lights from the lifts and the party noises are receding behind me, and it's getting darker and quieter down here. I've never been down here before. I think it's just all conference rooms that are rarely used. At least, not by telesales staff. Maybe the marketing bods, or the managers get more use out of them.

As I'm walking I'm trailing the fingers of one hand against one wall to steady myself in the dark. There are definitely sounds of activity coming from up ahead and finally I can see that two doors further down have got light coming out from under them, one on the right and one on the left.

I pause in between the two, then move right, placing both hands on the wood and leaning forward so my head is almost touching. All is silent within. After a second or two, I start to move away, but then freeze. I've heard a sound that stills my heart for a second. It was a cry, a gasping cry, and it came from behind this door. I'm almost entirely sure it was made by a woman.

I stand there, hand on the handle in an agony of uncertainty. Something is going on behind that door and someone could be in need of help. I look right and left but there is no one around. Something needs to be done and the only person who can do it is me. Weak, pregnant, solitary me. I brace myself against the door, grasp the handle more tightly, then release it and step back; then forward again, then before I have any more time to reconsider, push the handle down quickly, at the same time shoving hard against the door with my shoulder. I am sure that whoever is in there will have pushed something up against the door to avoid being interrupted, but they haven't and the door swings open easily, my increased momentum carrying me stumbling over the threshold and three or four paces into the room.

When I've regained my balance I look round. And instantly long to be anywhere else.

The two people who have obviously been, until my dramatic entrance seconds ago, the source of the strange sounds I heard are staring at me in horror, eyes and legs wide. I'm aware without really seeing that they are half-lying on the floor immediately in front of me and instinctively I take a step back. My eyes are jumping from place to place, not wanting to linger on anything, so I put the scene together in a series of very short close-ups. A bare thigh. Some undone buttons. Bent elbows. Damp skin. Baby-blue eyes.

In my confusion I understand that one of them is Paris. My eyes rest for a little longer on that haircut, taking in the wisps over the ear, the feathered fringe, the short tendrils down to the collar. It's gorgeous and very familiar. Then this view is blocked by the sheen on a shoulder, bones and muscle moving beneath the damp caramel skin, as its owner leans over to grab a shirt from the floor.

'What the hell are you doing, Rachel?' he says. I realize finally what no doubt you spotted immediately. It's Nick Maxwell, there on his knees in front of me, wearing nothing but his boxer shorts, his skin damp and his hair messy; but he's not begging me to take him back and he's not reaching up for a kiss. He pulls on a shirt aggressively as he spits out, 'For God's sake, bursting in like that. What, is there a fire or something?' Nick does seem to prefer the floor for his sexual liaisons, doesn't he?

I gape at him. 'What are you doing?' I say stupidly, quietly, almost just to myself.

'What does it look like, darling?' Paris says, buttoning up her basque with a smirk.

I'm still staring at Nick – his thick, dark hair, those full black eyelashes, that sensual mouth. My plan of being oblivious to him has pretty much gone out of the window – did you notice? I'm drinking in the view, rapt.

'For God's sake, Rachel, where's your dignity?' Paris sneers at me and finally I stir myself, turning to look at her.

'I'll tell you after you pull your knees together, do up your blouse and get off the conference-room floor,' I say cuttingly.

'Now now, come on, girls, be nice,' Nick starts saying, although I can see he's really enjoying this.

'He's married, you know,' I say quietly. Nick's head snaps up to look at me, horrified. 'You might want to ask him about that before you wonder about my dignity.'

'*What?*' Nick and Paris say together, Nick staring wide-eyed at me, and Paris staring wide-eyed at Nick.

I nod, feeling on the brink of something, teetering on the edge. 'It's up to you, really, Paris, but I made my decision four months ago. The question is, what sort of person are you? I know what I am, and now we both know what *he* is.' I incline my head in Nick's direction but don't look at him. I don't trust myself.

My throat is aching as if I might cry, but there are no tears coming. I feel calm and strong. It's FANTASTIC! As I go back through the door into the corridor, I hear his voice telling her in soft, loving tones that it's not true, I've made it up, I'm a seriously mad bitch, and I can picture him stroking her arm and kissing her ear and my throat aches like it's going to break. My head is down and I don't hear the door opposite opening, don't notice someone coming out until I practically walk into him.

'Whoa, there, heads up,' he says and I look up to find myself staring into the face of Rupert de Witter, the owner or manager or director or whatever he is of the whole company. I've only ever seen him before inside the back cover of all the brochures.

'Oh, Mr . . . Sorry, sir, er, Mr de Witt . . .' Can this night get any worse? Now all I need is for Hector to see me humiliated like this for the evening to be complete. I turn away and hurry off along the corridor as quickly as I can in these shoes. Behind me, Mr de Witter puts his hands in his pockets and watches me go, a bemused expression on his face.

'What's going on?' says a voice behind him, and fortunately I am too far up the corridor to know that Hector has now emerged from the same room as Rupert de Witter and is watching my retreating figure as well.

Rupert shrugs and smiles. 'Oh, something to do with the office party, I should think. You know what it's like, Hec, too much booze makes those simmering office passions boil over.'

Hector is peering down the darkened corridor towards the lift. 'But . . . I'm sure that's—'

'Rachel!' Hector and Rupert jump as the door opposite is flung open and a young man comes hurrying out in hot pursuit, pulling the edges of his shirt together, buttoning it up as he jogs off down the corridor. 'Come back here, Rachel,' he shouts out as he runs, '*Stop!*'

Hector sees this, hears the name, and in an instant pieces it all together. He knows in that moment that what he predicted, what he has dreaded, has happened. And as he returns sadly into the conference room with Rupert, he knows that, although it feels like his heart has been forced through a mangle, then minced, set on fire and jumped on, this is the best outcome for almost everyone.

'You all right, Hec?' Rupert says, watching his friend move slowly back into the room. 'You've gone a bit pale.'

Hector nods and forces a smile. 'Fine, mate. Just tired. Can we get this finished, please, so I can get back to my office?'

As the door to their room closes, so the opposite door opens again and out steps Paris – smart, rearranged, dignified. She holds her head high and rolls her hips seductively as she sways up the corridor behind Nick, a large hole clearly visible in the back of her black tights.

This is the corridor outside the lifts and here I come, hurrying towards the lifts and away from that scene. Quickly I stab the 'G' button, then, glancing over my shoulder, thump it repeatedly as I can sense from the left a bastard approaching.

He comes in fast, seizing my arm. 'What the fuck is the matter with you, you sick bitch?'

'Take your hand off me,' I say in a low voice without even looking at him. He does, too.

'Are you some kind of obsessive stalker or something? What the hell are you doing, bursting in on us like that? I mean, I can understand that you're upset I'm seeing someone else, but face it, it's been four months, for fuck's sake. You really need to accept that it's over, love.'

'Oh Nick, don't flatter yourself. I wouldn't touch you with a gloved hand holding a pair of tongs with a barge pole in them.'

'Yeah, sure. Whatever you say. But I've been here a few times before, you know. Dumped girl can't deal with the fact that there's a new girl on the block. Follows me around like a sad little puppy, calling me up at all hours, waiting outside my house, sending me things. But this. Hah.' He shakes his head. 'This is a new one on me. Telling her I'm married. I mean, for fuck's sake. What's got into you? Have you gone mad?'

I'm still facing forward while he's standing to my left, rambling on and on. From this vantage point, I can see the silver lift doors with my own calm, serene reflection smiling back at me, and Nick's profile at one ear, snarling and growling into it. Thank God the lift is here at last. The doors slide open and I hurry in, turning to face him once I'm inside.

'I'm sorry, Nick, it was very, very wrong of me . . .'

'Too fucking right it was.'

'. . . to waste a week of my life on you. I regret almost everything about it. Now get back to your girlfriend – she looks like she needs some attention.' And as if in a film, the doors close beautifully on time: just as Nick frowns in fury and opens his mouth to say something else; just as Paris flounces out of the corridor on the right and heads towards him. And I'm sealed away safely in the descending lift. I've said my piece and the curtains have closed.

Standing there in the lift, I am faced with my full-length reflection again, minus the snarling profile this time. My face is glowing and I am grinning now. My hair is longer and as I move my head from side to side, it sways with the movement, the lights in the lift glinting on its glossy surface. I look bloody good.

'I'm sorry about that, Plum,' I say, addressing the little bump in the reflection. 'What a nasty man. But you won't have to see him ever again, if you don't want to. I promise.' I smooth my top out over the bump, turning sideways so I can see it better. It's not big but it's there, and I like it.

This is the next Monday, three days later, and I'm arriving at work. You can see from the way I'm bouncing along, still faintly smiling, that I'm feeling pretty damn fantastic today. Over at station eight the seat is empty and I grin wider, wondering idly where they were now – men's loos? Stationery cupboard? Floor under Jean's desk?

'What are you looking so cheerful about?' Chrissie says, appearing in front of me suddenly. Today she's gone for tight white top and denim miniskirt with brown knee boots. It's still such a shock to see her dressed like this and for a second I can't think what she's just asked me.

'What?'

'You, walking around with a big grin on your face. I'm surprised to see you looking so happy today.'

Now I'm focused on what she's saying. 'What do you mean, surprised? Why shouldn't I be cheerful today?'

See that look on her face? It's her Gossip-versus-Guilt look. It's a complex one but I've known Chrissie for twenty years and can decipher her instantly. That look means she's heard something, probably about one of her friends – most likely me – and she is torn between feeling guilty because she didn't stick up for me, and thrilled that she's got some really juicy gossip to pass on. Her eyes don't meet mine – the guilt – but she's fighting against an excited grin – the gossip. 'Well, I heard—'

'Oh, here we go. It's not just Nick and Paris that have been banging all weekend, is it? It seems the office bongos have too.' I've got an image in my head that's probably from an old film – someone talking on a phone, and the screen splits so there are two people talking, then it splits again into four, then into eight, then sixteen, and so on, until the number of people gossiping on the phone is so great, you can't make any of them out at all, and all you can hear is the white noise of hundreds of voices all talking at once. 'Go on then.'

'God, you know about Paris?'

'Course. Is that it?'

'Well, no, there's something else. It's nothing bad. Just that you and Nick had a bit of a run-in at the party, and that you begged him to come back but he refused.'

'Hah! Well, that's not exactly how it went.' It's so far from the truth, I almost enter *X-Files* territory again. Is that how it went and I've had my memory altered by some higher being? Nope. I remember perfectly how it was. But I find, to my surprise, that I don't even care. 'Who told you anyway?'

Chrissie's eyes land on my left shoulder for an instant, then they're off again, buzzing around my head. 'Actually it was Paris. Does it matter?'

'Not remotely, Chrissie.' I smile then turn on my heel and call over to Val, 'The usual, Val?' She nods, and I turn towards the door. 'Oh, look, Chrissie, there is something I want to talk to you about. Can you come round to my place tonight, about sevenish? I'm going to ask Sarah and Sue to come too.'

Yep, I've decided at last, at over four months gone, that the time has come to tell people. I can't believe that I've managed to get away with it for so long, and I'm still reluctant to divulge it, although that's now more to do with enjoying the fact that only Hector knows. But these people are my friends: I owe them honesty. Even if it's late.

*   *   *

267

At seven p.m. I'm moving restlessly around the flat, touching things, straightening cushions, looking into the kitchen. The flat looks much better now, doesn't it, so I don't actually need to do any more tidying, but still I'm prowling. Of course, it's not up to Mum's standards any more, but I've decided that I can make better use of my time than to clean for an hour every day, and five hours at weekends. I keep on top of it, but the schedule has gone. Now I clean when it needs cleaning, and not a moment before. Occasionally a long time after.

Susan's here, and the buzzer has just gone, so that's either Chrissie or Sarah. Susan and I have made a bet who it is, although not with each other because we both want to bet on Chrissie. I answer the entry-phone and we both win because it is Chrissie.

'I want to wait and see if Sarah's going to be able to make it before I start,' I say as I get Chrissie a drink.

'Oh come on, Rach, don't keep us in misery,' Chrissie says. 'Tell us now, and then tell Sarah later when she gets here.'

'Leave her alone, Chris,' Sue says. 'Let her do it how she wants to do it.'

'I want to tell you all at once,' I say, passing the glass to Chrissie. 'We'll wait until half past, and then I'll call Sarah and tell you, with her on the phone. She did say that Glenn is working overtime again tonight, but if he gets home in time, she'll come.'

'More overtime?' Susan says thoughtfully to the room in general.

'Ooh, need a wee,' Chrissie says, getting up. While she's out of the room, the door goes again, and Sarah arrives.

'The overtime was cancelled apparently,' she says,

plonking herself down. 'I can't stay late, though. I've got to—'

'Get back for Jake. Yes, we know,' Chrissie says, coming back into the room. 'OK, Rach, come on, spill.'

Right. This is it. I don't need to tell you exactly what I'm saying; you know it anyway – Nick and the drinks machine, and the restaurant, and the hot night in July. But have a look at the four faces sitting there in my flat and the four different expressions as I tell the story. One looks hungry, soaking it all in, packing it away to be brought out and regurgitated first thing in the morning. One is clearly delighted, even silently clapping her hands together like a child at a party. The third looks sceptical, frowning, even slightly shaking her head. And the fourth – well, that's a little more difficult. It's so many different things at once: nervous, excited, pleased, terrified, anxious, impatient, thrilled, apprehensive. But mostly, if you look at me and know what I'm saying, I think you could say my face shows that I am happy.

Chapter Fifteen

I've never understood why every year you hear people remarking in astonished tones how Christmas has taken them by surprise. You can picture all the old dears in their fifties, scraping the ice off their windscreens in the morning, talking to each other over their front lawns.

'Morning, Marjorie, bit of a chill in the air this morning. Soon be Christmas again.'

'I know. Snuck up on us this year, hasn't it, Ralph?'

That's right, because of course we were all expecting it to fall in the middle of April. How inconsiderate.

Every non-pregnant year of my life, so all of them so far, I start my shopping straight after Bonfire Night, and have it finished by the end of November. I put my tree up on the first of December. I start attending the parties during the first week of December, and they go on until Christmas Eve. Christmas *never* takes me by surprise.

This year, I glance at the calendar one morning over my melon and notice that it's suddenly the twentieth of December. How did that happen? I didn't even notice that the government had cancelled November.

I'm twenty-two and a bit weeks now. My friends know about the baby, and as Chrissie is one of them, all of

Horizon knows. This includes people I've never even met. Hector, a virtual stranger, knows. The woman in the corner shop at the end of my road knows. It's probably about time I told Mum and Dad. Well, as it's Christmas in five days' time, I decide to do it then.

I phone straight away to avoid changing my mind.

'Hi, Mum, it's me.'

'Who's me?'

'Me. Rachel. Your daughter.'

'Rachel! You're alive! Dave! Dave, it's Rachel! She's alive!'

Yeah, all right, maybe I deserve it. And with the news I'm going to give them for Christmas, this is going to get worse.

'Mum, I was wondering if it would be all right for me to come and spend Christmas with you.'

'Course you can, love. That'll be lovely. Granny's here, she'll love to see you. Will you be wanting Christmas lunch?'

I remember suddenly that I promised myself I would go and see Granny to make up for pretending to Jean that she was dead. This will kill two birds with one stone.

'Yes, please. I'd like to come round in the morning this year, and spend the whole day, if that's all right.'

'Of course it's all right. We'll look forward to that, love. Got some big news, then?'

Did I tell you how insightful my mum is? She scares me sometimes. 'I'll see you on Monday, Mum.'

There's a kind of mini Christmas celebration on the last day the office is open before Christmas, which is Friday the twenty-second. There are a few nibbles and a glass of alcohol-free vinegar each. Jean is making the annual

271

league champion presentations. I'm in the top ten, so I get a 'Well Done' card. Val's third, which is a turn up for her. She gets a bottle of Blue Nun. And Marion from the other side of the room has got top. White rum for her. None of them has come close to Jean's old record, and Marion is still a hundred and twenty-two sales below my record from last year. She's had a good year, though, regardless of that.

Paris is not taking part in our mini Christmas party. Her jacket is draped over her chair, but she's pleasingly absent. She has spent so much time away from her desk since she joined, it's hardly surprising she's at twenty-fourth place. There are only six people between her and the part-timers. That's a poor performance.

Shall we have a look and see where she is? On her back in the stationery cupboard? Nope. Kneeling on the conference-room floor? Not there either. Hands and knees in the ladies' loos? Men's loos? Surprisingly, she's not in any of these places. There's only one other place to look.

If we go up three floors to the personnel department, we can see that most of the offices and desks are empty. This is not open plan, like the sales room, but the offices all have glass walls, so it's clear that Paris is not in any of them. Further along the corridor is a conference room where all the personnel staff meet once a week to discuss, well, personnel. It seems that everyone is crowded in there.

Here is Leo, the supervisor, and Carl, his assistant. Chrissie says they're having an affair, even though Leo has been married for twelve years. Next to them are Lauren and Pat, drinking but not talking. Pat is Lauren's mum. Over by the window on his own is Trent. He's about six feet five and nine and a half stone. He also has halitosis from hell. I expect everyone in the room can smell it, but if they stay far enough away and take quick, shallow breaths through their mouths, they can survive.

And here in the doorway to the kitchen are Nick and Paris; Nick's arm draped across her shoulders, Paris's hand tucked into the back of his waistband. She's actually got no business being here because she's Telesales, and everyone knows it. In fact, if you look closely you can see that everyone in that room is taking furtive glances at her and pursing their lips. The revelry is fairly subdued this year, because of the interloper in their midst. But do Nick and Paris notice, when they have eyes just for each other?

Yeah, I think they do because they're heading out towards the men's loos now. How romantic.

Horizon is closed now until the day after Boxing Day. We're approaching our busiest time of year, so it's nice to have four days off in readiness.

I've got a few cards through the post, which I open lethargically on Christmas morning. One from Susan, one from Chrissie, one from my uncle and auntie in Swindon. It's ridiculous but even at the age of twenty-four I am still disappointed when I wake up and find no stocking on the end of my bed. Santa doesn't visit single people.

Can you see that little package on the coffee table? I've left it there on purpose since it arrived a week ago, so that I would have something to look forward to when I woke up today. I've been walking past it for seven days, my eyes lingering on it longingly, wishing I could open it early. Well, I could, of course, but that would spoil the surprise.

I hold it in my hands for a few moments before opening it. At this point it could be anything, from anyone. All the

273

while it's intact, it's from Hector, but just in case it isn't I'm feeling reluctant to open it and destroy the image.

Curiosity always wins.

It's a little blue velvet jewellery box and inside is a pair of very light blue drop earrings. They're so pretty, they catch and reflect the light when I move. The card has a penguin on the front hitchhiking a lift with Santa's sleigh. It is from Hector. He writes, 'Have a truly magical Christmas and I hope everything in the New Year happens perfectly for you. H xx'

I love the way he signs it just 'H'. It's so intimate, as if we know each other so well, all that's required is a hint of who it's from. But of course, he and I are complete strangers.

I do hope it's not from Harriet in Marketing.

I'm wearing the earrings now, and I have chosen my outfit today based on them. Well, the top anyway. I'm still pretty much dependent on the black lycra skirt, but my top is pale blue. How do I look? I think I still look pretty good, considering I haven't had my highlights or eye-lashes done for several months and I look like I'm storing some small beanbags in my bra. Mum is bound to notice this time, but that's OK.

Here I am again, standing at the point where Sarah and Martin Kennedy made beautiful music together. It's particularly touching on Christmas Day, don't you think?

It's ten thirty and Mum and Dad are in the kitchen in a fog of heat and steam and alcohol fumes. They're both wearing paper hats pulled down low over their foreheads and they're giggling loudly as they read each other the lame cracker jokes. They're clearly both pissed.

'Hi, Mum: hi, Dad,' I say, coming in to the room. They

turn in unison to face me, then exclaim, 'Rachel!' also simultaneously, their red, grinning faces beaming at me like something off a cheap Christmas card. I am twenty-three weeks' pregnant now, and there is a definite bump, but neither of them mentions it, which is weird. OK, I think to myself, I'll make an announcement over dinner.

But that's easier said than done. You can't just bring this thing up spontaneously, you need some kind of opening. Well, even before an opening, I need there to be a break in the conversation. My granny is here too and she's a tenacious conversationalist. Once she's started, she absolutely will not stop until she's finished, no matter how long that takes and regardless of how many interruptions there are.

'So, Rachel, you're looking very well. How's that boyfriend of yours? Tom, was it? What a lovely young man he was. He was here last year, wasn't he, Clare? He reminded me so much of a lad who lived over the road from Grandad and me when your mum was still a girl. Before she had her childhood stolen from her.' She stares fiercely at my dad, who raises his glass at her. 'Do you remember him, Clare? I think he was called William. You were sweet on him for a long time.'

'No, I don't remember a William, Mum. Who wants custard and who wants ice cream?'

'Haven't we got brandy butter?'

'No, it wasn't William, that was the boy that lived next door to me when I was a girl. This one was called something else.'

'You know we haven't got brandy butter. We never have brandy butter. It's custard or ice cream.'

'It was one of those traditional names, though, like

maybe Philip or Albert. You must remember him, Clare. He had acne and a budgie.'

'Can I have both, Mum?'

'Ugh, James, custard and ice cream in the same bowl?'

'Or was it the budgie that was called William?'

Mum still stuffs the pudding with pound coins, I suspect just as much for my benefit as for James's, so you really have to have your wits about you while you eat it. The table falls silent for five minutes as everyone concentrates furiously on not breaking their teeth, or swallowing any money. At the end, I've got six pounds out of mine, James has got seven and even Granny has done well and found five. Mum and Dad put any they find straight back into the pudding so the last portion is always particularly dangerous.

The table is cleared, plates scraped and coffee made. We all sit down in the living room for a film or a snooze, or a bit of both. James gets his new remote-control tank and heads out into the street to liaise with the neighbours' kids and compare presents. It feels like the moment is coming and I've got butterflies, although I'm not sure if it's dread or excitement at the prospect of telling my parents.

'So, Rachel, how are things with you?' Dad says, leaning back and sipping his coffee. 'How's your life?'

It's perfect. I look at him and Mum, smile and say, 'Much better than I thought I would be six months ago.'

'Why's that, love?'

'Well, I've got some really good news. For all of you. Mum, Dad, Granny, I'm going to have a baby.'

Mum's mouth goes into a wide, open-mouthed grin and she looks immediately at Dad, to see what his reaction is. He's smiling too, and also looking at Mum. Then they both turn back in unison to me.

Dad says, 'Oh Rachel, love, that's fantastic!'

Mum says, 'I'm going to be a granny, I can't believe it!'

Granny says, 'I mean, it's a ridiculous name for a bird.'

'When then? When does it all happen? August? July?'

'Ah. No, actually it's the twentieth of April.'

'Twentieth of . . . ? But that means you must be about five months' gone already. Have you only just found out, then?'

I predicted this would happen and I decided in the car on the way over that I'm going to tell a teensy-weensy little white lie to save their feelings. 'Yeah, just about a week ago.' Well, they'll never know, will they? No need to tell them I found out back in August and told a perfect stranger the news minutes later. 'I didn't suspect a thing and then finally went to the doctor last week because of a slight pain in my tummy and he tells me I'm five months' gone. Can you believe it?'

Granny is looking at me shrewdly, her eyes narrowed. 'No, no, I'm completely wrong. The bird was called Cyril. The lad was called Henry. Henry Bateman. Last I heard of him, he was in prison, I think. Your Tom reminded me so much of him.'

Everyone looks at Granny, as if she's just made a valuable contribution to the conversation.

'Yes, of course, where is Tom, Rachel? He should be here with us while you break the news. Or is he telling his parents?'

I've predicted this, too. But this time, I decide to go with the truth. Well, part of it, anyway. 'Actually, Tom's not the father. We broke up.'

'Oh that's a shame. He was lovely.' She's so wrong about Tom. He had big curly hair and bit the skin around his fingers the whole time. 'So who is the father then? And when can we meet him? Is he coming round for a drink later or something, after you've had a chance to break the news?'

'Er, no. We broke up too.' No need to mention that he's blissfully ignorant of his imminent offspring. Or that he's spending Christmas with his wife.

Mum's disappointed. 'Oh, no. But he's going to be involved, is he?'

'Oh, I should think so. We haven't really discussed it yet. But there's plenty of time to work out all the details later, isn't there?'

'You need to make sure you get some money off him,' says Granny suddenly. 'Because you won't be able to work, will you? Or you'll have to have a nanny or something to look after it during the day. And those things cost money.'

This is not something I've given any thought to at all. I don't know how I'm going to manage financially but I hadn't considered asking Nick for money. I'll store that away for consideration after it's born. I guess his wife is going to have to find out after all.

So here I am later that night, back home and slumped on the sofa in front of *Sleepless in Seattle*. I love this film: it's so simple you can follow it while you worry about being a single parent with not enough money to keep the baby alive. There aren't many films I like that don't demand my full attention.

Remember those little worry lines that flitted on and off my face on a certain hot night in July? Well, they're back, and I think they're permanent now. I have made the decision to have the baby and I'm not going to change my mind, but telling Mum and Dad, and my three friends, has set that decision into stone somehow. All the while it was just Hector who knew, it felt as if it was happening in some secret, unseen part of my life and could therefore be kept completely separate. It didn't encroach on or affect my life at all, really. Apart from my clothes not fitting me any more. But now it's like I've brought the baby into the world already. It's out there now, real, solid, causing changes, making differences, altering the way people think, the way they behave. Mum and Dad were different after I'd told them. They sobered up really quickly and the topic of conversation didn't move on from the subject for the whole of the rest of the afternoon. What we will all be doing different next Christmas. What it will be called. Whether it's a boy or girl. They spent hundreds, if not thousands, of pounds on it, thinking about birthday parties and Christmas presents to come – things they've seen on telly and would love to buy for it. Dad was actually talking about teaching it to join wood. It was all ridiculous.

The film's finished so I've made myself a hot chocolate and am flicking through *Parenting*. There are those photos again. Red face, eyes screwed tight, legs akimbo. Christ, is that one of her internal organs coming out? I slam it shut and fling it on to the floor, and my eyes land on the blue velvet box that held my earrings. I pick it up and hold it in both hands and at that moment – did you notice? – those little worry lines smooth out again. I'm going to ring him. I need to thank him for the gift and I should wish him a Merry Christmas, seeing as how I didn't get him a present or card. Bloody hell, *why* didn't I?

There's no reply at his home number. He's probably round at Sarah's, having a few drinks with his family. It's eight thirty; I'll try his work number, just in case, and if I don't get hold of him there, I'll try Sarah's – just to wish her a Merry Christmas – and see if I can prise out of her who she's got round. I could even do a sob story about being on my own and see if she'll invite me.

It's answered on the second ring. 'McCarthy Systems, Hector McCarthy.' His voice is dull and flat.

'Hey, Hector. It's Rachel. Merry Christmas.'

Sitting at his desk, Hector closes his eyes and a smile appears for the first time that day. 'Hello, Rachel. Merry Christmas to you, too. God, it's good to hear your voice.' He closes the folder he's reading and drops it carelessly on to the desk.

Wow. Did you hear the difference in his voice then, once he knew it was me? He sounds like he's smiling now.

'I just wanted to say thank you so much for the earrings. They're absolutely beautiful.' I touch them absently as I speak.

'Well, they had to be beautiful. It's what . . .' He clears his throat. 'Are you having a good day?'

'Not bad. Been to my mum and dad's. What about you?'

'Well, I've pretty much been here all day.'

'Oh Hector, why? You shouldn't be sitting there all on your own on Christmas Day.'

He sighs deeply. 'I couldn't bear to be in the house today. I would have just been sitting there alone, thinking about things, remembering. No thanks.'

'But what about Glenn and Sarah? Why didn't you go round there?'

'Nah. They've got a houseful today. Lots of friends of theirs . . .' He trails off and I'm sitting here thinking that for all he knew, I might have been there. Is that why he didn't go? Then he says, really quietly, 'Did you go?'

280

'No.' I didn't even know about it.

Hector lets out a long breath and I have the feeling he's been holding it for a while. 'Oh. Oh, well.'

On impulse, I blab out, 'Look, Hector, don't sit there on your own for the rest of the night. I'm here on my own – why don't you come round for a Christmas drink? We could keep each other company. I've got a large Yule log.'

'I'm sorry to hear that,' he says with a smiley voice. Then there's a protracted silence during which I start imagining all sorts of things like he's married, he's got a long-term girlfriend, he's embarrassed by my obvious interest or the worst one, he's *irritated* by my refusal to leave him alone. I'm picturing his face, lips pressed together, brow furrowed, wondering how best he can let me down without hurting me. Then there's a long exhalation of breath, and he says, 'I don't think it's a good idea, Rachel.'

Looks like my imagination was spot on. But the fact is, although I was imagining all those things, I didn't really expect any of them to be real. Deep down – well, not all that deep, actually – I was still convinced that he does like me, does want to be with me. It's so new, so unprecedented, that a bloke would say no to me. He sounds regretful though.

'No? But why? What . . . ?'

'I'm sorry, truly, but I'd just feel uncomfortable. You know, what with you and—' He stops. What I can't see is how he's dropped his head down to rest his forehead on his hand, but I can hear that his voice is dull and flat again. 'It's too . . .' He shakes his head, then straightens up in his seat. 'I should never have . . . I'm sorry, Rachel.'

'Why are you sorry?'

'I just wish . . .' He's whispering now.

'What do you wish?' I whisper, tears pricking my eyes.

'I wish . . . you a very Merry Christmas, Rachel Covington. Take very good care of yourself and that baby, won't you? And I truly hope that your new year is everything you want it to be. Bye.'

The phone clicks and goes silent. And I'm left sitting here alone on Christmas Night, knowing that he meant that goodbye to mean for ever, and I'm never going to hear from him again.

Chapter Sixteen

The rest of the Christmas break passes quickly. Mum, Dad, Granny and James have been round to the flat on Boxing Day with a whole load of food and a pram catalogue. God knows where they got that from on Boxing Day.

'Oh, all the shops are open today for the January sales,' Mum said. 'You should try and get most of your stuff now, while it's all reduced.'

I can't face shops. Only a short while ago, I would have thought, Oh, Hector will come pram shopping with me, and I'd've rung him without hesitating. I had thought that he was almost as excited about this baby as me. But why would he be, for God's sake? I'm no one to him, and this is not his baby. He's shown an interest out of politeness, in the same way you would when you bump into the sister of someone you used to work with, and she tells you she's pregnant. You smile and say, 'Congratulations. When's it due?' and then you switch off. Who cares? It's nothing to do with you. You'll probably never even see the thing once it's out.

Back at work on the twenty-seventh and the news about my condition is hissing round the office. My baby is out there now and I can't take it back. Suddenly everyone's an expert with advice on how I should stand, how I should sit, what I should eat and what I should avoid. They've got ideas on birthing plans, nursery furniture, nipple cream and sterilizers. People who have done it want me to do it their way, and people who never will do it but once knew someone who lived next door to someone whose sister's friend was pregnant once want me to do it their way.

'Oh, Rachel, you should definitely have a water birth,' one of the Ms says to me one morning. 'My friend's cousin did that and she enjoyed every minute of it.'

'You obviously haven't seen the photos.'

'You what? Well, anyway, she had music playing, she was warm and comfortable, really relaxed. She says that she'd do it again tomorrow if she could.'

'But then her plans for tomorrow involve having her toenails extracted with pliers?'

'Eh?'

'Nothing. OK, right, thanks for that. I'll bear it in mind.'

'Well, yes, but she says you need to reserve the pool well in advance, all right?'

'Thanks. Can you tell your friend's cousin from me to fuck off and die, please? That's great.'

I didn't really say that. I'm keeping my temper, more for Plum's sake than anything else, but I'm keeping it.

I haven't seen or heard from Nick since the office party. Paris has been smiling smugly at me though. Either she believed him when he said I was lying about him being married or she's happy to continue their fling anyway. Or maybe she's going to shag him until she makes up her mind.

'It's no good, Nick, I've decided that I can't continue with this relationship knowing that you're married.'

'And you think my retirement party is a good time to tell me?'

Obviously she hasn't worked out that this bump is her boyfriend's baby and therefore likely to get in the way for the next twenty years or so. Silly girl. They're not too bright, are they, that pair? Apparently the fact that I announced it so long after our little fling must have been enough to confuse them. They've only got to look at me to know that it probably occurred around the end of July. Maybe they're in denial. Well, let them. Plum and I certainly do not want any more input from Nick Maxwell. It was his input that put me here in the first place.

I haven't heard from Hector either. I suspected that I wouldn't but it's on my mind constantly. Every time the phone rings at home, I rush to answer it. Every time my turret beeps with an incoming call, I wonder if it's going to be him. It's torture and I've got to get over it. He was like a guardian angel who helped me when I was at the lowest point in my life and set me back on my feet. And now he's gone to help someone else who needs him. That's that.

But that's not that. I can't stop thinking about him. Everything reminds me of him – Plum squirms inside me and I think of Hector, gazing at me in Pizza Hut. I see the midwife again and I think of him and our drive in the country straight after the first appointment. I sit on my sofa and think of him trying to sleep here the night of my accident. Oh God, that's the hardest one, imagining him lying here, within yards of where I was sleeping, watching over me. Just a guardian angel, that's all.

I'm ringing Sarah. Yes, another outgoing call, but I

couldn't care less. I'm not going to probe about Hector but I just want to make sure he's all right. Sarah doesn't even know that I know him so if he's ill or dead she wouldn't think to let me know.

'Hi, Sarah, it's Rachel.'

'Oh, hi, Rach. You all right?'

'Yes, fine. Sarah, is it all right if I pop round tonight? I'd appreciate a chat about babies and all the stuff I'm going to need. You can fill me in on everything I need to know.' She's bound to jump at this – a chance for her to demonstrate her superior knowledge. And this is her favourite topic of conversation so it's win win for Sarah.

'Oh, well, I suppose so. I've got a few bits and pieces that I've got . . . but I suppose it's OK. What time?'

I'm staggered. It seems she's really not bothered. In fact, I'd even go as far as to say that she's a bit fed up with me for asking.

'Sarah, is everything all right? You sound a bit down.'

'Yeah, yeah fine. I'll see you later then, shall I?'

I decide to go round about eight, thinking that Jake will probably be in bed by then. On the way there, I've stopped at the garage and got a box of Quality Street for Sarah and a slab of cheddar for me, which I open in the car and bite into with a squeak. God, delicious. I just love its rubbery texture, its smooth saltiness that lodges thickly between my teeth and leaves a nutty aftertaste coating my tongue.

As I'm driving, suddenly the image of Glenn embracing that mysterious woman at Sainsbury's car park pops into my head. It feels so weird to know something about Sarah's husband that she doesn't know. I mean, the fact that he's having an affair is one of the few things I do know about him. It's like it's poisoning my brain. I can't tell Sarah what I know because I also know that Hector was planning to talk to Glenn about it and get him to stop, so Sarah may never find out. But there will always be that little black kernel of knowledge nestling in my head. It is never going to go away.

And the image of what would happen to Sarah and Jake if she does find out is sickening. Sarah trying to cope alone, short of cash; Jake a child of a broken home, seeing his dad every second Sunday. I can't think about that. Maybe Hector has already had words with Glenn and the whole thing is in the past.

When Sarah answers the door five minutes later, I know that's not true. Her face is pale and blotchy and she has dark circles under her eyes, which are red and watery. I conclude in that second that she knows. But she can't know that I know. And I can't let on that I know she knows.

'Sarah, are you all right?'

'Crap as it goes. You're looking really well.' She turns away from the door and walks back up the hallway to the living room, so I follow her in, closing the door behind me.

In the living room, Sarah is sweeping a load of books, toys and clothes off the armchair, then she sits on the sofa, so I assume the empty chair is for me.

'Thanks. Where's Jake then?'

'In bed, Rachel. It's quarter past eight. He's only six.'

He's six. I must write that down in my diary. 'Is he all right?'

She shrugs. 'Same as ever – lazy, rude, unhelpful. The light of my life.' Obviously she catches sight of the expression on my face and adds quickly, 'Oh, but you know, he's brought so much joy too.'

I smile gratefully and she grins and we share a rare moment of connection – like when we were at school. I haven't had a laugh with Sarah since . . . well, since she started seeing Glenn.

'Come in the kitchen,' she says standing up. 'We can have a fag out the back door.'

This time my ears do the 'BAROOOOGA!' thing. 'You are *smoking*?'

The shrug again. 'Why not? It's a small pleasure when I'm here on my own in the evenings.'

'So where's Glenn?'

She pauses in the act of putting teabags into two mugs. 'Well, he says he's working . . .'

I don't like the way this is going. Obviously Hector has not done anything at all about Glenn – either that or Glenn didn't listen – so the affair is still going on. And now Sarah's lip is trembling. Oh no.

'What is it, Sarah? You don't look very well.'

She turns to face me full on and leans against the counter behind her. Her eyes are shining with tears. She sniffs.

'I could be wrong, and I probably am, which makes me feel really guilty, you know, cos what if he really is working all this overtime to get some extra cash together for us all? But then sometimes, when he comes in late from work, he's just so . . . you know, and then sometimes he smells like . . . oh . . . as if he's been . . . as if he's been . . .'

'As if he's been what?' Although I think I know the answer.

'As if . . .' She rubs her face and eyes roughly. 'As if he's been with a woman.' She lets out a huge shaky breath and smiles at me weakly. 'Do you think I'm being ridiculous? I am being ridiculous, aren't I?'

'Um . . .' Arses. What on earth am I meant to say now? Either way, we both lose. 'Oh, Sarah. How awful for you feeling like this. Have you been sleeping?'

She shakes her head.

'I didn't think so. You're torturing yourself with something that probably isn't even happening.' Dear God, please forgive me, it's for her own good. 'Have you spoken to anyone else?' In reply, God kindly sends me a flash of inspiration. 'What about Glenn's brother, have you spoken to him?'

'Hector? No, why would I?'

I feel a little surge just hearing his name spoken out loud. 'Well, I just thought he might know if there's anything . . .'

'Anything what?'

'Well, just that as their mum died recently, maybe that's got something to do with it.'

She stares at me for a few moments, and I'm bracing myself for the acerbic comment that's coming: 'Oh, yes, Rachel, of course, losing his mum will cause him to be out all night and come home smelling of perfume. Why didn't I think of that?'

But it doesn't come. Instead she says, 'You know, Rachel, I hadn't even thought of that. Hector has been behaving really strangely the past couple of weeks. He was very down on Christmas Day – well, that's understandable, so was Glenn – but he didn't come for dinner and it's the first time he's not had anyone to be with, since all that business with Miranda. And since Christmas he's gone all sullen and quiet. Even seeing Jake doesn't seem to cheer him up. Maybe he's not just grumpy, maybe he's suffering more over Celia's death than I thought. And maybe Glenn is too and I haven't even noticed, I've jumped straight to the wrong conclusion about him. So he's feeling desperate over the loss of his mum, and instead of supporting and comforting him, I assume he's having an affair. Christ, what kind of person does that make me, then?'

I heard none of that after the word 'Miranda'. I blink at her and she's looking at me, obviously expecting an answer. 'Um, well,' I shrug, non-comittally, 'could it have been the business with Miranda that was making Hector grumpy?'

She shakes her head. 'Don't think so. I mean, he was very bad at the time, I remember, moping around, hardly speaking. But he kind of snapped out of it suddenly during the summer. Got back to his old self almost overnight. He must have decided his grieving period was over and it was time to move on, I suppose. It was remarkable.'

'Really?'

'Yeah. He's been really cheerful and smiley the last couple of months – until just before Christmas, I guess. No, I reckon they're both suffering with the realization that she's really gone. There are stages of grief, aren't there? So the first couple of months it probably hadn't even sunk in, and now . . .' She smiles broadly. 'They're miserable because they're missing her so much. That's fantastic! Thanks, Rachel.'

"S all right.'

She reaches into a cupboard and brings out a metal canister that says 'Flour' on the front. Inside this is half a bag of flour with the top folded down, and inside this is a dusty packet of ten Silk Cut. She grins as she blows the white film off it and walks to the back door. 'Coming?'

These cigarettes are so floury they're like those joke ones you have when you're a kid, the ones that just empty powder everywhere when you blow through them. It's all right, stop fussing, one quick puff won't do any harm. Anyway the taste of flour mingling with the tobacco and smoke gives it a kind of wholesome, home-cooked flavour.

'So how did you know about Glenn's mum dying, anyway?' Sarah says suddenly, blowing a smoke ring, which might have been a flour ring.

'Well, you told me, of course.'

'Oh. I don't remember that.'

'Well, you did. Otherwise how would I know?'

'True.'

After two drags, I feel like I could puke up what I had to eat three weeks ago, let alone yesterday, so I flatten it under my shoe on the patio.

'Oh Rach, what d'you do that for? I could've had that later.'

'Sorry. Sarah, you said something about some business with someone called Miranda. What was that all about?'

Clumsy, aren't I? But I can't think about anything else. My brain has got snagged on this name and I can't get free. I can't even think about a better way of asking. But Sarah's feeling better about her own situation now, and is ready to discuss someone else's misery.

'Oh, yes. Poor Hector. I think he really loved her. Miranda Waters. They were together for more than three years. We thought they would get married. Little Jakey as a page boy, can you imagine it?' She takes another drag.

'And?'

'Mm. Well, she fell pregnant last year – no, year before last now. I was so excited about a new baby in the family. Little cousin for Jake to play with, you know. Anyway, everything was going along fine, Hector was all excited about it, and then suddenly she was off the scene completely. Just gone.'

'Bloody hell. What happened?'

She shrugs. 'Don't know. Hector never said and we didn't like to ask.'

'Did she . . . die?'

'Oh God no. Just left him. Or he kicked her out. Really, I don't know. He never talks about it. Never even mentions her name. Anyway, we heard from a friend of a friend that she lost the baby after that. Hector was pretty devastated.'

'How awful.'

'Well, yes, but like I said he seems to have got over it recently. But we never did find out why they broke up. Probably to do with Hector's work.'

'What exactly is Hector's work?'

'He's got this computer business out on the business park. He's never away from it – everyone and everything always come second. It's caused him quite a few break-ups in the past.'

'Hmmm.'

'Anyway, what do you want to ask me about babies?'

'Oh, yes. Shall we go inside? It's freezing out here. And I've got some choccies in my bag for you, to say thanks.'

'You didn't need to do that,' she says, heading back indoors eagerly.

'I know, but I stopped for cheese anyway, so I thought—'

'Cheese? Oh Rachel, you shouldn't eat that. It's far too full of fat and salt.'

Well, that was a close one. Somehow I managed to divert Sarah's suspicions, but it won't hold for long. It's like Val's husband's accountant all over again. Val was eager to believe anything that explained what was going on, so she didn't have to face what was actually going on. I mean, who pays their tax bills weekly? It doesn't sound very likely to me.

But Sarah did the same thing. She accepted the first life-line I offered her, but as soon as she remembers that Glenn's absence and mysterious overtime has been going on at least since Jake's party, which was weeks before his mum died, then it'll all fall apart again. There's only one thing to be done. I am uncomfortable contacting him after all this time – it's been three weeks – and he said goodbye so finally on Christmas Day, but this is a legitimate reason to call. I'm trying to convince myself that I'm not like one of those desperate types that keeps phoning me days or weeks after I've said that I don't want them to phone me any more.

'Hello?' I've called him at home. He sounds so tired.

'Hi, Hector, it's Rachel.'

'Rachel. Hello. How do you do that?'

'What?'

'Know the exact moment when I am at my lowest, in greatest need of a perk, and call me then.'

'I don't . . . I'm sorry, do you want me to call back later?'

'NO! I mean, no, this is the perfect time. Again.'

'Oh. Good. How are you?'

293

'Oh, you know, so-so. How have you been? And how's Plum? Getting big now, I expect.'

'Not too bad. I've had another ante-natal session with Katy.'

'Really? How did it go?'

'Great. She gave me one of those little yellow and black flags to pin on my arse when I go outside.'

He bursts out laughing. 'Oh, Rachel. I've really missed . . .' He stops suddenly and my ears are aching with wanting him to finish.

'You've . . . ?' I say, trying to coax the rest out of him.

'Nothing. No. So how was your New Year?'

'Pants. Yours?'

'Quite good, actually.'

'Really?' That is not what I wanted to hear.

'Yeah. Caught up with a few people I hadn't seen in a while, you know. Had a few laughs, swapped a few stories.'

I'm feeling all flustered and angry, thinking about him being with other people, like maybe Miranda, and then something occurs to me. 'You were at the office, weren't you?'

'Well, all right, if you must know, yes I was. I can't lie to you, Rachel.'

'So it was pants?'

He's laughing again. 'Yes, you're right. I was in the office, on my own, emailing someone in New York.'

'I was on my own too.'

There's a small noise, as if he's sat forward in his seat suddenly. 'Were you? But why?'

I shrug, even though he can't see me. 'Who wants to go out with someone looking like this?'

He makes a little sound in his throat, almost like a growl.

'Pardon?'

He clears his throat. 'Nothing. I just can't bear . . .'

I crush the phone to my ear so hard it goes pink and starts to throb. He's driving me nuts with this not finishing his sentences. '*Yes?*'

'Never mind. I just want you to be happy, Rachel. Are you?'

This sounds like friend mode again. Am I happy? Right at that moment, curled on my sofa with Hector McCarthy on the other end of the phone, yes, I am. My lips are millimetres from the mouthpiece and I imagine his, the same distance away at the other end. We're almost kissing.

'Erm . . .'

He's making end-of-the-call noises. Quick, think of something to say. And then I remember the reason why I rang him in the first place.

'Hector, I've just been to see Sarah and I'm a bit worried about her.'

'Are you? Is she all right?'

'Well, yes, she's not ill or anything. But she's very down and keeps crying. She thinks Glenn's having an affair.'

'Shit.'

'Yes, he is. I just wondered . . .'

'If I've spoken to Glenn about it yet?'

'Well, yes. I know it's really none of my business, it's between you and Glenn, but she's one of my oldest friends, you know? He's your brother and you love him; well, she's like my sister. My real brother is this really annoying ten-year-old kid who never stays in the same place for longer than a minute, so Sarah's my stand-in.'

'I love the fact that you really care about her. I do too. And the fact is that I have done nothing about it. I don't even know why. I was all set to do it and then Mum died and then . . . Well, since then, I haven't felt much of an interest in anything. I'm sorry, Rachel. I've let you down.'

'What are you talking about? Don't be silly. It's nothing even to do with me, so how can you possibly have let *me* down? In fact, from a purely selfish point of view, you've been the most . . . I-I mean, you've always . . . I couldn't have . . .' Oh God, now I'm doing it.

'Well, that's good to hear,' he says, a smile in his voice again.

'Thanks.'

'You're very welcome. Listen, I'll go and see him this week, OK? I shouldn't have left it this long, particularly if Sarah's starting to suspect something. I just hope I'm not too late and this can all be sorted out.'

'Me too.'

'God, it makes me so angry, what he's doing. It goes against everything I believe in. You don't mess around in a long-term relationship, especially where kids are involved, even if . . .'

'What?'

He pauses and I can hear movement at the other end. 'Doesn't matter. I'm not thinking straight, just ignore me. Over-work, probably.' He pauses and I'm about to speak and then suddenly he starts talking again and his voice grabs me and drags me in, pulling me down with him, it's so dark and intense. 'Rachel, do you ever get sick of doing the right thing? All around me I see people doing and saying things to suit no one but themselves, and they're happy and enjoying life and seem to have everything, and here am I, sitting alone in the office at Christmas, alone again at New Year, tearing myself into pieces, trying to do the right thing. God, why is it always so hard? What's the use of trying to be a good guy when all it gets me is misery? Don't I ever get to be happy? Isn't that what it's all for, so that I can enjoy some happiness one day? Because I'm starting to think I don't want to be a good guy any more, Rachel. Christ, I so don't want to any more.'

Can you see my goosebumps and the hairs on my arms and neck all raised? His voice is always heavy and low, but just then he sounded so raw and wounded, his voice all throaty and hoarse it took all the air out of my lungs and sent me plunging into an abyss of lust, and I don't expect to be coming out again. He's clearly dreadfully unhappy about something, struggling with inner turmoil, torturing himself every moment and in desperate need of some help.

It is a huge turn-on.

He's fallen silent now but is breathing heavily and I feel I should say something because he sounds like he's waiting for my reaction. Or he's as turned on as I am. All I know is Hector is a good guy and I don't want him to stop.

'But you *are* a good guy, Hector,' I say very softly. 'You're one of the best people I know. You can't stop being that because then you stop being Hector McCarthy. And that wouldn't be fair. On the world.'

He sighs deeply. 'I don't know about that. What do I owe the world? What about me, for once?'

'What's wrong, Hector? This is not you.'

'Rachel. I only wish I could tell you.'

'But you can! We're strangers, remember. You can tell me anything.'

'No. We're not strangers. We haven't been strangers for a very long time, you know that as well as I do. And I can't tell you this. Not while . . . Not ever. I'm sorry.'

I've closed my eyes and leaned back in my seat. And look at my face – lips slightly parted, cheeks flushed, head thrown back. Is there anything more sexy than a tortured man?

He lapses into silence again and I'm thinking the only thing I can say now is goodbye, if I can even manage to push that out. But then he seems to rouse himself suddenly. 'Hey, I've just remembered, I am coming over to Horizon the week after next to see Rupert. Maybe I'll see you then?'

'Oh, really?' Slowly I drag myself up from the depths and open my eyes. 'When exactly is that?' I get up, walk fast into the kitchen and take the calendar down from its hook.

'It's the twenty-sixth. A week on Friday.' And then he says, 'Ten days,' as he writes an 'R' on the calendar in his kitchen, and I say 'Ten days,' as I write an 'H' on mine.

Standing in his kitchen, Hector runs his hand over his face, shaking his head. He has to try and focus on other aspects of his life. Like speaking to Glenn, for example. He's neglected so much lately and it's got to the point where other people are starting to be affected by his lethargy. He picks up the car keys and goes immediately to his brother's house to put that right at least.

Here are Glenn and Sarah, slumped in front of the telly together, their bodies not quite touching at the sides. The doorbell has just rung so Sarah is getting up. Glenn watches her as she stands, then goes back to the film.

Sarah lets Hector in and offers him a drink. 'You look exhausted,' he says to her kindly. 'Let me make you one.'

'Oh, thanks, Hec. Great.'

'Glenn, come and show me where the cups are.'

Glenn looks up from the sofa. 'You know where they are – they're all in the cupboard next to the—'

'*Show* me,' Hector says meaningfully, so Glenn heaves himself up from the sofa and follows his brother into the kitchen.

Hector closes the door. 'I need to speak to you.'

Glenn raises his eyebrows. He looks calm, unbothered. 'Hec, can't this wait? There's a really good film on.'

Hector walks to him and says in a very low voice, 'I know about your affair.'

Glenn's face shows the smallest flicker. 'What affair?'

'And I want you to end it.' Hector's face is very close to Glenn's, although being taller he's bending slightly to look his brother in the eye.

'You want *what*?' Glenn spurts, finally losing his composure.

'You are damaging your marriage and potentially harming my nephew. It is selfish and irresponsible and I will not allow you to cause pain to—'

'You won't allow? *You won't allow!* Who the fuck do you think you are? You're only my bloody brother, not God of everything. *Je*-sus.'

Hector remains calm. He needs Glenn to pay attention to what he's about to say and if he gets angry, Glenn is likely to storm out of the room and out of the house.

'You will contact this woman and end it immediately.'

'I will not!'

Hector gets the cup out of the cupboard and starts

299

making tea for Sarah to keep himself calm. 'I'm telling you, Glenn, if you don't do it—'

'What? You'll what, big brother? Beat me up? Give me a Chinese burn? Make me do the washing-up for four weeks? Go on, tell me, what punishment have you got lined up for your naughty little brother this time?'

'I'll call in the loan.'

Glenn's smug expression falters. 'You'll . . . ?'

'You owe me money, Glenn. I want it back.'

'B-But . . . you can't.'

'Of course I can. It's mine.'

'But I haven't got it any more.'

'Oh, now there's a surprise. What did you spend it on? Holiday for Sarah? New dishwasher? Smart new car?'

Glenn is starting to look rather uncomfortable, his eyes darting around and settling eventually on the mug standing next to the kettle. 'My . . . The . . . She's . . . she's got . . . expensive taste.'

Hector's lip curls. 'Five grand? You spent the whole five grand on your dick? Money that I lent you because you're my brother and I thought it was to get you out of a spot. I thought I was helping you and Sarah and Jake to be more comfortable, maybe taking away some of your stress because that's one thing I can do for you all. Christ, Glenn. You disgust me.' He turns his back on his brother and makes Sarah's tea. 'If you don't end this liaison immediately, I will take whatever steps are necessary to recoup my losses, do you understand?'

Glenn tries to look smug again. 'You wouldn't do it—'

Hector swings round, his face distorted with fury. 'Do you want to try me, Glenn?' he snarls, lunging towards him so fast, Glenn steps back worriedly. 'Do you want to see what I would do? Well *do you?*'

Glenn is seriously discomfited now. He shakes his head.

'Good.' Hector hands the tea to Glenn. 'Now you take this in there and you start appreciating your wife and your son and your home because believe me, you shit, you have got everything. And first thing tomorrow, you ring this *woman* and you let her down. Right?'

Glenn nods and they return in silence to the living room. As they enter, Sarah is sitting down rather hurriedly and does not look at either of them. Glenn sits down next to his wife and this time sits close enough for their shoulders to touch.

Look at Hector outside the front door a minute later. He's leaning back against the door, palms pressed flat against the wood, breathing heavily, eyes closed. His face shows amazement, I think. And he's shaking a bit. Do you know what? I think he was bluffing. But he's managed to convince Glenn, apparently, and that's what counts. He rolls his eyes, smiles a little, then pushes off from the door and heads towards his car.

Chapter Seventeen

I'm nearly late for work the next day. I get up at the right time, get ready in the right amount of time, get my shoes on and reach for the car keys on the hook by the door . . . But they're not there.

They're always, always, on their hook. That's why there's a hook there. Dad put it up at Mum's suggestion, so that I wouldn't make myself late for stupid work looking for the stupid car keys. I hang them up, every day, the very second I come in through the door.

I spend several minutes flinging things around and slamming doors, but it doesn't help. Eventually, after some calming screaming and head pounding, I locate the keys in my tooth mug, looking a bit minty. I have a few seconds to wonder – and dread – where the hell my tooth-brush is, before charging out of the door.

It's gone five past nine when I arrive and everyone is already working. There's no sudden rush of movement this time, so obviously no one was gossiping about me. Well, they wouldn't be, would they, not after nine.

There's a steaming mug of hot chocolate on my desk, and I give Val a grateful smile as I sit down. She's had her hair done – looks like a perm and some colour. It really suits her – she looks younger. On the other side of the partition, Chrissie is already engrossed in a call, head down, flicking those pages, saying 'OK, OK.' Jean and Graham do not seem to have spotted that I'm late so after a brief hunt for my pen, which I eventually find in yesterday's coffee cup, I switch to 'F' and take my first call.

The only interesting thing this morning is a visit to Telesales from Vivien Attwood, the head of Planning. She announces that there will be a staff meeting on Friday, 26 January, in the canteen at five thirty. And as it's after hours there will be a full buffet laid on by Mr de Witter. Everyone has got to attend. I want to know if we're all going to be paid overtime for the extra hours. Vivien says no, that's why they're feeding us instead. What we save on food that evening is our overtime.

'Wonder what that's all about?' Val says, after Vivien has gone back up to the sixth floor. 'It must be really important if they're feeding us.'

'They're probably going to make us all redundant,' Marion says. We all stare at her. Could that be it? With free food as a sweetener. Better fill a few carrier bags while we're there.

'I wonder what the line is about not going,' I say. 'If we're not being paid, surely they can't make us go?'

'I shouldn't think so,' Val says.

'But you've got to go, Rachel,' Chrissie says, grinning. 'You'll hear it from the horse himself what colour the new tiles in the Ladies are going to be.'

'Hey, Chrissie!' It's Creepy Steve, from station eighteen. 'Can you get back to your desk, please? I've got a call for you.'

Our impromptu break is over and we all go back to our desks.

A few minutes later, I'm suddenly aware that there's no noise coming from Chrissie's desk. I stand up to look over the partition that separates us and find her holding her head in her hands, elbows on the desk, her turret switched to 'B'.

I'm in the middle of a call and can't speak to her, so I tap the partition with my hand to attract her attention. She looks up and I am shocked to see that her eyes are swollen and tearful.

'Have you thought about Fuengirola?' I say, raising my hands in a 'What's up?' gesture. She shakes her head. 'Well, are you dead set on Europe?' I say, gesticulating at her, but she waves me away, frowning, and switches to 'F' to get rid of me, it seems.

A few minutes later and it's this side of the room's turn to go for lunch. You can see on my face that I've made up my mind about something, and I'm looking around me for Chrissie, determined to speak to her during our break.

Wow, did you see that? I didn't even know Chrissie could move that fast, especially in a skirt that tight. She's out the door to the lifts before you could say split stitches.

Which leaves me going down to the canteen with Val again. I'm nodding politely and smiling while she's telling me about the gym she's just joined, and Finn, her twenty-eight-year-old, blond personal trainer, who was on the New Zealand Commonwealth Games swim team four years ago, but I barely hear her, I'm so focused on what's happened to Chrissie. She was obviously upset about something, but what could . . .

'. . . huge arms, the size of a small child . . .'

Once or twice, the odd word breaks through.

When I get back to my station, Chrissie is again already engrossed in a call so I don't have a chance to speak to her. I'm standing up watching her as I switch to 'F' , just in case she gets off the call and has a chance to speak.

Some of our clients have no intention of booking anything, they just ring up for a chat. There's a few regulars – a Mrs Holley from somewhere in Scotland calls about once a week to deliberate over the Isle of Man; there's a Miss Hatton, with a daughter in Australia that she's never been to visit; Mrs Harkness who wants to do a watercolour painting activity break in Crete, and Mr Silverside who just shouts. Their names and addresses are on the walls all round the office – Horizon Holidays' Least Wanted – to help us identify them quickly so that we don't waste any time on them. I've had Mr Silverside once and he was so unpleasant I just cut him off straight away. Right now, I suspect I've got one of the others because she's been wittering on about her daughter in Australia for so long but has made no mention of when she wants to go.

'What part of Australia are you thinking about visiting?' I ask half-heartedly, to remind her why she called. I'll give her two more minutes.

Siân at station nine shouts over to me suddenly that she's got a call for me, which makes up my mind. 'Well, what we could offer is a pack—' See that? I cut her off in the middle of a word. It's less suspicious if you do that. 'Stick it through, Siân!' I call back. My phone beeps to let me know the call has arrived.

'Hello?'

'Hi, Rachel. Hector.'

There's that plunging sensation again. Suddenly the day has become special and exciting; the other noises in the sales room fade away and there's only me on this end and him on the other end. I press the headset close to my face. 'Hi, Hector. How are you today?'

'I'm fine. How are you?'

'Fine thanks.'

'Good. I just rang to tell you that I spoke to my brother yesterday.'

'Yesterday? Bloody hell, that was quick. What did he say?'

'Well, he denied it.'

'Oh.' Quick flashback to Sainsbury's car park last year, me standing by the car watching someone in a red vest embracing a woman. Oh my God, was it definitely Glenn? I didn't see him close up, not really. Is it possible I made a mistake? *Is Glenn innocent?*

'And then he caved and reverted to being a snivelling little shit.'

'Oh, thank God.'

'What?'

'No, right, what I mean is, you know, thank God he owned up. Because then you told him to end it. Right?'

'Oh, I see. Well, yes, I did my best.'

'Do you think he will? End it, I mean.'

He sighs. 'I don't know. And if he doesn't, there's really nothing else I can do. I threatened him a bit, you know, to get him to promise . . .'

'Threatened him? Blimey.'

'Well, there's no need to sound so . . . impressed about that. It wasn't easy. I had to watch all three *Godfather* films before I went round there.'

'All three?'

'Well, I got in the car after One and Two, but then I had to go back indoors and watch the last one. For closure, you know.'

We laugh together, the headset still pressed so close to my ear I can hear him breathing. After a moment, abruptly he stops chuckling, as if he's suddenly remembered that what he rang me up for was a serious matter.

'Look, Rachel, if Sarah says anything to you, or you get the idea that she might . . . you know, *know*, or if you're worried about her,' there's an almost imperceptible pause, 'or about anything, anything at all, you will call me, won't you?'

He's gearing up for the end of the call but I don't want it to end.

'I'm wearing the earrings.'

There's a surprised silence. Then he says, 'You are? I bet they look fantastic on you.'

'They do. They're so gorgeous. Actually, I haven't taken them off since Christmas. I love them. Thank you so much.'

'I'm really glad you like them. I spent ages . . . Anyway, I'm sorry if it seemed a bit inappropriate, but I'd sent them before I knew about . . .'

'About what?'

'Well, about you and Nick, you know, at the office party.' He sounds uncomfortable, disgruntled.

'The office party? I don't understand – what on earth does that have to do with you getting me a present?'

'No, you're right, it doesn't have anything to do with that. It shouldn't matter but I'm afraid I find that it does. Just me I suppose – old-fashioned.'

I'm frowning now. He's not making any sense. 'What are you—'

307

'See, the thing is, Rachel, I'm an all-or-nothing kind of guy. Some people in my position might decide that they'd be happy with friendship, if it's all they could get. But for me that's like torture. Seeing someone, talking, spending time . . . knowing that it'll never be more . . . Well, it's too hard. I prefer to . . . cut myself off, lie low, wait it out on my own until the agony stops. And it will stop, in the end. It always does.'

Is he trying to tell me something about Miranda and the pain she caused him? The idea that he's talking about me is out there, but I don't grasp it. Not quite.

'Hector, what—'

'No, please, don't ask me, Rachel. I want so much to tell you, but I can't. You said last time that it's not me, and you were right, it's not. It seems I am destined always to want people who don't want me. Well then, if that's my fate, I'll face up to it, welcome it, embrace it, because I, as you said, am a good guy.'

'Yes, you are, but you're not—'

'It's been a pleasure, Rachel. Take really good care of yourself. Bye.' And he's gone. Again.

The rest of the day at Horizon is really dull, just boring holidays, holidays, holidays. Chrissie races off at five, faster, if it's possible, than when she sped off at lunch, so I've decided to leave it until tomorrow. If she wanted to talk to me about something, she would have. So let's go to me, at home later, lying on the bed with a bag of salt-and-vinegar chipsticks at my elbow. Don't look too closely at the floor – you might spot three or four more empty chipstick bags down there.

I'm trying to remember what Hector had almost said

today, but all that comes into my mind is him mentioning me and Nick at the office party. Why would me stumbling in on Nick and Paris have any effect on him? No matter how many times and in how many different ways I think about it, it always makes no sense.

And another thing. How did he even know that I had bumped into Nick at the party? I told Chrissie about it – no doubt Chrissie has told others, including Sarah most likely, and she will have told Glenn, of course; but will he have passed it back to Hector? I try to picture Glenn breaking this devastating news: 'Hec, I'm sorry to have to tell you but a random girl you don't know walked in on her ex and his new girlfriend having sex at some Christmas party or other. You're going to have to be brave, big guy.'

No, it's ridiculous. No one knows that Hector and I even know each other, so nothing I did would be gossiped back to him. I can't fathom it out.

Mum always says if looks were brains, I'd be a genius. Which I guess is a polite way of saying that I'm not one.

Just as I'm opening another bag of crisps the phone rings. Plum's fast asleep, but when I roll over to get up, he stretches and pushes in four different directions at once, one of which goes straight into my bladder. God.

'Rachel, it's Sarah.'

'My God, Sarah, what's happened?' Sarah's voice is thick and heavy, full of tears and distress. 'God, is it Jake?'

There's a series of sniffs, then, 'No, no, Jakey's fine. It's Glenn.'

'Oh no.'

'You remember what I was telling you, about how sometimes when he comes in, it seems like he's . . . been . . .'

'Yes, yes, I remember.' Cold dread is coagulating in the

pit of my belly. I know what she's going to say and I don't want her to say it, but I hurry her anyway.

'Well, I've found out . . . I know for sure now. He's definitely havinganaffair.' She runs all the words together as if she wants them to be in her mouth for as short a time as possible.

'Oh my God, Sarah. I'm so, so sorry. What are you going to do?'

'I'm leaving him. Me and Jakey, we're leaving him. Actually, we have already. We need somewhere to stay for a few days and I was wondering whether . . . ?'

'Oh, yes, of course, come straight round. I'll fit you both in somewhere.'

She sighs with relief. 'Thanks, Rach. I knew you'd say yes – I'm on the mobile outside your front door.'

She's a mess, isn't she? Glenn's got a lot to answer for, I know that. And look at little Jake, following his mum everywhere, making sure he's in physical contact with some part of her all the time. He's never seemed as small and pale as this before, and I wonder what he witnessed between his parents before Sarah and he left the house.

Sarah's brought a carrier bag with clothes screwed up inside and another bag with toys in it. I'm fearfully eyeing the large yellow plastic microphone that's tumbling out, but Jake pays it no attention. The Gameboy that he got for his birthday last year, his absolute favourite toy, is in there too, but he does not even look at the bag. His wide eyes are focused on his mum, who is slumped on the sofa, red-eyed and sniffly.

'I heard Glenn talking to Hector,' Sarah is saying quietly. 'Hector was telling him off about it, how selfish and irresponsible it was of him. And he says he's going to

310

get some money back off Glenn if he doesn't end it, so it seems my husband has been borrowing money from his brother to lavish attention on this woman.' Her voice breaks and she sobs into her hand for a few moments.

'Don't cry, Mummy,' Jake says, gazing up at her from his position by her side on the sofa, snuggled into her. 'Please don't cry.'

But she either doesn't hear him or ignores him. 'Look at me, Rach,' she says, looking down at her sweatshirt and jeans, which look like they might have come from Tesco's. A long time ago. 'Don't you think I could do with having something lavished on me? And Jakey, what about him? Doesn't he deserve the odd treat or two?'

I glance at Jake, who is vigorously wiping his nose with his hand, which is then smeared on to my carpet.

I look away quickly and focus on Sarah, who is still sobbing and shaking her head, saying 'Why? Why?' over and over, more to herself than to me. I'm not even going to think about answering, even if she's expecting me to.

Jake is trying to be the adult, rubbing her back the way she must have done for him countless times over scraped knees and bumped heads. He takes her face between his own tiny hands and says, 'Try to be brave, Mummy,' and it's clear that he's got no understanding of what's happening. Sarah smiles at him weakly and bundles him tightly into her arms, rocking him as she would have done when he was much smaller. I'm not sure if this action is to comfort him or herself.

Later on, she tries to settle him on my bed but he won't let her leave the room. As I'm trying to clear their things up a bit in the living room, I hear from along the hallway the low murmurs of Sarah's voice, soothing, reassuring, followed by the high-pitched staccato of Jake's anxious tones. Their words are indistinct but I feel sure she is telling him that no, they can't go home yet, and yes, Mickey the hamster will be fine without him. She doesn't reappear from the room and eventually I settle myself down on the sofa for the night, my legs bent double so my distended belly is compressed uncomfortably into my ribs. Plum objects immediately, pushing hard against the new smaller environment, but he's the lucky one – when I push against the arm of the sofa to try to get comfortable, it doesn't budge an inch.

Evidently the refugees manage to get some sleep. Can you hear that noise? That's one or both of them still snoring softly when I leave the next morning. I'm peeking in to make sure they're all right: Sarah has rolled away from her son and into the foetal position, the curve of her back facing towards him. Jake is making an exact small replica of his mum, a diminutive curled lump under the covers, knees drawn up tightly, mouth slightly open. I close the door and tiptoe out.

So now I have the dilemma of should I tell Chrissie and Hector or not? I'm going to leave thinking about Hector until I have enough time to do it justice.

So, Chrissie. I conjure up her face in the car and look at the expression on it as I'm telling her. What do you think? Is that a sympathetic look? To me she looks scandalized – but in a hungry way. I am swaying towards thinking that, although she will be shocked, horrified, sympathetic and attentive, there will be some very small, possibly even sub-conscious – and possibly not all that small – part of her that will get a kick out of it. Maybe I'm feeling this way about her because if I'm really, completely honest with myself and with you, I did get a little kick out of it when I saw Glenn in the car park.

God, it's good to get that off my chest. You know, I only felt it for a short time and since then I've tried really hard to make it up to her. I've phoned her and visited her loads more often than usual and now I'm sleeping on my own two-seater and I'm six months' pregnant. What more can I do?

Not tell Chrissie. That's what I could do.

But then we're a foursome, we're close friends. If one of us was in need or unhappy about something, and I was the only one that didn't know because the others didn't tell me, I'd be really fed up, and rightly so, I think. Plus, of course, it's probably very hypocritical of me not to tell her because I suspect her reaction will be the same as mine.

There is no dilemma about telling Hector. Glenn is his brother – he needs to know. I will call him as soon as I get to the office.

Oh God, more guilt. I am such a bad person. Can you believe I am actually grateful to have this reason, this *excuse*, to call him again?

In the office, I head quickly for my station. It's six minutes to nine, so I can ring Hector now, before the calls start coming in, and discuss what we can do together to help our good friends get through this crisis. We can take a bit of time over it, have a really long talk. As I'm heading eagerly to my station, I spot Chrissie at her desk, hunched over, apparently already on a call. She looks up as she spots me approaching, and I am shaken by her appearance. She has no make-up on, which immediately makes her look like she's dying of TB. She has dark shadows beneath her eyes, which are red-rimmed and puffy, her hair is flat and lifeless – it looks in need of a wash, actually – and she's wearing a dirty pink hoodie and big white jogging trousers.

She ends the call she's on and greets me listlessly.

'Hi, Rach. All right?'

I pause on my way to my turret, the call to Hector momentarily forgotten. 'Chrissie, are you all right? You don't look very well.'

'I'm letting my skin have a rest, that's all. God, if one more person . . .'

'But you . . . I mean, you look as if . . . Have you been crying?'

Chrissie pulls her handbag up from the floor and rummages around inside for a tissue. 'Yes, all right, I've been crying. I've had some bad news, that's all.' She puts up a hand as I start to walk towards her. 'Oh, nothing as devastating as your news, naturally, but it upset me. OK?'

I go over there anyway and stand by her desk. 'I thought so. You were upset yesterday but you rushed off before I had a chance to speak to you.' She's certainly got quick-exit clothes on today – much better for running than yesterday's ensemble. I perch my behind on the edge of the desk. 'What is it?'

She blows her nose loudly on the tissue and Jim from station fourteen looks up briefly. 'Nothing. Just a disappointment, that's all. I'll get over it – I always do.'

So it was a man. For I think the first time in all the twenty years of our friendship, I can actually understand. I had never experienced it before Nick and have always been a teensy bit, well, impatient with Chrissie or Susan or anyone else who routinely goes through these soggy

314

dramatics at the end of a relationship. Why didn't they just accept that it's a fact of life that can only be avoided by avoiding the cause? And that would be far worse than dealing with the consequences. Like getting old – no point crying about it, unless you want to avoid it all together and die young. Mum says I might change my thinking when I'm thirty-nine. Anyway, at least Chrissie hasn't been left pregnant by her disappointer.

'Well—' I start to say, but she cuts me off.

'Yes, I know, at least I'm not pregnant. Turn the conversation back to yourself.'

'That's not—'

'Fair? Maybe not, but just because you're in worse circumstances, doesn't make mine hurt less. We don't all feel what we feel in relation to you, you know.' She meets my eyes for a second, then turns away hurriedly.

I think the only other time you have seen this expression on my face was the moment when Dr Kant was giving me the wonderful slash dreadful news back in August. It's a combination of shock, hurt, anxiety, disappointment and, if I'm totally honest with you, and myself, deep down in there is realization of my own stupidity. The second time in six months. What a year.

I kind of stumble round the end of the desks, past Val and along to my own, my throat aching as I'm desperately trying not to cry. The rational part of me is telling me calmly not to be silly, Chrissie is just upset and lashing out at anyone because she's hurt, but the rational part of me is very small these days. All the other parts of me are shouting in unison, 'CRY! Go on, CRY!'

I keep my head low over my turret until the tears dry up. Luckily, there's an old, partially stuck-together but dry tissue at the bottom of my bag, so I wipe my eyes and blow my nose, in that order, on it. When I look up, there's a steaming cup of hot chocolate on my desk and Val smiles at me when I look over gratefully.

And now I don't have time to call Hector. I acknowledge to myself that if my intention is pure and centred only on Sarah and informing Hector about her well-being, I should call him immediately, even if I can only talk for ninety seconds, in between calls. That is what I should do. What I want to do is talk to him for ten, twenty, forty years. Minutes. I mean minutes. I decide I'll stop on the way home and call him on the mobile, in the car. That way, Sarah won't overhear, and I won't be interrupted by work calls.

As I'm shutting down my turret at five o'clock, I turn to find Chrissie standing there. She looks dreadful.

'I'm sorry, Rach,' she says immediately. 'I didn't mean it. I'm just fucked up at the moment.'

'Doesn't matter. I knew that. Look, why don't you come to my place for tea? We can open a bottle of wine, and I can watch you drink it.'

Chrissie smiles gratefully. She's got nothing else on tonight.

It's not until I'm driving home that I remember two things: one – Sarah and Jake are there, so now I'm cooking for four – well, five, technically, if you include Plum; and two – I can't really stop the car and pull over for a twenty- to forty-minute phone conversation with Hector, while Chrissie is following along behind in her car. Arses.

When we get in, we're greeted by the sound of a man explaining how to make a handy pen and note holder in the shape of a headless corpse. I'm hoping it's the television.

In the living room, Jake is not watching *Art Attack* but is hunched over a pile of Lego, talking to himself. He's still in his pyjamas and the bottoms have slipped down a little bit at the back revealing a miniature and untypically beautiful builder's bum. It is that more than anything, more than the small bumps of his spinal bones visible in a curve through his top, more than the quiet sound of his nonsense chatter, more than the velvet valley of the back of his neck, his messy hair or his reluctance to look up when I greet him, that wrenches into me just how tiny and vulnerable, how fragile, this little person is.

'Hiya, Jake. What you doing?'

He doesn't answer. Well, he barely knows me, even though I am his godmother, and that is my fault. In that moment, suddenly I wish that he was running up to me and flinging his arms around my knees, crying out, 'Auntie Rachel!', delighted to see me, feeling better for me being there. Indifference is excruciating. I'm determined to get to know him.

Chrissie's gone awfully quiet and still, hasn't she? She looks a bit appalled by what she's seeing – Jake here in my living room in his pyjamas, the mess of Lego and other toys, the carrier bag spilling out Postman Pat T-shirts and Spiderman shorts, the blanket on the sofa. The look of horror on her face is pissing me right off.

'Is Sarah . . . ?'

'Sarah and Jake stayed here last night. Sarah's left Glenn.'

The blood drains from her face. 'Oh Christ. Why?'

Her eyes have taken on a hunted look, wide and frightened. I'm looking at her quizzically. This is a strange reaction. What's it all about? I bet you've guessed, haven't you? But it's easier to see things when you're observing them and not in the middle of it all.

'She found out he's been having an affair.'

She starts to shake her head. 'Oh no, no. No. She shouldn't have left him . . .'

'I think it was the only thing she could do, Chrissie. He's treated her and Jake like dirt and Sarah does have some self respect.'

'But – but—'

'But nothing. He's a total shit and the slut he was with can have him. She must have known he was married, maybe even knew about Jake, but it just didn't bother her. She's obviously one of these people who go through life just thinking about themselves, taking absolutely no notice of how their actions are affecting other people.' For some reason, Hector's words pop into my head – about people who do and say things to suit no one but themselves, and I remember that he was talking about Glenn at the time. 'They're perfect for each other.'

'But it wasn't . . . I didn't mean . . .'

I turn slowly to look at her and she's gazing pleadingly at me and in that instant realization hits me like a plane crash. Stills of things I've seen and heard flash across my mind: the woman hugging Glenn in the car park, with a floaty lemon-coloured top on; the indistinct profile of the woman in the car he drove away in; Chrissie avoiding conversations about Glenn and his overtime every time they've come up; Chrissie's new hair, new clothes, new car. Revulsion floods through every particle of me at once and I narrow my eyes, struggling to keep composed in front of Jake.

'Get out,' I say quietly. 'I can't believe that you would do something like this. It's despicable.'

'I'm so . . . so—'

'Save it. No one wants you here. I don't think we'll ever have anything to say to each other.'

'Will you tell—'

'I should do. But I think that Sarah's suffering enough knowing that her husband betrayed her. I can't see any point in letting her know that she was betrayed by her best friend as well.'

'She already knows.' Sarah's appeared in the kitchen and has obviously heard enough through the open partition.

Chrissie turns to her, her eyes full of tears. 'Sarah . . .' It seems the enormous guilt is preventing her from speaking.

'Just go away, Christine,' Sarah says, refusing to make eye contact with Chrissie. 'Go away.'

As Chrissie stifles a sob – poor thing – Sarah walks over to where Jake is hunched on the floor. She sits down there with him and places her hand on his curved back. He looks up at last, drops what he's making and climbs on to his mum's lap. He looks into her face and seeing tears there, wipes them away with his own small fingers.

Chrissie can't watch this, apparently. She's at the door, so I go over there. 'Stay away, Chrissie. She doesn't want you here begging for forgiveness. Just try and live with yourself.' I shut the door behind her without saying anything else.

When I go back into the living room, Sarah and Jake are still cuddling on the floor. Jake is singing a song for his mum, his slightly nasal voice muffled by Sarah's shoulder, while she rocks backwards and forwards, tears falling into his hair. I leave quickly and head for the bedroom but I can't escape the sound of Jake's trembling rendition of 'Funky Town'.

Chapter Eighteen

When I was about twelve, my uncle Tony taught me to play 'Everybody Hurts' on his piano. I could bang it out fairly accurately but I had no sense of the emotion when I did. That didn't stop Mum making me do it whenever we went to Uncle Tony and Auntie Janet's. She'd get a tear in her eye every single time I thumped out the chorus.

'So true,' Auntie Janet would say. 'Everybody does.' Mum would nod, smiling and crying at the same time, and then would come over to me and gaze adoringly at me, from my shiny blond plait to my gorgeous nails, touch my face with her fingertips and shake her head sadly. I don't know what she was sad for – nothing bad ever happened to her. Or me.

The tune and words are going round and round my head at the moment. I fall asleep hearing it; I wake up hearing it; I drive to work hearing it. While I'm selling holidays I forget about it for a few hours and as I drive home listening to the radio, I start thinking about another tune – something cheerful and upbeat that you could really move around to, like 'Bat Out of Hell', or something by The Killers. Then I get home, see Sarah's face and everything except that tune is driven from my head.

This morning when I got out of the shower I was humming that song Hector and I were enjoying all those months ago, in his car: 'I get knocked down, but I get up again, you're never gonna keep me down.' I was walking fast along the hallway, moving my head from side to side, jigging a bit with the rhythm, enjoying the lift it was giving me. I rounded the corner into the kitchen and there was Sarah, moping over a bowl of porridge. The music in my head stopped abruptly, there was a slight pause, and then, sure enough, the gloomy, repeating notes of 'Everybody Hurts' began. Da-da-da-da-da, da-da-da-da-da-da. It's driven every other thought from my head. I even forgot all about ringing Hector. Can you believe that?

Can you also believe I didn't recognize Chrissie when I saw her with Glenn in Sainsbury's car park? I am totally obsessed with the fact I didn't spot what she was up to. I keep thinking about all the signs – the car park, the way she was behaving, the fact that she completely changed her look – how could I have missed all that? I'm trying not to be too hard on myself: it's not everyone who can spot other people's misdemeanours. Plus, I'm pregnant now too.

'What am I going to do?' Sarah keeps saying, holding her head.

'Be strong for Jake,' I say wisely, like someone who actually knows what it means to be a parent. Chrissie hasn't been into work since that day. She's been signed off by her doctor with stress apparently. Diddums. I hope she never comes back.

Sarah and Jake staying here is getting a bit difficult. They've been here for nine days so I have spent nine bad nights on the sofa. Look at my flat now. Can you believe all that is just from three people?

Well, two technically. All my stuff is pretty much where it always was.

Sarah didn't bring an awful lot with her, but what she did bring is on the floor. There are never any clean cereal bowls in the morning because she doesn't wash up after herself, and we're constantly running out of milk because Jake has a big mugful warmed up before bed, most of which gets poured down the sink the next morning. By me.

Plum's reaction to the cramped conditions at night is to rearrange his body clock. Now he's awake most of the night, practising Tae-Kwon-Do, and then asleep all day. I do love the sensation of him moving around inside me, pushing against the flexible walls of his confinement, but God I need to sleep. Can you see the dark circles appearing under my eyes? Don't say yes.

But I don't mind. I don't mind. I don't mind. It's become a kind of mantra. If I say it often enough, I will believe it. Less easy when I fall off the sofa at three o'clock in the morning, or when I stand barefoot on an upturned Power Ranger.

I have been hurrying home each evening after work, but if I'm honest my flat is not a very good place to be at the moment. Sarah is so down, she's constantly fighting against tears, and Jake just watches her and tries to take care of her. When they're not crying, they're cuddling each other. Jake doesn't ask about Glenn or when they're going home any more. I think he suspects that this is their new home and that he's never going to see his daddy again. I think Sarah has been avoiding telling him what's happened.

As I'm shutting my turret down and wearily picking up

my coat, already thinking about another suicidal evening ahead (da-da-da-da-da-da, da-da-da-da-da-da), Val says, 'You coming then?'

'Where?'

'Down to the canteen. It's the staff meeting, remember?'

'What, today? I thought it was nearer the end of the month?'

'Yes, that would be today, Rachel. Come on.' I have been offered a reprieve from the black misery that waits for me at home and I seize it. I'm walking down with Val with a bit of a spring in my step. She's looking good in a suede skirt and knee-high boots, and as we reach the lifts, a man called Keith from Marketing joins us. I don't know why he bothers – he's not my type, never will be. But then I notice that it's Val he's looking at, Val he's walking next to, turned towards her as we walk, their shoulders touching. Val's got a light flush on her cheek and her eyes are sparkling. She looks really happy. I am so thick sometimes.

I wish Chrissie was here, then I could walk off and ignore her. Actually, I wish I could tell her about Keith and Val; she would love to know about that. What I really want is for things to go back to how they were before she did what she did, so that we could still be friends.

In the canteen, five of the dining tables have been laid end-to-end against the back wall and covered with bowls and plates stacked up with food. The other tables have got white paper cloths on them, I suppose to make us feel valued. There are even people circulating in white shirts with trays of sparkling wine. Or is it cloudy lemonade? Seems that Rupert de Witter has gone to some expense. I'm starting to wonder whether we are all in for bad news.

I've sat next to Val and Keith, but look at the three of us.

We're not a threesome, we're a twosome and a onesome. And I am the onesome. Val is on my left but she's turned her body slightly to that she's angled towards Keith, and therefore away from me. To my right are empty chairs. Look at me, sitting there all on my own. Oh my God – I'm unpopular.

Look around the room – can you see anyone for me to sit with? Quick, before people notice that I'm on my own. Well, there are Paris and Nick, their open mouths pressed against each other so that every so often their tongues slide into view like a snake hatching from an egg. Jean is nowhere to be seen – no doubt outside for three or four quick fags. There is Craig from Data Processing and he's coming this way, looking expressively at the empty chairs. Oh, there are Marion and Penny, chatting in the middle. I wave at them and they come and sit next to me.

Here we go. A microphone has been set up at the opposite end of the room to the food tables, and the woman that's approaching it with a terrified expression is Jenny Wright, Rupert de Witter's personal assistant. She raises her arms and smiles nervously to make everyone look at her and be quiet. They don't, but she starts anyway. She's got a hundred-watt amplifier on her side.

'Right, well, good evening, everyone. I just want to say quickly thank you for coming . . .'

'Like we had any choice,' Marion says quietly.

'. . . and I hope the buffet at the back there goes some way towards compensating you for keeping you over your hours.'

'Not really,' Penny says.

'Rather have the money, frankly,' Marion adds. They snigger.

'Also, please make sure you all have a glass of wine. Mr de Witter wanted you all to be here as he has something important to tell you, and he would also like you to drink a toast with him at the end of the meeting. He's on his way here now from an earlier meeting, so if you could just bear with us for a few minutes, we'll get under way as soon as possible. Please have something to eat while you're waiting. OK, then. Thank you.'

Everyone heads for the buffet tables after me. We pick our way through and over the tables and head back to our seats.

'Wonder what this is all about,' Penny says.

'We're all being made redundant, I reckon,' Marion says, putting a sausage roll in her mouth.

'You reckon? Oh well, it saves cooking.'

'Have you tried these mushrooms?' I say. 'It's a kind of garlic—'

'You shouldn't be eating that stuff, Rach,' Marion says.

'Good evening, everyone,' the speakers boom out suddenly. We all look up to see that Mr de Witter has arrived, accompanied by a tall man with dark hair in a suit. Except he's taken the jacket off and rolled up his shirtsleeves. He's not even wearing a tie and one half of his shirt has come untucked at the front.

'Who's that, d'you think?' Marion says.

'Oh God,' says Penny. 'This has got prawns in it.'

'I'm sorry to have kept you waiting, and we'll try not to keep you for any longer than is absolutely necessary. I hope you're all enjoying the buffet.'

'I'm allergic to prawns.'

'Now some of you, probably most of you, will be aware that we have been conducting surveys over the past six months using stats and questionnaires, from staff and clients.'

'If I blow up like a balloon, can one of you stick me with adrenalin?'

'The results of these surveys have pointed me towards the realization that our computer systems are not what they should be in the twenty-first century.'

'Has anyone else got this black stuff?' Marion says.

'So what we did next was to put out tenders for the best company to rectify that situation . . .'

'Why? What's it like?'

'It's disgusting. Try it.'

'God no, it looks like lots of little eyeballs.'

'And the one that's offered the best set-up, in terms of . . .'

I've not eaten a thing. My fork is frozen, hovering just above the quiche on my plate. My eyes are fixed on the tall man standing just behind Rupert de Witter. My face is starting to feel hot.

'This wine is revolting,' Penny says.

'Tastes all right to me.'

'You *are* kidding?'

'No, it's fine.'

'God, you know nothing about wine.'

'Can I have a sip?' I ask. They all turn to me in horror.

'Of course not, Rach . . .'

'. . . shouldn't have alcohol . . .'

'. . . bad for the baby . . .'

'. . . to introduce to you the chairman and owner of McCarthy Systems, Hector McCarthy!'

Rupert de Witter claps loudly and enthusiastically and little by little other people in the room start to join in.

My hand is still holding my stationary fork. The tall man at the back steps forward and I can see now very plainly what I have been suspecting for the past few minutes: it is Hector. He smiles at the assembly, nodding, although he looks a little uncomfortable and keeps rubbing the back of his head. He hasn't seen me.

Rupert is speaking again, asking everyone to join him in a toast, so everyone stands up and raises their glasses. I don't have a glass so I just stand and stare. The image of the elderly relative sitting in a rented office, helping out answering the phone and shouting over the partition to see if Hector is there, pops into my head and is suddenly replaced by an idea of thick carpeting that you leave footprints in, and marble pillars.

I realize that everyone is sitting down again, and hurriedly do the same.

'Thank you very much, Rupert, and thank you, Horizon Holidays,' Hector is saying now. 'You've made me feel very welcome and I'm looking forward to working with you all in the future.' He pats his chest with both hands. 'I've got some notes somewhere . . .' he says, grinning. He rummages in his trouser pocket and finds a piece of paper, which he brings out with relief and unfolds. It's very small and irregular in shape and actually looks as if it has been torn off something. I think it's even purple on one side, which makes it look as if it might be . . . a chocolate bar wrapper?

'Here it is. Now, Rupert has asked me to say a few words about the new system we're installing for you. Sadly, a few words won't be nearly enough. The system I've designed is phenomenally powerful and yet extraordinarily easy to use, so no one out there will have any problems getting used to it. I'm aware of the differing needs of all the staff, from Telesales to Product Design, and I know that staff are likely to change departments very frequently. Because of that, I've tried to incorporate everything into one package, so that once you've had your training, you will be able to move . . .' He trails off suddenly. 'Er . . . to – to move . . .' He's stalled. I look up and find myself staring straight into his brown eyes. 'To, er, to move . . . to move, um, around, from department to department, without the need for additional training. The system I've designed will cover all Office applications, to include booking and reservations, personnel records, pay details and . . . er . . . anything else that you do here.' He stops and refolds the paper in his hand, while Rupert is looking at him questioningly. 'Thanks.' He steps back from the mic and walks to the side of the room. I lose sight of him.

'Ah. Well, thank you, Hector, and I'm sure we all appreciate you keeping that brief. No doubt everyone will find out a lot more about the new system and what it can do in the coming months.'

'Oh, that should make things a bit better, then, shouldn't it?' Penny says, going back to her pizza.

'You think so? I think that with all these computers, they'll need less staff.'

'Oh shut up, Marion.'

'Hello, Rachel.'

My head snaps up. He's standing right in front of me, hands in his pockets, a big grin on his face.

'Hello, Hector.' Can you see the expression on my face, there? I feel like a tiny iron filing near a great big beautiful magnet. 'How are you?' I have to crane my head backwards to look up at him from my seated position.

I'm not going to stand up though. Not while I look like St Paul's Cathedral.

He glances around then pulls a chair over from the next table. I can see that people there are looking at him, then at me, and nodding. Are they concluding that he's the father of the baby? I wonder idly what he would think of that.

There are at least two shocked expressions behind me, but I'm not looking at them. I'm looking at Hector, in his shirtsleeves, pulling up a chair to sit next to me. He sits on the edge of the seat and leans forward, sits back suddenly and hastily tucks in his loose shirt tail, then leans towards me again, hands clasped loosely, elbows on his thighs.

'It's good to see you,' he says quietly. His eyes are moving all over my face and hair, taking everything in. 'How have you been?'

'I've had better days,' I say.

'Really?' He's frowning.

'Yeah. It was on holiday in Spain – I won quite a lot of money in the casino, then we bumped into George Clooney on the beach.'

He smiles. 'That was a good day.'

'The best.'

'You look well. Have you changed your hair?'

I touch my mop self-consciously. 'No, only done nothing to it for a while. It's a mess.'

'No, no, it's lovely. It really suits you.'

'Thanks.'

He glances back towards Rupert, then looks at me again. 'How's Plum doing?'

I smile and pat the dome fondly. 'He seems fine. He's taken up martial arts.'

'Really?'

'Yes. Well, it's a tough world, you know. A foetus has got to know how to protect itself.'

'Of course. What's the instructor like?'

'Oh don't be ridiculous, Hector, he's still in the womb, there is no instructor. He's learning from a book.'

He laughs out loud, drawing the interested stares of people all around the room. I feel like I've been spotted having dinner with a celebrity.

'Same old Rachel. Still picking me up when I'm feeling low.'

I frown. 'Are you feeling low, then?'

'Oh, only always. Except when . . .' He clears his throat. 'Anyway, only three months to go now, I guess. Thought about names?'

Well, of course I have. If it's a boy, I want to call it Hector. And if it's a girl, I want to call it Hector. 'Not really. Wait and see what he looks like, I suppose. Maybe he's an Eric or a Toby.'

'Or a Cuthbert.'

'He's not a Cuthbert.'

'Wallace?'

'Nope.'

'Crispin?'

'Uh-uh.'

'Virgil then?'

'I'd rather die.'

He chuckles again. 'Of course.' He glances up at Rupert again who is signalling something. 'Look, Rachel, I have to go. I am so glad I've seen you.' He picks up my hand and stares at it for a second as he holds it gently in his fingers. He raises it a little, almost as if he's going to press it to his

331

lips, but he doesn't do that – of course he doesn't do that. 'Take care of yourself, Rachel. Bye.' He drops my hand, stands up and walks away from me.

Before he's even got back to where Rupert is standing, I am up and out of there like a hippo on rollerskates. I can hear Penny and Marion calling my name as I head to the exit, but I really don't want to face a load of questions about him right now. If ever. I can't bear to look at him and be in the same room as him and not be with him. It feels almost like actual physical pain and it's interfering with my breathing. I have to get away, get outside, to my car.

Here I am in the car with my head leaning on the steering wheel, weeping. This being in love with someone who doesn't feel the same is *awful*. Everything he's just said and done is playing through my mind in slow motion, on a loop. Every so often I pause it so I can have a better look: close-up of his face as he crinkles his eyes when he smiles at me; his eyes looking down at our hands while he's holding mine; his face when he spotted me in the crowd and fumbled his words. I've explained how good I am – well, used to be – at flirting and being sexy, and generally getting any bloke I fancied? Well, it goes without saying really that I am therefore pretty good at reading the signs when a bloke is interested – although, as I've said, I could generally take it as read that they were interested – and to me, Hector is showing signs of being interested. So either I'm misreading the signs, which is possible because this might well be the legitimate ordinary behaviour of a 'just good friends' friend, or he really is interested.

I don't often look puzzled, but that's it, right there.

Brows together, eyes moving around, fingers stretching out on the steering wheel. And tears still sliding down my face.

No, wait. There is a third option. He's interested in me, but not in Plum. Of course. He fancied me when he first met me, back in the summer when I was thin and sexy, but now that I look like Shamu the whale's big sister, he doesn't want to know. No, that doesn't work because he wouldn't be showing signs now, would he? So if the signs are there, and I'm reading them right, he's interested. But the fact that I'm carrying another man's baby is putting him off. That must be it. So he's not ever going to make a move, not even after Plum is born. That means that for me, it's either Hector or Plum.

Plum.

Or . . .

NO. Plum. No question.

I rub my hand over my mound again, feeling the hardness of the taut skin. 'Don't worry, Plum, you're the most important thing to me now.'

If you go forward five minutes, you'll find my car gone from its space in the Horizon car park. Go and look in the Ashton business park – that's where I am, hunched forward in the seat, snivelling as I peer through the darkness to see if I can find anything that looks like it might be McCarthy Systems. I have only ever been down here before to go to my doctor's surgery, and once to Cream Tease, so I have no idea what else is here. Hector probably does rent his office space, just on a larger scale than I imagined, so I need to look at all the boards by each building to see what companies are housed there.

Why am I doing this? It's torture, actually. Prying into

the different parts of the life of a man because I know he'll never show me his parts himself.

Oh, you know what I mean.

But I want to know all about him, as much as I can find out, every detail – where he works, where he lives, his hobbies, his friends – without arousing suspicion or being arrested for stalking.

I've driven past every building I can find, and I've read every sign outside every building, looking for the name McCarthy; and then as I round the corner having turned round for the third time, I spot it.

McCarthy Systems is not on one of the signs I've been reading. That's why I kept missing it. McCarthy Systems is written in huge, shining letters across the top of the building itself. Because McCarthy Systems doesn't rent office space inside a larger building. McCarthy Systems *is* the larger building.

I've parked on the side of the road and got out of the car to stare. Look at the size of the place. It's a four-storeyed building with glass sides and a staff car park. It's probably got a staff canteen and rest rooms with drink machines and water dispensers. There's probably a McCarthy Systems Christmas Party and people sitting at home with MS pens and MS stationery on their tables that they've pinched from the office. And Hector, my Hector, is their boss. He's their boss's boss's boss's boss. I'm gasping here.

In another place, a place that is felt but not ever seen, a tiny pair of black eyes flutter and slowly open for the first time. In vain they are staring into the impenetrable darkness, wet and sightless, now only waiting for the moment

334

when light will strike them and images will fill them, making them see.

I trudge back to my car and drive home, tears welling up again. I know that I have to choose, have chosen, Plum over Hector, but why, oh why, can't I just have both?

Let's leave me blubbing alone in my car for a moment – no need for you to see that – and go back to Horizon Holidays. Up at the front of the room, Hector is there, fidgeting. He's smiled and shaken hands with department manager after department manager, promising them all an easier more organized life with a virtually paper-free office, and now he has face-ache.

He'd known I was likely to be there somewhere, but he'd tried not to look for me, tried to keep his concentration. As soon as he'd seen me, of course, sitting there so tiny and sweet (*tiny?* bulbous more like), struggling to lean forward and reach the plate on the table because of the bump, he had longed to speak to me, longed to touch me, smell my hair . . .

It's a shame because I used some gorgeous cranberry and raspberry shampoo that morning, so my hair was smelling delicious.

No, he couldn't do that anyway, not in the circumstances. You can't go around smelling hair that belongs to another. He had tried to ignore me and carry on with his little speech, but it had proved impossible. He was like an alcoholic or a drug addict, unable to function until he had had a fix. He needed a fix now, dammit, but I'd already gone. He's frowning a bit, which with the fixed smile makes him look a little bit mad. But he is feeling mad. He acknowledges to himself that he needs a fix every bloody, damn day.

So now he's hiding in a corner, watching all the Horizon staff enjoying the free food and wine – courtesy not of Rupert de Witter, as everyone believes, but of McCarthy Systems – and tries to relax the muscles in his face. He is tense, though, and not just in his face. So he's fidgeting.

'Have a drink, mate,' Rupert says, nudging into him from behind. 'You did pay for it, after all!'

Hector smiles. 'No thanks, Rupe.'

'What's up?'

'Nothing. Just got to drive home later, that's all.'

'Oh.'

'Actually, Rupe, I do have a bit of a headache, so if it's all right with you, I'd like to . . .' He gestures towards the door.

'Course, mate, course. You head off. I'll see you in the week.'

'Yep, you will. Seeya.'

He claps Rupert gratefully on the back and starts to make his way through the crowd to the back of the room. He's glancing this way and that as he walks, desperately scanning the crowd. Who do you think he's looking for? Rupert's PA? The head of Data Processing? The toilets?

It's me, isn't it?

Anyway, I'm not there, I'm driving slowly home from the business park, my eyes swollen and bloodshot, my nose red and running. Thank God Hector can't see me. He continues to scan as he walks until eventually his eyes do fall on someone he recognizes. Can you make out who he's spotted? Or can you guess? He squints at the person, drawing nearer, trying to remember where he knows him. It was only recently, he's fairly sure of that. And of course it must have been inside Horizon's building. But where? In a corridor. In a darkened corridor, during the Christmas party, and at that moment, as he watches with loathing as this boy kisses and touches the girl next to him, his face contorts and his eyes narrow. Hector knows who it is.

This is the father of Rachel's baby, he's sure of it, and here he is, kissing some other girl. He is filled with molten fury and clenches his fists as he walks nearer, his eyes wild.

'Get up,' he demands in a low voice. They both turn to look at him.

'Mr McCartney, er – sir. Wh-what . . . ?'

'Just get up, please.' He's practically snarling. They both stand up and Hector looks at the girl.

'Not you. I suggest you go home.'

She looks at the boy and he nods, giving his permission. She glances up at Hector, then grabs her bag and jacket and hurries towards the door, glancing back over her shoulder repeatedly.

God, how seductive is that, that people just do his bidding? It's a good job I'm still booing in my car, all red nose and wet cheeks, and can't see Hector's command of the room. I would probably faint at his feet.

Hector bends slightly and puts his face very close to the boy's. 'Come outside, would you, just for a moment?'

The boy nods and follows him through the double doors and into the deserted lobby.

Hector turns to face him. 'You should be bloody ashamed of yourself.'

'Wh—?'

'You've got responsibilities, you little shit. What do you think you're doing?'

337

'I-I'm . . .'

'Don't answer that. It's perfectly obvious what you're doing. Messing around like that with her when you know you should be somewhere else.'

Nick receives a sudden moment of clarity and understanding, and a small smile turns up the corners of his mouth. 'Is this about me being married? Because it's not—'

'Married!' Hector puts his hands on his head in despair. 'Oh, this gets better and better!'

Nick puts his hands out. 'No, no, it's not like that . . .'

'Oh, just shut up. You're pathetic and disgusting. Why on earth she would want you . . .' He shakes his head.

Nick looks back towards the door, towards Paris. 'Why wouldn't she? And what's it got to do with you, anyway?'

'You don't know how lucky you are, you little bastard. You don't deserve what you've got.'

'Don't I?'

'No, you don't.' Hector lowers his head and brings his face eye to eye with Nick. He's at least four inches taller. 'Now you listen to me. You will end this relationship immediately, do you understand?'

'Or what?'

'Do I need to spell it out? You've probably noticed how much influence I have over Rupert de Witter. I'll leave it up to your imagination.'

'Are you threatening me?'

'Yes.'

'But you can't do that! I have a contract, and there's—'

'Do you want to try me?'

He hesitates. 'No.'

'Good.' Hector stares furiously at him for a few seconds,

then strides away towards the main door and out into the car park.

Nick watches him, then goes back through the double doors into the canteen where Paris is waiting.

'Oh God, Nick, what on earth was all that about?'

Nick shakes his head. 'I really don't know. Maybe he's heard this rumour about me being married or something.'

'But what's that got to do with him?'

'Maybe he's a really highly moral person and tries to stamp out adultery wherever he finds it. I don't know, babe. All I know is, he's threatened me with the sack.'

'Bloody hell! This is mad!'

'Yeah, I know.' He drapes his arm around her shoulders and plays with her hair. 'There's only one thing left for me to do.'

Here's Hector, marching violently away from Horizon. His face is twisted with anger and he is repeatedly clenching and unclenching his fists. He is thinking about that little shit who thinks it's all right to get someone pregnant, then fool around with someone else in plain view. Good God, she could have seen them there. Could that have been why she left in such a hurry?

He halts suddenly. Maybe she didn't leave? Maybe she just ran off into the Ladies to cry in private. He turns back towards the building. Takes one step. Then turns around again and resumes walking across the car park to his car. If she was in the Ladies, she would be surrounded by female friends all saying 'Oh God,' and 'It's awful,' while they surreptitiously check their hair in the mirror. She would neither want nor need him there.

But what if she doesn't know? Back in his car, he sits for a while holding his phone, staring at it. Should he tell her? What business is it of his? Well, she is his friend. Good friend. He is her friend. That's all. But is that all? Is there an ulterior motive? No, of course not. The fact that Nick is married – and therefore can't marry Rachel – is out there, but Hector is trying to do the right thing and ignore it. He just doesn't want to see her hurt. Is that all? Well, all right, he admits to himself, he would be delighted to see Nick out of the picture, but not if it means Rachel being hurt. So don't tell her. But she ought to know. What if he were in that position? Would he want to be told? Damn right he would and he would be bloody well annoyed if some-one he considered a good friend had known, and not told him. Right. Ring her then. OK. Good.

He dials her home number, which he took when she had her accident, and is taken aback when it's not answered by Rachel.

'Oh, er, hello. Is that the home of Rachel Covington?'

'Yeah, I'll just get her.' There are some muffled noises and as he listens he realizes suddenly that he had recognized that voice.

Sarah calls me to the phone when I am up to my elbows in hot soapy washing-up. I whip off the Marigolds and leave them on the coffee table in front of her, as a hint, and take the phone.

'Hello?'

'Hello again, Rachel. It's Hector.'

'Hi.' Sarah is settling back down on the sofa, the Marigolds dripping on to the carpet. I cradle the phone to my ear and go out into the hallway.

'Listen, was that Sarah who answered the phone?'

OH MY GOD! It hits me that in the nine days that Sarah has been with me, I have completely forgotten to tell Hector. I didn't even think about it at work today.

'Oh Hector, I'm so sorry, I completely forgot to tell you. Sarah has left Glenn.'

Remember when Hector was driving too fast to the hospital when I had my car accident, and he kept pulling out in front of lorries and cutting up taxi drivers? Well, here he is again, screeching out of the Horizon car park and speeding through the town. He arrives ten minutes later, and it's a journey that really ought to take twenty. But he knows how uncomfortable that two-seater is to sleep on and what he has heard has upset him a lot. I'm enjoying thinking that it's the thought of me on the two-seater that kept his foot firmly down on that accelerator.

He hammers on the front door until it's pulled open, then marches straight into the living room.

'Oh, hello, Hector.'

'I understand that your wife and child have left you?'

Glenn stares at a point in space in front of him. 'Yes, last week. Why?'

'Do you know where they are?'

'No. I don't even know where to look. I mean, she's got credit cards, passports, they could be anywhere in the world by now.'

'Did you try Jake's school?'

Glenn's eyes flick to Hector's without even moving his head. 'No I didn't. I didn't even think of that. I'm so tired all the time. Just can't stop sleeping. I haven't been to work, I can't eat. Look at me.' They both look down at his filthy greying dressing gown. 'I'm a mess. A complete wreck. I just can't . . .' Tears well up and spill over. 'I miss them, Hec, I just miss them so much. Please help me . . .'

Hector sighs. The sight of his little brother in this state has done a lot to cool his anger. He wanted to shout and scream at Glenn for being such a selfish idiot, but it's now obvious to him that Glenn is suffering for what he's done and doesn't need his brother telling him how stupid he was.

'They're staying with a friend of Sarah's – Rachel Covington.'

Glenn nods. 'Of course. Why didn't I think of her?'

'She's got a one-bedroomed flat, Glenn. Sarah and Jake share the bed while Rachel sleeps on the sofa. She's six months' pregnant.'

'Oh. What can I do to help? Do they need a new sofa or something?'

'No, of course not, you idiot. They need you to get out of here so they can move back in.'

Glenn is nodding vigorously. 'Yeah, sure, of course. I'll do that. Anything. But do you think Sarah will ever . . . ?'

'I can't say, Glenn. You'll just have to give her time. She's very hurt.'

'I know, I know. I've been so stupid. I didn't mean this to happen, I really didn't.'

'Oh shut up. You don't have an affair with someone by accident. The only thing you didn't want to happen was Sarah finding out and leaving you.'

Glenn looks hurt, and then looks sorry. He nods. 'You're right, Hec. I am scum.'

Hector puts his hand on his brother's arm and almost smiles at him with affection. And look at the effect that's having on Glenn. His face looks brighter, more animated, than it has since Sarah went, as if just knowing that he has his brother's support will help him cope. 'Glenn, you have to try to make this right again, do you understand? You have got to make amends.'

He nods again, more slowly. 'I will. I will do anything to get them back. Can I speak to them, do you think?'

'Eventually. But not yet. I think they will both feel a lot better once they are back in their own home. Give it a week or so, and then we'll try and set it up.'

'Right.' Tears are sliding silently down Glenn's face. 'I ended it, Hec. I swear to you. I ended it the day she left. Before she left. It was over. What am I going to do?'

Hector puts his arm around his pathetic brother. 'You are going to clean this place up, clean yourself up, and sort this whole thing out. All right?'

Glenn nods. 'All right. Can I stay with you?'

Chapter Nineteen

So Glenn moves in with Hector and Sarah and Jake can go home. It's too late to do anything that night, so Sarah and I agree that we'll spend the following day clearing up her stuff and moving her and Jake back in.

I am counting the minutes. I've even made a plan. As soon as they're gone, I'm going to lie down on my bed and have a snooze. In the middle of the day. I'm fantasizing about it. The smooth bed, clean, cool sheets, soft mattress. Silence and solitude. And sleep.

It's 6 o'clock on Saturday morning, the day after the staff meeting. I fell off the sofa again at half past five, which woke Plum up, after he'd finally dropped off about two, so I haven't been able to get back to sleep. My eyelids feel like they're made of hessian, scratching my eyeballs every time I blink, but I don't care. Later today, I will be inert on my own big bed.

I've made some toast and am standing in the warm kitchen, yawning and licking chocolate spread off my fingers. Outside it's all quiet and dark, apart from one or two birds starting to cheep sleepily, and the electric whine of the milkman's van. All the world is asleep apart from me and Plum, and it's lovely that it's just us two, sharing this peaceful moment together. I love the fact that from now on, I will always have someone to share these moments with; someone to talk to, someone to hug, someone to be with in the cold darkness of the early morning or the night's silent loneliness.

'Fucking awful night I've had,' Sarah announces loudly, coming suddenly into the kitchen. 'My child kept me awake half the fucking night.'

I jump and turn to look at her. Da-da-da-da-da-da, da-da-da-da-da-da.

'Yes, I know what you—'

'Clinging on, not letting me move even two inches away from him.' She yawns. 'I'm glad you're up. Any chance of some breakfast? I'll have what you're having.'

I make more toast and she munches away while I finish washing up the things from last night.

'Well, seeing as we're both up, we might as well make a start on the packing, mightn't we? You could be back home by . . .' I take a peek at my watch. It's nearly seven o'clock. '. . . half past ten, I should think. You must be dying to get home, Sarah.'

She shrugs. 'I suppose so. I do need to get a good night's sleep, I know that. Your bed is not very comfortable, is it?'

'Well, I've always—'

'Plus, this place is very cramped for the three of us, isn't it? I'm not criticizing – I mean, you've really only got room for one, haven't you, which is perfect for you, but it's not so great for us . . .' She trails off, remembering suddenly that I'm not going to be just one for much longer. 'I mean obviously there's enough room for you and a baby, but just not us as well.' She smiles weakly.

345

At this stage, I've got the feeling that there's a 'But' coming. She's listing all the reasons why she should want to be out of here, but if she really wanted to go, she wouldn't be listing reasons, she'd be packing. I'm not naive enough to think that she doesn't want to appear too eager to leave out of kindness.

'The thing is, Rach,' she says, not meeting my eye, 'I've never lived on my own.'

This is true. She went straight from living with her parents to living with Glenn. I don't see what relevance that little factoid has here, though.

'You won't be on your own. Jake will be there.'

'Oh, yeah, of course, I forgot about him. If there's a burglar, or a gas leak, I'll just send him out, shall I?'

'Well, no, obviously not, but what . . . ?'

She's fidgeting now, trying to smile and look . . . what is that expression? Pleading? I'm sure I'm not going to like what is coming. 'What I mean is . . . I really don't want to be in the house on my own.'

'Oh.'

If you could see crushing disappointment, it would look like my face. I have got little cloud pictures clustered round my head and they all show me stretched out asleep on my beautiful, big bed. Now, they all break apart and dissipate into mist, then vanish all together. Sarah's pleading face comes back into view, and behind it the microscope of my eyes zooms in on the tiny two-seater sofa – which apparently has a broken spring somewhere in its depths that corresponds exactly with the position of my arse when I lie on it – and behind that is the holocaust that used to be my living room.

I love my little flat but it's far too small for this many

346

people. I have accepted the fact that in a couple of years, when Plum needs his own room, I am going to have to think about moving. But right now, it's the perfect size, as long as it's just the two of us. Sleeping. 'But I really don't think it's a good idea for you both to stay here any longer – just because of the lack of space. As you said, it's far too small for more than one person – and their baby.'

'No, I agree.' Bells ring, the sun comes out and the birds start singing again. 'Actually, what I was thinking was maybe you could come and stay with me for a few days, in the spare room? There's a single bed and a small wardrobe, so you'd be very comfortable. And I'd really appreciate it. Please, Rach?'

When we were seventeen, Chrissie told me she was a lesbian. I stared at her in horror, thinking of all the things we'd been through together; everything I'd told her, everything she'd told me, the irreparable damage this was going to do to our friendship and how everything would have to change now. I was absolutely devastated.

Then she said, 'And I've lost your turquoise earrings. But that thing about me being a lesbian isn't true.'

What Sarah is suggesting is so much better than what I had imagined that I accept her proposal instantly. All right, I know, no peace or solitude. But right now, I've set my sights on a proper bed – a single will do – with a proper mattress and pillows and some sheets and blankets. The cloud pictures of me in a real bed pop back around my head like fireworks.

Getting into the car later – would you believe it's nearly half past *eleven* by the time we're finally leaving? – is an ordeal. If we go back an hour and a half, we can see that all Jake's toys are packed away into the carrier bag they came in and stuffed into the boot of Sarah's car. The clothes too. My packed bag has been on the back seat of my car since twelve minutes past eight. But you'll notice immediately what is missing from this quiet, still image of two parked cars in the cold winter sunshine – people. There is no sign of the three of us.

Back in the flat, Jake wants scuba-diving Action Man back out of the bag in the boot so he can hold him during the journey. It's a ten-minute journey, by the way.

'Oh, you can manage without him,' I'm saying, at exactly the same moment Sarah says, 'Oh, all right then, Jakey.' I snap my head round to glare at her, but she's already heading back to the car to unpack all the toys.

Scuba-diving Action Man, by the way, is an evasive bastard. He's not where he's meant to be, and is eventually tracked down at the bottom of the box of Lego. Good job he had oxygen tanks on.

Forty-five minutes after everything was packed into the car, it gets packed in again. At this point, I realize that I'll have to take Cosmo with me. I get his carry case down from on top of the kitchen cupboard. It's a huge grey plastic box with slatted holes everywhere to let light in and a swing door made of thin steel bars at the front. Sarah is eyeing it suspiciously.

'What's that for?' she says.

'It's my make-up case,' I say, unsnapping the barred door on the front. 'I need to look my best – you never know who you might meet.'

She frowns, either not liking the sarcasm or not understanding it. 'It looks like a pet carrier.'

'Yes, Sarah, that's exactly what it is.'

'For what?'

I bite my tongue. What I want to say is, 'Two lions, two giraffes, two peacocks,' but I leave it. Sarah knows that I have a cat, only one cat, and therefore is not asking who the pet carrier is for but more why I think I need to use it.

'He's got to come, Sarah. There's no one else to feed him.'

'I can't have a cat in the house, Rachel. What if it picks at the carpet or the furniture and does loads of damage? I've got enough on my plate to worry about without that adding to it. Plus, there are the germs. I remember that thing about toxoplasmosis in the pooh. It's a really serious bug – it can cause brain damage or even death in children.'

'Sarah, for heaven's sake, you and Jake have been here for over a week and it didn't bother you. Why is it likely to be any different at your house?'

She pouts. 'Well, what if it does some damage?'

I've seen Sarah's house. I don't think there's much damage that Cos could do there that Jake and time haven't already done. The milk, food and juice stains that now appear on my living-room carpet (*I don't mind, I don't mind*) feature much more heavily on hers. Plus, I'm doing her a favour, moving in with her for a few days. If she wants me, she has to put up with my cat too.

But when people's husbands have affairs, you don't tell them how unreasonable and selfish they're being. She could park three caravans full of bag people on her front lawn and dance naked round the garden in a drug-induced high while playing loud slash-metal music until two o'clock in the morning, and the neighbours would all tolerate it behind their curtains and say to their horrified visitors, 'Her husband had an affair.' To which the visitors would all nod their understanding, 'Oh, I *see*.'

Anyway, I am trying to do Sarah an enormous favour by giving up my home and moving across to the other side of town, to sleep in a strange bed, even though I'm heavily pregnant, and she is being difficult, unreasonable and selfish.

'What if he stays in the garage?'

She tuts, sighs, makes a big show of thinking about it for ages, then says, 'I suppose so.'

I chase Cos into his box, feeling very guilty about what I have just agreed for him. Still, it's only a few days.

'But if it makes a mess, you clear it up.'

I'm not even going to remind her that the toxoplasmosis bacteria are more harmful to unborn babies.

When we arrive, we are both delighted and relieved to find that the house is immaculate and there are vases of fresh flowers everywhere. Glenn has obviously gone to a lot of trouble to welcome her back into her home, even though he's not doing it in person. It's a nice touch and from Sarah's face, I think he scored a few Brownie points, even though she mutters, 'Stick some flowers in a vase and everything's all right again . . . ?'

Cosmo sprints off across the garden, belly low to the ground, tail flat. I wonder if I'll ever see him again.

I carry my bag up to the spare room, where there are more fresh flowers and clean sheets. The January sun is slanting across the bed, putting it into a spotlight, and it seems to get bigger, filling the entire room until it's the only thing I can see in there. It looks so wide and smooth, the quilt pulled neatly flat at the edges, as inviting as a field of freshly fallen snow.

I sit on the end and bounce a couple of times, pushing my shoes off with my toes and rubbing my feet over each other. I yawn mightily, stretching upwards, then flop backwards with my arms above my head. Yes, it's a very comfortable bed, but compared to my two-seater sofa, Sarah's kitchen table looks pillowy. Now that I've tried it out, I should go back downstairs and see if Sarah's all right, but I can't breathe properly lying on my back any more, so I shuffle up the bed until my head's on the pillow, roll on to my side and close my eyes. Relaxed exhaustion descends on me and all my limbs grow heavy. I picture them made of warm lead, sinking deeper and deeper into the softness of a marshmallow mattress.

A sudden jolt brings me fully awake, eyes wide with surprise. Plum seems to be having a tantrum in there, lashing out with his hands and feet, blissfully unaware of how it feels from this end. I sit up and put my hands on my belly, feeling Plum move past. 'You all right in there, Plum?' I say out loud, and the thrashing stills for just a moment. 'Can you hear me, little baby?' I say in wonder. 'Are you listening to your mum's voice?'

'Don't get used to that,' Sarah says going past on the landing, 'once he comes out, he'll never listen to you again.'

Looking at my watch, I'm amazed to find that I've been up here for about two and a half hours. I go out on to the landing and see Sarah's bedroom door close, so I head downstairs to see what my godson is up to.

Jake is in the living room, slumped on the sofa, eyes glazed as he watches a strange programme about a boy who looks like a bath sponge. He does not look very happy to be home, which surprises me. I thought he would be much more comfortable in familiar surroundings, with all his toys and books to hand. But he's slumped on the sofa, watching television, eyes glazed. Under one arm he's clutching a brown furry thing that could be a teddy bear. I notice that he's sucking his thumb, which is something I haven't seen him do since he started school over two years ago. There's a funny smell in the room, too – a rather unpleasant, acrid smell that wafts over to me in bursts. I can't identify it so I presume it must be something outside.

'Hey, Jakey, wotcher watching?' I say, bouncing into the room, trying to be his godmother. He's having none of it though. 'Is it good?' I try again, but he still doesn't reply. He doesn't even look at me. I walk over to where he's sitting and the smell becomes stronger, a pungent, ammonia smell and suddenly I identify it. It's urine. I glance at Jakey and sure enough there's a large dark area on his trousers around his groin.

God, now what do I do? My first thought is Sarah, but she hasn't emerged from her room, so I'm assuming she's having a kip while Jake is busy watching telly. I can't disturb her. So I'm left with two options: leave him like it, or sort him out.

Looking back at him over my shoulder, I walk out of the room and head back upstairs. I'm going to run a bath, for heaven's sake. You didn't think I'd leave him like that, did you?

In his room, which is also beautifully tidy, I find some clean pants and trousers in a chest of drawers. As I turn to walk out, I notice some bright red, shiny paper in tatters on the floor, and a cardboard box that says 'Bear Factory' on it. It's the only thing out of place in there, so I crouch down to have a look. The red paper has a tag attached to it that says, 'Jake, please look after this bear for me. His name is Bert. He needs lots of love and cuddles. All my love, Daddy. xxx' The Bear Factory box has been pulled – or pushed – open, and its contents lifted – or climbed – out. It reminds me for a second of one of those monster movies where the scientists find the cage empty, with the bars prised apart, and start to look around worriedly. Bert is at large in the house.

Getting Jake to come upstairs for a bath isn't as hard as I thought it would be. I just said to him, 'Come upstairs for a bath, Jakey,' and he stood up. He's still clutching the brown furry thing under his arm and I deduce that this is Bert, thankfully now captured and restrained. I leave Jake in privacy while he gets out of his clothes and into the bubbly water, and once I hear that he's safely submerged, I knock and go back in. I've found a book in his room called *Harry's Half Adventure*, so I sit on the toilet seat. Bert is peering at me intensely from the window sill.

'Would you like me to read you a story?' I ask him.

''Splease,' he says and I get a huge whoosh of pleasure. He spoke to me! And he seems to have good manners.

'All right then. This is called . . . *Jake's Half Adventure*.' As I read the story, I'm changing all the Harrys to Jakes, which is not as easy as it sounds. I suspect that Jake has heard this one already, and once or twice when I accidentally say, 'But Harry didn't go left, like he always does,' Jake calls out, '*Jake!*' He smiles at me and we share a small moment of connection. It leaves me almost unable to carry on reading.

When the story is done, I tell him he needs to get out now and I stand up, ready to leave him in privacy to wrap himself in a towel, but he stands up in the water and puts his arms out to me, waiting to be lifted out.

'You want me to pick you up?'

He nods.

'What, a great big fourteen-year-old like you?'

'I'm six.'

'Oh. Well, in that case . . .' and I swoop down on him with the towel, bundle him up and lift him out. He's not giggling, but he is smiling a little. Just a little.

Between us we get him dry and dressed and head off back downstairs – not forgetting to retrieve Bert from the window sill. As I follow him down, Jake looks so much younger to me now than he did at his party nearly six months ago. He has Bert under one arm and the thumb of his other hand plugged firmly in his mouth. His hair at the back is damp still around the collar and his little neck looks so tender and precious as he bends his head forward. I don't know if it's Plum inside me or the sadness of what's happened, but I'm feeling a very strong urge to wrap this little boy up in my arms and protect him from ever being hurt again.

Towards the bottom of the stairs, he stumbles slightly and as he recovers his balance his arms go out and Bert falls from his grip. As it hits the floor, a strange thing happens. It speaks.

'I love you, Jake,' it says, in a growly bear voice.

Jake and I freeze, staring at the thing lying on the floor in the hallway as if it's been possessed by the evil restless spirit of a long-dead doctor who liked to disembowel people and stuff them at the weekend.

'Bert can talk!' Jake eventually exclaims, turning round to me with a great big grin on his face. 'Did you hear that?' And he leaps over the last remaining stair to land at Bert's side. Apparently it was just me that thought it was possessed. Jake picks him up and squeezes him hard in the belly.

'I love you, Jake,' says the bear, although this time, because I'm expecting it, I realize that it's not a soulless, demonic voice that strikes terror and dread into the heart of every man, woman and child. It's Glenn.

'I love you, Jake,' it says again, and again, as Jake presses and presses and presses. After the fifth time I am sure, and I think that Jake is sure too, whose voice that is, even though it's been disguised to sound growly and bear-like.

Sarah comes down after a couple of hours. I've done my best to wash the damp sofa cushion and it's outside on the line. Sarah looks at it quizzically, turning towards Jake with a frown.

'I spilt some coffee,' I say hurriedly, wondering as soon as I've said it why I did. Surely Sarah needs to be aware if Jake has started wetting himself? It might be linked to Glenn's departure. I'll tell her later, after he's in bed. 'Sorry.'

She shrugs and heads for the kettle.

Jake looks at me and smiles again. I really am starting to feel like a godmother.

'I love you, Jake,' says Bert suddenly, and Sarah jumps. 'What the hell was that?'

'It's Bert,' says Jake, pressing his tummy. 'I love you, Jake.'

Sarah of course recognizes the voice instantly. I hear her muttering, 'Few flowers and a recording in a bear, still doesn't . . .'

I notice that once Jake and Sarah are reunited, Jake's whole demeanour changes. While Sarah was sleeping, he definitely perked up, once I'd got him away from the telly, and he actually smiled for the first time I've seen since they turned up at my flat. But now, sat snuggled up in front of the telly next to his mum, he's become withdrawn and subdued again. It's obviously having a bad effect on him to see his mum so sad all the time. Maybe, after nearly two weeks, he's adapted to his dad not being around now, but can't deal with his mum's depression.

We phone for pizza. No one wants to cook and no one should have to.

The three of us settle into an awkward routine over the next few days. I'm usually awake by six o'clock, so I get Jake up and let Sarah sleep on.

'Good morning, Harry.'

'*Jake!*'

Then I drop him off at school before heading on to work. It's great practice and now I'm wondering why I always used to think I didn't know how to talk to him.

In the evenings, I've taken to soaking in a hot bath after Jake's in bed. It's one of the few places where I can get comfortable these days as the bump kind of floats to the surface, and it gets me away from the black hole that is Sarah. She's sucking all the life and light out of everything at the moment. Five minutes in her company and you start to feel lethargic and cheesed off. She's like that thing in *Star Trek* that makes all the crew start fighting with each other.

This routine goes on the same for about three weeks, so we can skip forward a bit. You can see from her face that Sarah's mood hasn't really improved, but I feel like I am actually doing some good here. Jake's talking a lot more, although still silent and miserable around his mum, and Cosmo's got a good social life going with the other moggies in the neighbourhood. I'm proud of him for making the effort to get out there and make friends.

Anyway, I'm sleeping as well here as I would in my own bed and the truth is, Sarah's house is a bit nearer Horizon. Those five minutes make a difference when you're on your way home from work thirty-two weeks' pregnant.

Here I am, in the bath, relaxing, eyeing the tip of the iceberg that is my belly. Don't come in, just stay at the door. The days of me not minding being seen naked are long gone.

Plum doesn't have much room in there now, so he's constantly trying to get comfortable, stretching his arms and legs out as far as they'll go. I love to watch this activity under my skin, his limbs and head fading in and out of view like a seal glimpsed through dark water. It's the most peculiar thing I've ever seen, like a slow-motion miniature earthquake. I can't look at my belly button any more since it popped out into a hard, pink marble, but there are other changes going on that still surprise me.

'Hey, Sarah, my nipples have gone brown,' I announce, walking into the living room in my dressing gown ten minutes later, and come eye to eye with Hector. I freeze in the doorway. He is sitting in the chair by the fire, his eyes smiling at me and I can feel my face going red.

'Good news, then?' he asks, a smile just visible at the corners of his mouth.

I nod. 'I've finally done it, after months of trying.'

'You must be very proud.'

I laugh. 'So, so proud.'

'Hector was just telling me how you two know each

other,' Sarah's saying in the background somewhere. 'You kept that quiet, Rachel.'

We're still smiling at each other. I cross the room and sit down on the sofa next to Sarah, my eyes on his the whole time.

'Rach? I said, you kept it quiet, that you've known Hector all this time.'

'Oh, er, no, not really. I mean, I didn't know for a long time that he was Glenn's brother, and then, when we found out, well . . .' I stop smiling as I remember suddenly how we came to find out the connection with Sarah and Glenn. It was back in August, when I blurted out that I'd seen Glenn with another woman.

'It was around the time that Mum died,' Hector says smoothly, coming to my rescue. 'Which is also about the time that you found out you were pregnant.' He turns back to me and his voice softens. 'We didn't really think about alerting all our friends to the fact that we knew each other, did we?'

I shake my head.

'Oh,' says Sarah. She's not really listening anyway. *Casualty* is on and the television screen is filled with the image of a blood-smeared shard of glass sticking out of a leg. Hector and I continue our conversation around her, in hushed voices.

'You look amazing,' he says to me. I know he means, 'You look like a bungalow!'

'Hmm. Thanks.'

'Are you all right? I mean . . .' He inclines his head towards Sarah. 'Comfortable?'

'Oh, yes, yes, it's fine. Actually, it's nearer work so—'

'But further from the hospital.'

'Yes, but it won't be a panicky journey, when I do go.'

'How will you get there? Is Nick taking you?'

I stare at him. I don't even remember telling him the name of the father. Or did I? 'No, no, I haven't even—'

'Look, you two, I'm really shattered. Would you mind if I go up?' She doesn't wait for an answer and leaves the room.

Hector and I are alone. We look at each other, smile and then quickly look away. The way that he's looking at me makes me feel eighteen, thin and sexy again, not a huge, bloated lump of lard, with a baby swimming around inside.

'How's everything going at Horizon?' I ask him.

'Yes, good, so far. The people in the IT department that have seen the programme are pleased . . .' He trails off. 'I haven't seen you there at all.'

'I've been there! Come on, you can't miss me.'

'I do though,' he says and I'm all flustered, wondering if I really know what he means.

'You just need to look harder. There aren't many places where a person this size can hide out. Luckily I'm in Telesales, so the office is open plan. I don't know what I'd do if I worked in one of those tiny DP cubicles. I'd probably just have to stay there until the baby comes out.'

He puffs air out through his nose in a tiny acknowledgement of me trying to be funny. 'Listen, Rachel, you're not neglecting yourself, are you?'

I look down at my rather faded and shabby orange dressing gown, with a faint egg-yolk stain on the front, and my cheerful sexy smile droops suddenly. What on earth was I thinking of, feeling thin and attractive? 'What are you trying to say?'

'No, no, I don't mean that. I'm just worried that you're so focused on helping your friend that you're not thinking about yourself. You should be resting, taking it easy, not worrying about someone else.'

'I know, but—'

'It's the last chance you'll get for a while to be selfish.'

I really don't know what to say to this. I'm sure he's right, but I don't feel stressed or tired, and Sarah's spare bed is very comfortable. Plum elbows me hard in the ribs suddenly, as if to remind me that I need to say something, and I gasp, clutching my side.

'You all right?'

I nod quickly. 'Yes, fine. It's just this one, moving around. He's got sharp little elbows.' I hesitate for a moment, looking at Hector. He's slid to the front of his seat, as if he was about to get up. 'Would you . . . like to feel it?'

His eyes widen. 'Can I?' I nod again and he moves from the chair over to the sofa next to me.

'You're going to have to get nearer,' I say, and he shuffles right up next to me so there's a line of contact between us all the way down one side, his left and my right, from our shoulders, down our arms to our thighs. I can feel the warmth of his leg pressing against mine. Look how close his face is to mine. And you can see, even from here, what effect it's having on me. I'm jittery and keep looking at him, then quickly looking away. It's very hard to meet someone's eyes from this distance, even if they're short, ugly trolls.

I take his hand and lay it gently down on the part of my belly that's quaking. After a few seconds I feel the pressure of Plum from the inside, and Hector gasps as he feels it from the outside.

'Wow! It's exactly how I imagined it would be.'

This is a bit odd, that he has been imagining what my baby will feel like in my tummy. I stiffen and he removes his hand quickly.

'No, no, God no, I don't mean yours.' He shuffles away from me on the sofa again. 'Oh Christ, please don't think . . . I'm really not a . . .' He stops and rubs the back of his head. 'Perhaps I had better explain.' He leans forward and stares at the carpet.

'I met Miranda at work. One of my department managers took her on in the advertising department. She walked into my office one day . . .' He smiles a little and looks up at me, head bowed. 'I'm not trying to impress you or sound arrogant or big-headed, but you have to imagine how inappropriate this was. I mean, do you think one of the people who work in advertising in Horizon would simply walk into Rupert de Witter's office?'

'God, no.'

'Well, there's an established protocol, isn't there? Even the department managers don't simply walk in. I mean, I'm not one of those remote managers that's never seen by their staff. I go to all the meetings, I make sure I walk around each department at least once every week.'

'Uh-huh.'

'But they still make appointments to see me, when they need to. It's just a courtesy. So anyway, she walks in. I have seen her before, you know, when I was doing the rounds, but I can't really remember her. She tells me she's Miranda Waters and starts really flirting with me, right there in my office. I've got this mountain of work to get through but I'm sitting there talking to this woman about what we like doing in our spare time. She intrigued me.'

'When I left the office that evening, she's there, all alone in the lobby. It turns out she's waiting for me. I mean, this was getting on for nine o'clock in the evening, so she must have been there for a long time.' He rubs his face with his hand. 'I think she made me her little project.

'Anyway, after six months she decides we're perfect for each other and moves in with us. I wasn't sure about how this would affect Mum, you know, but Miranda wouldn't listen to my objections. To be fair, I didn't voice them very loudly. I was weak . . .

'Well, it wasn't a grand passion, or anything, but we were together for four years, all together.' He's staring at his hands. 'Just over two years ago, she told me she was pregnant.'

I kind of suspected this was coming.

'I was . . .' He looks up at me. 'I was stunned. I'd been having second thoughts about the relationship, and then she tells me she's having our baby. Of course, I couldn't tell her then that I wasn't convinced we should stay together, so I carried on as if everything was fine. The one good thing about our relationship at this point was the baby. I was delighted about it, thrilled, but I had reservations about Miranda. Sometimes she seemed a bit . . . unstable. She would fly into a rage about nothing and I would think about the stress of a crying baby and whether or not it would tip her over the edge. I tried to convince myself that it would be good for her – the responsibilities of motherhood to bring her down to earth, you know.' He laughs bitterly and shakes his head. 'I needn't have worried. A month or two later we had a blazing row – one of many – and she tells me the baby isn't mine. Then she shrieks that she's going to kill it and storms out of the house.'

He stands up and walks over to the fire.

We have to pause a moment here. Fix your eyes on Hec's face. He seems to be a bit tortured, doesn't he? Just look at the pain behind those eyes, the agony he must have suffered, the anguish he went through. I love that look. You can tell just by looking at me, gazing at him hungrily. George Clooney could walk in behind me in a pair of boxer shorts and say, 'Hey, Rach, great to see you again, wanna get married?' and I probably wouldn't even notice him.

'I can't begin to describe my feelings at that moment,' Hector says. 'I have never been as low, either before or since. I stood there in the hallway of my home after she had slammed the door and I actually felt like I didn't want to go on with my life.'

'Oh, Hec.'

'Well, thank goodness I had Mum. She gave me a reason to keep going.' He clears his throat and turns round to face me. 'Anyway, that wasn't the end of it. She came back that same evening, all apologetic and contrite, so we carried on.'

'Even though . . . ?'

'Yes, even though she had thrown this huge boulder of doubt into the air. But I was so desperate for the baby to be mine, I just avoided it.'

'So what . . . ?'

'Ah, you haven't heard the best bit yet. I didn't realize quite how unhinged Miranda was, you see. As the weeks went by, she didn't . . . she didn't get bigger. Just stayed the same. She was very thin.

'So finally I asked her if she'd been to the doctor, and was the baby growing properly. I was genuinely worried

363

about the baby, and about her. And she looks at me and says, really calmly and matter-of-fact, as if it's the most ordinary thing in the world, "Oh you didn't believe all that rubbish about a baby, did you? I'm not pregnant, you idiot. I made it up."'

'Fuck.'

'Yes, that's what I thought. So all that stuff about the baby not being mine, and then insisting that it was and that she'd only said it wasn't to hurt me, and all the time there was no baby at all. I was staggered. I mean literally. I just sat in the kitchen for two hours to get this new information into my head. We broke up that day. She moved out and resigned from her job. I haven't seen her since. I suspect that she's still mystified over why I was so upset.'

I stare at him. I remember Sarah telling me about 'the Miranda business' but she had said that Miranda had lost the baby.

'Sarah told me that Miranda had a miscarriage.'

'Well, the truth is, I was embarrassed to admit to having been so easily deceived. I told everyone that it was a miscarriage. It was easier than the truth.'

'But why did she . . . ?'

He shakes his head. 'I can't imagine. There was nothing to be gained by making that up. The only thing I can think is that she sensed I was considering ending the relationship and came up with a pregnancy to keep us together. She was always going to get found out, though, so it really only delayed the inevitable. And she made no attempt to fake the symptoms, you know, to convince me it was real. But then, I think sometimes people believe the thing they really want to be the truth, even if the evidence points to it not being.' He smiles and looks at me pointedly, and I wonder if he's trying to say something else. 'So, there you are. I was nearly a father once. Except that I wasn't. I've never told anyone that, not even Glenn.'

'Thanks for telling me.'

'Who else would I tell? You're the only complete stranger in my life.'

The next day at work, I've decided to make my pregnancy official, especially after what Hector said about taking more care of myself. I mean, of course everyone already knows about it – there aren't any blind people in Telesales – but I need to get maternity leave and things sorted. I've only got seven and a half weeks to go before it's born.

I manage to speak to Jean over by her desk. Hector told me that my employer is obliged to offer me a package, seeing as I've been working there for seven years, and he says it's probably something like eighteen weeks on ninety per cent of full pay, followed by six months on statutory maternity pay.

'How much is that then?' I asked. He said it was about a hundred pounds a week, and that might cover seventy per cent of my rent. Great. He suggested that I think about going back to work part time after it's born. Apparently, if I'm on a low income, which I will be, I can get tax credits from the government. And I'll get about fifteen quid a week child benefit too. Let's not forget that.

'I need to speak to you about maternity leave, Jean,' I say, and Graham jumps out of his chair and hurries off to the other end of the office.

'Oooh, aren't you getting big?' Jean says and puts her hand on my belly. I flinch. This is so intrusive. Apparently, when you're expecting, you become public property.

When that woman in Complaints had to go on steroids and blew up like a barrage balloon, did people walk up to her and say, 'Ooh, Linda, aren't you getting big?' and put their hands all over her to have a feel? No, they bloody well did not.

'When are you due?' Jean asks me.

'My *baby* is due on the twentieth of April, Jean.'

'And will you be breast-feeding?' Now she's asking me about my breasts!

'I haven't decided yet. But I do need to sort out my maternity leave.'

'Got a leaving date yet?' she asks abruptly, looking over my shoulder.

'Erm, well I suppose around the middle or end of March. Do you need a specific date now?'

'As soon as possible please.'

'Oh. Right. And what am I entitled to in terms of —?'

'Yes, yes, all right, I'll have to look it up. Leave it with me.'

You know, she's not a very nice person. I used to idolize her – she's so great at making the sales – but actually she's quite unpleasant. I suppose that to make lots of sales you have to be unpleasant, using guilt to persuade people to part with money and buy something they don't really want. If you really love your husband/wife/fiancé, you'll spend a bit more on your honeymoon/anniversary/trip to visit your daughter, won't you?

'You're not forcing them to do anything they don't really want to do,' she always says, but I disagree. If they wanted a two-week holiday in Las Vegas, they wouldn't phone up and ask for a week in the Algarve, would they?

As I'm standing here, let's just have a look at the sales

figures. You can see that I'm way down at nineteenth now. Val has slipped from her third-place spot back to fourteenth. Good. She's obviously got more things to think about again, than just making the sales. Marion is still at number one and look! Paris is fifth! I'm quite chuffed to be at the bottom.

I don't think Jean has ever been married, or had kids. I guess that her ancient sales record will remain until some other socially inept, single-minded loner comes along and takes it from her. I thought it was going to be me. I'm glad that it isn't.

Val is absent from her desk when I get back to mine. In fact, there seem to be a lot of people missing from their desks. I crane my head up over the partition to look around the room and spot Val, over in the corner, huddled together with Simon, Mike and Martin, poring over something. At that moment, she spots me looking and signals to me to come over.

'Have you seen this?' she says, sniggering as I walk over.

I look at what she's holding. It's a blue ring-binder, with lots of loose sheets inside it. 'Yes, of course I have.' It's the daily bulletin folder for Telesales. The Product Design department and other parts of Sales put messages in there whenever they want us to push a particular resort, or if there's a special offer we need to know about. We're all supposed to read it every day, but I haven't looked at it in over a week. I've been trying to give people the holiday they've phoned up for.

'Have you looked at it *today*?'

'No, of course I haven't,' I say, laughing. 'Should I have?'

'Here you go, there's a chair, read it immediately, I want to see your face. And you might need a moment or two to

367

recover afterwards.' I look at Val and I notice for the first time that she's wiping away a tear. 'You'll love it!' she adds, giggling as she drags a chair over and motions for me to sit down.

Simon, Mike and Martin chuckle as they head back to their respective desks. Val raises her eyebrows expectantly, so I turn to today's date, and start to read.

From: Nick Maxwell, Personnel Dept.   ·   27 February
To : All Departments

Can I please advise everybody that the malicious spreading of untrue rumours about other people is libel, and anyone found to be doing these rumours will be spoken to about them. To this can I add that the above mentioned rumour about me being married is wholly untrue and without foundations, so whoever is doing it should be aware that I am not bothered by it, so you are wasting your time. I am not, I repeat not married, so everyone please ignore any further repeat of this rumour.

Thank you for your attention.

I blink at the page a few times, then read it again. Is this *real*? Has Nick Maxwell actually gone into print and circulated a memo to the whole of Horizon to inform all three-hundred-odd staff how totally *un*bothered he is by this rumour? I snort out one fat laugh, then a few more come.

'Methinks he doth protest too much,' Val says suddenly. I turn to look at her.

'Well, I think he's a cock,' I say, and we both collapse into undignified giggles.

Chapter Twenty

See that strange asymmetrical mountain of white jelly quivering over there? That's me. I'm in another ante-natal appointment and Katy is checking the baby's heartbeat.

I've decided to work until the end of March, which is in just under two weeks. Just two weeks to go at work. It's so strange to think how going to work used to be everything to me – well, apart from all the parties, shopping for shoes, having my highlights done and the fortnightly waxing – and now I can't wait to stop going there. After Plum arrives, I'm going to work part time and use either a child minder or my mum, depending on whether I want the child minded or my lifestyle criticized. Katy says that mums need social interaction with other adults to keep them sane. I think she means that with their only human contact for four years being a person who only eats, sleeps and shits, a woman would go mad. Presumably that's why two out of four marriages end in divorce.

Katy is very good at her job, isn't she? She reaches around my very own Taj Mahal, threads the monitor straps behind me, velcros them together, locates the heartbeat, measures it, checks the digital display showing beats per minute, assures herself that it's fine, writes it down, unstraps me, wheels the monitor machine away and helps me up, all while she's asking me if I'm keeping well.

'Not really. A friend of mine has been going through a tough time so I'm staying in her spare room at the moment. It's OK though – I don't think I would be able to sleep any better in my own bed.'

Katy is looking serious. 'It's not just about the sleep, though, Rachel love. Are you managing to put your feet up during the day?'

'Well, I'm still working full time. And then I help Sarah out with her little boy most evenings. And mornings. And I'm helping her keep on top of her ironing pile. And the hoovering and dusting. And I cook a couple of times a week. But, you know, only spag bol or something. Nothing fancy.'

Katy takes hold of both my hands in hers and rubs them together. 'It's time for you to go home now, Rachel,' she says, and you can see on her face how serious she is. 'I'm not trying to be funny but you've got a massive, painful, physical trauma ahead of you, which is going to flatten you and leave you drained and exhausted, possibly depressed and tearful and feeling totally shitty. But you are not going to be able to recuperate properly because you are going to be the sole person in charge of a tiny, vulnerable and needy baby, which will terrify you.'

Why would I think she was trying to be funny?

'You won't get another chance to be selfish for a very long time,' she's saying, but I almost don't hear her. Look at my bloodless face and wide staring eyes – I'm seriously traumatized here.

But her words do eventually filter through, only because

I recognize them. It's almost exactly what Hector said. My eyes are refocusing gradually and I am coming back into the room. I see Katy picking up my pink folder, now thick with eight months of notes, tests and graphs.

'Now then, today is the nineteenth of March. I'll need to see you every week from now until she's born.' He, I correct her silently. 'I'm afraid that she's still head up, and probably won't turn round now, so you're going to have to make a decision, poppet.'

Is this the choice to end all choices? Have a baby the size of a basketball pulled through a 'canal' (at this point its name changes from 'vagina' to 'birth canal', just so you are in no doubt at all what God made it for) the width of a mobile phone; or have three thicknesses of your abdomen – and that means skin, muscle, womb, the lot – sliced open and introduced to the world, leaving you in agony and paralysed. Hm.

'Yes, I've been thinking about this. A lot. Almost every moment.' Those pictures in *Parenting* magazine flash past my eyes like police evidence – exhibits A to M, a case for the defence. 'I'm pretty sure I want to go for the caesarean.'

'Sure?'

'No. No, actually I'll have a vaginal delivery.'

She frowns at me. She thinks I'm messing around. 'Rachel?'

You know, at this point I've decided I'd rather not do either one. I've changed my mind. I don't really want to have this baby after all; I'll just leave him up there.

'Caesarean.'

'Good, all right then, come back and see me again next Monday and we'll check to see if she's turned. If she hasn't, we'll book you in for the caesarean. You might have your baby in two weeks, Rachel.'

Terrific. I don't think I'll be ready in two years, let alone two weeks.

So I go back to work knowing that whatever happens, caesarean or not, Friday of next week will definitely be my last day there. Until afterwards, that is. At the moment, the birth itself is so huge in my mind that I can't see past it. It feels like I've just got to get through this one unpleasant thing, and then it'll all be over, like having your tonsils out. I have to keep reminding myself that after the birth is when everything starts.

I'm at my desk, look, and I'm on the phone you'll be pleased to note. Don't look too closely or you'll see an 'O' in the display window, telling you it's an outgoing call, to social services. I ask the woman to send me a list of registered child minders.

'While you're at it, can you send me information about having a baby put up for adoption?'

'What?'

'Just kidding.'

There's a sudden small pressure inside me as if Plum has anxiously pressed his little hand against me. 'It's all right,' I say to him softly, rubbing the place he pressed, 'you're staying with your mummy.'

Skip forward to me arriving home – or rather, back at Sarah's – at half past five. You can see that I'm looking anxious and the reason is that I'm dreading Sarah's reaction to the news that I'm moving back home. She's so miserable at the moment, with only me and Jake for company, so when I'm gone she'll only have Jake. I'm not sure she will be able to handle not having me around.

'OK,' she says.

I'm trying really hard not to feel pissed off about that. 'Sarah, listen, there's a very good chance I'm going to have to have a caesarean delivery—'

'Really? Why?'

'He's upside down. Anyway—'

'I had a Caesar with Jake.'

'Yes, I know. I wanted to ask you—'

'Bloody agony. People who have natural deliveries think that we caesars have it easy, but they don't know the half of it. It feels like someone's shoved a white-hot pitchfork into your belly and they're twisting your insides round like spaghetti. You feel like, if you stand up straight, you'll tear at the seams; if you cough, you'll blow apart . . .' (just look at my white face a moment while she's talking!) '. . . and every move you make is like knives. Getting up at two o'clock in the morning is bad enough, without the searing pain across your entire abdomen when you try and get up or pick the baby up or hold the baby on your lap. And I bled for twelve weeks afterwards, you know.'

My throat's working, trying to get up enough fluid to moisten it. 'I know, Sarah. That's partly why I wanted to ask you—'

'What?'

'Well, I'm thinking about having an epidural so I can stay awake, which means I get to have someone to come in with me to hold my hand. Obviously, it won't be the father, so I wondered . . . Will you come into the operating theatre with me and watch while they slice me in half?'

And that is why I've asked her: she's smiling for the first time in ages. 'Really, Rachel? You want me in there with you?'

'I do.'

'I'd love to!' She gets up off the sofa and comes over to me for a hug. 'Thank you so much for asking. This is going to be amazing.'

Move your gaze away from Sarah and me embracing a moment, and look at the other person in the room. He's on the sofa, sprawling on his side where he tumbled when his mum got up suddenly. Sarah and I are now talking quite animatedly about the horror and bloodshed we're both excited to be a part of, so we can't see Jake's dark, troubled eyes watching us closely, following Sarah's every move, brows drawn together with hurt. Why do you think he's so upset? I think it's because all he's seen for weeks and weeks is his mummy either crying or mute and all he wants is for his mummy to hug and kiss him and love him like she used to. And now she's hugging someone else and not him and not daddy either. He wants to be the one who makes his mummy smile; he wants to be the one being hugged. He is sure that when his daddy comes home, everything will be all right again. His mummy will smile again and love him and Daddy can play Star Wars with him like he used to.

'I love you, Jake,' comes a growly voice. 'I love you, Jake. I love you, Jake. I love you, Jake.' Jake presses the bear again and again, holding it up to his face as tears fill his eyes. Unseen, he gets up and rushes silently from the room.

It's easy to pack my few clothes away ready to go home. Sarah's given me some of her old clothes, which should see me through the last few weeks before the birth. Her maternity clothes are all far too big for me, but a pair of her old stretchy trousers fits me perfectly. She's a few inches taller than me too, so the waistband sits nicely under my boobs and they're still a good length. She doesn't look too happy, does she, that a pair of her everyday trousers would fit someone who is eight months pregnant.

At work, no one seems to expect very much from me, which is insulting but terribly convenient. I do have a few things to sort out while I can still think without being interrupted, not least of which is what to do about Nick.

I have spent some considerable time over the past eight months wondering what role Nick should play in Plum's life. I don't really want him to be a father figure, and I suspect that he won't want that anyway. I fully expect him to deny that he's in any way connected to the baby, or me. The simplest thing seems to be just not to tell him and keep the two of them apart for ever and that's what I've been sticking with. But lately, as Plum becomes a bigger and bigger part of my life and makes his presence more and more felt, I've started thinking that not telling Nick is not right. Not for Plum. Frankly, I don't really care what Nick thinks about the whole thing – whether he is horrified, or it ruins his marriage, or he laughs or denies any responsibility, it's all the same to me. Unless he ever hurts Plum. I can't allow that. In the end, though, I think it's Plum who needs to decide what contact he wants with his father, not me, and not Nick.

Katy says every baby has a right to know its origins, and that means its mum and dad. 'Secrets staying secret only do damage in the long run.'

Penny at work is adamant I should *not* tell him. 'God no. Have nothing to do with him. Cut him out of your life. Never let him know he has a child. Involving a man will only lead to stress and unpleasantness. We women can manage perfectly well . . .'

'Better,' says Siân, coming up behind Penny and touching her arm.

'. . . better, then, on our own.' Penny turns towards Siân and smiles at her affectionately and they walk out of the room hand in hand. I think that perhaps their opinion is a bit biased.

I've asked Sarah what she thinks.

'Yes, you bloody well should tell him,' she spat. 'He thinks he's got away with it, the low-life, shit-eating waste of space that he is. Banging some overdressed bimbo behind his wife's back. That'd teach him a lesson he'll never forget, wouldn't it? Slimy, piss-faced little worm wanker.' She pauses for breath. I think she'd momentarily forgotten that I was the overdressed bimbo that was banged. 'And, you can screw him for every penny he's got, can't you? You'll need financial support, you won't be able to work any more, so first you should tell him and destroy his life for ever, then make him pay. *Make him pay!*' I expected her to throw her head back and laugh maniacally to the sound of cracking thunder, but birds continued to sing and cars drove past outside.

I think that perhaps her opinion isn't as objective as it might have been.

I've been to see Susan in her shop to see what she thinks. I thought she was bound to be more objective than Siân, Penny and Sarah. In fact, she was so detached, she wouldn't even tell me her opinion.

'Rachel,' she says, folding up a gigantic bra, 'I could not possibly presume to advise you on that one.'

'What?'

She looks at me. 'This is one of the most momentous, important, life-long decisions you will ever have to make.

What you decide to do now will affect you and Plum for ever and ever. And that is why I think you should make it completely on your own.'

I think that perhaps Susan is so convinced she herself made the wrong decision all those years ago, she doesn't want to be involved in any more decisions. Ever.

So here I am now, floating about in the pool, mulling over what everyone has told me. I haven't bothered to ask my parents – they'll probably just say, 'You must do what you feel is right, Rachel,' which, if you've ever needed sound, objective advice from people you respect who are older and wiser, you'll know is useless.

In fact, as I bob aimlessly around the pool like a mini iceberg – except that there's much less of me under the waterline than above it – I know that there's only one person who I know would give me really good, sensible advice, without trying to persuade me one way or the other, and that's Hector. Of course. I haven't seen him since he told me all about Miranda and that was about three weeks ago. Now that I've moved back home there's no chance of seeing him at Sarah's any more, and I don't phone him and he doesn't phone me. He did say I could call him whenever I wanted anything, so I could, but it's uncomfortable. I still can't get the idea out of my head of him rolling his eyes as he puts his hand over the mouthpiece of the phone, shakes his head and whispers to his colleague 'Sorry, it's this crazy woman who won't stop calling me and I don't know how to put her off. She's having a baby,' before saying cheerfully, 'Hi, Rach! How are you?'

I do all my thinking in the pool. I can breathe more easily and Plum's weight is largely supported by the water, so I'm much more comfortable there. I lie on my back and drift about, trying to imagine what Nick's reaction would be, if I tell him.

'Oh, so that's why you've got so fat,' is one possibility, although I'm sure Paris must have told him the happy news by now.

'So what?' is a possible. I think I can probably deal with that one too.

'Wahey, I knew I had it in me. What a stud,' also seems fairly likely, although to be fair, I don't really know the guy, so I might be doing him a disservice.

I kick a foot as I float a bit too close to the side, and I'm propelled backwards, diagonally across the middle of the pool, rotating as I go. I just assume that other swimmers will get hurriedly out of the way when they see me hove into view.

There is one thing that worries me about telling Nick and that's his wife. She may be so plain and boring that her husband has to seek fun in another's arms the whole time, but she is innocent in all this. How will it affect her? Does she even suspect that her husband is as faithful as an internet surfer? Well, that's not my concern. Besides, she needs to dump him, big time. Once she finds out . . .

Yikes! I've hit something. There's a sickening jolt and I'm sure I feel, just for a second, the softness of an eyeball coming into contact with my elbow.

'Ugh, oh God, oh,' I'm half shouting, arms flailing, trying desperately to tread water before realizing that this is proving difficult because I keep banging my feet on the ground. I stand up and look round to see what I've hit.

It's Hector.

Incredibly, wonderfully, breathtakingly Hector!

In this part of the pool, the water is up to my armpits, which I'm glad about. On him, it only reaches up to his ribs, which I'm very glad about.

Can we pause a moment here, please, and have a good look at him in his trunks. He's a big bloke, isn't he? Compare this to Nick Maxwell, emerging from my shower seven months ago. Makes Nick look rather, I don't know, puny, really, doesn't he? My eyeline is just about at the level of his chest and I'm trying not to look at his nipples. Although I do love a hairless chest. And those broad shoulders. And well-formed arms.

Oh, sorry. Where was I?

Right. Hector hasn't realized it's me yet as he's got both hands clapped to his left eye, and his right eye is streaming in sympathy. And I'm just standing there, gawping.

'That'll teach you for stalking me,' I say eventually, when the five-second silence is starting to become awkward.

His head snaps round to the sound of my voice. 'Rachel? Is that you?' His lips produce a smile, in spite of his obvious agony.

'Yeah, freak. I've got a gun and it's pointed at your head.'

He smiles more broadly. 'Yep, that's Rachel. How are you?'

'Swollen beyond all recognition. You?'

'Temporarily blinded. You look good to me.'

'Thanks. You, on the other hand, look terrible. Do you want me to take a look?'

'Yes please.' He bends down and prises his eye open. I move forward and try to look up into his face, and our bare arms touch accidentally. Christ, we're both nearly naked. There's a huge amount of exposed flesh here and

379

I know that all of mine is tingling self-consciously. Or is it lust? He feels something too, because he's moving away from me at the same time.

'I can't really see . . .'

'Actually, I think it's all right now . . .'

'Good.'

'Yes. Well, I think it's time for me to get out. I've had enough anyway,' he says, stepping backwards to go to the steps, but not quite striking out in the right direction.

'OK. Bye.'

'No. Not yet. Will you join me in a cup of coffee upstairs?'

'I'd love to, but I doubt there's room.'

He chuckles. 'Meet me in the café?'

'Lovely. But you might want to go a bit to your left if you ever want to get out of this pool.'

Ten minutes later, and here I am, hanging my head upside down, desperately trying to make my hair do something other than just lie there. I'm blow-drying it and as soon as I straighten up again, I stagger and nearly fall over with dizziness.

'You know you shouldn't really do that while you're pregnant,' says a total stranger walking past.

Hector beats me to the café. His hair is still a little damp and messy-looking, and he's wearing a white T-shirt and jeans. If you look at his chest closely, like me, you can imagine what's underneath that T-shirt. As I draw nearer I can see that his left eye has a large patch of red veins clearly visible in the white. I bite my lip as I sit down opposite him. 'I'm very sorry about your eye. It looks really sore.'

'No, it isn't. It's just sore.'

380

'I'm glad about that. Makes me feel much better.' There's a cup of coffee on the table in front of me, steaming away. 'Is this for me?'

'Yeah. That guy over there in the window left it for you. Do you know him?'

'No. Decent of him, though.' I raise my cup towards the stranger in the window, who gives a surprised look, then smiles.

'You've made his day,' Hector says quietly.

'Well, I try to do a good deed every day. Trouble is, Hector, he obviously doesn't know that everything except water tastes like washing-up liquid at the moment . . .'

'Say no more.' He leaps to his feet. 'I'll go and see if they've got any washing-up liquid.'

'I'm not an invalid, you know. Sit down, I'll go.'

'I know you're not an invalid, but by the time you've hauled yourself out of that chair and shuffled over to the counter, I could have got six glasses of water. Just stay there.'

I watch him chatting easily with the lad on the drinks counter and I'm smiling automatically.

'What are you looking so soppy about?' he asks, returning to the table.

'Nothing, just thinking what a good friend you are.'

He pauses as he places the glass in front of me and meets my eyes frankly. 'Am I?'

'I hope so. You are, aren't you?'

'I thought we were strangers.'

'No, you can't keep bringing that up, not after we've known each other for eight months.'

'Seven months, ten days.'

'Oh. Oh.' I take a sip of water and try not to think about

what that means. 'I'm really glad I bumped into you today, Hector. I need your advice. Do you mind?'

'Mind? Of course I don't mind. What can I do for you?'

Here goes. 'Well, you may have heard me mention someone called Nick once or twice?' He nods. 'He's the . . . father.'

'Right.'

'Right. So. I'm in a dilemma. What I'm wondering is, and you have to bear in mind he's immature and un-reliable and, I'm ashamed to admit, married . . .'

'Really? Oh dear.'

'Yes, bastard. Anyway, so now you know as much about him as I do. And bearing all that in mind, what I wanted to ask you was . . . do you think I should tell him about the baby?'

Hector splutters around a mouthful of coffee and then starts to cough, trying hard to keep his lips together to avoid spraying it all over me. Eventually he manages to swallow the coffee and stop coughing. 'He doesn't *know*?'

Ah. Obviously Hector's opinion is that I should tell him. 'Well, I haven't seen him to speak to, you know, properly, in private, for months, not since last year.'

'Wha—'

'In fact, the last time I saw him was at Christmas and at that point I just looked like I'd put weight on. Which I had, of course, but not for the reason he was thinking. Although I don't know what reason he was thinking, if he was even thinking about it at all, which he probably wasn't because when I happened upon him he was rather engrossed in . . . What? What are you grinning about?'

'Stand up.'

'Why?'

'Please, Rachel, will you just stand up.'

'OK.' I stand and he walks around the table, his eyes fixed on mine, but he doesn't stop, he just keeps coming until my belly touches him and we look down at it but then we both look up again and he reaches out his hands and puts them on my cheeks and his fingers stretch around the back of my neck and cup my jaw so softly, and then he bends his head down and I tilt my head back and he kisses me. Right there, in the middle of the Waterside Café.

I'm driving home. Look at me, I look like I'm about to burst. I'm bouncing around in my seat, rocking from side to side, singing that song again as loud as I can with the window open.

'I get knocked up, but I get up again, you're never gonna keep me down!'

Someone on the pavement shouts out, 'Put a sock in it,' but I don't care.

Hector loves me! Has loved me for ages, months! Did you spot it? Because the signs were there, weren't they, and I did read them right, after all, which is just so fantastic, because it means he loves me – *he loves me*! He was just keeping his feelings to himself because he thought I was trying to make a go of it with Nick. That prick. He almost ruined my life that time. But he didn't! HE DIDN'T!

I really need to concentrate on driving. I glance yet again in my rear-view mirror and sure enough there are the twin beams of Hector's beautiful headlights, and I smile at them and give him a wave. The lights flash lovingly at me. He loves me.

When we get to my flat, he meets me on the pavement and bends down to kiss me again, right there outside my block. 'I can't believe I can just kiss you when I want,' he says, and kisses me again. I can't feel the pavement any more.

I make us some cheesy pasta and we sit cross-legged on the sofa as we eat. We are so close, our heads are almost touching.

'So tell me,' I ask him.

He knows exactly what I mean and lays his fork down, studying my face. 'Probably almost from the very first moment we spoke.'

'"The Blooding?'

'No, no, I mean when we first spoke, on my old phone.'

'Really? What, straight away, without even seeing me?' That's a first.

'Absolutely. I didn't have to see you to know that I . . . could really like you. Love you, even.'

'No way! There is no way you loved me before we'd even met. You're teasing me!'

'No, no, I don't mean that I fell in love with you then. I just knew, straight away, that I could love you.'

I'm frowning. 'I don't get it.'

He leans back a little and puts his knuckle on his chin. 'Let me try and explain. Let's see. The truth is, you inspired me. Inspire me.'

Holy crap, did you hear that? I have never, ever been told that before, by anyone. I inspire him! 'Really?' I'm whispering.

'Yes. I mean it. It's because . . .' He shakes his head. 'No, I mean . . .' He frowns for a moment. 'OK. Have you ever cracked a joke to someone you don't know, like in the street or in a lift, and they totally don't get it?

It's so uncomfortable. Let me give you an example. I was queuing up in the Early Learning Centre once, years ago, with a plastic birthday cake for Jake—'

'You know he craves sponge that he can actually eat.'

'I had no idea. Poor kid. Anyway, in front of me in the queue was a woman manoeuvring an enormous box that evidently contained a play first-aid station, complete with play bandages, play stethoscope, play syringes, that kind of thing.

'We were standing in the queue together for about three or four minutes and it always seems rude to me to stand so near to someone for any length of time and not speak to them. So I looked at the box she was holding and said, "It's a really good idea to have one of those in the house, isn't it?"'

A fat giggle bursts out of me. 'Fantastic! Did she laugh?'

'No. She barely even smiled. She just did that look.'

'What look?'

'You know, one of those fake, half smiles that means, "I know you said something to me, but I don't know you and I don't understand what it was, so please don't speak to me again."'

'Oh, yes, I know the one you mean. I do that one all the time. It's like, "I'm too polite to ignore you outright."'

He nods knowingly. 'Yeah, that sounds about right, you witch. Anyway, it was excruciating because now she thinks I'm slightly mad, or one of those nuisance strangers that won't stop telling you really boring facts about themselves when you can't get away, like when you're in an Early Learning Centre queue on a Saturday close to Christmas and there's a school child operating the till who has to keep buzzing for assistance because he doesn't know how to do credit cards.'

'A long wait, then?'

'Someone handed round tea and sandwiches.' He's grinning, but watch now as he shifts his expression, just a fraction, around the mouth and eyes so that they're fixed on mine, like twin tractor beams. It gives me that plunging feeling in my chest again.

'But you. You. You didn't know me; you didn't know anything about me, or what I was going to say, but you never gave me the look, even down the phone. I could tell. I was feeling buoyant the day we finally spoke; cheerful, a bit optimistic. That was the day Rupert finally signed on the dotted line for the Horizon system. So on the spur of the moment I started off a little joke about a kidnap and ransom for the phone, not really expecting anything to come of it, thinking that the other person would say something like, "Look, dude, I didn't steal your phone and I'm not holding it to ransom, but now that you mention it, is there a reward?" But you didn't. You just flung yourself one hundred per cent straight into the spirit of it.' He shakes his head. 'It was amazing.'

'Really?'

'Absolutely. It inspired me. That's what I mean. Right there, talking to me on the phone with, I might add, the sexiest voice I had heard in years, was someone else in the world who wanted to have fun. Someone who could see the point in a pointless joke. Someone who wasn't too caught up in the daily grind of life to join in with something ridiculous.

'Even before we met, I looked forward to those conversations. I planned them, put time aside for them, tried to make sure I was going to be available. I kept my phone in my hand when we were due to speak. I smiled for half an hour beforehand, and grinned for hours afterwards. And I didn't want to have to cut it short because of work or something else intruding. I wanted fun to be my top priority, just for those precious moments. It – they became incredibly important to me.'

'Wow.'

'I know! I could not wait to meet you. I had butterflies in my stomach, sitting there on that fountain. You know I was there from just after five fifteen that day? We weren't due to meet until six. But I couldn't concentrate on my work so in the end I just gave it up as a bad job. By the time six o'clock came round, I was a wreck. I felt sick, I was sweating. Mind you, I drank about four cups of coffee in that café while I was waiting.'

'I wondered why your eye kept twitching.' I'm joking but look at my face – I can't take my eyes off him.

'And then I finally saw you, sitting there. You were so small and pale, so terrified. I felt drawn to you, as soon as I saw you, but of course I couldn't approach you because I was there to meet . . . well, you. So I just had to try and ignore you, while I waited for you to turn up. When my phone rang in your bag . . .' He trails off and reaches up to tuck my hair behind my ear. 'I knew I had to do something to keep us connected. I couldn't just take the phone from you and never see or hear you again.'

I whisper, 'I'm so glad you did. I mean, didn't.'

'Oh Rachel, so am I. I can't believe how close I came to letting you go. When I saw you and Nick at the Horizon party—'

'I've explained about that, you softhead.'

'I know you have. I know. It was just so . . .'

Give us a moment here, please. We need our privacy and there's probably only so much kissing you can take. I hate seeing it when people do it in public.

'You know,' I say eventually, 'Sarah told me years ago that you were a really controlling older brother who likes to think the whole world does his bidding.'

'Did she? Well, that's a bit upsetting. I thought she liked me.'

'Hector according to Glenn?'

He nods. 'I'm absolutely sure that's what it is. I wonder why he thinks that.'

'Did you lend him some money recently?'

'Yes, I did. Five grand.'

'Did you tell him to end his affair with Chrissie?'

'Yep.'

'Did you threaten him?'

'Well, yes, I suppose I did.'

'Still wondering why he thinks you're controlling?'

He smiles at me. 'You really are a sorceress, aren't you?'

'Of course. How else do you think I persuaded you to leave your phone on the trolley?'

'That was you? God, you're good.'

'So I've been told. Do you want any more cheesy pasta? There's plenty left.'

'Mmm, yes please. It's delicious.'

'Don't you ever eat?'

'Well, since Mum went, I don't bother much. Not really worth it for one person.'

'But isn't Glenn staying with you?'

'Mmm-hmm, but he doesn't want to eat, he just sits

around the place feeling sorry for himself. He's a mess, the place is a mess, the whole thing is a mess.'

'Sarah's the same.'

'I know.'

'Well, don't you think it's a bit silly that they're both sitting in different houses feeling miserable?'

He looks at me then brushes a stray hair away from my eyes. 'What are you suggesting, witch?'

I shrug. 'I don't know. But we need to get them talking, I think.'

He lays down his fork and puts the plate on the coffee table. 'You're right. I am sick of seeing his limp face everywhere I look. He's off work at the moment with stress, so it's there at the window when I go out and it's still there when I get back – facing me on the sofa, passing me on the stairs, coming out of the bathroom. It's even starting to invade my dreams now.'

'Let's go and see Sarah,' I say suddenly. 'It's awful that we're feeling so happy, and they're both so miserable.'

'So fucking miserable.'

I laugh. Look at the expression on his face – he really has had enough of looking at Glenn's face, hasn't he? 'All right, so fucking miserable. So what do you think? Shall we see if we can inject a little magic into their situation?'

'OK, sorceress, we'll go straight away. You can cast a spell.' He's staring at me again, as if in wonder. 'My Rachel,' he says; then I kiss him.

I drift off in Hector's comfortable car. I've reclined the seat and tilted the head rest forward and the smooth motion and quiet engine have soon lulled me to sleep. I am wrenched awake suddenly by ghastly, grisly images of split skin and tearing wounds that look like red screaming mouths. I jerk and open my eyes, heart thudding. The car has stopped and Hector is leaning over me, his face inches from mine, stroking my cheek.

'Hello,' he says.

'Hi. How long have I been asleep?'

He looks at the clock on the dashboard. 'About two minutes.'

'Oh. Two minutes?'

'Yep. We're here, come on.'

Standing on Sarah's doorstep, I lean comfortably against him. The top of my head barely reaches his chin. He dips his head and puts his lips in my hair. As Sarah opens the door, we spring apart.

'Oh, hi, you two.' She is apparently completely unsurprised to see us together. She turns and walks back down the hallway, sniffing. Did you notice that her eyes are red and puffy? She's obviously just been crying.

'What's the matter, Sarah?' I ask her as we arrive in the living room.

She looks up at me. 'Oh, my husband has been having an affair with one of my best friends. Did I not tell you?'

The living room is pretty untidy. There are toys, clothes, dirty cups and plates, magazines and newspapers scattered around, and in the midst of it all is Jake, curled up in a ball on the sofa. I glance at the clock. It's nine o'clock – way past his bedtime.

'Hey, Harry, wotcher watching?' I call over. He doesn't stir.

'Harry?' Hector says to me softly, a quizzical look on his face.

'Tell you later.'

390

Sarah sits back down on the sofa and Jake shuffles right up next to her again, laying his head in her lap. Absently she puts her hand on his hair. Hector and I sit down on the armchairs.

'Glenn's been round,' she says suddenly.

'That's good,' Hector says. I'm watching Jake. He looks so pale and worried. A little boy of six should not be worrying about anything other than how to work out which shoe goes on which foot.

'Not really,' Sarah says. 'He wants a divorce.'

'What?!' Hector almost shouts. I see Jake flinch with the loud noise, but his eyes remain fixed on the television screen and he rarely blinks. His hair looks unkempt and dirty and he has no shoes or socks on.

'Yeah, bloody cheek. I should be the one divorcing him. He reckons we have irreconcilable differences, and I think he's right. Like he wants to sleep around and I don't want him to.' She does a mirthless 'Hah'.

'I'll talk to him, Sarah,' Hector is saying. 'I know that's not what he wants. It's just a knee-jerk reaction.'

'Well, I'm not so sure it's a bad idea,' she says miserably. 'What's the point of carrying on with a relationship where there's nothing left between us? You know, Hector, we don't speak any more, we don't laugh, it's just like, "What's for tea?", "Did you pay that bill?", "We need oven cleaner."' She shakes her head wearily. 'I think it's just naturally reached the end. That's that.' Tears start to slide down her cheeks and she sniffs loudly, smearing them away with her fist. On her lap, Jake raises his head and looks at her face. Seeing her crying, he sits up and picks up Bert the bear, then presses it into her hand. 'I love you, Jake,' says Glenn's voice. Jake watches his mum but Bert has no effect on her, so he climbs down from the sofa and leaves the room. I glance at Hector, then I follow.

Upstairs in his room, Jake is kneeling by a large red plastic toy chest. The lid is thrown back and Jake is rummaging furiously around inside. He's talking away so I move nearer to the door to listen.

'. . . get the . . . sky-diving Action Man, that's the best one, and, and, and the giant pirate ship. No, too hard to carry . . . Oscar the owl, he's my favourite, except for Bert, and maybe the alphabet desk. Take Bob the Builder's remote-control scrambler, that's good, and my Thundersaurus Megazord . . . What about Maurice the Monkey? No it's stupid, doesn't even look like a monkey, not a proper tail . . . Spiderman ball . . . Just got to get these . . .'

He's pulled a number of toys out of the chest and tossed them into a rough heap to one side. Now he's loading them into his arms, scrabbling and struggling to carry them all. He's obviously getting his favourite toys together to go somewhere, but where? His little pale face is crumpled with concentration as he stands up, arms full of toys.

I back into the bathroom as he heads towards the landing, and hide behind the door. I hear him pass, still muttering.

'All my best things, gonna let her play with all of them, gonna make her happy again. Dropped the Spiderman ball, bouncing down the stairs. Get it later. She can play with all these, whenever she wants, and all my other stuff. But these are my best ones.' And he heads off down the stairs.

I was thinking that he was planning on running away and was packing what he saw as the most important things to have with him when he's alone and fending for himself in a world where child killers seem to lurk on every corner: a Spiderman ball and Oscar the Owl. But as I tiptoe down the stairs behind him, it becomes suddenly very clear what's going on.

He lurches into the living room, head tipped back to allow room for the things in his arms, bumping into doors, sofa arms, Hector's outstretched feet; then crouches slowly and allows all the toys to tumble out of his arms on to the floor. Hector and Sarah are watching him curiously. Hector glances at me: I'm standing in the doorway, arms wrapped round myself, tears flowing, eyes fixed on Jake, who has selected an Action Man from the pile.

'Mummy, do you want to play with my sky-diving Action Man? It's my best one. You throw him up in the air and his parachute opens and he floats down again. Look.' He holds the toy out towards his mum, who looks at it for a moment, then takes it and wafts it in the air a couple of times.

'That's great, Jakey, thanks,' she says, smiling wetly, and puts it on her lap. Jake watches her, then goes back to the pile of things. 'I-I've got Thundersaurus Megazord. Look, it morphs into three different dinosaurs.' Nimbly he demonstrates exactly what the toy does, then folds it all back up and holds it out to his mum too. It joins the Action Man on her lap.

Over the next few minutes, we all watch with astonishment and sadness as Jake returns to the pile of toys, selects one and holds it out to Sarah with a brief description of what it can do. She stretches his stretch Homer ('You can pull his arms and legs out really far, and he always goes back to how he was'), drives his remote-control car ('When it bangs into something, it flips over') and pretends to battle on his treasured Gameboy ('It's got Pokemon Yellow game') until eventually she leans down and opens her arms to him, smiling through tears.

'Come up here, Jakey, come on, come and give me a cuddle.'

He puts down the Magna Doodle he's holding and climbs on to her lap, wrapping his arms tightly round her neck, pressing his face to her cheek.

'Oh, thank you so much, Jake. Thank you, my darling boy.'

Hector and I stand up and head towards the door.

'Sarah, we're going now,' Hector says. 'Don't get up – we can see ourselves out. Let me know if you need anything.' She nods at us over Jake's shoulder. 'Good. And I will talk to Glenn. I promise.'

'Thanks, Hec. See you later, Rach,' she whispers, rubbing Jake's back. As we're walking back down the hall, I hear Jake's voice saying, 'Did you like playing with my best things, Mummy?'

Sarah smiles over his shoulder and rubs his back. 'Oh, Jakey, yes I did, and it was so kind of you to bring them all down for me. But you know, I'm a grown-up and grown-ups don't really play with toys any more.'

Jake sniffs and leans back to look at his mum's face. 'But Daddy used to play Star Wars with me. I was Darth Vader and he was Obi Wan Kenobi. We always used to play that.'

'I know, love. I wish we could go back to that too. But Daddy's not here at the moment, it's just the two of us. Just you and me, the terrible two. OK?' And she pulls him forward for another tight hug.

But look over her shoulder, at Jake's face. Have a really good look. Can you see his face slowly changing? His eyes open wider and his mouth turns up from desperate sadness to grim determination. And unheard, he whispers one word into his mummy's hair: 'Daddy.'

Chapter Twenty-one

So today is my last day at work. At least for a while. I've
had a letter signed by Vivien Attwood telling me that I
am entitled to eighteen weeks' paid maternity leave, after
which time I may take unpaid leave or return to work part
time, details to be arranged when it's convenient to me.
I'm to phone in and discuss it with Jean nearer the time,
once I know for sure what working pattern suits me and
the baby best.

Can you believe that I'm not even worrying about it?
What, worry about money and work, when I'm due to
be cut open and have a human being dragged from my
depths? I don't think so. There is no room left in my head
to worry about anything else.

'Fuck, Rach, your hair looks awful today.'

'Oh my God, Rachel, have you heard that we're all
getting a twenty-five per cent pay cut?'

'Quick, Rachel, there's a carnivorous dinosaur loose in
DP, we've all got to evacuate.'

I'm oblivious to everything. I just hope Val drags me
out of the building if there's a fire, because I know I won't
notice the screaming alarms, the freezing-cold water
sprinklers and the panicked stampede of everyone else

towards the stairs. I will be still sitting there at my desk, dripping with water and smoking slightly, when the fire-fighters burst through the door from the corridor.

The operation is next Thursday, by the way. Did I mention that? Six days away. Yep, 5 April. A date that will from now on and for ever be significant in my life. Just the plain old fifth of April.

When I come back to my desk after a toilet break, there's a yellow square of paper stuck to my screen saying 'Chrissie rang', in Val's handwriting. It's Val's last day today too. Oh, only for a week though. She's off to Lake Garda with Keith tomorrow.

Anyway, I take the paper off my screen and stare at it in my hand for a few seconds before screwing it up and dropping it in the bin. Chrissie is still off sick, bless her. It must be so stressful being a selfish, home-wrecking bitch. Anyway I really don't want to hear anything she's got to say at the moment. The image of Jake's desperate attempt to cheer up his mum with his best toys the night before last is still haunting me.

I'm going to call Hector. I haven't spoken to him yet today. And now I have no fear of him pulling a 'for-God's-sake-what-now?' face. I needn't have worried about that anyway.

'I have a very sensible telephonist,' he told me yesterday, when I told him about the scene I imagined of him with his colleagues, making faces at the phone. 'I can always leave your name with her, and when you call, get her to tell you that I'm in a meeting or out of town or something. Job done.'

'McCarthy Systems,' the receptionist says. I'm trying to picture where she might be sitting, what her surroundings are like. Obviously it's not a pasting table on the other side of a partition. I'm thinking yucca plant, pictures of Sydney Harbour, red carpet with footprints in it.

'Hello, may I speak to Hector, please?'

'Who is calling?'

'It's Rachel Covington.'

'Oh, I'm sorry, Miss Covington, Mr McCarthy is out of the building just now. Would you like me to give him a message?'

'No, no, it's all right. Could you just tell him that I called, please?'

'Of course. Although I should warn you he isn't due back in the office until after lunch.'

Great big bums and balls. 'No problem. Thank you.' Arses. I really want to speak to him now.

'You shouldn't sit like that, Rach, you'll get varicose veins.' I turn to see Martin or Mike walking past.

'Arse,' I say out loud to him.

'Right you are.'

I'm dithering a bit, trying not to resort to taking a call to pass the time, when Simon comes to my rescue.

'Rach, got a call for you!' he shouts, loud enough for everyone who's called Horizon this morning to enquire about apartment availability to hear.

'No, no,' I hear Val saying as I walk past her on my way to Simon's desk, 'it was someone outside the window. I'll just close it . . .'

Simon nips off for a few minutes so I can take the call in privacy.

'This is Rachel.'

'Hi. It's me.'

Notice that he didn't say 'It's Hector' to identify himself

from other men who might be calling me. He doesn't need to do that any more. I sink down on to Simon's chair with a smile.

'Hi, you.'

'How's it going?'

'Far too slowly. I tried to call you earlier but your receptionist . . .'

'Moira.'

'Moira said you were out of the office for the next ten years. I'm sensing a subtle message there. Something you want to say to me?'

He's chuckling. 'I told her to say two months, bloody woman. Ten years is just so blatant, isn't it?'

'Oh, definitely. You need to be far more subtle when you dump someone without telling them. Just so that they're not ever completely sure whether you dumped them or not.'

'Wow. You really know what you're talking about, don't you?'

'I have a fair amount of experience in that area. People say that ambiguous dumping like that is cruel and that it's much kinder just to do it outright, to their face, you know: You're dumped, end of.'

'I can see that some people would think that was kind.'

'Nah, it's not. Mum says that I shouldn't leave people hanging but I disagree. It preserves their pride, gives them a sense of dignity.'

'What, even when they phone you up two weeks later and sob down the phone, begging to see you again?'

Spooky. That's actually happened to me, more than once. 'Absolutely. Gives them a chance to be all eloquent and noble.'

'Remind me never to be dumped by you.'

I smile. There's no chance of that. 'Hey, as long as you have a decent speech prepared, it's a breeze.'

'Somehow I doubt that.'

'Listen, did you call me up for a reason or is it just to taunt me over how you're ambiguously dumping me even as we speak? Anyway, I thought you were out of the office until after lunch . . . ?'

'Yes, I am out of the office until after lunch. I am out of the office right now, in fact.'

'Oh . . .'

'Actually, I am outside *your* office. By the door.'

'Really?' I jump to my feet and look over towards the door but there's no one there. 'I can't see you.'

'Look again.'

I am looking, haven't stopped looking, but there's . . . Oh wait a minute! Did you see that? Something appeared for a moment there. It's an arm! Just an arm, waving. No, beckoning. It's beckoning me over. I start laughing.

'No, I still can't see you, but there is a huge crowd of people all going towards the door for some reason – maybe they're obscuring you.'

The arm is snatched back behind the door quickly and a head appears briefly then disappears again.

'You are a witch, Rachel Covington. I knew it the moment I saw you, sitting there with those hounds of hell behind you, poised and waiting for your next instruction.'

'You're right. I told them to stand very still and slaver, and they did my bidding.'

'Come and meet me?'

'I am at work, you know, I don't know if – OK then.' I

press 'End', yank the headset off and walk briskly over to the door.

On the other side, he walks to greet me and comes right inside my personal space. 'Hi,' he says, bending his head down so our faces are close.

'Hi.'

'Come with me. I've got something for you.' He takes my hand and leads me off towards the lifts.

'A pres?'

'A wh—? Oh, yes, yes, a pres.'

'Ooh, goody. Why can't I have it now?'

'Because it's downstairs, silly. Come *on*.'

'All right, all right keep your very nice Van Heusen shirt on. It's not me, it's Plum.' I'm doing the pregnancy saunter – you know the one, with your legs slightly too wide apart and your hand in your lower back. I've seen *Casualty* and I always thought that was one of those myths associated with pregnancy, like eating coal, but it isn't, it really seems to help me put one foot in front of the other.

'Whoops, sorry, not thinking.' He stops pulling on my arm and puts his hand around my waist instead.

OK, we've gone into the lift and the doors have shut. Let's skip over this bit and go down to the ground floor, as we are coming out of the lift again.

He brings me along the corridor to the canteen, which is virtually deserted, and takes me to a table in the corner of the room.

As we get nearer to the table he's guiding me towards, I want you to think back for a moment to the sight of his business premises in the business park. That massive glass building with a car park and water dispensers and a pension plan. Remember it? OK, now you've got that in your head, what do you think the owner of that business will have bought me as a gift? I'm guessing he's at least a mono-millionaire, if not a multi-, so I'm not ruling out the possibility that he's got me something outrageously huge. And I'm not sure if I like that idea or not.

'Close your eyes,' he says. 'Go on. I'll guide you.'

'OK, but if you leave me standing in the middle of a crowded room with my eyes closed for ten minutes, I will not find it funny.'

'Don't worry, I promise I will never intentionally humiliate you.'

'Why do I not find that reassuring?'

'Well, you should. I've never promised that to anyone before.'

'Oh. I am flattered. Although to be honest, I'm not sure that the fact that you feel it is necessary with me, and no one else, is a good thing.' We are making our way very slowly across the room, and I've got my hands out in front of me, like a game of Blind Man's Buff. I feel like a first-class tit. 'Can I open my eyes yet?'

'Nearly.'

'You know, I don't need gifts, Hec. Your promise not to humiliate me is enough.'

'Rachel, my darling Rachel, you have made me happy for the first time in months, years probably. I am stunned that I've got you in my life. I want you to stay there. Please, let me get you a little something now and then, will you? Please?'

If it's something really huge, like a car, I know Mum would tell me to do a *Pretty Woman* and turn it down. But I so don't want to and anyway, why should I? I'm not a paid girlfriend; I'm here out of choice. But I don't want anyone to think I am a sponge. Which they might, given the shape of me at the moment.

Look at my face? So serene and tranquil. You wouldn't believe the spinning tornado of panicky thoughts going on inside there, would you?

He guides me to a chair and I sit down unsteadily. There's a sound of slight movement and then he says, 'Open your eyes.'

I almost can't. The image of Richard Gere is so vivid. But when I do, I am greeted with the sight of Hector sitting on the other side of the table on which are standing two steaming mugs. I look at the drinks, then back at Hector. He looks like a dog with the tail of the cat that's had the cream. 'It's . . . You've . . . bought me a . . . hot chocolate?'

He nods enthusiastically.

I stroke the side of the mug. 'Oh, Hector, I love it. You shouldn't have. Thank you so much.'

'That's not all.'

'It isn't?'

'Nope. Rachel, I don't want you ever to feel like I'm trying to patronize you or demean anything that you do for Plum. That's why I haven't rushed straight round to Mothercare and bought it.'

'Bought what?'

'Mothercare. Are you even listening? Anyway, I respect you and I respect that you, of course, want to do everything for your little Plum yourself. But the fact is that I am only ten minutes behind you in the length of time we have known of Plum's existence and, well, I'm fond of the little tike.'

'Are you?'

'Yes, I am. So, anyway, without wanting to . . . step on any toes, meaning yours, I have bought the little ankle-biter a, er, pres.' He reaches under the table and brings out a small parcel wrapped in yellow paper covered in tiny white bootees. There's a tag attached that says, 'Dear Plum, Good luck next Thursday, mate. Looking forward to seeing you. Give your mum a kiss from me. love, Hec.'

I glance at him with a smile, then pat my bump. 'Listen, Plum, I'm going to open this for you, seeing as you still haven't tidied up your room,' and I rip open the paper.

Have you ever seen anything so perfect? Inside is a gorgeous white velveteen sleepsuit, with tiny silver stars all over it. It has five-centimetre feet on the end of the legs. I hold it still in my hands for a few seconds, just staring at it; then I lay it out flat on the table. 'It's beautiful,' I whisper. On impulse, I pick it up again and lay it down in the crook of my elbow and along my forearm. 'Look, it fits.'

'You like it?'

I look up at him but he's gone all blurry. 'It's perfect.' I look down again at the suit slumbering peacefully in my arms, waiting to be filled. 'I'm going to have a baby.'

'You are? Well then, I'm really glad I bought that, and not a Sodastream.'

'Hector, tell me something?' Subconsciously I have begun rocking the sleepsuit in my arms. 'Why did you have to bring me down here to give it to me?'

'Truthfully? Truthfully, I just wanted to see you. On your own. I missed you.'

'I only saw you yesterday.'

He nods solemnly. 'Yes. Well. I . . . love you.'

Oh, God, I love hearing that. Those words just float out of his mouth, almost without him even saying them.

'I love you too.'

See him swell a bit when he hears me say it? It looks like he can't quite get his breath.

We watch each other sip our drinks, and I remember that it's my last day at work today and I still haven't told Nick about Plum.

'You never answered my question at the pool the other day.'

'What question was that?'

'About whether or not I should tell Nick – Plum's father.'

He exhales deeply. 'Ah yes. I remember. It just seems so odd thinking that he doesn't know about it yet.'

'Yet?'

He leans forward on the table. 'Rachel, he's the baby's father. He has a right to know about it. And his family should know about their grandchild, nephew, cousin . . . brother or sister, even.'

Ah yes, of course. Nick's other children. Well, I don't know for sure that there are others, but with a wife it's a possibility. Plum, of course, will want to know his brothers and sisters, which will mean I will have to meet the wife at some point. There are going to be rows and unpleasantness about where Plum goes for Christmas every year, probably for the next sixteen years or so, until he's old enough to decide for himself. Years of resentment will build up and finally explode in a nasty punch-up at Plum's wedding when Nick gets drunk and his wife calls me a filthy name. That's if she comes. Well, she can be invited, just to keep the peace. Whether she accepts the invite or not is up to her.

'Yes, I know. I've thought about them more thoroughly than you can imagine. I pretty much knew I'd have to tell him, sooner or later; I just wanted to know what you thought. I . . . respect your opinion more than anyone else's.'

He's swelling again.

We drain our cups and stand up, me still clutching the sleepsuit to my chest. 'Have dinner with me tonight?' he says suddenly.

'Yep. Where?'

'I'll meet you after work.'

'OK. Thanks for the drink and this beautiful thing. I love it.'

'I'm so glad.'

Back upstairs, I want to show everyone what I've got, but they're all busy on the phone. Paris is watching me blankly, so I smile sweetly in her direction. Val's absent, presumably in the loo or paying one of her bi-daily visits to Marketing so I fold up the sleepsuit and tuck it safely into my handbag.

At five o'clock I shut down my terminal for the last time. I think I might have sold two holidays today but compared to the carnivorous dinosaur rampaging around downstairs in Data Processing, it hardly matters. I pick up everything that belongs to me, which is one magazine from my desk drawer and my Betty Boop mug, and turn round to find Val standing there with everyone else crowding round. She's got a huge box balanced on the desk in front of her, with a big pink bow on top.

'Rachel, we had a collection and got you some things for the baby. There's some nappies, blankets, bottles, a bouncy chair – it's flat packed – and a few things for it to wear.'

'Oh . . .' I put my hand on my mouth and feel too full of emotion to speak.

'Just about everyone from Telesales wanted to contribute, and quite a few people from other departments, which I think is a measure of how much people wish you well. Good luck, Rachel. We'll all be thinking of you.' She leans forward and kisses my cheek and rubs my arm. And after she's gone, everyone I've worked with for the past seven years comes to say goodbye and give me a kiss. Simon, Siân, Penny, Marion, Jean, Graham, Mike (who's short and fat), Martin (tall and fat), and even Paris comes over. She doesn't kiss me and barely cracks a smile, but she does shake my hand and wish me good luck. Well, good luck to her. I just hope she's using condoms, otherwise we might be seeing an awful lot more of each other in the future.

For old times' sake I do one last pathetic female act and ask Martin to bring the box out to the car for me. I think on this occasion it's justified, though. It's bloody heavy, and I'm already carrying something. Duh, a baby, remember?

As we approach my car, I see there's a gorgeous tall person leaning against it. It's Hector, of course, and as we draw nearer he stands up and I can see that he's watching Martin with narrowed eyes, frowning.

Martin puts the box down on the bonnet. 'Do you want me to put it in the boot for you?'

'No, it's fine there, thanks, Martin. Hector can move it

for me now. I really appreciate you bringing it out here, though.'

Martin glances at Hector and nods at him. 'OK, well, I'll be off then. Best of luck, Rach. Come back soon.' After a quick peck on the cheek, he hurries off towards his own car.

'Who's that then?' Hector asks immediately.

'It's just Martin.'

'Uh-huh,' he says, still watching Martin walking away. 'And what's this?' he nods towards the box.

'It's my leaving gift. I haven't even had a chance to look inside yet, but they've bought me a whole load of baby stuff.'

'Oh, have they?' He sniffs as he picks up the box, feeling its bulky weight. 'I see.'

'Oh, Hector McCarthy, you're not . . .' Suddenly the breath is sucked out of me as an iron clamp tightens around me and my stomach clenches like a fist. 'Umph.'

Hector is at the back of the car, putting my box into the boot. His head jerks up. 'What is it?'

I can't answer. The tightness isn't painful but it's making my heart pound loudly in my ears and throat. It feels like something is wrapped around my whole body, gripping me so tightly that the blood can't move any more and my heart is beating harder and harder to move it on.

Hector appears at my side. 'Are you all right?' I nod and try to smile. 'I'm calling an ambulance,' he says decisively, but doesn't. 'Shall I?'

I shake my head, although I feel like machinery that's had a metal bar shoved into it. I stand, frozen, for several seconds. Eventually, the hardness dissolves and I can release the breath that was stuck inside me. Hector's gripping both my upper arms, his face bent towards me.

'Wow, that was weird,' I say, trying to produce a reassuring smile.

'What was? What happened?'

'I think it was just Braxton Hicks. I'm pretty sure that's what it was.'

'*Who?*'

'Braxton Hicks. False labour pains. It's perfectly normal, apparently.'

He blows out a long breath. 'False . . . Jesus. So what did . . . ? I mean, how is . . . ? How are you going to know whether it's false labour or real labour, then?'

'You tell me.'

'Oh my God.'

'I know.'

He stares at me in horror for a few minutes. 'Right, you're not going further than five minutes away from the hospital for the next six days.'

'OK.'

'Now. Dinner. You ready to eat?'

'Oh yes.'

I follow him in my car along the bypass to the outskirts of town where it becomes very rural and villagey suddenly. After turning off the roundabout the road narrows dramatically and runs between low hedgerows with fields behind them and large farmhouse-style dwellings in the distance. Every so often an opening in the hedgerow shows a fleeting glimpse of a huge stone-built house with three storeys, four cars and a huge front garden accommodating a curved driveway and sculpted hedges.

After about fifteen minutes along this road, Hector

signals and pulls into a dirt road on the right. It's a very odd place for a restaurant to be situated – I can't imagine that they get many customers down here. Unless it's one of those really expensive exclusive places that's only known to a select few, where all the staff know the clients' first names and everyone has a regular table. God, I'm not dressed for a place like that. I'm wearing black leggings and outsize skin.

A few minutes along the track there's a sudden large opening in the hedge on the left and Hector pulls in. I follow him and find myself driving up to one of the enormous stone farmhouses, complete with gravel drive and crisp circular lawn. He parks and gets out, smiling at me as I approach. I'm fairly sure that this is no restaurant.

Inside, his hallway is about the same size as my living room. It has a solid wood floor and a wide staircase, which curves up out of sight. He takes my hand and leads me into the kitchen, which is roughly the size of Old Trafford.

'Would you like a drink?' he asks.

'If you set out now, I will do by the time you get back,' I say, staring around me in wonder. He's got one of those rack things with herbs and plants hanging from it over an island in the middle of the room that has stools round it. I climb on to one. At one end of the room is a large chunky wooden table with six chairs round it and a big bowl of green apples in the middle. Beyond the table the wall is made entirely of glass, which opens out over something that looks like a sports field. It's almost six o'clock so the light is fading fast, but the sun is still clearly visible, dark salmon pink and melting on to the horizon. The sky above and around it is still lit but beyond the reach of the weak rays the sky is indigo. The field, though darkening rapidly, is gilded briefly and the low golden light slants through the window in bars, glinting off the gold dust floating in the air.

'Just water, is it?' he says, heading across the room.

'Lovely.' He brings a glass over to the fridge, which is about the same size as my car and fills it from a tap that's set into the door. He adds a slice of lemon and ice cubes and puts it in front of me.

'Do you like it?' he asks me, leaning his elbows on the counter where I'm sitting.

I sip the water. 'The lemon adds a certain—'

'I mean the kitchen, you sorceress. The house. What do you think?'

'I knew that. I'm stunned, Hector. I've never seen anything like it.'

He grins, obviously pleased with my answer. 'Thanks. I spent a long time slaving over the Yellow Pages to get this effect.'

We talk about the house as he prepares the food. Apparently it was nothing like this when he bought it five years ago and he's done a lot of the designing himself, including that amazing window. While we eat, Glenn puts his head round the door with a small, white aromatic bag in his hand. I glance at Hector as the familiar tune starts up in my head. Da-da-da-da-da-da, da-da-da-da-da-da . . .

'All right, Hec. Oh, hi, Rachel.' He doesn't seem at all surprised to see me there. 'Chinese,' he says, holding up the bag.

'Great,' Hector says, and Glenn disappears. Hector turns

to me. 'See what I mean? That flaccid face everywhere I look. It's driving me . . . Rachel, are you all right?'

The tightening is happening again, robbing me of breath, clamping my lungs. I put my hand on my tummy and it feels like concrete, with a thin layer of skin stretched over it. I nod, not able to speak for a moment. Hector puts his hand on the back of my neck. When it eases I sit up again and breathe more easily.

'False or real?' he says straight away.

'Only one way to know,' I say, going back to my food.

'Really? Well, what is it?'

I chew for a moment. 'Well, if a baby comes out, it was probably a real one.'

'Uh, Rachel. I'm trying to be serious. I'm worried about you.'

I smile. 'You don't need to be. There'll be plenty of time if it is real labour. I've read magazine articles.'

'Oh, good, that's very reassuring.' He eats for a while then says, 'What does it feel like?'

'What, the false labour?'

'Yeah, what you just had, false, real, whatever. What's it like?'

'Hmm. Let me think a minute. Ooh, I know. Did you ever see that old film about gorgons or titans or something? Had a character in it with snakes for hair? What's her name?'

He frowns. 'Medusa?'

'That's it. Well, in this film, Medusa is so ugly, apparently, that it's said that if you look once into her eyes, you'll be turned instantly to stone . . .'

'Yes . . .'

'So, the film builds up to the point where the hero has

412

to face Medusa and fight her, but he can't look into her eyes.'

'Otherwise he'll be—'

'Turned to stone. Right. So he holds up his shiny shield instead, and Medusa looks into it and sees her own reflection.'

'I remember that!'

'And then in the film do you remember they did some kind of poor, sixties-style special effects to show her gradually turning grey, like water soaking into a sponge, and the hardness creeps up her legs and down her arms and gradually spreads all over her body as little by little she turns into stone?'

'Yes?'

'Well, that's what it feels like.'

There's a stunned silence. Then Hec says, 'Wow.'

The telephone rings from the table in the hallway. 'Excuse me,' Hector says, getting up and going to answer it. He's got such beautiful manners, hasn't he? He brings the handset back into the kitchen and sits back on his stool before pressing the button. He reaches out to touch my hair as he speaks.

'Hello? . . . Oh, hi, Sar—' I watch as his relaxed, smiling face hardens, and gradually greyness soaks into it. He removes his hand from my hair and turns partially away from me, eyes widening in horror. 'Hold on, hold on, say that again, only slower . . .' He puts his free hand on the back of his head, begins to rub it, stands up, takes two steps, turns, walks back. He looks at me – his eyes are wild. And I know, from that look, that something truly terrible has happened.

'All right, look, we'll be there as soon as we can.' He

curls his free hand around the mouthpiece of the phone as if to comfort the person at the other end. 'Try to hang on, Sarah, OK? Just hang on.'

He hangs up the phone and dashes into the hallway where he shouts, in a voice that sounds like it has been clawed from raw stone, 'Glenn! Glenn, come down, come on, *now*.'

He strides quickly back to me in the kitchen and takes my hand, pulling me to my feet. 'Come on, Rachel, quickly, we've got to go. Come on.'

'My God, Hector, what's happened?'

As we rush into the hallway to find Glenn halfway down the stairs with a quizzical look on his face, Hector lays his hand on the banister, looks up at his brother and says softly, 'Glenn, it's Jake. He's gone missing.'

Chapter Twenty-two

Running feet; pale, shocked faces; doors slamming; paralysing, sickening, terror; unwelcome images that pour into my head no matter how hard I try to stop them. We're in Hector's car, the three of us, heading too fast and not fast enough to Sarah's house. We're in silence, Hector and Glenn in the front, the tension in the car so enormous I almost expect to see lightning crackle from the head of one brother across to the other.

I can't look at Glenn for long. The sight of him hurts my eyes. Even the back of his head is raw and agonized, his shoulders tense and hunched, one hand pressed permanently over his mouth. He is like an enormous open wound, as if someone has flayed the skin off him.

A lorry joins the road in front of us and we are forced to slow down. Glenn and Hector both lean forward slightly, urging the car, the traffic, to move faster. 'Come on,' Hector says quietly. 'Move . . .'

We arrive at Sarah's. Every light is on, the house glowing like a beacon in the dark for a lost child. Glenn leaps from the car and rushes to the door, which is pulled open and Sarah collapses into his arms, sobbing, talking, gasping out words, her voice high and mostly unintelligible.

'Out there . . . didn't come . . . didn't know what . . . Dark . . . hasn't come . . .' Glenn supports her back into the house, Hector and me following on behind.

Inside, Sarah sits on the edge of the sofa, hunched over, picking at the skin around her fingernails. Look at her face – she's got the same wild look that I've seen in photographs of Holocaust survivors, like she's witnessed a horror. Glenn sits next to her, their sides pressing together, holding hands. Hector crouches in front of them.

'Now, Sarah, can you tell me what happened?'

She nods, swallows, takes a breath, pressing down her voice so that it doesn't shriek with hysteria. When she speaks she sounds like she's desperately holding the two edges of herself together, but they're slipping from her grip.

'We . . . ate our tea . . . about half past five. I – I cleared the plates . . . Jakey . . .' She gasps, covers her mouths, closes her eyes, then recovers enough to go on. 'Jakey . . . went upstairs to his room. I . . . I was reading . . . I was just reading. I didn't think . . . I just didn't think. After maybe . . . an hour, I went up to see if he was . . . But . . . he wasn't . . . he wasn't in his room, Glenn, he wasn't in his room. Oh God, where is he? Where's my little Jakey? He's so small, Glenn, he's just a baby . . .'

She turns to Glenn's shoulder and sobs silently.

'Have you phoned the police?' Hector says.

She raises her head. Her face is blotchy, puffy, pale. 'No, I didn't . . . I wasn't thinking . . . I just rang you.'

'OK. Glenn?'

Glenn nods and gets up, taking the phone into the hallway with him. After a few seconds we hear his voice, low and urgent. Hector turns back to Sarah.

'Have you looked all round the house?'

She nods. 'Yes, I did. There aren't many places to hide . . . I've checked everywhere. I even . . . ran round the garden, looked under all the plants, behind the shed . . .'

'In the shed?'

'No, no, it's padlocked.'

Hector nods. 'Is there anywhere you can think of he might go? A friend's house? A special place? Favourite park . . . ?'

She's shaking her head. 'No, no, I can't imagine that he would do that. He just wouldn't go out on his own . . .'

Hector puts his hand on her arm. 'Sarah, he has done it. He has gone out, hasn't he? Can you think of any reason why he would?'

Her eyes flick almost imperceptibly at the spot on the sofa where Glenn was just sitting. 'Only . . .'

Hector follows her gaze, apparently understanding, and nods. 'OK. Do you have all the phone numbers of his friends?'

'Yes. But why . . . ?'

He looks at me. 'Can you ring them all, Rachel? Just in case?'

I nod, but Sarah is speaking again. 'No, no, there's no point, he doesn't know how to get there.'

'No, I know that, Sarah. But if he knows their address, or even the name of the road . . . someone might . . .' He pauses, obviously unsure whether or not to say what he's thinking. 'Someone might pick him up . . .'

She doesn't react. 'That's what terrifies me most.'

Hector moves forward and takes her hands. 'Sarah, try and remember that just about everyone out there will help him, if they find him. OK? Most people are good people.'

She nods mutely but it's small comfort.

417

Hector stands up as Glenn comes back into the room. 'What did they say?'

'They're on their way. They said we should check in his room to see if anything's missing. If he has run away, we might get an idea of where he's gone by what he's taken with him.'

'Right. Sarah, can you go and have a look upstairs with Rachel – check all the rooms – while Glenn and I have a look down here? Make a note of anything that seems to be missing.'

This is better. Sarah feels it too – actually to be doing something positive. There's a huge well of pent-up energy, adrenalin, urge to act, which we finally put to use as we hurry up the stairs. Jake's room looks exactly the same as it did two nights ago. There are no obvious empty spaces on shelves. We go in and stand in the middle of the floor, looking around.

'What do you think?' I ask Sarah. She's got her arms wrapped around herself, her mouth open and twisted down as if she's crying, although she isn't.

She shakes her head. 'I can't think. I don't know . . .'

'Right, well, what's his favourite toy?'

She looks at me helplessly. 'I can't . . .'

'It's all right, Sarah, you're mind isn't working properly at the moment. What about that thing you bought him for his birthday last year – Gameboy?'

She nods. 'Yes, that's probably it.'

'Where does he keep it?'

She walks over to the bed. 'It's usually here on the bed-side cabinet. He plays with it in bed.'

Well, it's clearly not there. 'OK, is there anywhere else he might keep it?'

She shakes her head. 'There might be, but it was on there this morning. I don't think he's played with it today. I can usually hear it, you know, when it's on.'

'So it looks like he's got that with him. Can you see anything else that's missing?'

She looks around the room, shaking her head, trying to remember. 'Oh, that bear that Glenn gave him is missing. The one that talks. He's always got that with him. And his rucksack. His little green frog rucksack. It hangs from the end of his bed and he hardly ever uses it so it never gets moved. It's gone.'

It's really hard to think about a six-year-old boy putting his Gameboy and a teddy bear into a frog rucksack, with some kind of plan in his head. It's so secretive of him, which is terrible for me to grasp, let alone for poor Sarah.

Downstairs, Glenn and Hector have not been able to find anything obvious that's missing. Sarah checks the fridge and other food cupboards and weeps when she finds almost a whole Angel cake and a mini packet of Coco Pops missing. This tiny child believes he will need food while he's carrying out his plan, and what he chooses to take is cake and Coco Pops.

There's a five-pound note missing from Sarah's purse, and her mobile phone is gone. On this discovery, Hector dials it immediately, but it's not switched on.

'Of course,' Glenn says bitterly, sagging under almost unbearable disappointment. 'How would a six-year-old know that it needs to be switched on?'

'Right,' Hector says. 'Glenn and I will go out in the car and look for him. Can you two deal with the police when they get here?'

'Course.'

He looks at me and jerks his head towards the hallway, so I follow him out there. He touches my arm. 'Are you all right?'

I nod.

'Listen, do you think you'll be all right to look after Sarah, while we're out? I mean, if we find . . . If it's bad news . . .'

'It won't be.'

He puts his hands either side of my face. 'Rachel, can you cope here with Sarah, if it's bad news?'

How can I answer that? No one knows whether they will be able to cope with that situation, and no one should ever have to find out. I don't even want to try and imagine what it would be like, as if somehow thinking about it will make it happen. But Hector needs an answer so he can go and hunt with a focused mind. He doesn't want to be worrying about what's going on here while he's out there. Finally I nod, even though I am far from sure that I will cope, I am more sure that I absolutely will not cope, will not be able to think or move or be any use to anyone, least of all my friend Sarah who will be reacting to the worst news she could ever receive.

'OK,' he says and gives me a smile. 'I've got my mobile phone . . .'

I nod again. 'I'll call you the minute he turns up.'

He strokes my cheek with a sad smile, hesitates just a second, then turns and strides to the front door. 'Come on then, Glenn.'

Glenn emerges from the living room, rubbing his eyes, and the two men leave.

As soon as they're gone, my belly solidifies again and freezes my breath in my lungs. Only this time it's showing me what it can really do. It's tighter, longer and beginning to be slightly painful. I clench my teeth and fists, holding my breath until it passes. Then I put the kettle on.

Thousands of images crowd into my mind as I wait for it to boil: a tiny dark shadow, curled in a cold corner, shivering, arms wrapped round himself, angel cake crumbs mingling with the tears on his face; cars that speed along the darkened streets too fast, not expecting suddenly to see a wide-eyed six-year-old out at this time; predators of all kinds, seeing only too readily how to make use of a discovery like this. I know that he is longing for his mummy by now, freezing and frightened, lost and alone, unable to remember his way back, thinking that he'll never get home again. I shake my head and take two cups of tea through into the living room. As if this is going to make Sarah feel better, but I don't know what else to do.

She's at the window, staring at the dark road, one hand holding back the curtain. I hear her voice, mumbling something quietly and it's a moment or two before I can make out that she's saying, 'Where are you, Jake, where are you?' over and over.

'I've made you a cup of tea, Sarah,' I say, holding out the cup.

She turns to me and takes it, saying, 'Oh God, Rachel, he's out there somewhere. Where is he? What's happening to him? What's he going through, right this minute?' I shake my head, but she doesn't want an answer. 'And why did he go? What's he thinking? What on earth persuaded him that he needed to do this? *Where's he going?* He doesn't know the way, wherever it is.'

She drops the curtain and moves back to the sofa, putting the mug down on the floor.

'He hates the dark so much he has to have a Thomas the Tank Engine light on in his room all night.' She says this to the floor.

I sit forward and touch her arm. 'Sarah, try and picture all the mums and dads out there. Thousands and thousands of them. Far more than . . . other people. More good people than bad people. I mean, if you found a lost six-year-old what would you do? You'd make sure he was safe, wouldn't you?' She looks at me and nods. 'So that's probably what will happen. Someone will find him and take him straight to the police station. It's very unlikely that anything bad . . .' From the terrified expression on her face, I decide to stop. Just the words 'anything bad' immediately makes us both realize what bad things could happen to him. I know that the good people outnumber the bad people, but it's dark now. Good people are locked safe inside their homes while the rats and night-walkers make the streets their domain until the sun comes up again.

I'm stroking Plum protectively. He's pushing a leg, or arm, into me fiercely. It feels for a moment as if he's going to make a hole. Looking at Sarah, I know that she will not be able to function without the survival of Jake. The end of his life would effectively bring about the end of hers. It's not occurred to me until now how vulnerable you are once you're a parent. You become totally dependent on the continuing survival of your child. The child himself, of course, will survive, whatever happens to his parents. If you die, he'll be cared for by someone else and will recover from your absence in time, scarred by the loss, but not destroyed by it. No amount of time or care will ever mend the bereaved parent.

These morbid thoughts are interrupted by the doorbell. Sarah's head jerks up and she looks anxiously towards the door. 'I'll go,' I say, leaping to my feet the way an elephant would, and hurrying along the hallway. I can see through the glass that it's two police officers standing there, but they might have some news and it might not be good.

'Good evening, Mrs McCarthy, I'm Lorna Daniels and this is my colleague Steve Sparks.' For one completely brainless, disconnected and self-obsessed moment I am about to say, 'Oh no, we're not married yet.' Then I realize she means Sarah. Of course.

'I'm not Mrs McCarthy, she's in here.' I indicate for them to walk down the hall. 'Is there any news?'

'No, not yet Mrs . . .?'

'Miss actually. Rachel Covington.'

'Ah. Well, Miss Covington, no news yet, I'm afraid, but I'm sure he'll turn up. They usually do.'

I stop. 'Sorry? What did you say?'

'I said they usually turn up.'

'Ah. So six-year-old boys run away a lot, do they?'

'Er, well, not as—'

'And in your experience, they fend for themselves quite successfully out there, do they, overnight?'

They've stopped just outside the living-room door and turned to look at me. 'Um . . .'

'I imagine there's a little community out there somewhere, where all the under-seven runaways gather together and look out for each other? Take it in turns to heat milk, read each other a bedtime story? Keep the paralysing terror at bay?'

They look at each other, then Steve Sparks says, 'Ah,

423

Miss Covington, I'm sure my colleague didn't mean any offence by—'

'The point is,' I interrupt, 'that Jake's parents just want him found. They don't need to hear "He'll be fine", or "He's bound to turn up", because it won't make the slightest bit of difference to how they feel all the while their precious child is out there, on his own, at night. All it does is belittle the strength of their feelings.'

Lorna Daniels is going red. She says, 'Well, I apologize, Miss Covington. I really didn't mean to upset anyone.'

'Just stick to the facts from now on, please. That's what Sarah needs. Not your opinion.'

I am roaring inside. I feel like I could rip someone's arms off and swing them round and round my head, shrieking, *You're a fucking imbecile!* I have to content myself with clenching and unclenching my fists as the two officers carry on into the living room.

I hear Sarah stand up, her voice anxiously asking them if they'd heard anything, and the voice that replies is calm and low as it says they haven't got anything to tell her, but all squad cars in the area have been alerted and as soon as they hear anything, they'll pass it on. There's a pause, as if something isn't being said, and I imagine Daniels pressing her lips together to stop herself from saying something like, 'Try not to worry, Mrs McCarthy.' Then Daniels asks Sarah if she wants a cup of tea.

I've got this almost overwhelming urge to be doing something, like a big ball of energy bouncing around inside me, trying to get out. I can't sit still; I can't stand still, so I shift from foot to foot, swinging my arms, looking about. My scalp is tingling and my hair feels as if I've been rubbing balloons on it. My eyes land on the cupboard under the stairs and on impulse, I open it and pull out the broom, Hoover and dustpan. Daniels comes out of the living room carrying Sarah's mug, the tea I made her earlier cold and untouched. She smiles at me weakly, "Scuse me,' then heads towards the kitchen. Right. I'll go upstairs then.

Halfway up the stairs, my stomach goes into spasm again, clenching tighter and tighter around poor little Plum, as if condensing him into a tight ball. I try to bend over and this time the pain intensifies a little, moving another couple of notches up the 'Uh-oh' scale. I'm very surprised that it would hurt this much – from what I'd read, Braxton Hicks contractions are meant to be painless. And that's all they are. Just false labour. Nothing else.

I'm really rubbish at facing facts, aren't I? I think I'll call this baby Denial. I mean, Daniel.

Bending over on the stairs clutching the Hoover in one hand and my belly and dustpan in the other is not easy even when you're not eight months' pregnant.

As soon as it eases, I come back to life and resume dragging the Hoover upstairs. I'm going to give Jake's room a spring clean. Clear all the shelves off, wipe them down, rearrange the books, give all the other surfaces a polish, clean the windows, make the bed, hoover—

'Er, Miss Covington . . .' It's Sparks, standing at the bottom of the stairs.

I turn. 'Yes?'

'If you're going to do some cleaning upstairs, could you please not go into Jake's room? We need to preserve it as it is, just for the time being.'

Arses. 'OK. Fine.'

Sarah's room is a bit of a mess. It's mostly just dirty

clothes on the floor so I scoop them up and push the Hoover round. There's a few cobwebs on the ceiling, too, which are very satisfying to suck up the tube.

I don't think there's much point dwelling on what's going on in the house. I'm on a one-woman cobweb annihilation exercise, and Sarah is silent and tearful on the sofa, chewing her fingers. She is brought cup of tea after cup of tea, but they all grow cold on the floor. She gets up and walks to the window, pulls the curtain aside, looks out. She goes back to the sofa and sits down. She gets up again. Time ticks on agonizingly slowly. Eventually it is almost eleven o'clock at night and Jake is still not found.

Let's go to where Hector and Glenn are, snapping at each other in the car. Looking through the windscreen from the front of the car, we can just make out two pale, frowning faces, hunched forward as near to the dashboard as they can get.

'Here, turn down here,' says Glenn, pointing at a road on the left. 'His school is down there.'

'We already tried the school,' Hector says, going past the turning.

'So bloody what? Maybe he's arrived there since we last looked.'

'Is that what we're going to do then? Spend the entire night checking places we've already looked in?'

'Oh and have you got a better idea, big brother?' Glenn's voice is getting louder.

'I just don't think it serves much purpose to keep going over the places we've already been.' So is Hector's.

'Well, what do you bloody suggest then?'

426

'I haven't got a fucking clue, Glenn. Do you want to drive?'

'No I don't,' he says grumpily. He needs to be able to peer constantly into all the dark shadowy corners where a tiny person might be crouching.

'Right. Tell me where his friends live.'

'Oh, for fuck's sake. What's the point of that? He doesn't know how to get there, even if I can remember.'

'Glenn, give your boy a bit more credit, for crying out loud. Children soak up information like a sponge. He probably knows his way to lots of places just by paying attention when he sits in the car.'

'Right, fine. Whatever. One lives in Albion Road, I remember that. One lives right near the school, in Mayfleet Close.' He jerks as he spots something outside. He points to a turning on the right. 'Wait, there's a sweet shop down there that Sarah sometimes takes him to after school.'

'We drove past it the first time we tried the school,' Hector says with exaggerated patience. 'And anyway, Glenn, we have to think about what motivated him to do this in the first place. What does he normally do if he wants sweets?'

'All right, all right.'

They lapse into uneasy silence, Glenn leaning forward in his seat, squinting into the darkness, his head turning all the time, to the right, the left, behind, back to the front. Hector wants to drive really fast, his pressing sense of urgency to rescue his little nephew flinging adrenalin through his veins, pumping his heart at twice its resting rate. But he knows he has to drive very slowly, so that they can spot every undersized shadow that cringes in a doorway or huddles in a hedge. His hands are gripping so tightly on the steering wheel, his fingers have gone white.

The brothers have not discussed what they both believe is the reason behind Jake's disappearance. Glenn doesn't dare to open up that particular package – he knows that if he even touches it, he will not be able to survive the shockwave. Hector is keeping silent on the matter. He knows that too.

Slowly, slowly, the brothers crawl through the cold streets, at times reassured by the absence of many people; at times disturbed by it.

'What was that?' Glenn barks suddenly.

'Where?'

'Back there, next to that letter-box.'

'What did it look like?'

'Fucking hell, Hector, *turn the car round.*'

At the house, Sparks is getting a message on his radio. I've come down now and am whipping round the living room with a duster. I'll need to hoover after this – the dust is really quite thick. Is there a limited amount of dust that can collect on your furniture? Does it reach that depth and stop, like saturation point; or if you leave it for a hundred years would it just keep getting thicker and thicker and thicker?

'Excuse me,' Sparks says, getting up and leaving the room as an incomprehensible voice hisses out of the radio on his shoulder.

Sarah jumps and watches his exit with wide eyes. She stands up and takes a step towards the door to follow. Daniels gets up too and takes Sarah's arm. 'Best leave it a minute, Sarah,' she says kindly.

Sarah looks at the police officer with wild eyes. 'B-but . . . He . . . he's . . .'

Daniels nods. 'If it's any news, he'll come straight back and tell you. Try—' She bites off the end of that sentence with a glance at me. We lock eyes for a nanosecond, then I resume polishing the mirror over the fireplace.

Sparks re-enters the room, his expression unreadable. Our three anxious faces turn to him expectantly.

'They've found his rucksack,' he announces tonelessly.

When he said 'found' Sarah jerked out of her seat with a small sound, but now she sinks down again, looking at me helplessly.

'What does that mean?' she asks, and I'm wondering the same thing. While Sarah is gazing pleadingly at Sparks, take a quick look at Daniels. Did you see it? For just a moment, a fraction of a second, her face showed freezing dread at Sparks's news. But then she composes herself, re-arranges her reassuring smile and touches Sarah's arm.

'It doesn't mean anything, Sarah. Don't read anything into it, honestly. It means nothing.'

But we saw her face, didn't we? We know she's lying.

The radio crackles again and we all jump. For a moment Sparks doesn't move, as if he knows what is coming, and it's not good. He shoots a meaningful look at his colleague, then retreats to the hallway again.

For twenty-three seconds, Sarah and I live in a world where Jake is dead. My scalp freezes, my mouth dries and burns; Sarah's eyes lose the ability to see, her ears to hear. Everything is a thunderous rushing sound and all the light in the room closes in around the one thing I can't look at: Sarah's frightened face.

'They've found him! He's found!' Sparks re-enters the

room suddenly, speaking as he enters. He bounds over to Sarah and flings his arms around her, squeezing her tightly and bouncing her up and down. I am touched by his obvious enjoyment in imparting this wonderful news. Sarah grips his arms and stares intently into his eyes, as if trying to reassure herself that he is telling her the truth. 'Your husband rang in just a few moments ago—'

'Glenn . . . found . . . ?'

'He found the rucksack, on the pavement by Jake's school. Then within ten minutes of that, we had another call from a member of the public saying he'd witnessed . . .' He pauses, just for a second, stumbles, then carries on. 'He found a small boy, only a bit further along. The description matches what you've told us about his clothes and appearance.'

Witnessed what? I'm thinking. And why match him to his description? Why not simply ask him who he was?

'Steve, what else did they say?' Daniels says calmly. 'Where was he found?' I don't see how this matters right now. 'How is he?' That's a good point. 'And where is he now?' Very good point.

Sparks and Sarah disengage. 'They've taken him to hospital,' Sparks says, looking at Sarah.

'Ho—?'

'He has been injured,' Sparks goes on.

'Wh—?' Sarah's hand goes to her mouth. She looks as if she's about to vomit. I drop the duster and go to her side as her legs buckle under her and she collapses on to the floor.

Chapter Twenty-three

We're in the back of the police car, speeding towards the hospital. The siren's on and the lights are flashing and inside the car it is absolutely deafening. We can't hear anything, we can't speak to each other, we can't even think. Yet the howling siren is somehow the perfect accompaniment to the squeezing agony that's going on in my belly. If there was a sound equivalent of that pain, this is it.

Before we left the house, Steve Sparks told us what he knows so far. It seems that the motorist who phoned the ambulance was driving along Church Road behind a motorcyclist. He claims that he saw the motorcyclist swerve suddenly and wobble dangerously, and at the same moment he saw something flung backwards on the pavement. He assumed something had fallen from the motorcycle's pannier. He didn't know it then, but he had just seen a six-year-old boy being struck by the speeding motorcycle and left bleeding and unconscious in the gutter. He continued on for another hundred yards or so but couldn't escape the feeling that he had seen something that wasn't right, so eventually turned round and went back. He walked up and down in the darkness for a few minutes before finally finding Jake's battered little body under a hedge. He was so shocked and horrified, he threw up on the pavement. He must have thought Jake was dead. I know how that feels. He called an ambulance and went to the hospital, though, so he knows he's not dead now. Sparks and Daniels have to speak to him when we get there. God willing, they will also speak to Jake himself.

When Sparks said it was Church Road, the first thing I could think of is that he was on his way to school, as it's very near to there, but what would make him want to go to school on his own, at night? The more I think about that, the more I am convinced he was on his way somewhere else, not to school. I have a theory, but I'm not going to talk to Sarah about it until I have a chance to see what Jake says.

Sparks said that there is the possibility that he was picked up by someone, and dropped off on Church Road, before the motorcyclist struck him. It's a line of enquiry, although it seems unlikely that anyone would do that and not contact the police, or at least make sure that he got safely to his destination.

'Umph,' I say and you can see from my poor face that another searing pain is ripping through me. No one hears me, though. Not even me. The siren's screech is louder than mine and, if I'm honest, wailing to myself as the pain grips me does help somehow, even though I can't hear it.

I'm not thinking what you're thinking. I am having a caesarean next Thursday. In six days' time. The plain old fifth of April. I'm booked in already, so I can't do it now.

Five minutes later, we're arriving at the hospital. Sarah's acting as if her clothes are on fire. She practically flings herself out of the police car even before it has stopped properly, and rushes into the Accident and Emergency department, her eight-month pregnant friend hobbling in awkwardly behind her in the company of two police officers.

As we enter, everyone in the waiting room turns and looks at me with interest, the dark blue of a police uniform instantly drawing every eye, even those whose heads were turned away. How do they do that?

Sarah is standing at the receptionist's window, having just shouted out Jake's name apparently.

'Would you mind keeping your voice down, please?' the receptionist is saying. 'We do have some very sick people here.'

'I know that,' Sarah says, really slowly. 'My six-year-old son is one of them. Now can you tell me where he is, please?' Look at her face – she looks like she could rip a few arms off herself.

At this point the receptionist notices the two police officers come in and is momentarily distracted, smiling at Steve. 'All right, Steve?'

Sarah leans down to the window. 'Jake McCarthy,' she says through gritted teeth.

Turns out he's been taken to Intensive Care, which is on the third floor. 'Follow the yellow line,' the receptionist says, pointing at the floor.

We follow the line until it comes to a lift so we get in. When we come out on the third floor, there is the yellow line again, reassuringly familiar. Comforting, Sarah says. The colour yellow in a hospital context makes me think of pus and fever, but I don't say this to Sarah. She's walking extra fast and won't stop talking.

'I can't believe it, Rach, he's been hurt, my poor little baby was out there all alone and got hurt by someone and I couldn't help him, I've never been to this part of the hospital before, I've only been to the maternity area, which is only on the first floor, really good place to put it too cause when you're heavily pregnant you don't want to be hauling yourself up three or four flights of stairs when the lift breaks down. Oh God, I hope Jake is all right. I just can't bear the thought of him out there all on his own wanting his mummy so badly and me not coming.'

The two police officers are following along behind. I'm assuming the man who found Jake is up in Intensive Care, waiting to be interviewed. I really don't like the idea of this stranger hanging around our boy. Yeah, thanks for finding him, now clear off home and mind your own business, it's got nothing to do with you.

Do I sound ungrateful? I don't mean to be. It's just losing Jake like that for all that time has made me so fiercely protective of him. I want to claw out the eyes of anyone who hurts him. And as we arrive at an archway with a sign hanging in it saying Intensive Therapy Unit, I am starting to feel that way about the man who found him too, hanging around where he's not wanted. I feel like telling him, when I see him, that he's bloody well in the way, this is a private family matter and we need our privacy, so he should just—

'Nick!'

Just inside the archway, sitting hunched on an orange vinyl chair with a rip in it that's been mended with black tape, is Nick Maxwell. Doesn't he look pale? And small, somehow. The expression on his face is frightened, anxious, those beautiful eyes wide and dark, his lips trembling as if he wants nothing more than to have a good cry. His eyes widen further when he sees me. They have to, to fit me in.

'Rachel? What are you doing here?' He stands up and approaches me eagerly, some of the strain in his face smoothing away. What was that, then? Was that *relief*? Is he relieved to see me? Why?

'I'm with my friend. Her little boy has been injured. What about you?' Behind me, Sarah has hurried on past to the nurses' station.

'You won't believe this. I've just seen a bloody awful accident, right in front of me. Some motorcyclist hit a little boy on the side of the road. Right in front of me. It was awful. The bastard didn't even stop.'

I stare at him. I really don't want Nick Bloody Maxwell to be the hero of this story. '*You*? You found him?'

He looks back at me. 'Yes, me. Oh, God, Rachel, it was so awful. I thought—' He breaks off, taking in what I've said, the fact that I've arrived with two police officers who are, even now, moving in. 'Wait a minute. Is it your friend . . . ? Is it her child . . . ?'

I nod.

'Wow. Small world.'

'We'd like to ask you a few questions, please,' says Daniels, stepping forwards.

'Course, course,' Nick says, edging closer to me. 'I've already told the guy on the phone everything, though.'

He glances at me, as if he would really like me to stay with him, but the two officers are clearly waiting for me to leave, so I do.

It's not until I'm round the corner by the nurses' station

that I realize I completely and utterly forgot to go and see Nick at work today (God, was it only today?) and tell him about his imminent fatherhood. I go back and peer round the corner at him, talking to Sparks and Daniels. He raises his right arm above and behind his head and puts his head to one side, obviously demonstrating the position Jake was lying in when he found him. Perhaps now is not the best time.

The Intensive Therapy Unit is a hushed, low-lit environment where people talk in muted tones and walk slowly in soft-soled shoes, so that the peace is not disturbed by raised voices, or loud footsteps. Even the rattle of the food trolley and the clatter of stacked plates make no impact here; none of the patients is on solids.

At the nurses' station, a very young male nurse points me towards Jake's bed. I approach with small steps and held breath. Sarah is sitting on a chair by the side of the bed, holding a tiny white hand in hers and stroking the hair away from his eyes.

Jake is lying on his back, bare to the waist with blankets over his legs. He looks so out of place here. The tubes that go in and come out of him are adult-sized; his body is too small for the bed; huge machinery pumps vigorously up and down; giant bleeps appear on a screen; everything is white and silver – there are no bright primary colours. His eyes have been taped shut. The treatment he's receiving looks as though it will do him more harm than good.

'Sarah,' I whisper in horror, approaching the bed, tears blurring the sight of him. I can't bear to look at him, but I can't take my eyes off him. One side of his face is scraped and raw, all the way from his forehead to his chin. There are other bruises just turning blue on his arms and chest.

But these are minor things that will heal. The real terror lies in the enormous dressing on his head.

Sarah looks as if someone has drawn all the blood from her veins. She is empty, a pallid lifeless shell of herself.

A nurse comes over and smiles. 'Are you his mum?' she says softly to Sarah, who nods mutely, not taking her eyes from Jake's white face. 'Don't be too concerned about the tape on his eyes. It's just to make sure they stay shut while he's unconscious.'

'Uncon . . . ?'

The nurse rubs Sarah's arm. 'I'll get someone to come and talk to you.' She walks away.

'Look at him, Rach,' Sarah whispers. 'He's so small . . . His little body . . . so fragile, so . . . unprotected. How could such a tiny, delicate little boy survive all on his own?' She leans forward in her seat and presses her lips on to Jake's unmoving cheek, lingering there for several seconds. Even when she moves away, she does not sit down but stays, bent over him, her face inches from his. 'You'll be fine, my brave little boy,' she says. 'Mummy and Daddy are here now, you'll be good as new. I promise.'

I start. Bloody hell! Glenn. Glenn and Hector, to be more precise. They're still out there, searching, worrying, terrified. I look at Sarah, nuzzling her boy's cheek. I must go and ring them and get them here. I touch her arm. 'Sar, I'm going to go and ring Glenn and—' I stop as my stomach closes in again suddenly, constricting everything, cutting me off. I wrap my arm across my belly and feel the iron-like mound beneath the skin. I wonder if Plum can feel this – and what it feels like. My head is pounding and the pain almost takes me off my feet. I lean heavily on the bed, doubled over, eyes screwed shut, immobilized until eventually it eases off and releases me.

Very near by, in an unreachable place, tiny black, sightless eyes are wide open and tiny arms push uselessly at the walls. A small heart beats faster with anxiety as the sensual being understands a change is happening. The walls are squeezing and squashing, tightening and holding, and doll-sized legs try in vain to straighten out. The walls will not stop pushing in, on to chin, shoulders, arms and toes. The legs cannot stretch out and the body cannot move, so it stops, and waits.

'All right, Rach?' Sarah whispers across to me, dragging her eyes away from her son's face for a moment. I nod.

'Mm-hmm, fine, just Braxton Hicks. No problem. I'm off to call Glenn.'

She dismisses me and turns back to Jake. 'Oh, yes, Glenn. Please ring him. Daddy will be here really soon, little man. Really soon now.'

I wander off, one hand pressed into the small of my back, which is aching like crazy. It must be the stress, I tell myself, starting not really to believe it.

There's a pay phone back along the corridor near the lifts. I pass the ripped orange chair on my way out, but Nick and the police have gone. I ponder for a moment what that could mean. Has he been arrested? Was it him who hit Jake and he's made up the motorcyclist to conceal his own guilt?

No, I don't believe that. He's a filthy, two-timing, cheating little scumbag, but a very considerate driver. And he did seem genuinely upset just now.

On the way down the corridor, I'm rubbing absent-mindedly at the small of my back as I walk, breathing through my mouth. The young male nurse who was at the station in I.T.U. earlier is walking towards me. He grins at me. 'Good luck!' he says with a wink as we pass each other.

'Th . . .' I start to say, but then I'm not sure whether he means with the phone call, with Jake's recovery or with . . .

No, can't do that now, must call Glenn and Hector. That is going to happen next Thursday. Fifth of April. Not now, can't do it now, too much going on, it's just false labour.

The anxious expression on my face says different.

Hector's phone is answered on the first ring.

'HELLO?' It's Glenn, shouting down the phone. The car noise is very loud.

'Glenn, it's Rachel. Jake's been found, he's here, he's alive.'

There's a pause. In the background I can hear Hector shouting frantically, '*What?*'

'WHERE ARE YOU?' Glenn shouts.

'In the Edward Hospital. Get here as soon . . . Aaaaaaahhhhhhh!' This time it takes my breath away as white-hot pain knifes through every part of me with Plum, my precious little Plum, at its epicentre. I bend over as far as I can, feeling instinctively that the pain will lessen if I can wrap myself around it, cradle it with my body. I'm breathing hard, a little whimper escaping me on each exhalation. The receiver is still in my hand and I can hear Glenn's voice coming out of it, calling to me, then shouting at Hector to turn towards the hospital. Then it clicks and goes dead and I let go of it, watching it dangle backwards and forwards on its metal rope.

'You all right there?' I hear a man's voice nearby but I can't look up or answer. There is nothing but pain. 'OK, listen, try and hold on there, I'm going to get you a chair. All right?' I can't even nod. 'Hold on, I won't be a second . . .' The voice recedes, and with it goes the pain, fading back like the tide. I concentrate on my belly for a moment and now it seems impossible that the pain was ever as bad as all that. I shake my head. I feel guilty because that man has just rushed off somewhere to get me a chair, but I'm perfectly all right. It'll be embarrassing when he gets back; perhaps I'll just be gone by then and we need never even see each other's faces. I pick up the telephone receiver and hang it back up properly, then turn round ready to go back up the corridor to Sarah and Jake.

There's a male nurse – the same one I've seen before – standing behind me with a wheelchair. He smiles brightly at me. 'Here we go then. Pop yourself down here and I'll take you down to Maternity.'

'Oh, no, really, there's no need. I'm having a caesarean in six days, and right now I have to get back to I.T.U. My friend—'

'I.T.U.? No, love, I'm taking you down to the labour ward. Sharpish.' He spins the chair round expertly and we head towards the lifts.

I feel like I'm being kidnapped. 'No, no, please, I really need to get back to my friend in Intensive Care. Her little boy is in there. She's all on her own – I can't go . . .'

'Look, don't worry, er . . . ?'

'Rachel.'

440

'Rachel. It's all right, I'll come back up here later and tell her where you are. All right?'

'But she's—'

'She knows you're pregnant, right?'

'Yes . . .'

'Well then, she'll understand, won't she? She's got a little boy herself, she probably knows only too well how babies decide to come at the most inopportune moments. Although your little bundle couldn't have picked a better one, could he now? You were already here – that's a great start!'

We come out of the lifts and this time we're following a white line. I feel like a complete fraud being wheeled along when I'm perfectly all right, but it is a relief to get the weight off my feet. Thank God I was able to tell Glenn and Hector where Jake is before the pain came. In fact, Glenn will be with Sarah soon, so she won't be on her own for long—

'Aaaah!' Abruptly the pain whooshes back in and the world around me fades out. My breath is gone, there is nothing but pain, coming on and on, pain on top of pain, throbbing, grinding, shattering. There is a rushing sound in my ears and I know it is the sound of pain and death, I know I am dying and right now I want it, I want death because then the pain will stop.

'. . . out, in and out, nice big breaths as slowly as you can, soon be over, and there you are. Well done.' As I come back into the world, a world of no pain and life continuing, I realize that we've stopped moving and the nurse is crouching in front of me holding my hands, his voice calm and hypnotic. It's very soothing – I just wish I'd noticed it earlier.

And now we're arriving at the labour ward. Bit different

from the dim, hushed corridors of I.T.U., isn't it? People rushing everywhere, calling to each other, carrying things in and out of different rooms. Did you hear that? The crash of something large and metal hitting the floor, followed by a loud curse. And suddenly the air is slashed by a terrifying shrieking wail that rises to the point where the hair on the back of my neck is standing up and I have tears in my eyes.

'Here we are, labour ward,' says the nurse with me, wheeling me up to the nurses' station. 'I've got to go now but you'll be fine here.' It feels like he's brought me to the depths of hell and is now abandoning me. 'What's your friend's name?'

In the lulls of sound between blood-curdling screams, I tell him quickly about Sarah, and he rushes off. I watch his receding figure with terrified longing.

'Well now, and what do we have here then? Everything a'right with you, precious?'

Another nurse has appeared, this one in a dark blue dress. She's wearing a name badge that says 'Rosie', and she certainly is. She's rounded with lots of frizzy ginger hair escaping randomly from a thick plait. 'What's your name, honey?'

'Rachel Covington. Actually, I'm due to have a caesarean next week, on the fifth of April, so I shouldn't really be here.'

'Ah,' she says, looking at me. 'The ting is, precious girl, my friend who brought y'in says you've been getting contractions about every three to four minutes, bad ones. Is that right?'

'Well, I haven't timed them, but they have been quite painful.'

'Right then. Well now, can you tell me how many weeks you are, darlin'?'

'Thirty-seven.'

'Ah. So your wee mite is a wee mite early. Not to worry, he'll be absolutely fine, I promise.'

I hadn't worried until that moment.

'And who's your GP, my pet?'

'It's Dr Kantha—' I'm cut off by yet another fierce, overwhelming, ripping-me-in-half-and-stomping-on-the-pieces pain.

'Are y'getting pain now, precious girl?'

I don't answer.

'I'll take that as a yes then, will I? All right, poppet, just let your breath out, nice and slowly, that's the way, there y'are, all done. Now then, Dr Kant, did you say? Right. Let's get you into a delivery room.'

She takes hold of the handles and wheels me towards the screams. The sound is unholy and I wonder about the horrific agony that is causing them. Sarah thinks the Caesar women have it bad, but I wonder if she's ever heard anything quite like this?

'Ah, one of our ladies is making a bit of a racket today, isn't she? Poor ting. She'd do better to keep her energy for the pushing. That she would.'

She wheels me into an empty room. 'Here we are. Now then, you just pop yourself up on there, honey, and I'll come back with the doctor. All right then?' And off she goes.

I am clearly in no condition to be popping anywhere at the moment, least of all on to that bed. What do you make of it? It looks like an instrument of torture to me. Or a magician's prop, with stirrups and foot pedals, a dividing lower half that comes completely away from the top half, and a nice big absorbent pad across the middle. On trays, shelves and hooks around the room are gathered the other presumably essential giving-birth equipment. It seems all the best pregnant women are squatting on footstools or over buckets, or rolling around on giant inflatable spheres. And the rear-opening nightie is the item to be seen in.

Another contraction comes – yes, yes, you were right the whole time – and I fall against the bed. The pain travels down into my thighs and groin and I crouch down, holding on to the bed with one hand for stability. I lose all sense of where I am and what is going on, only clenching my teeth together, tensing every part of me, waiting for the pain to pass. What if they don't know about Plum being breech and try to make me deliver him normally, all the time expecting to see a head pop out while his feet are tangled up in my pelvis? What if I can't do it? Why have they all left me alone?

As I'm rapidly turning back into a four-year-old, I think we would do better to go back to Intensive Care and see how things are up there. Sarah has been visited by the doctor who is treating Jake, and by a very young male nurse who tells her that I am in the labour ward. She gives me a moment's thought, then goes back over what the doctor said. Severe concussion, causing some swelling internally, probably from the impact of his head with the ground. *His head with the ground.* She can't get that image out of her mind.

'His injuries aren't too severe, from what we can see. He's fractured his arm, but not seriously. We're keeping him unconscious at the moment and the ventilator is breathing for him to give his brain a chance to rest and mend. We're monitoring his progress constantly and when the swelling has gone down sufficiently we'll let him wake up. That's when we'll be able to see if there's any long-term or permanent damage.'

Sarah shivers as she hears those words again in her head. Brain damage. She moves nearer to her tiny son, clutching his arm. 'Please, please,' she whispers, tears in her eyes. His face seems whiter than ever, apart from the red grazed area, and she can't stop herself from seeing, over and over again, in a slow-motion replay in her head, Jake's sweet, soft little face thudding into the ground and sliding along it, the skin being torn away, the arm being broken. She forces herself to think about the pain and fear her precious child must have known in that moment, then closes her eyes as tears slide down her cheeks.

'Oh my God!' comes a cry behind her. Sarah's eyes fly open and she looks around to see Glenn and Hector arriving.

'Oh Glenn!' she says, standing up and rushing to him. He wraps his arms around her, holding her close for a moment then releasing her and moving nearer to the bed. He is holding the frog rucksack, and carefully places it on the end of the bed. Jake's feet don't reach this far.

'What did the doctor say?' he says shakily, taking in the bruises, the red scrape, the taped eyes, the terrifying bandage.

'He's got concussion and some swelling in the brain. They're keeping him unconscious to give his brain a chance to recover. When the swelling goes down they'll let him wake up and then we'll know if there's any . . . damage.'

'Damage?' Glenn turns to face her, horror-struck. 'Do you mean brain damage? They think he'll have brain damage? Oh Jesus.' He leans over the bed, placing his cheek against Jake's, stroking the hair back gently from his forehead. 'Oh Jakey, my little Jakey, I love you so much, matey. My precious little boy. I'm so sorry.' He stares at the tape over Jake's eyes for a few moments, then turns to Sarah. 'Are you . . . all right?'

She nods, then her face crumples as she starts to cry. Glenn moves nearer, enfolding her tightly in his arms, rocking her gently as she sobs.

'Oh, Glenn, it's all my fault, I should have been watching, I didn't even notice . . . I'm so sorry.'

'No, no, Sarah, it's my fault,' he says, his lips in her hair. 'I'm the one that's in the wrong, not you. I have put you through hell, both of you, and I don't deserve to have . . . I don't . . . Sarah, I love you. I don't want a divorce. I have missed you so much. You and Jake. You're the best things in my life. I don't want to lose you.'

She sniffs, pulls back so she's looking into his face. 'I've missed you too.'

They lean forward gently and rest their foreheads against one another.

Don't look at them for a moment. Look at Hector. See the expression on his face? He is standing a few feet away, glancing around the ward anxiously. What do you think he is searching for? He looks very worried about something. He turns to his left, scans the room, then turns again, peering through the low light into the corners of the ward, the other beds, the corridor. Finally, he turns back to Glenn and Sarah.

'Ahem, sorry to interrupt you two, but do you know where Rachel is?'

*   *   *

Here's Hector, fourteen seconds later, tearing along the corridor to the lifts. He thumps the call button repeatedly but no lift arrives in the two seconds he allows, so he bursts through the adjacent door on to the stairs, descending them two, three, sometimes even four at a time.

After two flights, he explodes out of the stairwell into the first-floor corridor and begins to sprint along it, heart thudding wildly, breath coming fast, eyes darting up, down, right and left looking for signs to the delivery suite. He realizes quickly that he does not need to see a sign as he can simply follow the coarse, inhuman shrieking he hears every minute or so. It makes the hairs stand up on the back of his neck with terror; he wonders with dread if that voice is mine.

As he runs along the white line, it crosses his mind fleetingly how many feet before his have pounded along this corridor, rushing to be by the side of the woman they love as she delivers their child? He wonders how many men have run to be by the side of a woman who is delivering another man's child? But it doesn't feel like another man's child to him.

At the nurses' station, he almost shouts out Rachel's name, then fidgets and shifts for ten seconds while the nurse looks her up on the computer. Eventually, she leads him deeper into the hellish place, screams and swearing rending the air.

'You must be excited. First baby, is it?' she says conversationally as she walks, apparently oblivious to the sounds of human torture going on all around.

'I can't fucking do this any more, I can't take it, will you just get the bloody thing out of me, cut me, please God just cut me, get it out, get the bloody thing out!'

447

'Yes,' says Hector distractedly, shivering.

She leads him through a doorway and he finds himself in a small room, in the centre of which is a high bed with bars either side, pedals underneath and lots of machinery on all sides. He looks at all this before finally noticing the tiny pale person sitting atop the bed.

'Hector!' Oh my God, am I glad to see him! 'Thank God you're here.'

He looks over at me from the doorway, his face a mixture of relief and concern. 'Rachel, there you are.' He comes over to the bed and leans down to embrace me, and he's all hot and damp as if he's been running. His arms are warm and tight as they enclose around my back, and he smells so reassuring. He looks into my face. 'Are you all right?' he says really softly, touching my cheek with his thumb.

I nod. 'Not in half yet. Do you know how Jake is?'

'The same as when you saw him, I think. You know he was found in Church Road? That's near his school, isn't it, where we found the rucksack. God, we must have driven right past him, lying there . . .'

'Don't think about it. It's not your fault.'

He rubs the back of his head. 'I can't help it. I've got these images in my head that won't go away . . .' He closes his eyes. 'That poor little boy. He must have been desperate . . .'

'Do you know who found him?'

'No. I haven't spoken to—'

'Nick Maxwell.'

He stares at me. 'What, you mean . . . ?' His eyes flick to my bump. I nod. 'Bloody hell. Christ. What a small . . . Hey, did you see him here?'

'Yeah.'

'So, what did he say about the . . . ?' He indicates Plum again. I bite my lip and look shifty. At least, I feel shifty. Hector is looking disapproving. 'You did tell him, didn't you? You didn't? Oh, Rachel, that's not good.'

'Oh, Hector, I completely forgot about it. I forget things all the time at the moment. I forgot something this morning.'

'Did you? What?'

I stare at him. 'I've forgotten. That's what I'm telling you.'

'Oh, yeah, right. I get it. But how could you forget this, when it's right there in front of you?'

'Well, I didn't remember at work, and then when I saw him upstairs I did remember but he was talking to the police. The time didn't seem right, somehow.'

'All right, point taken. But you must tell him the first chance you get. If not before.'

'I will, as soon as I finish this.'

The nurse comes back in with a trolley laden with terrifying implements. 'Right, Rachel m'lovely, you'll soon feel more comfortable.' I look at the equipment at hand and somehow doubt it. 'The anaesthetist is on his way to pop your epidural in. Do you want Dad to go or stay?'

'Stay.' I look at Hector who is eyeing the trolley uneasily. 'Is that all right?'

He smiles at me, realizing that I haven't corrected her assumption that he is the father. 'Of course, Rachel m'lovely. As long as I don't have to do anything.'

Hector has agreed to come into the operating theatre with me. I'm not sure that he is entirely comfortable with the plan, but he couldn't really refuse. Sarah, of course, is otherwise engaged and I can't face going in alone. I have never known fear like this. I know that I won't feel any pain, but it's the knowledge that parts of my interior workings are going to be shown to daylight that disturbs me. I keep thinking about the cut they are going to have to make in me, a very, very deep cut that goes through flesh, through muscle, through tissue. I'm going to have an extra opening for a while. The thought is almost enough to make me puke. Except I am numb from the chest down so vomiting without the use of my stomach muscles would be virtually impossible. Oh my God, I hope I don't have to throw up while I'm split open from hip to hip. I might lose some bits.

Anyway, here I am, flat on my back in the operating theatre. It's like a scene from *E.R.*, with the big circular lights above me, and people moving around just outside my field of vision. If only George Clooney was here.

They gave me some kind of sedative to drink about half an hour ago, which is supposed to calm me down enough to endure being conscious while they slice a new hole in my belly. If they'd have given me a crate of diazepam and a bottle of gin to wash it down with, it might have worked. Hector's gone off somewhere for the moment and I think they're about to start, so I wish he'd hurry up and come back.

Can you hear that buzzing sound, or are my ears ringing? No, no, it's definitely there. There's a green curtain hung up by my chin, and some activity is going on on the other side of it. How strange is this, being able to hear what's happening, but not feel it.

'Can you make it a heart shape?' I call out. They chuckle but I know they are shaving the lot off.

450

A nurse appears at my right shoulder with a blue gown and scarf on and crouches down to eye level. I look at him, thinking that he'll be wanting to look at my pupils to make sure they're dilating, or not dilating, or whatever they're meant to be doing, and I realize with a start that it's Hector.

'Woo, get you, Dr Kildare.'

'Thanks. The Batman costumes were all gone.'

There's a sound like heavy Dralon curtain fabric being cut, and the bed starts to rock around suddenly, making the green curtain in front of me flap. We both stare at it disconcertedly for a moment.

'How did you think Sarah looked?' I ask quickly, changing the subject.

'When I saw her, she had Glenn there, so probably better than when you did.'

'Oh, yes, of course. I hope they're all right.'

'Me too. When I came down here they were hugging and saying how much they had missed each other, so I'm hopeful.'

'Oh, thank God.' There's a loud sucking sound, like a Hoover pipe sucking water out of a bowl. Hector clears his throat loudly.

'So does this mean that the false contractions you were getting earlier on were probably real after all?'

'Well, I certainly hope so. I don't want to have to do all this again on Thursday.'

'Good point. I'm busy on Thursday anyway.'

'Are you? Doing what?'

'Sitting by the bed of a heart and lung transplant first thing; then hysterectomy at half two.'

'Heavens, you are in demand. Maybe you ought to go full time.'

'Nah, there's no money in it.'

'Job satisfaction, though.'

'Here we are then, Rachel, look who's here!'

It's the surgeon talking. We both fall silent and our eyes move upwards to the other side of the curtain. The surgeon is just visible, in a mask and a scarf like Hector's, and he's holding something up, something blue and pink and red and white and I realize suddenly, all in a rush, that this is my baby, this is the little life I had inside me, this is my Plum, my precious little Plum. The surgeon's hands are under the arms and around the chest, his fingertips almost meeting in the middle; the little pink legs are bent up, the knees round as peaches, the feet dangling, ankles crossed; and the head is lolling to one side, the face screwed and red. There is a giant blue hose coming out of the belly and down, disappearing behind the curtain and as I watch, one of the arms raises slightly, jerkily, then flops down again. My baby waved at me.

The surgeon cuts the blue hose and passes my baby to someone behind me who does things out of my sight. Then she hands a heavy, warm little bundle to me and lays it on my chest.

'There she is, Rachel, your new baby. Isn't she beautiful?'

'She?'

I stare into the miniature face, inches from mine, and can just feel tiny hot breaths touching me like prayers. She is all closed up, sealed against the world and my breath catches in my throat.

'Oh, my little daughter. My precious little daughter. Hello, my gorgeous darling. I'm your mummy.'

452

Chapter Twenty-four

Remember ages ago when I said that I was happy last year, with my fabulous, flirty life full of parties, clothes and hairdos? Did I say 'happy'? That's not really what I meant. It would be closer to say fucking stupid. The fact that I thought I was living a perfect life didn't actually mean that there wasn't something wrong; it just meant that I hadn't spotted it.

I don't particularly want you to stay and watch me being stitched together again, so let's move forward a couple of hours, to the post-natal ward.

Picture a darkened, quiet area, populated by bay after bay of sleepy mums gazing into cribs at their snoring babies, gently lifting a blanket to cover the little bodies, softly stroking a perfect tiny cheek, touching a velvet head.

Post-natal is nothing like that.

There are never less than two babies crying at all times, because when one starts, it wakes up the one nearest to it, which in turn wakes up the next one along, and so on, creating a domino crying effect. This never happens in reverse; one satiated tummy sending its owner swiftly off to the land of nod does not, unfortunately, send the others. And, of course, the more babies that are awake, the more mums are awake trying to calm them. The air is filled with the deafening roar of low, soothing voices.

The ward is in semi-darkness, leaving just enough light for the nursing staff to move around safely and keep everyone awake.

'You doing overtime this weekend, Abby?' says a loud voice walking past, accompanied by the slosh of a bed-pan.

'Not sure yet. Mark wants to go to Monster Trucks.'

The ward is made up of four beds on each side of enormous bays, of which there are three or four. I have been assigned to the first bed on the left in the third bay along from the door. Go past the nurses' station and head into the bay almost opposite. Look, there I am, lying wide-eyed and exhausted on my back. Two of the other beds in the bay are empty and all but one of the other babies and their mums are asleep at the moment – one is being fed – so our bay is blissfully peaceful. For now.

Come a bit closer to me. Right in. Now look at my daughter. Isn't she just the most amazing, the most beautiful, the most miraculous thing you've ever seen? Her face is so perfectly oval, her lips so full and kissable. She is going to have the boys queuing up at her door, just like her mum. And have you ever seen eyelashes like that?

Don't say, 'Yes, on Nick Maxwell.' It's not helpful.

The mum opposite is looking at me as her baby suckles – perhaps she wants to chat – but I can't sit up yet, so I've turned my head to gaze unwaveringly into the Perspex crib at my sleeping daughter, watching over her, protecting her from harm. My legs are still paralysed, so if harm comes this way I will shout very loudly.

It's four a.m. I'm pretty much immobile for the next three hours, so let's move on and have a look at how everyone else is doing on my daughter's birthday.

At six o'clock, Hector is up, singing in the shower. There he is, look, cheerfully rubbing shampoo into his hair, eyes shut tight as white foam runs down his face, drips off his chin on to his chest, trickles down his belly . . . OK, stop there – no need to see where the foam goes next.

'I get knocked *up*, but I get up again, you're never gonna keep me down!' he's singing loudly. That makes me smile – it's like our song, isn't it? He hasn't slept much since he got into bed three and a half hours ago, with all the events of the day running ceaselessly through his head. Suddenly he stops himself singing and his face becomes grave and concerned. And there's a flicker of guilt, too, isn't there? I bet he's thinking about Jake at that moment, feeling bad for feeling so good.

He's out now, rubbing himself dry, so I think we should leave him some dignity and see what news Sarah and Glenn have got. Hey, come on – leave.

Here they are, slumped on plastic chairs either side of Jake's huge bed. The intensive care unit is everything that post-natal isn't: peaceful, quiet, dark. But Sarah and Glenn have been kept awake by something else.

Look at poor Sarah's face. She's not so white any more – she's now got dark circles under her eyes that give her face its only colour. She's resting her head on the bed, her arm across Jake's legs, and at intervals she jerks and raises her head suddenly, looks him up and down, checking every inch of him from the top of his bandaged head to the ends of his toes. Then, after staring at him for five solid minutes, she slowly lays her head down again. She is restive while he rests, stressed by his sedation, made anxious, for once, by his total inactivity.

Glenn has not slept at all. Right now, at six o'clock, he is back in the chair opposite Sarah, staring at his wife and son, hands clasped between his knees. At intervals during the night he has paced the room, looked out of the window, stood and gazed at his dozing wife, touched Jake's foot. Do you think he feels responsible for all this? Well, he bloody well should.

Only Jake slumbers on, undisturbed.

Back in post-natal and it's seven-thirty. The nurses decide it's morning and open the curtains in every bay to the sound of 'Good morning, ladies!' as if we've all been snoring lazily in our beds well past the time that we should decently have been up and about. Around the ward, eleven pairs of swollen, bloodshot eyes peer resentfully up from their pillows at the cheery greeting.

Here comes the mum opposite me, dressing gown on, for a chat hopefully. I'm still dead from the waist down – not in that way, cheeky – so if I want company or attention, I'm utterly dependent on people coming to me.

'Keep an eye on Keanu for a minute, would you?' she says to me, lying encased in concrete. 'Just popping outside for a smoke.'

'I can't do anything,' I say, but she's already gone. As I watch the back of her off-grey dressing gown retreating towards the main door out of the ward, I am suddenly more sure than I have ever been about anything that her name is Michelle. But her friends call her Meesh.

God, this paralysis in my legs is so frustrating. I really want to go over and peer at the baby in the crib, just so I can make a mental note of how much prettier Plum is.

And I'm still dying to cradle my new daughter properly in my arms. They placed her on my collarbone when she was first born, but she was far too close to my face for me to see her properly. From here, I can just reach out and touch her in her crib, and rub her back when she snuffles, although the side of the crib digs into my arm. Her back feels so solid, so complete. I can feel shoulder blades and the bumps of a spine and tiny ribs that go in and out with each gasping breath. My splayed hand is the width of her back, which curves and fits perfectly into my fingers.

Think back to that green two-dimensional image Hector and I looked at four months ago on the scan day. Isn't it amazing that now it's this firm, warm, breathing person, with her own bones and lungs, blood and hair? She will have her own personality, her own identity, she will like things and dislike things and make choices and feel happy or sad or disappointed or confused. It's a life, a brand-new life, for her, and for me. She has made the jump with me into this new, fragile place and I wonder if she's as glad to be here as I am.

My fingers are going numb. I wonder why that is. Maybe I'm having a massive allergic reaction to the anaesthetic and my air pipes are going to swell up and seal shut, suffocating me in my bed. It could even be a blood clot or something and it's even now making its slow, emotionless way to my heart where it will block all the little valve thingies and give me a heart attack and I'll be cold by the time the woman opposite comes back from her fag. I'm calling the nurse.

'Take your arm out of the crib,' she says two minutes later. 'You're cutting off the circulation.'

While there's not much going on, just take a look at the

windows of the bay. They're all closed, and locked, would you believe? I asked earlier on if they could be opened as it's so hot in here – apparently new-born babies are perfectly safe in blistering sub-tropical heat as long as you count the togs – and the nurse told me they weren't allowed to open the windows 'because of the babies'.

'What do you mean?'

'Well, we don't want the babies falling out of the window, do we?' she said, as if she has witnessed first hand the tragedy that ensues when one of these flaccid, unaware little beings get an idea into their head. She raised her eyebrows at me, as if I really should know better. I'm staring at her and all I've got is the *Mission Impossible* music going through my head to the image of a determined line of babies climbing on to each other's shoulders to reach the window ledge so they can catch their first glimpse of the outside world.

I guess I've got a lot to learn about being a mum.

Ooh, did you see that? It's weird, but I think I just spotted my toes moving. I can't actually feel them moving, it's more like I'm imagining that they're moving. Wow. Oh, thank God for that. I might be able to get up in a minute.

Let's move forwards an hour. It's almost nine now and look at me, sitting up with my darling Plum in my arms! What I hadn't thought about when my toes were defrosting was the white-hot, searing agony across my belly that would follow. I got some strong pain relief pretty quickly, and it didn't come with a glass of water, if you know what I mean. The nurse pulled the curtain round the bed to give it to me, thankfully. I need to try and preserve the gram of dignity I have left.

Plum is warm and heavy in the crook of my arm. She's

had a bit of a feed and now she's dropped off again. I love the fact that she obviously feels safe with me. Her body and mine fit together.

Have you seen what she's wearing? It's the little white starry sleepsuit that Hector gave me in the office canteen yesterday. It was still folded up in my handbag. She looks like a princess in it, doesn't she? It's so perfect. I'm holding her foot in my other hand. It's as small as a mouse.

There's someone standing at the end of the bed and it makes me jump. But it's all right, it's Sarah, looking pale and tired. I'm guessing she's had a bad night's sleep too.

'Sarah! Hi. Come and sit down.' She smiles as she looks at my daughter and gently runs a finger down Plum's cheek.

'She's gorgeous, Rachel. Really beautiful.'

'Thanks, Sarah. How's Jake this morning?'

She sits on the chair and becomes more animated. 'The doctor came first thing and took him off for a scan. He said that the swelling had gone down so much they would let him wake up.' Her eyes fill with tears and I get a sick feeling. 'He opened his eyes about twenty minutes ago and asked for some ice cream.'

'Oh, Sarah, thank God!' I half lean forward and embrace her with one arm. I'm grinning like a fool.

'I know.' She's nodding but can't speak for a moment. I hold her hand as she cries. 'I can't tell you . . .'

I look at Plum. She doesn't have to tell me.

'Have you spoken to him about why . . . ?'

She shakes her head. 'No, not really. Church Road is right near his school, so I can only imagine he was trying to get there for some reason. It's so strange.'

459

'Sar, you know where Church Road leads, don't you?'

'Yes, on to Yew Avenue. Why?'

'Think about it. Yew Avenue turns into the bypass after the Hickman Roundabout, doesn't it? And what's on the other side of the bypass to Church Road?'

She stares at me for a moment, trying to work it out. Then suddenly her eyes widen and she pulls in a breath. 'Mill Lane? Do you mean Mill Lane?'

I'm nodding. Do you remember when I drove to Hector's house yesterday after work, we drove into a much more rural road that had fields on each side, and huge farmhouses glimpsed through the hedgerows? That's Mill Lane. Very close to Hector's house.

'It's just a theory, Sarah. You'll need to speak to him about it, but it doesn't seem likely that he would be trying to get to school in the middle of the night, does it?'

'No, no. You're probably right. Oh my God, he was just trying to get to his dad, wasn't he? Christ, my poor little mite.' She rubs her eyes roughly.

'Do you know who found him?' She shakes her head. 'Nick Maxwell.'

'Who's he?'

I look meaningfully towards Plum.

'What, you mean . . . ?' I nod and Sarah's eyes widen further. 'Jesus. Jesus. That's incredible.'

'I know. He witnessed the whole thing – the motorcyclist wobbling, Jake flying back . . .' I get a sudden vivid slo-mo image of Jake's little body falling on to the pavement, hitting the tarmac, skidding along it, his face, his downy cheeks torn and damaged by the rough surface. This is what has kept Sarah awake all night.

'I know. Thank God someone saw it – hopefully they

460

can prosecute the motorcyclist. He must have known he'd hit something.'

'Of course he did. You'd know if you hit a hedgehog on a motorbike, let alone a child, even in the dark.'

'That's what I thought too. God, Rach, I hope your Nick can remember some details about it. I hope they catch the bastard that hurt my boy and lock him up for ever.'

I've got my doubts about that, but I'm not going to tell Sarah. 'Yeah, me too.'

Sarah falls silent for a moment, then looks up at me again. She seems calmer now, doesn't she? More at peace than I have seen her for weeks. It's a relief.

'You know what, Rachel? Now I think about it, I'm not sure that I even care. Compared to everything else that's happened, it doesn't seem important. Jake's survived, he's fine. What else matters? Oh, yes, I know, he's got injuries but they're just physical, they'll heal. I am just so relieved that he has no psychological damage, nothing that will affect him his whole life. I couldn't have borne it if someone had . . .'

She doesn't have to say it. I'm relieved about that too.

'And Glenn's coming home.'

She's looking at me sideways, as if she's expecting me to disapprove, but I think she's right. I've always thought that men who cheat should be speared with hot barbecue tongs, dismembered – I mean separated from their member – and have their toenails and nasal hair pulled out with pliers on alternate days until there are none left. And dumped. Something like that, anyway. You can vary the details. But that was in my old life – my empty, selfish, pointless life. Now that Plum is in the world, I can see that nothing is as important as her happiness.

'I'm happy for you, Sarah. Jake will be ecstatic.'

'He will, won't he? Particularly when we tell him he's off to Disneyland.'

'Wow!'

She looks shattered. She's pale and has dark circles under her eyes and her limbs are too heavy to move easily. But her eyes are shining and she is bright inside. Sarah's life is back in the place where it belongs. With Jake and Glenn, together.

Before my second visitor, I have to make a phone call. I'm still not great at walking but fortunately there's a pay phone on wheels. Finally Meesh in the bed opposite is back, which is a relief because Keanu is squawking. She leaves him to cry and helpfully brings the phone over to me with a smile.

'Guess where I am?' I say, when the phone is answered.

'Hospital?' she says. How does she do that?

'Ye-es. And I've got someone here who wants to meet you.'

There's a pause. Then, 'Oh my God! I'm a granny! Oh my God! Where are you? Which hospital? Which ward? I'm on my way!'

I haven't even told her she has a granddaughter.

My next visitor arrives. Thankfully it is just moments after the nurse takes out my catheter and removes the wee bucket from under the bed. Urine travelling through a clear plastic tube across the blankets over your legs is not the most fetching accessory I've worn. I've got my back to the archway that serves as entrance to the ward so I don't notice anyone there until I've picked Plum up and am turning to sit back down with her in my arms. The tall figure standing at the end of my bed staring at us makes me jump again. I am so much less poised than I used to be, now that I've got more to worry about than what my hair is like.

'Oh!'

'How are you, Rachel?' Actually, he's staring at Plum, not at me. 'What did you have?' He dumps an enormous purple dinosaur on the end of the bed and I eye it uneasily. It's three times the size of Plum and if it fell on her would probably suffocate her.

'A little girl. A daughter.'

'A daughter,' he whispers, perhaps more to himself than to me or Plum. 'A daughter.' Is it my imagination or is he a bit taller since last summer?

'Why are you here, Nick?'

He looks up at me. He's holding a bunch of daffodils and crocuses that remind me of spring and new life. 'Come on, Rachel, you know why. She's my daughter too.'

I feel cold suddenly and pull Plum closer to me. She does not feel like anyone's daughter except my own. I don't know how he has worked this out but he has not been involved in any part of this, except the initial set-up. Surely he doesn't think he can just come along now and expect . . .

'All right if I sit?' he says, perching himself on the edge of the bed. A nurse appears to change the water in the jug by the side of my bed and he looks up and smiles as she passes. She colours and smiles back, lingering a moment.

'Beautiful, isn't she?' she says, staring at him. I am, apparently, invisible.

'Oh yes,' he says, flashing that confident, almost arrogant smile at her. For God's sake, why doesn't he leave? I do not want him here, do not want him being near my daughter.

The nurse leaves eventually. He watches her go appreciatively then turns back to me and Plum. He pauses for a moment to regain his thoughts.

'How's the little boy today?' he asks suddenly. 'Has he—'

'He's conscious,' I say harshly. I don't add 'No thanks to you', because actually it *is* thanks to him. But I don't feel that way. I feel as though he's personally responsible for Jake's injuries. I feel as though he's personally responsible for drought, disease and acne at the moment.

'Oh, thank God for that,' he says, relaxing visibly. 'I haven't slept a wink all night. I've just been thinking about it all the time, what he looked like when I found him, his little arm all twisted, the blood on his face . . .' His voice trails off and he concentrates hard on his lap for a few moments. 'I went up there first thing, but no one would tell me anything.' Good God, look at his face – do you think he's going to cry?

'Nick, he's fine. He bumped his head but he's absolutely fine now. Really.'

He nods but he doesn't look up and his lips are pressed hard together. 'Thanks,' he whispers.

I leave it a few moments before asking, 'Did you manage to give a description to the police?'

He nods and clears his throat, looking up at me. 'Yeah, quite a good one. I followed the bike for a few minutes before it happened, so I noticed the registration plate. I can't remember all of it but I did notice . . .' He trails off suddenly and his cheeks fill with colour.

'What? What did you notice?'

464

'Well, it's a bit embarrassing. I noticed that all the letters made up a kind of sentence, or statement, if you made a word out of each of them.' I'm frowning, so he carries on.

'It was S, then three numbers, then AAB. I was looking at it for a few minutes, trying to make words, which is a little game I play sometimes when I'm driving. Anyway, eventually I came up with: Sex in August, April Baby. The police reckon they'll be able to track the owner down, from that.'

'Oh, well, good.' I'm more than a bit taken aback. Couldn't he have thought of any other four words starting with those letters, especially as he had several minutes to think about it? Like maybe Stupid Arsing Arse Bastard – I came up with that one in a matter of seconds.

'I was thinking about you, about the baby, when all this happened,' he says suddenly, apparently reading my mind. 'I wanted to speak to you at work yesterday but it was difficult – you were down in Telesales and I was upstairs and I didn't really have an excuse to come all the way down there, you know. I didn't want a scene but it was impossible to get you on your own, without other people . . .'

'Paris, you mean?'

'Yeah, all right. I didn't want her to know about . . . to overhear . . .' He stops, then looks up at me earnestly. 'I love her, you know, Rachel.'

'Oh.'

'Yeah.' He smiles as he thinks about her. 'Anyway, someone in ITU told me you were here so I've come here now to talk to you about . . . everything. I am your daughter's father. I've worked it out. I'm right, aren't I?'

This is it. This is the moment I set Plum on one path

or another. She is not yet one day old and already I have the power to make life-altering decisions for her. For me, I don't want Nick Maxwell in my life. I can use this moment to deny him, get rid of him for ever. But what would Plum want? I'm looking at Nick, but then I look down at her lying comfortably in my arms and I find that her liquid black eyes are open and staring at me. I look into their depths and I can almost read what it says there. She is imploring me to do the right thing. She can't speak, can't act for herself, so she is relying on me, her mum, her fierce protector, to help her and do what is right for her. How can I deny those eyes?

I look back at Nick and smile. 'Do you want to hold her?'

To his credit, he looks a little surprised and very pleased. Perhaps he wasn't so utterly sure that he was the father. 'Can I?' he says, holding out his arms.

'Make sure you support her head.' I reach over and place my daughter in her father's arms, leaving my hands there too. 'Just, just . . .'

'It's all right, Rachel. Don't worry.' He bends his head and gazes into her face. Reluctantly I withdraw my hands. 'Hello, er—' He looks up at me again. 'What's her name?'

Bloody hell! I haven't even thought about it! I've been calling her Plum all night, but she can't go to school with a name like that. 'I don't know. She's just Plum at the moment.'

'Plum? OK. Hello, Plum. I'm your father.' I'm really glad for some reason that he didn't say 'daddy'. Father is exactly what he is. 'It's totally amazing to meet you.' He looks at me again and he's grinning. 'She's got your nose.'

He's saying exactly the right things, isn't he? 'Oh, do

you think so? I think she's got such a lovely little button nose but I really can't see any resemblance.'

'Oh yes, no doubt about it. Just like you. A total stunner.'

Oh, for goodness' sake. Look at me. I'm blushing. He really knows how to turn it on, doesn't he? And I am *pathetic*! Get a grip.

'When did you find out anyway? You've not said anything all this time.'

He doesn't raise his head. 'Pretty much since I saw you at Christmas, I suppose. I heard some rumours, then I saw that you'd put some weight on. I started thinking then, but I wasn't sure until you let Personnel know what your due date was.' He looks at me with that lopsided grin. No, it's not having any effect. 'I work in Personnel. It wasn't difficult to count back from the twentieth of April.'

'So why didn't you speak to me about it?'

His eyes flick up at me, then back down to Plum's sleeping face, as if he can't bear not to be looking at her. I know how he feels. We're holding this entire conversation with our eyes locked on Plum.

'Well, I couldn't speak to you about it at work because of . . .'

'Paris.'

'Well, yeah. Plus I didn't want everyone there knowing my personal business.'

'OK, so why not ring me?'

'I lost your number.' He shrugs. Just like that he dismisses the weeks of misery I endured last summer.

'But it's in my personal records at work. You're in Personnel, why not retrieve it from there?'

'Yeah, I know, you're right. I did look it up once, even

wrote it down in my diary. I was going to call you that night, from home, but it was awkward. I wasn't entirely sure that I wanted to be . . . I don't know. I didn't want to intrude. No, no that's not it exactly.' He sighs and looks up at me. 'I didn't want—'

'You didn't want your wife to find out,' I finish for him, rolling my eyes.

'Oh, for crying out loud, not you as well! Where the bloody hell is this stupid rumour coming from?'

'Keep your voice down.' I notice that some of the other mums and their visitors have looked round at us briefly. 'Look, it's no use keeping up this pretence. There's no one else here to convince, so you might as well just come clean.'

'Oh, Jesus, for the last time, I am not married!'

The ward falls silent suddenly and many more heads turn our way to stare. Nick's words hang suspended in the air for a few moments, then dissipate like smoke. I am concentrating very hard on straightening Plum's blanket around her.

'OK, right,' I whisper angrily, 'so the woman who answered the phone when I rang you up was who exactly? The cleaning lady?'

'When did you ring me up?'

'Oh some time last year, just after we . . . It doesn't matter anyway. The point is, who answered the phone? She said she was Mrs Maxwell. Explain that.'

He sighs, he fidgets, he strokes Plum's soft leg. Then he raises his head and looks into my face. 'So it *was* you, all this time. Just because of . . .' He shakes his head. 'You're right, she's not the cleaning lady. Well, not in an official capacity, anyway.'

'What?'

'She's not my wife either. She's my mum.'

I stare at him. Suddenly he looks very, very young, sitting there with our daughter in his arms, head bent over, slight flush on his smooth cheeks. 'Your mum? But I thought . . .'

'I know what you thought. But you got it wrong, didn't you? Rachel, I'm nineteen.'

'Nine . . . ?'

'No, not nine, for Christ's sake. That's ridiculous. I'm nineteen. In fact, I'll be twenty next week.'

'Y . . . ? You . . . ?' Fucking hell. He's nineteen. Jesus, that's almost illegal. But just look at him – the full sensual lips, the long black eyelashes, the beautiful hair, the student card that's fallen out of his jacket on to the bed. Oh dear God.

'I never said I was older, did I?'

'Well no, you didn't, but you never said you were a nineteen-year-old student living with his mum, either, did you? My God, Nick. I don't know what to say to you. Christ, you're a father and you're barely old enough to wet the baby's head.'

'I am not a kid, Rachel. Did I ever behave like a kid? Did you ever think for a second that I was only nineteen? Well, did you?'

'Well, no, but . . .'

'There you go, then. The actual number of years since someone was born doesn't matter. What matters is how people behave, their actions. It's maturity that counts, not actual years.'

I've gone all quiet and thoughtful. Actually, I'm thinking about what Nick was like last summer. Was he mature?

Did he act like a responsible adult, in spite of his age? Not really: there are two strikes against him.

'You're not old enough to be anyone's father, Nick. Yes, you are right, it's maturity, not age, that counts, but you fall down on both counts.'

'Why do I?' Look at him pouting now. Shall I ground him for a week?

'Because you did not behave maturely, did you? Firstly, your behaviour at the end of our relationship was very childish, just ignoring me without any communication at all.'

'So?'

'And secondly, you got me pregnant. That's totally irresponsible and immature, isn't it? So your argument about your maturity just doesn't stand up. Forget it.'

He stares down at our daughter, his bottom lip stuck out. Then he looks up at me. 'You hypocrite.'

'What?'

'You. You're a total hypocrite. I know for a fact that you have dumped people without telling them why in the past. Yes, I have been speaking to people at Horizon. At least three of them told me that you dumped them by not returning their phone calls. And you blame me for getting you pregnant, as if your actions had nothing to do with it? If I remember my biology GCSE correctly—'

'It was only last year.'

'Actually, it was two years ago. But that's not the point. You know as well as I do that it takes two people to make a baby. And you didn't use a condom either. How responsible is that?'

Just focus on Nick for a moment, because I am opening

470

and closing my mouth like a hungry baby, but no words are coming out.

Do you think he's right? Have I been irresponsible and immature?

I don't think you should answer that. We all know, deep down, if we think about it hard and long enough, what the answer is going to be, don't we?

I turn to Nick. Look at my face now – I think that's probably the most friendly I've been towards him since – well, since 28 July last year.

'So. You're not married, you're just nineteen.'

'Nearly twenty. But yes, that's the situation.'

'Hmm. Well, I have to admit, weird though it is, it certainly uncomplicates things.'

'Does it? How?'

I shake my head with a smile. 'You wouldn't believe the soul-searching I have been doing about your poor wife. How Plum's birth will affect your relationship; where Plum will go for Christmas; how she will get on with her half brothers and sisters, particularly if their mum is permanently resentful about your affair and brainwashes them into thinking Plum is the enemy; what kind of snide remarks or even underhand thumping she will be subjected to every day if she comes to stay with you during the school holidays; who will sit at the head table for her wedding because as her parents we should both be there, but no doubt your wife will have her own idea about that; whether Plum will have to put up with rude comments about me from your wife's family for the rest of her life. All that stuff.'

With his face like that – eyes wide and staring, jaw slack – you can really see just how young he is, can't you?

'Jesus,' he says, shaking his head. Then, 'Jesus,' again. It seems he is momentarily unable to say any more.

'OK, can I have her back now, please? I think she wants to go back to her mummy.' I reach out my hands and wiggle my fingers.

'Bye bye, Plum,' he says, not handing her over. 'At least for now.'

I look up sharply. 'What do you mean?'

'Rachel, I want to be part of her life. You can't deny me that. I'm her father.'

Shit. This is what I have been dreading. Although the whole idea of Nick seeing Plum regularly has lost a lot of its horror now that his wife is no longer on the scene.

'OK. We'll work something out. But she's living with me.'

He puts his hands up. 'Fine. Absolutely fine. I think that's definitely best.' Yeah, because a three-year-old toddler with vomit down her pyjamas bursting unannounced into a room can kill a romantic mood stone dead.

'Good.'

'And I'm going to give you money for her. That's what I want to do – it's the right thing to do.'

You know, maybe he is more mature than I thought after all.

I smile at him and lean towards him to touch Plum's head. 'Thank you, Nick.' Quickly I kiss his cheek, then draw back, and our eyes lock for a moment. Then we both look away, look down towards the beauty of our daughter, our heads almost touching.

What I can't see, but you can, is Hector, standing just on the other side of the archway. He's got a troubled look on his face as he watches us. See that carrier bag? It looks excitingly bulky, doesn't it? But now he looks as if he's not so sure. He glances at the bag then focuses back on Nick Maxwell, sitting on the side of my bed, holding my baby, and enjoying an intimate moment with me. And as he watches, I lean forward and kiss Nick on the cheek and he can hear me, quite plainly, as I say, 'Thank you, Nick.'

It's just after nine fifteen now. Let's go back a couple of hours and see what Hector has been doing since we left him getting out of the shower.

We know he was up early, so he was ready to leave the house hours before anywhere was ready to receive him. Here he is now, standing at that huge glass wall in his kitchen with a cup of coffee. The clock says seven thirty, so still hours to go before visiting starts at the hospital.

Half an hour later and here he is again, with the Hoover out, cleaning up the living room. He's still glancing repeatedly at his watch, though. How much do you want to go and put your arms round him right now and give him a great big kiss? I know I do.

Eventually it's eight thirty and he's in his car, driving into town. The shops don't open for another half an hour so he parks outside the one he is most excited about and stares at the locked door for twenty-eight minutes until the manager appears inside and unlocks it. He spends an hour in there, deliberating over a very special purchase, then makes one more quick stop before heading straight to the hospital where everything in the world he cares about are.

On the ground floor he gets into a lift and then hesitates over which floor to visit first. His anxiety for Jake struggles with his joy for me and in his mind he pictures the neo-

473

natal ward next to the I.T.U. One is a bright, sunny place, filled with smiling faces and cheerful nurses carrying vases full of fresh flowers; the other place is dark and shadowy, a quiet place where the nurses wear grim expressions and carry nothing but tubes and thermometers and bedpans. His future lies in the sunny place, his love, his life. But there is no fear there, no anxiety, and he has no doubt that his brother and sister-in-law will be feeling both this morning. He must go to Glenn first. His finger goes to the '3', but wavers again without pressing it and moves to the '1'. It pauses there too, then moves decisively to the '3' and presses it firmly.

In Intensive Care he strides quickly to the bay where Jake's bed is, rounds the corner and stops in horror. The bed where Jake lay unconscious last night is empty, stripped of all personalization, the blankets folded up on the end, the sheets in a heap on the floor. Nearby is a giant laundry basket on wheels, other used sheets hanging loosely over the edges. Hector spins and looks frantically around the ward. He sees a nurse and hurries over to her.

'The – the boy, the little boy, Jake McCarthy, he was here, in that bed . . . where is he now? He's not . . . ?'

'Oh, yes, little Jake. Yes. He went downstairs, about an hour ago.'

'Downstairs?'

'Yes. He came round this morning so the doctor said he could be moved down to the paediatric ward. There are other children there, and it's much brighter, so he'll—'

'Oh thank you, thank you!' He touches her arm briefly then turns and hurries back towards the lifts.

'You're more than welcome,' she says, flushing as she watches him go.

This is Spencer Ward, the children's ward. It's much more cheery, isn't it? I love the way they paint Tigger and Pooh on the walls in every children's ward in the country, to give the kids that move around from hospital to hospital some sense of continuity and familiarity. Or maybe there's a single set of NHS Winnie the Pooh stencils that tour the country.

Hector locates Jake's bed and arrives to find Jake sitting up in bed eating ice cream, Sarah and Glenn sitting either side of him, grinning.

'Hec!' Glenn shouts and stands up to embrace his brother. 'Look at him, Hector, look! Doesn't he look fantastic?'

Hector looks at Jake's ice-creamy lips and bright eyes and has to agree. 'My God, Glenn. He looks amazing. Is he . . . ?'

'They said his brain scan is clear. He's fine, absolutely fine. The doctor says he has hard bones.'

Hector looks from Glenn to Sarah and Jake. Jake is still very pale but he is animated now, eagerly tucking into the ice cream with one hand while Sarah holds the bowl still for him. His other arm is hanging in a foam sling that's round his neck. 'All right, Jakey? Good to have you back with us. How are you doing?'

'I'm having ice cream for breakfast and ice cream for lunch and ice cream for tea,' Jake says enthusiastically. 'And then we're going to Disneyland.'

'Wow, that's fantastic. You're very lucky, aren't you?' The boy nods. Hector turns to Glenn and says very quietly, 'Do you think there's any danger that he might link running away from home with loads of presents and treats, and try it again?'

Glenn shrugs. 'Maybe. I think it's more likely that he'll link running away with fear and pain, and coming home with treats and presents. Anyway, it's never going to happen again. We won't let it, will we, Sar?'

Sarah gazes up at her husband and smiles. 'No way.'

'Great,' says Hector, 'because I've bought him a present too!'

And so here he is, right now, standing outside the neonatal ward, watching me with Nick. As he bounced down the corridor only a few moments ago, everything was right, everything was perfect, in fact, and he had an excited, bubbly feeling inside. Today, early this morning, Plum's brand-new life started, and he wants to start a brand-new one too. His old life of loneliness and worry, with just his mum to care for, was coming to an end. Very soon, he would have two new beautiful people in his life, two very precious, very loved people to kiss goodbye, and come home to, and worry about, and devote his life to. He is grinning broadly as he walks, swinging the carrier bag, nodding and saying 'Good morning!' to any stranger he encounters. People are looking at him and smiling, particularly as he is heading towards neo-natal. There goes a new dad, they are all thinking with a smile, How lovely. He doesn't care. He is a man in love.

But it all freezes into greyness as he arrives at the ward and sees Nick on my bed. Worse than seeing Nick there is the fact that I look totally comfortable with him, and that he is holding little Plum. With a sickening jolt Hector is reminded that Plum is not his daughter and in fact he is *not* a new dad at all. He is nothing to this baby. He sags and instinctively takes a couple of steps backwards.

'Everything all right?' says a voice behind him. He turns to find a cheerful-looking nurse standing there holding a vase of flowers. Just as he imagined.

'I'm working on it,' he says, smiling at the nurse who turns faintly pink and smiles warmly back.

'Need any help?' she asks him, although she is clearly very busy herself.

He bows slightly. 'You are very kind, er . . .' he glances at her name badge, '. . . Maggie. But I feel that really I should be asking you that.'

She blushes more deeply. 'Oh, er, ha ha, not really, don't be silly, it's no trouble at all.'

He inclines his head again, then turns back to look into the ward. Nick is still there, although he looks as if he's getting ready to leave. He's standing up and now Hector has a clear view of Plum, in my arms, which means he can see that she is wearing the little white starry sleepsuit he gave to me yesterday, and this sight fills his chest with air and returns nearly all the bursting feeling. He grins again as he watches Nick leave and his fingers twitch on the carrier bag. He lifts it up to take out the small, red velvet box inside, which he slips into his jacket pocket – plenty of time – then walks confidently around the corner to the bed.

My third visitor is Hector who arrives seconds after Nick leaves, and he is by far the most welcome. I have been smiling so much today that my face is hurting, but still I manage a wide grin when I see him.

'Hector! Oh, I'm so glad to see you!' He comes over to the bed, leans down and kisses me warmly on the mouth. His face stays kissing-close as he looks at me.

477

'Morning, gorgeous. How did it go?'

'I didn't sleep a wink and neither did she, but it was the most fantastic night of my life.' He leans over the crib and touches Plum's curved back. 'Oh I'm so glad to see you.' It's Saturday, but he's dressed up smartly in a shirt and tie anyway. I frown. 'Are you going to work later?'

He turns to me, a serious expression on his face. 'No, Rachel, I'm not. Why do you say that?'

'The tie, the suit. You look like you're off to a job interview.'

He smiles and sits down on the edge of the bed where Nick has just been sitting. Only much closer. 'Of course I'm dressed smartly. It's an important day, isn't it? Plum's first full day in the world. I'm going to meet her properly soon, when she wakes up.'

'Oh.' The ache of tears comes into my throat. Isn't he just so wonderful, to dress smartly to make a good impression on my ten-hour-old daughter?

He's fidgeting now, though. He clears his throat. 'The thing is, Rachel, there is another reason why I've dressed smartly today.'

'Is there?'

'Ahem. Yes.' He puts his hand into his jacket pocket, then pulls it out again. 'But first things first.' He lifts a carrier bag on to the bed and pulls out a beautiful plush snail, covered in patches of different textures. Somewhere inside is a bell that rings as Hector passes it to me. 'I bought a little present for . . . for who? Who is she? She can't be Plum all her life, can she? She'll be terribly bullied at school.'

'Ruby. Her name is Ruby.'

'Ruby? That's very pretty. I like it.' He turns to the crib.

'Hello, little Ruby. I'm really happy to see you again. I hope you like your present.' Gently he places the snail at the end of the crib, then strokes Ruby's head with one finger. 'You're so lovely,' he says, almost not loud enough for me to hear.

'She is, isn't she?'

He turns to me. 'I mean you, Rachel.' He's looking at me earnestly now and his hand is back inside his jacket pocket. Suddenly I feel as if I know what is coming but at the same time I'm terrified to believe it. He slides off the bed and gets down on the floor, then kneels up. The ward has gone silent again and I can feel all heads turned towards us, but I can only look at Hector, lovely, wonderful Hector, the man I have loved for a lifetime – Ruby's lifetime.

'Rachel, you inspired me, you still do and I think you always will. I am madly in love with you. I don't want to live another moment without you. Please, please, say I can be your husband, and Ruby's daddy?'

I burst into laughs, or sobs, or a combination of both, and nod vigorously, smiling and crying. He leaps up and engulfs me in a hug and everyone on the ward claps and cheers and at that moment my mum arrives and wakes up all the babies.

THE END